"An intriguing m
dystopia, written
recommended."

"Yes, this is noir, dystopia and erotica – a unique story with a unique New Orleans setting. Hard to put down as the action runs straight and hard. Throw in great characters and dialogue and you have a winner. Go get this book right away. Maxim Jakubowski is a master."

—O'Neil DeNoux

"A new book by Maxim Jakubowski is always something of an event… *The Louisiana Republic* might be said to be something of a genre splice with New York a very different place after a mysterious global upheaval known as 'The Dark.' Jakubowski's protagonist here has become a detective after working as a researcher, and is hired to find the missing daughter of a local gangster… the book has a variety of entertainingly bizarre elements, and the whole has a phantasmagorical quality that keeps the reader mesmerised."

—Barry Forshaw, *Crime Time*

"*The Louisiana Republic* is a massively addictive book which delivers on so many levels… shocking thriller? urban noir? dark comedy? dystopian road trip novel? Brutal gut-punch commentary? It's all of these and it's very very bloody good."

—*Mumbling About…*

"…the hard edge of Henry Miller and the redeeming grief of Jack Kerouac."

—Ed Gorman, *Mystery Scene*

"Tough and tightly-written fiction as hardboiled as Hammett."

—Edward Bryant, *Locus*

"This novel is dark, very dark. I could feel the dense darkness ooze from thc pages, lightness failing to emerge at every turn. The characters themselves are dark, full of menace and danger, the women somehow fiercer, more brutal than their male counterparts, which I found altogether quite refreshing… Just as I thought I knew what was going to happen the novel took a twist that caught me off guard, surprising me, sending the novel into a totally different direction. It was an ending I did not expect, but one that was totally in keeping with this sometimes strange and unique novel."

—*GoodReads*

"*The Louisiana Republic* is a darkly engaging read with a speculative world building that is genuinely compelling… I want to call it speculative noir – the heart of the plot is very old school but with a modern twist – the further you get into *The Louisiana Republic* the more insane it gets… If you want something a little different, a little crazy, then *The Louisiana Republic* is a book for you."

—Liz Barnsley, *Liz Loves Books*

"Highly original and wonderfully dark with strong touches of the taboo and obscene without descending into tackiness or vulgarity. A rich and well-crafted tale that mixes Orpheus with hard-boiled noir detective fiction and occasional forays into magical realism. Like all Jakubowski's work, the heroes are as flawed as the villains, making them strongly relatable. Louisiana, and particularly New Orleans, come to life in Jakubowski's hands and the place forms one of the strongest characters in the novel. Nearly had me booking an airline ticket to visit."

—*Amazon.com*

"*The Louisiana Republic* is a brutal, no-holds barred book in which sex and violence bloodily collide, there are scenes which are viscerally disturbing and this is most definitely not a novel for cosy crime readers… if you're looking for something different, the twisted, genre-defying *The Louisiana Republic* is well worth checking out."

—Karen Cole

"A bold, hugely original, multi-genre, cracking read. A private eye in a reimagined New York, where the internet and electronic data is as dead as a dodo, is asked to trace a woman… a raw, provocative, unique experience for lovers of the written word."

—Liz Robinson, *LoveReading*

"*The Louisiana Republic* is not going to be to everyone's taste. It is dark, violent, sweary, shaggy, though I think "erotic" is the official designation… but when a story like this comes along I cherish the opportunity it gives me to enjoy something so very different."

—Gordon Mcghie

"The deeper I got into *The Louisiana Republic* the more I lost the link to a relatable reality – and the more I enjoyed what I was reading. It is not easy to create a new world and breath such compelling life into the society you have built whilst also keeping the main story spinning along… when a story like this comes along I cherish the opportunity it gives me to enjoy something so very different."

—*Grab This Book*

"Both savage and tender, Jakubowski leaves no perversion unturned…"

—Ian Lowry, *Desire Magazine*

Other Fiction by Maxim Jakubowski

NOVELS

It's You That I Want to Kiss (1997)
Because She Thought She Loved Me (1998)
The State of Montana (1998)
On Tenderness Express (2000)
Kiss Me Sadly (2002)
Confessions of a Romantic Pornographer (2004)
Skin in Darkness [omnibus edition of revised versions of *Because She Thought She Loved Me, It's You That I Want to Kiss* and *On Tenderness Express*] (2003)
I Was Waiting for You (2010)
Ekaterina and the Night (2011)
The Louisiana Republic (2018)
The Piper's Dance (2021)

SHORT STORY COLLECTIONS

Life in the World of Women (1998)
Fools for Lust (2006)
A Washington Square Romance (2011)
The Music of Bodies (Ebook only; 2011)
We Mate in the Dark (Ebook only; 2011)
Hotel Room Fuck: The Best of Maxim Jakubowski (Ebook only; 2012)

The Louisiana Republic

Maxim Jakubowski

Introduction by O'Neil De Noux

Stark House Press • Eureka California

THE LOUSIANA REPUBLIC

Published by Stark House Press
1315 H Street
Eureka, CA 95501
griffinskye3@sbcglobal.net
www.starkhousepress.com

THE LOUISIANA REPUBLIC

Published by Stark House Press by arrangement with the author.

ISBN: 978-1-951473-63-1

Cover and book design by Mark Shepard, shepgraphics.com
Cover photo by Roxy Aln
Proofreading by Bill Kelly

First Stark House Press Edition: March 2022

WOMEN IN A HALL OF MIRRORS
O'NEIL DE NOUX

In a chaotic, near-future dystopian world with no technology, no internet, a researcher becomes a detective on a wandering sister case. Begin in a nightmare version of New York, where gangs have divided the city into turfs and a mass of wild illegal immigrants and refugees have been parked uptown and are about to spill our from Central Park and create further chaos. Different. Give it a noir twist with supernatural elements and take it to New Orleans, which has separated itself from the rest of America, and you're on a unique ride with quirky people where libraries are valued as they are the lone source of information. This is no cozy mystery but hardboiled with strong language and graphic violence and descriptive sex, written by a master writer.

In Jakubowski's bravura noir piece everyone is flawed, most are losers and prone to primitive desires. It has a fierce femme fatale on the prowl and a duly creepy villain. Part crime fiction, part dystopian fiction, the story takes the reader along a scary path with enough surprises to keep it more than interesting. What the hell's gonna happen next? Conflict. One damn thing after another.

From New York, the story travels south where we encounter an oversexed daughter, a lost love, a murderous woman as the story continues on a surreal erotic journey. A master of erotica, Maxim Jakubowski does not shy from sexy scenes. He knows how to serve up alluring and enigmatic but seductive, dangerous females and equally desperate men. The women are the most interesting, the most diverse, like a retinue of frightening femmes fatales waltzing through a hall of mirrors. We see every facet, all the beauty and the flaws.

The accurate use of setting in *The Louisiana Republic* is one of its strongest points. Maxim Jakubowski elevates New Orleans into one of the central characters of the book. Lesser writers give the reader a tourist's view of New Orleans, what's seen in a brief holiday visit and worse – what's seen in TV shows and movies filled with clichés. Not a New Orleanian, Maxim is able to give us more than what's seen by his characters, but vivid, accurate details of the city, the tastes, smells, feel, sounds of the city, the sweat and feel of the city. His use of setting is more than a backdrop, he uses it to create mood and tone.

In *The Louisiana Republic*, as in his previous works set in New Orleans, Maxim gets it right. Back in 1999, when my wife Debra Gray

De Noux edited the anthology, *Erotic New Orleans*, Maxim was one of the few non-native New Orleanian writers included. His story, "Bottomless on Bourbon" was the lead story in the anthology, drawing readers into Maxim's penetrating and perceptive views of a city's "nights that smelled and tasted of sex." Moist, clammy embraces and voyeuristic pleasure. He is no tourist slumming his way through the guide books but someone who effortlessly captures unique senses of place but also manages to transform them into something dizzy and fantastical while never letting go of the human factor. He once described in a wonderful short story a shady, illegal club in a remote area of the French Quarter, which my NOPD colleagues and I in real life had never been able to pin down and raid; when I confronted him over a meal by Lake Pontchartrain of crawfish boil regarding how he had heard of the establishment in question, he confessed he had actually invented it, but the way he described it and situated it geographically chimed perfectly with what us policemen knew about the real one!

In Maxim's many trips to New Orleans over the years, he and I have nurtured our mutual passion for the city and beautiful women over countless plates of food, which like any true New Orleanian he is passionate about. He has sometimes inspired my writing, drawing stories out of me from my experiences as a homicide detective and private eye. He has become not just an editor but a good friend, stirring me to write better crime fiction stories as well as occasional erotica by the example of his own craft and by his encouragement.

Although in an eerie dystopian fashion, *The Louisiana Republic* shows the multiple faces of New Orleans, from the languor of the Garden District to the hustling French Quarter, as well as the dangerous attraction of a city which draws one to innumerable pleasures. I've heard Maxim referred to as the "King of Erotica"; he often uses New Orleans as "his city of sex." His erotic stories inspire other writers like me as well as stimulate readers. In this dark noir story, the city is the one of the most interesting characters in the book, equal to the gallery of women without whom there would be no story, or in the case of the main, struggling protagonist, no reason to live.

As editor of the long-running Mammoth Books of Erotica (*The Mammoth Book of New Erotica, The Mammoth Book of Historical Erotica, The Mammoth Book of Short Erotic Novels* among others) Maxim has encouraged writers like me to spread our wings and write erotic stories without holding anything back.

Now Chair of the Crime Writer's Association and a veteran publisher who not only knows the book trade inside out, Maxim has a long history writing crime fiction, science fiction as well as erotica and shifts between genres like a literary chameleon, although he never moves far, whatever the narrative context, from singing about the beauty of women. He is the editor of many crime fiction anthologies from *Constable New Crimes* Anthology (October, 1993) through the more recent *The Book of Extraordinary New Sherlock Holmes Stories, Invisible Blood, Daggers Drawn,* and upcoming anthologies about *Femmes Fatales and Dangerous Women* and *Black is the Night*—a Cornell Woolrich tribute anthology, a homage to the noir writer he considers one of his main influences.

The surprising twists and turns in *The Louisiana Republic* kept me turning pages, reminding me of Raymond Chandler and also Alfred Hitchcock's *Vertigo*. But at the end of the day, it is typical Maxim Jakubowski, a modern master of pulp fiction who always manages to combine thrills with a recognizable intimacy of feelings, through fallible characters you cannot help rooting for, even the baddies and those ever-balanced between good and bad.

—December 2021

THE LOUISIANA REPUBLIC AN INTRODUCTION

MAXIM JAKUBOWSKI

I think it was Bob Dylan who came up with the expression "You are what you eat". Or maybe it was someone else? It basically means that you become the sum of everything you have absorbed during your lifetime. Now I'm confident you have no interest in knowing what I've digested food-wise over the past years, but when it comes to this curious novel of mine, there is no way I can hide the fact it was created under a variety of influences, literary, cultural and even musical.

I will try and guide you through the labyrinth my brain travelled through during (and before) the writing of *The Louisiana Republic*.

Even though I am better known these days as a crime and mystery author (and editor, reviewer, ex-publisher and ex-bookseller) it's no secret that my career began in the welcoming swamps of the science fiction and fantasy field.

I was an only child until the age of thirteen and lived in a foreign country, since my parents had found employment in Paris, France when I was only three, and I naturally followed. I've actually never been to school in England, my own country and; when I speak French these days no Frenchman would ever guess I am British; which has sometimes distinct advantages!

I grew up as so many only children do a voracious reader. From an early age I was captivated by the adventures conjured up by Jules Verne, although I also read Agatha Christie and as I became older more contemporary SF and hardboiled crime by the likes of Mickey Spillane, Peter Cheyney, James Hadley Chase and others. To be totally honest, my initial interest in the dark side of crime on the page was certainly provoked by the fact that the sleuths and heroes on display met women and the sweet scent of sex lingered in the air, or between the pages, even if the fade to the next chapter always came too suddenly and I had to exercise my imagination to conjure up what sex was actually all about! I learned all about the birds and the bees in books, or at any rate about gumshoes and willing femmes fatales or helpless damsels in distress, seeing that my parents were either too busy or too embarrassed to give me the statutory talk on sex education!

I came across science fiction fandom when we eventually returned to

London and that heady environment encouraged me in trying to become a writer. I began publishing my own fanzine at 15 and was soon churning out short stories, selling one of my first attempts to *Satellite*, a minor French SF magazine for which I had done a few translations (of Clifford D. Simak and Philip K. Dick). This was all arranged through the post and none of the editors at magazines or publishing houses had the slightest clue I was so young... When a modest check was due I always asked for it to be made out to M. Jakubowski as my father and I shared the same initials and I, of course, didn't have a bank account. As a result my first book was published in France when I was only 16, a gallivanting space opera which deservedly fell on deaf ears (and will never be republished unless I am totally desperate). If that makes me sound like a child prodigy, let me temper the fact by mentioning it would take another 15 years before I managed to publish another book.

Eventually, I would tire of writing SF & fantasy as I came to realise I was not truly an ideas person, and was more interested in characters than actual plot—what makes them tick; their relationships—although I to this day remain a great reader of the genre. The other drawback was that a consensus of opinion amongst acquiring SF editors (and, maybe less so, readers) revealed an underlying criticism that mild sex scenes or examples of sexual interaction in my stories were possibly too strong and out of place. Which, for me, was actually the point: characters of flesh and blood inevitably, I felt, could not draw back from the attractions of sex even within a science fictional context. True, few other writers were of the same opinion: Philip José Farmer maybe, but he was a big 'name' and I wasn't.

By then, I had begun to work in book publishing, following a lengthy foray into the well-remunerated field of the food raw materials industry where I toiled on the export side, and promptly renewed my contact with the crime and mystery field, becoming responsible for a succession of imprints and, in the process, reviving the careers of many hardboiled writers who were, at that time, better known in France than in the US or UK, alongside working with a wide range of mainstream literary authors and creating illustrated and music-related books. To this day, even though I worked on books by Nobel laureates, award-winning literary authors and celebrated film directors, I am probably best remembered for having been the publisher of all the authorized Sex Pistols books and the notorious *Cluck; the True Story of Chickens in the Cinema* and *Rock Stars in their Underpants* by the late Paula Yates, though...

It was inevitable that after editing crime and reissuing forgotten classics, I should want to try my hand at it. But again, I was not much of a plotter, and unlikely to come up with ingenious puzzles or deep-layered psychological thrillers, so my first crime novel was actually a road movie!

I've always been an inveterate film fan, ran for several years a mystery film festival and attended other foreign ones and curated a season of road movies for London's National Film Theatre. I began *It's You That I Want to Kiss*, with two accidental lovers on the run from dreadful gangsters; they departed Miami for a drive across the United States, which afforded me the luxury of actually having a soundtrack for their journey, listing and describing some of my favourite music at the time. Initially, I didn't even know where they were headed to, improvising both their route and their encounters along the way, with no idea of final destination or outcome. It was an improvised novel all the way along and a pleasure to write. It quickly found a publisher. When I look back at it now, it suffers from the stop and go nature of its plotting and although I love the central characters, I find their foes a touch caricatural, and the violence sometimes slightly gratuitous; I felt compelled to rewrite and tone down a particular torture scene for its US reissue some years later.

But all my obsessions were nakedly on display: *amour fou*, American highways, rock music, and uncensored sex.

Two things came out of *It's You That I Want to Kiss*. The Seattle rock group The Walkabouts whose music I had mentioned several times in the book contacted me, and I was asked to do a reading on stage to open their next London concert and I became friends with them, to the extent that a later song "True Crime Story" was, according to their singers Chris and Carla, directly inspired by my writing, and I was invited some years down the line to write the liner notes for their *Best Of* compilation. More importantly, I challenged myself to write further crime books, each in homage to a particular sub-genre I enjoyed. Having tackled the road movie, I followed up with *Because She Thought She Loved Me*, which was pure hardboiled noir in the tradition of James M. Cain and Cornell Woolrich, and completed the trilogy (minor characters recurred throughout the three novels) with *On Tenderness Express* which featured an ambiguous private eye as its main and unreliable protagonist and narrator. Some years later, the three novels were collected as *Skin in Darkness*, an omnibus volume which is still in print.

The books' reception was mixed, with yet again the customary criticism being the surfeit of sexual action! A good friend of mine even penned a short parody in which my characters invariably shed their clothes on every page like clockwork! I was pretty philosophical about this as I had also written a number of specifically erotic books (with little crime involved) between each volume in the loose trilogy, one of which came to the attention of Nicole Kidman who acquired the film rights; two decades later it is still in development hell, although every edition worldwide of *The State of Montana* still proudly proclaims that it is "soon to be a major movie"!

But in my own mind, my next three novels, *Confessions of a Romantic Pornographer*, *I Was Waiting for You* and *Ekaterina and the Night* were not specifically crime, even if my favourite character, hit-woman Cornelia, made fleeting appearances and the books veered strongly towards fantasy and mock autobiography.

I was toying with the idea of returning to writing crime fiction in some fashion that suited me when the *Fifty Shades of Grey* phenomenon broke and several months ahead of its first publication there was a distinct buzz in the air and all of a sudden publishers who had always tut-tutted about the amount of sex in my books had changed their mind and began laying siege to my literary agent with a view to convincing me to write something in the same vein so they could compete with *FSOG*. I was initially reluctant, but then teamed up with a friend and came up with a two-book proposal which went to auction and sold for a ridiculous advance. The next two years saw us frantically writing ten volumes in our Vina Jackson series, which sold several millions of copies and was translated into 31 languages, before the erotic tsunami created by E.L. James quickly subsided. I am still proud of those books, even if *FSOG* fans initially found them rather shocking and the characters and their practices too real compared to Anastasia Steele and her millionaire tormentor. Someone said they were the literary version of *FSOG* and when after six volumes we were allowed to make a radical U-turn and allow the series to explore the fantastic and leave reality behind in *Mistress of Night and Dawn* in a bid to stop repeating our inevitable "are they or are they not together" relationship pattern, I think my collaborator and I reached a sweet nirvana spot which I am still inordinately proud of.

But all good things come to an end, and I think that we were both relieved when it did, after toiling in the erotica galleys over well a million words in two years, leaving us with our imaginations tapped out, and in the case of my collaborator with repetitive stress injury in her wrist from all the typing under deadline pressure!

It took nearly three years for both of us to recover completely and attempt any new full-length book, but as the royalties kept on coming in on a regular basis this was not so much of an imposition. I stuck to writing short stories and editing and my erstwhile partner in erotica got married and moved away from London. My wife had just been diagnosed with an incurable disease, and we took the opportunity before her condition worsened to spend our time travelling extensively, visiting over 35 countries and, finally, cruising around the world on which occasion I finally began writing another novel whilst onboard as I came to the conclusion that a writer never retires and the bug was biting me hard to resume.

Which is how *The Louisiana Republic* came to be, mostly written on deck during the day and in our stateroom in the evening as we sailed steadily between Tilbury and Sydney.

The coming of the Internet had changed the way we all function during my lifetime and the idea of how the world would react should it disappear overnight is what triggered the plot, as whilst at sea there were days when our boat satellite link weakened and we were unable to go online for hours on end. It was a science fictional concept, but I knew I didn't want to write a truly apocalyptic novel in the vein of Cormac McCarthy's *The Road* or my good friend Emily St John Mandel's beautiful *Station Eleven*, so I came up with the twist of making the main protagonist an involuntary private eye whose talent for research proves an invaluable skill following the global catastrophe, which I called "The Dark" and vowed to deliberately never explain as this was never the point of the book. He is fallible, fragile, human and has lost the love of his life. I'd long come to the realisation that, at heart, all the books I've written are basically love stories, concealed in the hall of mirrors of popular fiction genres. Call me an inveterate sentimentalist, but love makes the world go round, doesn't it still? So it begins, like so many hardboiled thrillers with a beautiful if enigmatic woman knocking on his door asking him to find her errant younger sister. This is of course a naked homage to Raymond Chandler. You borrow from only the best!

So I had myself a dystopia and a classic private eye premise. And a love story that paralleled Orpheus and Eurydice. How could I muddy the waters and include more of my personal obsessions?

I have long enjoyed a beautiful relationship with New Orleans, one of my favourite places in the world for a variety of reasons, and where I had already set various stories and sections of previous novels. Slight spoiler here: I decided to take my protagonists there, in a country riven by anarchy and where Louisiana has, alongside some other states, seceded from the rest of the country, and New Orleans sits behind a wall (shades of John Carpenter's *Escape from New York*) in a bubble outside time, like a magical place which draws my characters like a vortex and sets the scene for a bittersweet conclusion. Having already used the context of the road movie in *It's You That I Want to Kiss*, I replaced the journey by an eventful sailing down the Mississippi, no doubt inspired by the fact that I was travelling over water while writing most of the book.

Once a novel is published, I seldom look at it again but I still feel strongly that what became *The Louisiana Republic* is the quintessence of all the themes and characters I have written about in my career. A strange brew which probably fits nowhere else, the kitchen sink of my obsessions and I hope an intriguing read. As to the ending, I see it as a fever dream, a version of America gone mad as seen through English eyes (there are a few hints that the protagonist even though he is initially based in New York might actually be British; hence a few instances of what might be termed UK-isms scattered along the journey, for which I hope US readers might forgive me).

It was initially turned down by most of my editors. Some loved the criminal element but hated the science fictional context; others loved the dystopian world I had created but felt I had spoiled it by introducing a private eye scenario. And, as ever, some criticised the abundance of sexual matter. It's long been a tenet in book publishing that you should not mix genres, but I've always believed that it's a law that marketing and sales minions have created for no other reason than making things easier for themselves. It sold to Caffeine Nights, a small independent house in the UK, but failed to make an impact as shortly after publication they decided to stop publishing crime and concentrate purely on horror henceforth and the book became semi-orphaned and benefited from little publicity.

Which is why I am grateful to Greg Shepard at Stark House for agreeing to reissue it and arrange for it to be available for the first time in the USA. I hope new readers take it to their heart. Having read this preamble so far, you will realise it's not a straightforward crime thriller, and it's ironic that it should appear in a list where it will sit alongside so many genuine crime classics of the type I used to publish when I still worked as a book editor. And despite being the current Chair of the UK Crime Writers' Association, I must confess to feeling like something of an imposter as the other novel I've written since *Louisiana*, *The Piper's Dance* is all about the children who followed in the footsteps of the Pied Piper of Hamelin and features mermaids, belonging wholesale to the fantasy field. But yet again, I see it as love story. Will I ever write anything else?

Enjoy the ride.

The Louisiana Republic

Maxim Jakubowski

1- THE LITTLE SISTER

She visited my office on the 10th anniversary of the Dark.

It wasn't much of an office. You couldn't see any sky through the window. Just the well on the way to the derelict side wall of the building opposite, some ten feet away across the street.

Patchy rendering, crumbling at the edges, as dull as a Rorschach test with even less to say.

The sky outside was the colour of lead. It always was. Every single day of the year.

She was tall and blonde with cheekbones as sharp as a razor blade. Most women would have killed for such deadly beautiful geometry—men too—but there was a coldness in her cobalt-blue eyes that made her appear dangerous rather than beautiful.

She wore an ankle length fur coat that looked expensive and provided no clue about the body lurking underneath, and my gut instinct told me to not even speculate about that particular subject. But the sort of women who concealed their shape usually had something spectacular to show off, and the price to pay would be out of my league. And if someone visited me these days, I expected them to pay.

Peering through the minimal gap between her coat and a pair of white designer shoes with a hint of red soles and stiletto heels fierce enough to be used as a lethal weapon, was the contour of a shapely ankle.

She looked me up and down, her gaze never faltering, cold, as if she were appraising a side of beef hanging from a metal hook in an abattoir. It didn't make me feel wanted. Then she allowed herself a rapid glance at the modest office where I worked and quickly deduced the furniture could only have originated from IKEA and was second-hand at that by the looks of it. Which was a giveaway as the company had gone out of business after the debacle and it meant I hadn't been able to afford anything new since. It was an admission of weakness and she knew instantly that she wouldn't have to pay me much.

I half-expected her to turn round and go back through the door now that she had made up her mind about the sort of investigator I was—not good enough for the likes of her or whoever had sent her—but instead she stepped forward, sat in the chair facing my desk, which was providentially empty of the usual mess of papers and stuff I often piled up there. She flashed me a wide, insincere smile. Those teeth were so damn white and shiny, witness to the fact she relied on more than just expensive toothpaste.

"My name is Alexandra," she said.

"Hello, Alexandra."

"Never call me Alex."

"That had never even occurred to me," I said.

"Good. I wish to employ you."

"I don't do cats," I explained.

"What the fuck?"

"I don't take on jobs involving the tracking down of domestic cats. Or any pets for that matter."

"Too prosaic for your professional standards?"

"No. I just don't like animals."

"Well, I don't think any pets are involved this time around. In that case, you might be the sort of man I'm looking for."

"There's no better time to get down to business."

"I need you to find my sister."

I was about to break the news to her that this measured rigmarole sounded rather familiar, that I'd read the book or seen the movie, but I held back. She sat down in the chair as if reassured by my lack of repartee.

She opened up her coat and I had to take a deep breath.

Alexandra wore a tight tunic of a dress, white, zipped on the side, it looked like silk and adhered to every single curve of her body like glue, a second skin that revealed more than it even covered. She was definitely not wearing a bra. Further below I had no idea as the desktop screen blocked my sight, but with a body like that, she was bound to have legs that were both endless and perfect. Her skin was a delicate shade of pale, an imitation of porcelain. White against white, talk about colour coordination! But the dress was cut to bare her shoulders. Her right shoulder was a forest of pink scars as if she had once been in a fire and the skin had never healed. It was impossible not to stare. The contrast between the large, affected area which seemed to continue further under the fabric all the way down her front and back of her upper body, and the rest of her skin was striking. Hypnotic even.

I made an effort to draw my gaze away. I reckoned she was familiar with this kind of reaction. Even expected it.

I was rapidly revising my opinion of her.

Most women would take care to conceal such a spectacle under layers of clothing. Which would have been easy; after all, most available garments normally cover the shoulders. So, it was a deliberate choice. To demonstrate that the awful scars were something she was proud of, a badge of honour or an act of defiance.

"You're allowed to stare," she said, noting my reaction.

"I'm sorry."

"Things happened," she partly explained.

And that was the end of that.

I had to remain professional, take some pride in my own craft.

"Your sister, then… Tell me."

"She is three years younger than me. Her name is Cherise. Actually, it's Tiffany Cherise, but she's never really used her first name."

I kept silent, imperceptibly leaning back in my frayed black leather chair. It was always better to allow the clients to talk, keep the interruptions to a minimum. Hang on their every word.

Empathise.

Alexandra and Cherise came from a wealthy background but had never been close as children. Their temperaments were opposite: while Alexandra was cool and collected and distant, Cherise had been the wild child, always testing boundaries, selfish but bright, vivacious but secret. There was no mention of their parents at this stage and I didn't insist. It sounded like a familiar story. Though I did wonder whether the burn scars on Alexandra's shoulder had any connection with the past actions of the younger sister. Maybe that would come later in the story.

They had both still been teenagers at the time of the Dark, but where the terrible events had affected people in so many different ways, for the young Cherise it had been a signal to release, almost overnight, all the recklessness she harboured inside her. She had, shortly thereafter, become near uncontrollable, prone to all sorts of mood swings and irresponsible actions. Not that she had been a saint, let alone a nun before by any means, as Alexandra soon explained in answer to my queries.

"Was there anything specific about the Dark that could have caused her to change so radically?" I asked Alexandra.

"I don't think so."

□ □ □

Some said it was a form of electromagnetic wave that had swept out from the sun like an invisible wave of destruction and washed over our planet. Others believed the origin of the disturbance had come from further outer space, while hordes of crazies emerging from the woodwork believed it was all a conspiracy engineered by the government, the Arabs, the ethnic minorities, the communists, the feminists, the anti-feminists, the White supremacists, the Chinese, the Jews, the Freemasons, little green men from Mars, take your pick, just about anyone they were wary of. But you can't explain unexplained things. It had happened. Overnight, and things had changed.

We had fallen asleep in a world that was familiar and the next morning it had all gone. The Internet had been wiped out and with it, our material soul, our data, our records, our memories, our photos, for many their money, basically everything that made us who we were. Initially, there was panic. Riots.

Demonstrations. The army on the streets. Barricades in Wall Street that spread to the rest of the city, then, like a forest fire spreading wildly with nothing to contain it, then the illness had moved to other cities, the rest of the world, even to the lands of our enemies. The eradication of data affected the faceless enemies we believed were responsible, and then they blamed us in turn. There were local wars, larger conflicts, massacres, ugliness, but nothing brought back what we had possessed and never valued enough before what we now called the Dark.

Governments fell, factions emerged from the ruins, to the extent that right now the country had two Presidents, three capital cities and conflict reigned. And a controlled form of anarchy, a situation that was fluid and prone to changes at the drop of a dice or the shot of a gun.

Every piece of data stored in the cloud, on personal computers, in the deepest of technological storage units in official buildings, under mountains, below the concrete and the ice, was stolen from us. There were no surviving back-ups, nothing left to retrieve but the information we held in our heads, our brains. They tried. Oh, they tried, but the slate had been swept clean and there wasn't a byte or a pixel to retrieve from the depths of despair.

It was then we realised how reliant we had been on one thing and had mistakenly entrusted our lives to the permanence of technology.

A few weeks later, some hardy techs managed to get it started up again, at a huge cost and insomniac nights of combined effort around the planet, but no one trusted the medium any longer or even wished to use it, or go anywhere near it for fear of getting their fingers metaphorically burned, just in case the same scourge happened again out of the blue. You can't build a wall over and over again once it has a habit of collapsing.

We changed. We had to.

Information had now become a currency, now worth its weight in gold.

I was one of the first to adapt and take, in some small way, advantage of the situation.

Before the catastrophe, I'd been happy as a writer and researcher for a popular magazine. I'd always preferred gathering my facts, doing my checking, my investigating in the pages of old newspapers and in books rather than use the Internet. Now my skills had become invaluable. Similarly, librarians, from once being on the lowest step of the ladder had become indispensable.

And they knew it. The Guild of Librarians had been created, an exclusive group of men and women who knew where the treasures and the dirt lay. The New York Public Library on 42nd Street became a fortress of knowledge which was heavily guarded and anyone in need of information had to pay and pay again. The Library even set up its own security force. The tables had truly been turned.

The people who loved books were now at the top of the evolutionary ladder, while the bankers and their ilk had sunk to the bottom.

Once, cyber jockeys had ruled the world, now it was the turn of the pen and paper brigade.

In other cities, the change in the social order wasn't as seamless. In Paris, the Bibliothèque Nationale was burned down by an envious mob when its staff brazenly attempted to wield their newly-acquired power, as were many other repositories of knowledge in other major cities who suffered a similar fate or were looted by the have-nots.

I knew enough people at the Library and became a de facto associate member of the Guild, even though there was no badge or membership card. They trusted me.

I'd read so many detective novels over the years that it soon became obvious to me that, once the magazine I worked inevitably collapsed as did most publications, I would badly require another job involving fishing for facts and clues and becoming a private investigator, an information retriever of sorts, would suit me perfectly.

So, I found myself a small office in Prince Street, in SoHo and set up in business.

I was well suited to the job. I knew where to look, where the paper records were stored and was confident that in the real life we were living in following the Dark, my new profession would not require me to walk into dark rooms waiting to be bludgeoned by villains or get involved in car chases. Little did I know that some things never change.

Just like after 9/11, many people had taken advantage of the upheaval to disappear, get away from wives, debts, relationships, obligations. Others, however, had disappeared for no reason.

You couldn't even blame the overnight destruction of the internet for their vanishing from the face of the earth.

Giulia was one of them.

She was the young woman I had been in love with.

Her thick, dark hair curled all the way down to her shoulders and her eyes were the colour of coal and shone in the dark like a diamond in a mine. She was from Rome and was on a two-year post-graduate course in Catalan literature at Columbia. I knew nothing about Catalan writing and wouldn't even have been able to quote you the name of a Catalan writer, whether historical or contemporary, with or without access to the Internet. They say opposites attract. We'd met at a poetry reading in a subterranean warren of rooms on the corner of Hester Street.

Her breasts were slight and her nipples a dazzling shade of demure pink that darkened as they hardened slowly when they were touched by finger or lip. She had a birthmark, twice the size of a thumbnail, in the shape of Sicily on the inner side of her left thigh.

Giulia was only twenty years old at the time and made me feel like I was snatching her from the cradle, from the vantage point of my extra two decades. It made me feel guilty, but it also brought me joy. She didn't mind the age difference, she said. At least for now. I was sorely conscious of it, fear burning my soul, that it harboured already the seeds of our future, inevitable parting.

She had a unique style of dress, combining second-hand clothes she'd picked up in Goodwill or its Italian equivalents, or vintage stores in the West Village, something of a gypsy-style, and she always walked too fast, as if in a hurry and despite the fact I was also a head taller than her and had longer legs as a result, I was always obliged to lengthen my step when walking outside with her.

She fucked hungrily, enjoyed straddling me and impaling herself on me, her glorious wetness and heat gripping me like a sheath, allowing me to fill her to the fullest before she began, or was it me, the inevitable up and down and up again movements of lust unleashed. Giulia when she spoke. Giuli when she fucked.

Jiu Lia when she sang. My Jools when she smiled. Giulietta when she cried. And all of her when she laughed and looked at me.

We were happy. Or so I thought.

Within a day or so of the Dark, she had vanished into thin air.

The clothes and toiletries she left in my apartment had gone. She had her own key. When I visited her university lodgings I was told she had moved out and left no forwarding address.

At that early stage, telecommunications were still an unholy mess, iPhones just good enough for taking photos you couldn't save anywhere else, I was unable to contact her.

Vanished. Without a word.

Or, to make things worse for me, even a reason.

I tried to recall our last few days and what had been said, by her, by me, hunting for clues, moods, minor disagreements, but could pinpoint nothing of significance.

I wasn't yet a private investigator and was failing abominably.

Not very promising, was it?

Meanwhile, the Dark was taking its toll.

First California seceded from the rest of the United States and declared independence. Chicago followed but was retaken, at bloody cost, by the National Guard and Home Security when the government decided to reassert its authority. Until it splintered into separate, warring factions.

Shortly after, the news filtered through that Louisiana had declared itself a Republic and closed its borders and that its inhabitants were armed to the teeth and resolute in resisting any invasion. The state had little strategic importance or economic value, so no one was overly concerned.

Later, we would learn that not only had Louisiana reinforced its borders with the rest of the country but that a series of massive walls were allegedly being built around New Orleans, securing the city from all sides, coast and land-wise. At the time, it felt more like a curious appendix to the troubles dominating the news, and we had much more important things to worry about. Other states soon followed suit. Like dominoes falling.

I found it fairly easy to track people down, although trailing errant husbands and wives proved more problematic and sordid, and I soon made it clear that I wouldn't accept potential divorce cases any longer. I learned on the job, began establishing a trusted network of informants, bartenders, hotel staff and railway station employees in addition to the dexterity I already enjoyed delving into public records or anything that had been available in print at a given time. My success ratio soon proved more than satisfactory and the news spread of my relative prowess by word of mouth.

"So, where did you hear about me, the services I provide?" I asked Alexandra.

Apart from the sign on the door downstairs, I did not advertise.

"Friends of friends," she said enigmatically.

I didn't insist. I would never find out who did, what felt at the time, as a favour.

□ □ □

Cherise had dabbled in drugs from an early age, made a habit of frequenting the wrong people and places and quickly established she had a knack for choosing the wrong man at the wrong time.

A familiar story; from life and books.

Alexandra listed her younger sister's pranks and ills, as I listened attentively.

There was something on her face, as she enumerated the petty and dangerous goings-on of Cherise, an expression I couldn't quite read. At times, disapproving of the tales she was narrating, she appeared almost in admiration, as if she sometimes envied her sister the freedom she had grabbed for herself with both hands, or her audacity in embracing the wrong things.

The more she told me about Cherise, the more I wanted to learn about Alexandra.

She must have sensed my unasked question. She interrupted her monologue and looked me close in the eyes.

"Do you think I hate my sister?" she asked me.

"It's not for me to say."

"She slept with my husband. It was only a game to her. To show me she could do it. To hurt me," she said.

"I'm sorry."

Mentally noting this as an avenue to investigate further if I was ever allowed.

"She was driving the car when we had the accident and the fire did what you see to my body," she added. "She was both high and drunk, and sometimes I think she did it on purpose, not even worried what would happen to her. She never even apologised. He didn't survive. I didn't miss him much."

I tried to nod in sympathy, but Alexandra saw straight through me.

"No need," she said. "Just find her."

I warned her. "This is something I say to all clients, so don't take it personally: think very hard, do you genuinely want her to be found?"

"Oh yes, I do. Anyway, she's taken something of mine which I really want back," Alexandra said.

"What?"

"It's immaterial. Find her."

As long as it wasn't a falcon figurine, I could deal with that.

More likely jewellery, an heirloom, something of the sort.

"I can find her, locate her, but let me be clear we are on the same wavelength: you also wish me to bring her back?"

"You understand me."

We agreed fees and expenses and how to remain in contact and she closed her fur coat, the white screen of her body curtained away and rose imperiously from her chair, turned on her vertiginous heels and left me sitting there with not even a goodbye. The woman had style and attitude to spare. The sound of her shoes clicking away down the corridor faded.

The investigation had begun.

I could preface the story by beginning 'had I known', but I won't.
I had no one to blame but myself.

□ □ □

Sleuthing is not as difficult as it sounds. As long as you can think laterally, and are persistent, mule-headed and determined.

Know your employer as well as you know your prey. It always pays dividends.

My initial port of call was the local post office on 12th Street.

It had fallen into a sad state of disrepair. A lone federal employee, grey hair, untidy chignon and thick glasses partly obscuring a maze of wrinkles that snaked between forehead and lips, sat in a corner as if enveloped in cobwebs.

She looked up at me as if I were a freak. Reminded me that the postal authorities could no longer accept any responsibility for the safe delivery of letters and parcels and expected me to turn around and leave.

"I just want to consult your phone directories," I said.

"Feel free," she said, pointing vaguely to a corner of the room where prehistoric levels of paperwork, files, and volumes stood, shrouded in dust. "Be my guest." And returned to the Sudoku puzzle she was busy working her way through.

Alexandra had deliberately not provided me with an address, just a telephone number ('it's a pre-Dark network,' she had indicated, 'it does work.') I knew her family name: Helmsmark. It made sense that the number she had given me was still listed in the old directories. Had she purchased the number, and the actual phone which must have been something of a museum piece, from someone else, the path leading to her whereabouts would have been more complicated, but not impossible if time-consuming. I was lucky right away.

Helmsmark was listed at an address on Park Avenue, close to Central Park. A rather expensive patch of Manhattan. It made sense.

The preceding initials were neither hers, nor Tiffany Cherise's.

Commander W. Helmsmark.

Interesting.

The name did ring a vague bell.

But best be accurate.

I left the ancient postal counter and the attendant didn't even acknowledge my departure or my muttered thanks.

My next port of call was the newspaper archives on 40th Street, where the customary, token bribe allowed me unaccompanied access to the underground vaults where back issues were kept. They hadn't been catalogued for ages, but Commander Helmsmark appeared on a regular basis in ancient clippings.

Now in his 80s. Navy, distinguished service in Vietnam, advisory role during the Iraq invasion, involved in the private security business, sometimes philanthrope, evidently wealthy, wife deceased many years past, two daughters. All correct and present.

One cutting led me to another and a picture began to emerge.

There was more to Commander Helmsmark than the record showed. Vast swathes of years unaccounted for. No information as to how he had amassed his fortune. CIA, I assumed, where the pursuit of the mighty dollar could easily run in parallel to service to his country.

The only mention I could find in my initial sweep through the indexed back issues to Alexandra was the announcement in the society pages of her marriage to an investment banker in New Haven, Connecticut and the fact that following her wedding she had moved to Cold Springs. I couldn't pin down anything about the car accident she had mentioned, her sister, or whether she had married again, divorcee on to her nth husband already.

Going through the unindexed years would be a slog. I would have to return and do the job properly if the necessity arose.

The following day, I parked myself on the first floor of an indie coffee shop across the road from Commander Helmsmark's likely address. I observed the front door for several hours, while making a coffee, and drinking a cola that bore no resemblance to the colas I'd enjoyed before the world had fallen apart. I made the drinks last as long as they could, pretending to read the sports pages of the daily giveaway newspaper I'd picked up by the subway entrance on Astor Place.

By evening, there had been no sighting of the Commander, whose 15-year-old photograph I had illegally snipped off one of the newspapers in the archive, but I was finally rewarded by the appearance in mid-afternoon of Alexandra herself exiting the building, with an obsequious doorman tipping his hat towards her as she passed, regal, straight as a rod, now in jogging clothes, the Lycra outfit outlining every single curve in her body like a curtain letting in the sun. She ran off toward the park but I didn't follow her.

Now, I had an address.

That night, I began jotting down notes on a large sheet of paper I pinned to my office wall.

Names. Some of the facts I knew were true. Those I was still unsure about (the car crash, Cherise's affair with the husband, the possible spooks connection). Lines and arrows connecting what I had so far, which wasn't much but was at least a beginning. It was, as ever, like a jigsaw where you begin to assemble the outline contours before you fill in the middle.

Cherise was the spider in the middle of the web I now had to unravel.

The following morning, I walked over to Barnes & Noble on Union Square. I took the moving runway to the top floor and the cafeteria, where a mural of all the famous writers of the past overlooked the students, passers-by and nannies with prams.

Most of whom were killing time chatting to each other or reading books and out of date magazines for free.

I knew Mike O'Carlson came here every day.

He was one of the few journalists whose career had not been affected one single iota by the Dark. His patch was American Football and even the end of the world had not tempered people's enthusiasm and fanaticism for the game, so Mike always had an outlet for his writings and commentary. If there was one thing the Dark had been instrumental in, it was the revival of print and newspapers, however void of real news they were, were now all the rage, with half a dozen appearing regularly in Manhattan alone.

He sat at his usual table, overlooking the Square, watching the Farmer's Market being set up, vans emptying their contents, trestle tables being assembled and produce carefully laid out.

He greeted me like a long-lost brother, openly welcoming the company.

I got him a coffee refill and a Snaffles lemonade for myself.

They didn't even serve bad cola here. Bookshops still displayed a touch of class.

"Cherise Helmsmark? Heard of her?" I asked him.

His eyes twinkled. I knew I had hit pay dirt.

"Who hasn't?" he exclaimed.

"Me for beginners."

"Where have you been living, man?"

"In a parallel world that has no visible connection with yours, it appears," I answered.

"Ah, you have your priorities all wrong."

"Educate me. I'll keep the coffee coming."

"You're kidding me, aren't you? She is Princess Sensuality."

"Who is she when she's at home?"

"None other than the lovely Cherise."

The story of Cherise, a variation on what her sister had revealed.

The woman who made the Internet vanish. Or so said some of the more imaginative conspiracy theorists.

Young socialite goes bad in the nicest possible way. A true exhibitionist who decided one sunny day to share her body, her beauty with the world at large and, as Princess Sensuality, sets up Tumblr, Flickr and

Instagram accounts on which she posts nude photos of herself and garners a devoted fan base that grows exponentially by the day.

The more fans she had, the more the photographs became explicit.

She actually advertised for photographers, professional or amateur, to come to her, barely even charged for her services, to fulfil their wildest imagination of fantasies with her at the centre of their most perverse dreams. Travelled all across the country, at her own cost, disrobing here, stripping there, impudent, provocative, available.

She quickly became a cult.

Short blonde hair, an aquiline nose, like her sister a porcelain white complexion, not quite as opulent, but her nipples pierced, two miniscule steel studs traversing them horizontally, on most images her mons pubis shaven, on her own or with other models in lascivious postures by beds, by the sea, in forests, her strong thighs more often than not held wide open, the pink lips of her cunt meaty and shocking, peeing on demand, the strong stream of her urine describing geometrical ellipses as it surged from her innards against the bathtubs in which she crouched and squatted, or down her legs as she stood proudly beneath the waterfall of the showerhead, liquids splashing, mingling against the cubicle's glass walls, shower water or piss becoming undistinguishable from each other.

But, however obscene or compromising any of the photographs were, always the same detached smile and a bruised look of innocence, the princess of fairy tales and privilege exposing herself for the sins of the beholder, exposed, devoid of any vulgarity, serene, her face a mask of serenity, her private parts an offering to every stranger who knew where to Google her.

Men fantasised wildly about her, speculating whether she lived with any one of the many photographers she worked with, whether she fucked every single guy (and the occasional woman) who snapped her, why she behaved in such a compromising way, who she was?

And one day, probably a better investigator than I was had unveiled her true identity.

Princess Sensuality was none other than Tiffany Helmsmark.

A society scion.

Educated, independently wealthy, wanton, beautiful, unattainable.

The fuss had proven momentous, with her family intent on making every trace of her disappear from the Internet, to little avail as collectors and fans eagerly shared the photos and they moved from site to site as fast as they were eliminated from one or the other. It was estimated the Commander had spent a fortune in his efforts to eradicate the damning evidence, had even suborned law protection agencies to assist him in the process, or accelerate it.

And then, the miracle had happened. The Dark.

Providential, with most traces of Princess Sensuality's very existence wiped off the face of the net overnight.

Although there were still rumours that a handful of collectors had actually printed off some of the images and protected their treasures with the intensity of Ali-Baba. Collector's items, her face, pierced breasts, heart-shaped rump and unadorned sex had become legends in their own time.

Mike had waxed rhapsodic.

"And what's known of her since?" I asked O'Carlson.

"Very little. Just rumours. That she returned to her family with her head bowed in shame, maybe even married, had children. Hasn't been heard of publicly for ages now."

I'd never heard the story before. But then I had been so busy with Giulia that the naked bodies of other women hadn't even flown close to the edges of my perception in those days of old.

"Fascinating."

"So, do I deduct from your presence and questions, that she has made a reappearance?" O'Carlson speculated with a smile that was closer to a leer, indicating quite evidently that he had been both a devoted fan and a frequent onlooker at the altar of Cherise's photos.

"Not quite," I told him.

Even as a shadow, the essence of the sheen of her bare skin and more on a piece of paper, she remained one of the disappeared. Until I could find her.

2- CANDY'S ROOM

Year minus 10.

When most people now reflected on their lives, it was in terms of "before the Dark" and "after the Dark".

For me, it was before Giulia and after Giulia.

The fact that the dates almost coincided made no difference.

It's the way you look at things, isn't it?

Before Giulia I was a holy fool, with no appreciation of life, blind to the glare of beauty.

After Giulia, I was still a fool, but the mourning shadow of the fool I used to be. Empty.

With Giulia, I had been happy like never before, a state of joy I didn't think was possible. Simple, obvious, serene in the acceptance I had found her, and we were together.

I can't listen to the music of Bruce Springsteen any longer.

Imprinted on my mind are the strains of "Candy's Room" while we made love on Pamela's sofa in the small apartment they once shared beyond Columbus Circle, while Pamela revised in the next room and pretended to ignore our rather obvious sounds, our chamber music of fucking below the undulating surge of Springsteen's music. I don't know if you know that particular song: it's melancholy, thus made to measure for me, sad but also jagged in its rhythm, the surge of the E Street Band falling and rising until the whole band took its flight, loud and triumphant, and the music's wings took me to a higher place as did my orgasm and the tightness with which Giulia gripped me, her fingers dug hard into my rump as I lowered my whole weight down on her, drowning her, crushing her and she responded with a sigh, a perfumed breath of pleasure. Later she had to move away from Pamela's, after her friend returned to Florida, and music in her university lodgings couldn't be played so loud.

Neither can I listen any more to Pink Floyd, haunted that I am by the memories of Giulia playing "The Dark Side of the Moon" in its entirety on her laptop the very first time we made love, exploring our bodies with exquisite slowness and detail in the hotel room at the ski resort in the Rocky Mountains where we had arranged to meet.

The music, now, only served to evoke her and make me experience her loss even more, to the point of torture, leaving me in despair.

She also loved The Clash, but I didn't, so I am least spared an additional emotional connection when their music comes on over the radio.

She appeared to be on a voyage of discovery, as if all that music hadn't existed until she arrived in New York from Italy, as if she was new to the world.

I go about my data work, my people tracing with my feelings switched off at the tap, like an automaton, with no feelings left.

It's the only way to survive. I'm indifferent to all the other nameless victims of the Dark, all the terrible atrocities committed since, the despair, the desolation; I am detached, the ghost of me.

Feed me the money and I function, pretend I'm a human being.

But I know the truth.

Without you, Giulia, I am nothing.

I unmoored. Allowed myself to drift away on the tides of memories, carried by waves of evanescent sensations, alternately choppy waters and quiet streams of images, feelings, retrieved moments that vanished as soon as I focused on them, to be replaced by further shimmering, out of reach shards of life who cluster inside a bright form of darkness only to reform in different shapes, quicksilver photographs of the past.

The clothes she had worn.

The skirt dotted with sunflower patterns.

The silver band in her hair barely taming the mass of dark, wild curls that others would have paid a fortune to own but which came to her free and which she always complained about.

The cheap Swatch watches she switched between, mostly acquired on eBay.

The way her Italian accent wormed its way around new words, as if tactile, determining the right way for her to pronounce them, her eyes interrogating me silently to assess whether she had got them right.

The determined, hurried walk that saw her legs bounce across cobbled stones like a panther in movement.

The way she looked at me, echoing the quiet gaze I set loose on her nudity, drinking in every single detail in order to fix it in memory, like a photograph cast loose from the digital world.

The rooms.

The streets.

The places we had been together.

The restaurant on Bleecker Street for which she had insisted on wearing her finery, black high heels that helped her reach my shoulders, the strapless dress baring hers, the textured trace of her nipples against the thin fabric, the lipstick like blood, her untamed eyebrows, thick and straight.

The places we had never been together.

Which she wanted me to discover.

Which I wanted to take her to.

The Amalfi Coast.

New Orleans which I wished to share with her, the tarot readers and psychics sitting on their rickety chairs at sunset around Jackson Square, the Café du Monde at three in the morning, the windows of the antique stores on Royal Street. I'd once fallen in love with the city and its French Quarter and wanted to share its quirky beauty with her. We were making plans.

This was of course before the Dark.

I wondered what New Orleans looked like now, behind its new shield, its changed status as an independent, and, I had heard, pretty unruly state, a refuge for crooks, pirates and the hopeless.

My mind tried to focus on her face, but I knew that day after day, my memories would fade until details would merge with dreams, features and colours would dull, and she would eventually become the ghost of a ghost.

A shuffling sound behind my front door. I rose from my waking slumber. Walked over to the door. Someone had slipped a piece of scrap paper under it. I opened the front door but the corridor outside was empty.

I picked up the note.

A message from O'Carlson, suggesting we meet later at our usual place. I didn't even realise he knew where I lived.

I wondered who he could have used as a messenger.

He was sitting in his customary corner, the naive, child-like portraits of Mark Twain and William Faulkner on the wall fresco overlooking him.

"After all your questions about the lovely Cherise, I thought I'd enquire a bit more," he said, a sarcastic smile spreading across his features.

"So, tell me. I can see you're aching to do so," I said.

"If I surmise that, from our previous conversation you are looking for her, I fear my news will prove disappointing. She is still untraceable."

"Oh." Nothing is ever easy in my business. Only trouble.

"As I thought."

"So, what can you do to help me?" I enquired.

"Not so much her whereabouts, but her past reality…" his smile leaked a trace of sarcasm.

"Can you be a bit clearer?"

"I've found someone who knows someone who still has prints of some of her more infamous photographs."

"Really?"

"Those that everyone assumed were wiped from the web after the Dark."

"A collector?"

"Some might call him something of a pervert," he added. "But then everyone has a role to play, no?"

"I reckon so."

Alexandra had only given me two demure photographs of Tiffany Cherise. Face shots. High school album pics. Maybe it would prove useful to see the rest of her.

"What will it cost me?"

O'Carlson reflected briefly. He knew I wasn't in the habit of paying much for information. After all, I was only a second-rate investigator, never had much of a budget.

"Nothing. Just an understanding."

"About?"

"Should my information prove correct, perhaps you could arrange for some copies of the prints to be made. I'd love to see them again. Call it nostalgia."

"You dirty old so-and-so..."

"That's me."

"I can do my best," I assured him. "But no promise. I'll have to see how it goes."

In a twisted sort of way, I thought I understood him. When we were together, I'd often considered taking some nude pictures of Giulia, and I am sure she would have readily agreed, but I never did get round to it, and was now left with just crumbs of memories, snatched visuals tumbling inside my head, her stepping out of our bed, her back to me, bending over to pick something up from the floor, displaying more than she thought she was, or did she? Wonderful personal pornography. Her walking out of the shower cubicle, water dripping in cascades from her hair, her small breasts firm and impudent, nipples hard from the spray of the showerhead, their colour that ineffable shade I never tired of and found impossible to describe, like a brand new original colour from the rainbow spectrum between pink and brown that only she owned.

"There's only one problem..." O'Carlson said. Frowning.

"Tell me?"

"It's a no-go zone."

"Which one?"

The no-go zones were areas of New York which had come into being shortly after the events that followed the Dark.

Residential blocks that did a Louisiana of sorts and isolated themselves, protected by high security, and proved highly nervous about strangers. The normal rule of law was usually suspended within their perimeter and the city authorities adopted a laissez-faire attitude to the no-go zones. They were aware of the fact their resources were limited as far as enforcement went and, preferred to forfeit the property taxes they were owed there than get involved in trouble they could ill afford.

"The Angelika Block."

It was a block of buildings bordered by Houston, Mercer, the further reaches of Bleecker and Broadway, in which once upon a time the Angelika art cinema had been sited. Every movie house in Manhattan had of course long gone out of existence.

It could have been worse.

Some no-go zones were impenetrable whether by force or by use of hard cash. This one, less so. I knew someone who once worked as a cashier for the actual movie house. Maybe I could track him down and gain some intelligence as to how to get past the perimeter security?

"There might be a way," I told O'Carlson.

"Fantastic."

"If I can get hold of something, I'll share it with you. It's a deal," I told him.

We parted.

I walked down Broadway toward Houston. Two-thirds of the stores were shuttered or had their windows broken, and visible signs of squatter occupation inside. On the sidewalk, wonky trestle tables, frayed carpets and cardboard boxes were loaded with junk, which school-aged kids who had visibly not set foot in a school for ages were trying to sell. The real, valuable stuff that people wanted wasn't sold on the streets, but more privately.

These were just the leftovers of the feast of looting and theft that had followed the catastrophe. The dregs.

At the old Angelika entrance, beyond the steep set of concrete stairs, two dangerous-looking sentries in khakis, stood guard, sharp knives hanging from their utility belts, halted me.

I asked for Gareth.

"Who are you?" one asked.

"A friend of his."

They turned their heads away from me and conferred. Then returned their attention to me.

"He's not around."

"Will he be back any time soon?"

"Sure. He's normally here in the early evenings."

"I'll be back then," I told them and made my way back to the office. Spent time sorting through the known facts of the Cherise story, jotting down a note here, a question mark there, in an attempt to make the case clearer faster than it already was.

There was something about it that concerned me, that rang false, but I couldn't point my finger at it. It was different from other cases of a similar nature I had taken on. As if a rain cloud was hovering over it, threatening to open its trapdoors and flood me with all the contents of its heavenly sewer.

□ □ □

Gareth greeted me. "I thought it was you," he said. The goons on the block's protection detail appeared to have a talent for describing visitors.

I was pleasantly surprised: I didn't think I was that distinctive in appearance. Maybe it was the way I dressed. As if I cared.

I explained who I was hoping to make contact with inside the Angelika block.

"That old coot," Gareth said. "He's quite harmless, you know."

"I never said he wasn't," I pointed out, wanting to make him think this was just a casual request and I couldn't be bothered one way or another whether I succeeded in meeting the collector in question, whose name was Pochoda. "I hear he has some old documents I'd like to take a look at," I added.

"I'm confident we can manage that," Gareth said. "But he has to agree to see you first."

"Of course."

Gareth nodded to the bouncers and I was allowed in to the basement of what used to be the cinema.

"You still live here?" I asked him.

"Yes, Auditorium 4, the smallest one, but good enough for me. Cosy, practical, private." He grinned.

Beyond the screens, a warren of dark and narrow corridors, rumbling pipes, and noisy machinery kept the block alive and functioning. We reached a door, like a spaceship docking room, which Gareth opened after punching in a number on the control pad. We emerged into a white-painted hall, lit like a beacon of whiteness.

"It's the building at the back of the cinema," Gareth pointed out, as I followed him through. "An emergency exit, or entrance point, depending on the situation," he smiled at me knowingly.

"Helps bypass the doormen in the main Broadway lobby; they can be a bit fierce and protective."

He escorted me up to the right floor, but then left me to my own devices. "Just don't let on that I provided you with access to the building," Gareth requested. I agreed and walked up to the collector's door.

The bell didn't ring so I had to knock. Repeatedly.

Finally, I heard a shuffle on the other side and a voice:

"Who is it?"

"You don't know me, Mr Pochoda, but I'd like to speak to you."

"I have no wish to see anyone," he answered, in a whiny tone.

It took some cajoling, but he finally opened the door. I'd explained that I was a professional tracer and pretended I could possibly help him locate some rare items for his collections, appealing to his instincts.

He allowed me in. The hallway was in darkness. He was a small man, balding, with a comb-over, wearing a brown dressing gown tied around his waist with an old leather belt. His slippers dragged along the parquet floor. He was unshaven and once we reached a room where every shelf was bursting with books and magazines, every item of furniture buried under folders and old newspapers, I noticed the contusions on his face. He had recently been beaten up badly. A deep cut on his left cheek, a swollen eye, and dark bruises dotted around his cheekbones.

He gave me one brief look and saw through me.

"It's about the Cherise pictures, isn't it?"

"Yes."

"You've come for nothing," he said. "I don't have them any longer," he stated, his shoulders slumped, an air of resignation colouring his damaged features. "I told the other guy. But he still did this," he pointed to his face.

Who had Pochoda's other visitor been?

He raised his right hand towards me, showing me a heavy bandage wrapped around it. "He broke one of my fingers, even though I'd told him the truth. Tall guy, built like a tank. Cauliflower ears and a severe crew cut. Black suited…"

"When was this?"

"Two days ago. I had a set of the photographs, obtained them some time back from another collector in Cedar Rapids, but the photographer who originally took them insisted he wanted them all back."

Before O'Carlson had put me on his trail. I was struggling for some understanding of the situation and the precise chronology.

"What photographer?"

He looked at me and there was fear in his eyes, as if he thought I was going to inflict additional physical damage on him if I didn't believe him.

"Hilton Willis."

"Who's he when he's at home?"

"The photographer who initially took the majority of the Cherise set. Came to see me a month or so past, argued I had no right to keep the copies. Insisted he had to have them back. I kept on telling him I had no intention of making any commercial use of them; just wanted to own the set. I just love those classic pics; I also have a wonderful selection of Bettie Page ones in my folders, you know… An old man's hobby. Willis had somehow found out I'd acquired them from the Iowa source."

"And this is what you told the guy who beat you up?"

"Yes. No one wants to end up dead for a set of girlie pics," Pochoda protested.

I left him. Could almost hear his heavy exhale of relief as he closed the door behind me.

□ □ □

Hilton Willis was easy to track down. He'd once been a much in demand fashion photographer. Word on the street was he'd fallen on bad times since the demand for women's mags and glamour had greatly diminished since the Dark. He was doing other work, of a more dubious nature. His studio was situated in Brooklyn, just a dozen subway stops from my Greenwich Village office. Although I had a bad feeling about things, I knew that I had to pay him a visit.

It was an old converted warehouse. The front door of the building barely held on its hinges, its lock dangling, rusty, unused for ages. I assumed the individual spaces on the floors above would have their own separate, secured entrances. The service elevator was also out of action and I had to climb the stairs.

Willis's studio occupied the top storey.

HILTON WILLIS PHOTOGRAPHY
By Appointment Only

I hadn't called ahead for an appointment. His number had been disconnected already. As I had discovered when searching for the studio's whereabouts.

The stairs were steep and dusty. I was out of breath by the time I reached the top.

The door to the warehouse space the photographer occupied was a pockmarked slab of metal. Industrial chic in its heyday, now just another sign of urban dereliction.

It yawned open.

I knocked.

Shouted out his name. There was no response. I ventured beyond the studio's threshold.

The place was vast and cavernous. High ceilings where the sound of my voice trailed an echo alongside the red brickwork of the building's walls.

In one corner, a random, busy pile of rolled up material, projectors, twisted lamps and long abandoned equipment.

Beyond it, past a moth-eaten curtain, a small kitchen and, I assumed, a dark room area. All empty.

At the other end of the space, metal lockers, low-slung filing cabinets and a zone of relative darkness. I stepped in that direction, tiptoeing across debris, shattered cameras, a mess of wiring. I wanted to open the drawers, see if they still contained any photographs filed away for some personal purpose. As I approached, I noticed in the shadows of the upturned drawers a mountainous clutter of prints scattered across the floor, torn, creased, deliberately destroyed, and further afield a pile of ashes where some had actually been burned to erase all traces of the images they had once captured, like insects in amber. A hillock of destruction.

Whoever had disposed of Willis's archives had been thorough, systematic in savagely tearing up all the prints into shreds, a dark dress's hem visible here, an eyelash there, a hat, the soiled map of a body. It would be the jigsaw from hell to reconstitute a single image from what remained. My movements disturbed the almost ankle-high pile of scattered papers and photographs that lay at my feet. I cautiously moved my leg in an effort not to spread the field of detritus further. My sole stuck to the floor. I pulled my foot up to extricate it from what was sucking it down.

A metallic tinge reached my nostrils.

I then knew what I had stepped in. Blood.

Moving my foot away from the area where the floor was adhering to it, I struck something soft.

Holding my breath, I knelt down, timidly burrowing my hands through the jungle of papers and shards of photographic prints.

I reached the body.

I had guessed this was what I would find from the moment my foot had encountered it, blocking its path, buried beneath the mess of papers.

It was still warm.

White shirt soaked in blood, shoulder length hair, a face as pale as a sheet, drained, lifeless. I had no wish to move the body.

I rose and stepped over to the other side where I could see its face.

Throat slashed. The blood now congealing around the edges of the savage cut.

Hilton Willis.

Fuck!

A bolt of fear ran through me. Too many coincidences. Too much bad voodoo.

I was careful not to touch the body any further. Weighed my options. To get the hell out of here or to get the hell out of here.

I chose the only option possible and rose to my full height in readiness to walk away as fast as my feet could take me and hope against hope there had been no witnesses to see me entering the warehouse building or noting my imminent departure.

I only got as far as the stairs.

He was sitting on the top step. Waiting for me.

Relaxed, unhurried, dressed in a coal black wide-lapelled suit and a white shirt with black tie, just out of *Reservoir Dogs*, this year's fashion for villains. His hands were the size of concrete pancakes. I guessed the hands that had inflicted the damage on Pochoda.

He was wiping a butcher's carving knife clean with his handkerchief. Cleaning the blood off it.

He must have been here all along. Had I arrived just a few instants earlier, I would have witnessed the murder. My throat tightened.

"I was expecting you," he said. His voice was higher than the basso profundo I could have expected from someone of his bulk and size.

I was struck dumb. There was no way I could rush by him and run down the stairs. Not enough space; he would nonchalantly catch a leg or trip me and I would go tumbling down to the next landing where he would leisurely catch up with me and complete the job with ease.

A smirk cauterising his face, he slid the knife out of sight into a leather holder which he returned to the inside pocket of his jacket.

"Follow me. I have a car waiting for us around the corner," he said. "Don't want to linger here, do we?"

I did as I was told.

Standing, he was even larger and infinitely more menacing, as if violent pheromones were suspended in the air around his unholy bulk like butterflies, an invisible suit of armour.

The vehicle, a four-door metal grey SUV was parked two blocks away from the warehouse. The streets were empty as we made our way towards it with not a soul in sight I could appeal to for help.

He opened the rear door for me.

"The boss wishes to speak to you," he said, slammed the door, locked it electrically and we drove off towards Manhattan. I was alone with confused thoughts as we sped over the Bridge.

□ □ □

I should have guessed where I was being taken.

The Helmsmark mansion by Central Park.

But it wasn't Alexandra who had me summoned there.

The Commander's study was an exercise in shades of dark.

The light was muted and dull so I, at first, had to squint to make out what was there. It was as if he were suffering from an eye ailment and had been ordered to sit in semi-darkness by his physicians. As my vision grew accustomed to it, the surroundings came into view. Plain walls painted grey, heavy furniture and chairs, brown curtains veiling the window that, if my sense of orientation was right, looked out onto the park, a single bulb Anglepoise lamp above his desk, lighting his severe features from below. Behind him, the wall was a black and white kaleidoscope of rectangular-shaped picture frames of varied sizes displaying the Commander with famous politicians—I recognised at least three presidents—and other figures of authority whose faces looked familiar but to whom I couldn't immediately put a name.

On a corner of his desk, a small American flag floated in solitude next to a crystal inkstand and a set of pens.

The chair I was led to was too low and the Commander overlooked me from the other side of the desk, his face a mask of annoyance.

"You know who I am?"

"Yes, Commander."

"And I know who you are," he declared. At least I wouldn't have to hand over my business card. "You're the investigator my daughter Alexandra hired."

"I would normally plead client confidentiality, but I have a feeling you'd ignore that," I responded.

"You're nothing," he said. His features were frozen. He looked the same, whether he was threatening me or being jocular. But I knew it was the former. He was the sort of man who had no need for plastic surgery to look Botoxed to the max.

I kept my counsel and my silence.

For now.

"It's about her sister, I assume. She wants you to search for her?"

I nodded. There was no point in denying it.

"Let me tell you, young man: I only have one daughter."

That went against the facts I had collected so far. I'd seen the newspaper cuttings. He definitely had two daughters, albeit late in life, but two all the same. Had he forgotten one?

Noting my puzzlement, he made things clearer.

"In my heart, the other one died a long time ago. She has no right to call herself my daughter. I ordered Alexandra to forget her, erase her from her life, and mine. She brought shame to our name."

"I see..." was all I could say. Where was the instant wit and repartee when you need it? But I also recalled the dead photographer with his throat slashed. For the sin of having kept a record of Tiffany Cherise's shortcomings. Or had he been more to her than just a photographer?

"The record is expunged," the Commander proclaimed. "I thought all those filthy photographs had gone with the Dark, and that I'd managed to have any remaining evidence destroyed. And then you come along..."

"It's not as easy to erase people's memories," I pointed out.

"There are ways," he stated. And I remembered his thug standing in the room behind me. And the knife in the leather sheath. Maybe it would be better to keep the irony on the backburner and not irritate the Commander any further.

"I take your point."

"I will pay you what Alexandra promised, and you will cease your investigation with immediate effect," he said and slid a light brown envelope across the desk towards me. I was reluctant to take it. "Right here and now," he emphasised. Coughed. Gasped for breath for just a moment. The heavy in the dark suit rushed over with a glass of water, his elbow brushing against me as he did so. Having delivered the water, he picked up the envelope, turned towards me and stuffed it forcibly into my jacket's side pocket, making it clear I had no choice but to accept it. It was non-negotiable.

"My assistant will see you out," the Commander said. His silhouette was framed against the wall of mementos in chiaroscuro lines and, for a brief moment, I wondered whether he was in a wheelchair, but he brusquely got to his feet, stepped aside from the tall armchair he had been sitting in and disappeared through a side door carved into the wall which I hadn't noticed until he opened it.

There was a tap on my shoulder. I was being escorted from the premises like an unwelcome salesman who'd failed to make a sale. Disposable.

Even though it was a grey day, the light over Central Park was dazzling to the eye and I had to squint a moment before I got my bearings. I walked all the way down 5th Avenue, needing the time to think.

By the time I reached my office, I still hadn't thought of pulling the envelope out of my jacket and checking how much I was being bribed to forget about the case. How much, what was left of my ethics, was worth these days.

On one hand, it would be supremely foolish to proceed further with the investigation into Cherise's disappearance. On the other, there was something about Alexandra that both attracted me and puzzled me.

I hadn't reached a conclusion when I noticed another envelope, white and thin, that had been slipped under my front door. Not another summons from O'Carlson, I hoped.

Reminding me that I'd agreed to bring him a Cherise memento.

My name was scrawled across the envelope in a spidery handwriting that I knew wasn't O'Carlson's.

I picked it up.

Just a scrap of lined notepaper.

'I found this after you left. Not a typical Princess Sensuality shot, but thought you might appreciate it.'

Signed P with a flourish. Pochoda.

There was a small 5x5 photograph. A Polaroid if my memory served me right.

A bench on some cobbled Square. Two women, nude, in a chaste embrace, one's head leaning against the other's shoulder.

The curve of a breast obscured by the line of an arm. A flash of thigh. Almost demure, even artistic.

A blonde cuddled up to a brunette.

The blonde was definitely Cherise.

I took a closer look.

My heart rushed up to my throat.

The other woman was Giulia.

I think I stopped breathing.

Looked again.

There was no doubt about both the women's identities.

I was so blinded by the two nude women sitting on that bench that for an eternity I didn't peer beyond at the building against which they had been posed in the pale light of what must have been an early morning.

Then I recognised it.

There could be no doubt.

The Pontalba Building.

In New Orleans, off Jackson Square.

A place I knew all too well Giulia had never visited and which I had promised so often to take her to. Which indicated that this particular shot had been taken since the Dark.

I sat down, in a daze.

How could I drop the case now?

3 – THE KING OF WASHINGTON SQUARE

The northwest corner of Washington Square, by the angle of McDougall and Waverly Place, had gradually become a market.

Shortly after the Dark, some enterprising kids had taken over the tables hitherto reserved for the old, black chess players who had previously made the area their own, dislodged them after a few scuffles and then other, less salubrious, traders had quickly moved in and now the heteroclite market had taken over the whole north side of the Square occupying the length of the alley, annexing the children's play enclosure and every single wooden bench going all the way to the Arch, beyond which stood a newly-created no man's land, bordered by razor wire and patrolled by Home Security personnel, with goons in camouflage uniforms armed to the teeth, manning their searchlights aimed straight at the lower half of 5th Avenue, ever present, patrolling the roof of the arch, looking down on the helter-skelter landscape.

You could find anything there, from pre-Dark electronic wares to ancient porn magazines which had suddenly become in demand again after the disappearance of the Internet, spare parts for cars and household appliances, vintage clothing which never went out of vogue, and rumour had it any kind of illegal weaponry if you knew the right people and the right words to say. The market thrived during the day, but it was at night that its activities went into overdrive, in the shadows of the trees that squirrel tribes had long since abandoned.

I knew folk who worked there, or others who made it a regular port of call around the midnight hour. When they slipped out of their urban lairs and took the air, seeking solace in the company of other outlaws of our new society.

The sort of place you took care to walk through, just not wearing a suit and tie.

At the opposite end of the Square, in the shade provided by some of the old university buildings, the dog track was still in use in late afternoon, lit by the glare of bonfires, hosting dog and cock fights where people roared, gambled and took out their frustrations as the animals fought in the dust and blood soaked the ground which never seemed to dry long enough to absorb all of it.

The market had often proven useful for snippets of information and contacts in the past.

I wandered around, glancing at the goods on display and stealing curious glances at what lay under the benches, trestle tables and chess tables, which I knew would always prove more interesting and expensive, if not legit.

Timkins was a regular, a wide boy wheeler-dealer in old magazines mostly, with a sidebar in photographs of vintage cars, parts, and old vinyl 45s from the Golden Age of rock 'n' roll. He was always bemoaning the fact that there were less and less record players around that could be used to appreciate his treasures in full. "A bloody shame," he said, "Folk just have no respect for tradition."

He never appeared until six in the afternoon, claiming that he was spending the earlier hours scouring Manhattan and beyond for 45s and other material he could see fit to find a buyer for, but from the tired look on his face and the bags under his eyes, I got the strict impression that he never woke up until midday at the earliest. I indulged him.

He was tall and lanky, a head higher than me at least, even when he stooped.

"I'm a bit low on magazines right now," he said in answer to my query. "Some rich Brooklyn socialite bought up nearly half of my stock the other week. I had a ton of National Geographics and Esquires," he pointed out.

"Not those sort of pictures," I indicated.

His grin widened.

"Oh, oh, are we talking the same language?" he said, sotto voce, brushing his long greying hair back. "Girlie stuff?"

I nodded.

"Would never have expected it of you," Timkins said, with a note of surprise. "I always thought you had no problem attracting the right kind of women." If only he knew how good I also was at losing them.

"Research," I said.

He chuckled. "They all say that…"

I explained to him about the Cherise pics. He'd never heard of her and was adamant they'd never seen the light of day in magazines anyway. "I never deal in prints, but I know a guy who does," he continued. "A Rasta dude from New Jersey, but he only comes along at weekends."

He pointed to a bench further down the alley, close to the arch.

"That's where he trades."

Right now, the bench was occupied by a middle-aged woman in 70s gear which did anything but flatter her, selling batik, silk scarves, fake jewellery and watches, seemingly without any success as passers-by didn't give her wares a second glance.

I returned on the Sunday afternoon and, right on schedule, the guy was there, knitted hat in the colours of Ethiopia, or was it Jamaica, crowning his Afro with added braids. He was even taller than Timkins and towered above me. His eyes were bloodshot and you could smell the ganja fumes from several yards away.

Scattered across his bench was a series of cardboard shoe boxes.

I feigned interest. Looked through a couple of them, old postcards in one and a repetitive series of prints of ancient naturists at rest and play, all black and white and with their genitalia brushed out of existence. The images were almost innocent in an unhealthy sort of way.

"You like? You collect?" he asked me. I'd expected a Caribbean accent or a variation on one, but he was straight undiluted New Jersey.

"I was looking for something more modern, recent," I looked him in the eyes. "Anything you don't have on display, maybe?"

He had. I thought it best not to be too precise about the images I was seeking for now. It would only serve to raise his price, had he something of interest which would help me pinpoint Cherise, or Giulia.

He asked me to return the following day. He would bring the good stuff along, as he put it with a broad smile revealing a row of white teeth, too dazzling to be natural.

"Make it two in the afternoon," he said.

I agreed on the time.

I was corralled by dreams that night, unable to find sleep for hours. Images of Tiffany Cherise, images of Giulia dive bombing my anxieties, encircling my panic attacks with fine-tuned cruelty and accuracy.

When had that photograph been taken?

It made no sense.

Before the Dark, she had always told me she was so madly looking forward to my taking her to New Orleans one day when we both would have the opportunity to travel. Since then?

What about the association with Cherise?

And if the photo I now kept on my bedside table was faked, doctored in some way, why? Could you even Photoshop Polaroids?

I should visit Pochoda. Ask him questions.

By the time I reached Washington Square at the agreed time on Monday, I had created a web of nonsensical explanations, of answers to impossible questions that left me even more dazed and confused.

The white Rasta was standing by the bench, looking furtive and worried, casting nervous glances around him, at the other traders, the passers-by, the potential customers.

"Hi. Remember me?"

He looked up. Recognised me.

"You were going to bring me some of the good stuff?" I reminded him.

"Not here," he said. I followed him to one of the alleys that bisected the university buildings nearby on the south side of the Square. A few garden chairs, rusting, wonky, were scattered around. We sat.

He pulled a bundle of prints from the inside pocket of his cavernous coat.

"Maybe I have what you want here?" he asked. "Bettie Page, Nettie Harris, Vex Voir, Mistress Matisse, Madison Young, Casey Calvert, Gemini June. I've got them all."

I took out the image showing Tiffany Cherise and Giulia in a chaste embrace. "I'm seeking more photos of these two young women. This one is called Cherise. I gather she was once quite famous." I didn't want to mention Giulia's name.

He took one hurried look and cast further worried glances towards the alley's entrance, as if concerned someone would come upon us, swapping porno pics or drugs. Not that that sort of merchandise was of any concern to the cops these days.

"No, no," he stated peremptorily. "Nothing like that. Absolutely not…" He looked down at me as if I was the devil, hurriedly slotted the bundle down into his coat's cavernous pockets and walked off without a further word.

"Hey…?"

He didn't look back.

Had the Commander put the word out on the street, I wondered?

Too many coincidences, I reckoned. No smoke without fire.

But who held the matches?

First thing the following morning, I trooped off towards Mercer Street and managed to convince a now reluctant Gareth to smuggle me into the block through the subterranean areas below the old Angelika.

I knocked on Pochoda's door.

There was no immediate answer.

I knocked again, louder.

A door opened further down the landing and a face peered out. An old man holding himself steady with a cane.

"You're looking for the collector?" he asked.

"I am."

"He's gone. Left yesterday. Seemed in something of a hurry. I gather he's even left most of his mess behind."

It felt as if I was chasing my own tail.

Back on the street, still puzzled and trying to figure out my next step, I heard a voice over my shoulder, whispering my name.

I looked back.

She was wearing a man's trench coat, grey and cloudy, and couldn't have been more than sixteen and five feet tall. Straw-coloured hair cut short and a fringe that obscured her forehead.

Rounded, with large violet eyes that shone like a beacon in the landscape of her paler than pale skin. Standing behind her were two heavies, clad in jeans and bulky sweatshirts, under which their six packs and finely attuned muscles screamed for attention.

If, for any reason, you didn't take her seriously, there were a thousand reasons not to ignore her sidekicks.

"Yes?"

"The King wishes to see you," she said.

I had a good idea who she was referring to.

"And who are you?" His emissary, his Girl Friday?

"I'm the King of Washington Square's daughter," she stated.

What was it about daughters of dangerous men that attracted them to me right now?

□ □ □

The self-proclaimed King of Washington Square was one of the men who ruled the island south of Astor Place. He had a bad reputation and wasn't the sort of guy you wanted to cross. I'd never met him but knew enough about him not to wish to do so.

He occupied a building that was once a boutique hotel, close to the market by McDougall and Waverly Place. It was there he held court and it was unwise to turn down an invitation. I followed his daughter and her escorts there. The top floors were now derelict and abandoned but the lobby had maintained its art deco tiling and stylings. Glossy studio photos of old movie stars like Ingrid Bergman, Marlene Dietrich and Bette Davis hung from every wall, alongside other faded memories of times past I couldn't identify as readily.

Two Home Security soldiers were stationed behind what was once the reception desk, their semi-automatics laid out across the dark brown oak of the counter. The King had serious connections.

He was sitting in the bar.

"Here's the guy," his daughter said and nudged me ahead.

The King was as large and bulky as his daughter was petite and delicate. A hulk of a man with eyes full of menace and florid-coloured skin that made me think he was just days away from a heart attack. It seemed impossible that this pachyderm of a man had fathered a creature so small.

His lips were feminine, like a soft scar dividing the top half of his face from his bearded chin. His hair had turned grey and was cut short, but his beard was incongruously jet black. He looked to me like a pirate gone to seed.

"So, you're that private investigator?"

I nodded, kept my counsel.

"I've been hearing a lot about you these past years. Some people speak highly of you while others think you're just a nuisance factor," he said.

"Nobody's perfect."

"Hold back the wisecracks; I've heard them all."

I blinked in acknowledgement.

"Word reaches me from the park that you're looking for certain pictures."

"The word is right."

"Just the pictures or also the woman?"

He said the woman, not the women, I noted.

There was no point denying it. You didn't contradict the King of Washington Square.

"Both."

"Any luck so far?"

"Not much."

He fell silent, his brow furrowed, pondering over what to say next. I was as anxious as he was to know whether it would affect my immediate state of health or not.

"A word of warning… You're setting foot in perilous territory. Maybe not worth the bother. You're asking questions and some important people might not like the answers. I'd steer clear if I were you?"

"That's already been made clear to me by other concerned parties," I told him.

A hint of a smile lengthened his thick lips.

"Ah, so the Commander has already been in touch?"

"None other."

"I'm not like him," he said.

"I'd hoped not," I answered. "But then it's not your daughter involved either." I looked back, she was standing by the door next to the King's security, listening in silence to our conversation, her eyes intent.

"Exactly. Anyway, you're free to go. I was just curious to see what you looked like after all this time. Tread carefully, young man."

He appeared more amused than hostile. As if he thought it would be fun to witness me thrown, struggling into the lion's pit and was quite looking forward to the spectacle unfolding.

"I don't suppose you'd be able to provide me with some information?" I asked him. Why not?

"You suppose right."

He made a sign and one of his guards stepped out of the shadows and poured him a glass of cold water in which cubes of ice were packed to the rim.

"I'm sure you can find the way out."

"Into the hotel lobby, past the reception desk and I have no intention of paying my bill on the way out," I feebly joked.

He smirked. "As if you could afford it…"

I was dismissed.

It was dusk outside and the wind was picking up. A heavy storm was heading our way. I began my walk home, hoping I could beat the rain. I avoided crossing the park and headed for Broadway. There was electricity in the air as I reached the Bowery, the heavens about to open in no doubt a spectacular style, when I heard her voice again.

"Hey, Mr Detective!"

It was the King of Washington Square's daughter. This time she was alone.

I took refuge under the tattered awning of a long-abandoned store and faced her.

I'd never seen eyes so round and striking.

"So, what are you doing next?" she asked me.

"Rushing home so I have a roof over my head before all hell breaks loose," I replied, glancing at the menacing clouds above.

"I meant about this case you're involved in?"

"Tell you what: right now, I just don't have a clue."

The rising wind loosened a strand of her yellow hair and brushed against her forehead.

She looked at me with the same air of curiosity as her father, but without the underlying menace.

"When you go looking for people, I assume you only take on one case at a time?"

"Depends on my financial status," I pointed out. "Sometimes multitasking is the only sensible option."

"When all this is over," she said. There was a crack of thunder. "I might want to give you a job…"

"Are you acting on behalf of your father, or yourself?" I queried.

"Just me… And it would have to remain confidential between the two of us. Absolutely."

"Can you afford it? Is he generous with your pocket money?"

"Depends what you charge. Maybe I could pay in… kind?"

She unbuttoned her trench coat. She was small but perfectly formed, narrow-waisted, proportioned like a doll.

"I have a feeling he would disapprove."

"He would, but he wouldn't have to know, would he?"

"I'm not sure I'd enjoy becoming a eunuch if he found out, or having other parts of my anatomy modified," I pointed out.

She looked down at the pavement, tightened her trench coat closed again.

"So, what did you have in mind. It'd be good to know?" I asked her.

"I'd like you to find my mother," she said, with an air of defiance.

Daughters, mothers, what the hell! All I had managed so far was to be hounded by scary fathers. Would it be country cousins next?

"Ask me again in a few weeks."

It was neither a yes or a no. Weighing my options. She could prove a useful ally.

Right then, the skies opened their heavy gates and the rain poured down on the Village like a waterfall.

"Stay in touch," she said, walking off into the curtain of grey rain.

"How?" I sort of guessed my visiting the hotel and publicly asking for her would not be advisable.

She never answered, and her slim silhouette was devoured by the downpour. So that's why she wore the trench coat. I was stuck under the awning for almost an hour until the storm passed.

□ □ □

I was puzzled.

And realised I had forgotten to ask the King of Washington Square's daughter for her name.

It was rumoured that she was the one who controlled the dogfights in the park, even held some form of supernatural power over the dogs. I had never given much credence to the word on the streets. So many tales of the fantastic now attached themselves to the island post-Dark that it was problematic to separate the truth from the stuff of lies. Having now met her, confronted those eyes like saucers, that skin and its impressionistic canvas of freckles and the yellow pallor of her hair, I found it difficult to align her with all the things I had previously heard. She appeared vulnerable beneath her outlaw persona, as if she didn't fit in, hailed from another world altogether.

I kept on asking around about Cherise, hoping that my continuing enquiries might not reach the ears of the Commander or the King, expecting some form of violent retribution to crash down on me at any moment. I had to.

There must be a way to find out where Giulia fitted into the puzzle I was hoping to unravel. That was more of a motivation than Alexandra's money or allure. One I was determined to crack open, at whatever the cost to myself.

However, all it did was guide me through contacts, friends of friends and total strangers only to reach a series of dead ends, tall walls of ignorance.

The paper trail that I was so accustomed to investigating quickly ground to a resounding halt; most of it I had already exhausted anyway at the time of Giulia's disappearance. I must have done a thorough job in the throes of my initial despair as it seemed I hadn't overlooked a single fact, but still I went all over the work I had done again, but to no avail.

I lurked in the vicinity of the park, stood on corners watching, monitored the shady trades that went on under the cover of darkness, kept on answering questions that no one had an answer for or, in most instances even understood, knowing all along that no doubt inquisitive eyes were following my every move.

It reached the point where even people I knew and trusted began to avoid me, as if I smelled foul, trailed the rich aroma of garlic in my wake, had become a cumbersome pariah who would inevitably attract the worst kind of trouble and taint them by my presence.

I watched the steps and glass doors of the King's residence in the old hotel, until I saw his daughter leave one morning. I'd posted myself on the opposite side of Waverly Place in the shadow of a doorway. It had been a cold few hours. She was wearing her usual trench coat, her blonde hair trailing over the collar. She began to walk, straight-backed and determined towards 6th Avenue. I followed her. On the corner, where the still operating pharmacy once open 24 hours a day now only functioned in the afternoons protected by heavy security, the steps to the subway opened like a jaw leading to the gates of hell.

No one sensible took the subway those days, if you knew what was good for you. It was a subterranean world with laws of its own. I thought for a moment she was about to walk down the steps, unescorted by her father's acolytes but she stopped there and merely lit a cigarette, the metal enclosure of the stairway protecting her from the wind.

She began to puff away.

Noticed me watching her.

"Hey, it's you!"

"Yes."

"I know you're still asking around. I've heard my father and his crew complaining about it, so I guess you're not yet in the market for another job, so what are you doing here?"

"You never told me your name," I said. "It's been bugging me. Can't call you Princess of Washington Square, can I?"

"Why do you want to know?"

"For no specific reason. I just like being able to put a name to a face."

"He calls me Vienna."

I must have looked puzzled, so she continued. "Like the city. Heard of it?"

It was one of the trinity of European cities that had been erased from the map in the events following the Dark.

Terrorism. Collapse. War and barricades and fights to the death.

Genoa and Bristol were the other two. How it all happened, as if it'd been brushed under the carpet and was no longer the subject for polite conversation, no one knew any longer. But she must have been born long before, I realised.

"An unusual name…"

"Indeed. I've often asked him why he named me after a city and he always says it's because I was conceived there. But I know it's a lie. He once said he'd never set foot outside America. But I know it's better not to challenge my father."

"So, hello, Vienna. Listen, I'd offer you a coffee, but there's nowhere open around here at this time of day."

"Why?"

"I want to talk."

"About what?"

"Stuff."

"Shoot," she dropped the little that was left of her cigarette to the ground and ground her clumpy boot across it.

"Maybe not so close to the park," I suggested.

She nodded her understanding and we walked along, crossing Americas and taking Greenwich Avenue, which was now a parade of Japanese noodle soup dives, interrupted in places by raw produce stalls which had spilled out from the school playground that had once hosted a farmer's market, after the school had closed due to a severe lack of kids now being brought up in Manhattan.

"Why is the King interested in me and my enquiries?"

"Is that what this is about?"

"I've a one-track mind."

"They say dogs think that way…"

"Is it true what they say about dogs and you?"

She laughed. Her features beamed joyfully as she did so.

"No way. I haven't a clue how that one started. But then I've never denied it since, have I? Let fools believe the legend. I like to go watch the dogs and they seem to like me. Who knows why? Maybe it's the blonde hair? At least it keeps some of the wrong folk from approaching me and cramping my style. Sometimes I think maybe my father spreads the word too, to keep trouble off my back. There must be some privileges to being the King's daughter…"

I interrupted her. "You're not answering my initial question."

"I ain't sure. Just things I overhear. They never tell me much, treat me as if I'm part of the furniture. It's to do with the Commander…"

"That I know already."

"It's all connected with New Orleans. You know, in Louisiana..."

The name of the city was like a dagger to my heart as the Polaroid of Cherise and Giulia sitting on that bench in front of one of the Pontalba buildings, locked right now inside my safe, burned brightly in my short-term memory.

I needed to learn more from Vienna, assure myself of her cooperation somehow as an insider at the court of the King.

"Maybe we can help each other?" I suggested.

"You'll seek out my mother?" she asked.

"I could try. Help me puzzle out all the connections in this case."

From what she could piece together, both the King and the Commander had important business interests in the Crescent City. They had even been associates of some kind before the Dark. Had since badly fallen out but kept a close eye on each other's current activities and plotting. Which is how her father had become aware of the fact that I was seeking the vanished Tiffany Cherise. There must be more, she confessed, but she'd have to ask around discreetly, inconspicuously connect the dots.

"Do you think the Commander's daughter might have travelled to New Orleans?" Vienna asked.

"Possibly," I pointed out, my grey cells still speculating wildly while the jigsaw I was beginning to assemble was still much too fuzzy and lacking sense. "I'd also love to go down there, take a look see. I hear it's a fascinating place."

"It was in days of old. I'm not so sure it's anywhere near as attractive nowadays."

There remained one not insignificant problem. Louisiana had closed its borders and, reputedly, no one was allowed in and rumour had it that the city itself was blockaded behind high, heavily-fortified newly-built walls. No one had made it in or out of New Orleans in living memory, with just unproven stories of wild debauchery and total chaos beyond human understanding filtering out on occasion. Not the place you'd go to for a picnic.

It would be easier to penetrate Fort Knox or the Pentagon underground vaults than enter New Orleans, I told Vienna.

"There are ways," she said.

"Such as?"

"I've heard hints of smuggling routes. Some of my father's associates have spoken of such. No place can survive in total isolation."

"Could you find out more?"

"I can try but why should I trust you?"

"You're the one who came to me," I pointed out. She frowned, debating with herself. I tried to put her at ease by asking about her mother. "When did it happen, her leaving you?"

Her face darkened.

"I've never known her. Just the stories they've told me. He refuses point blank to speak of her. Something must have happened after I was born. He pretends she never existed even."

"Not even a name, photographs?"

"Nothing. I just thought, you know, when I heard you were a guy who found missing people…"

"A tough one. I need to start somewhere. And I guess my asking your father is not an advisable option. I get the feeling he already sees me as a nuisance and poking around his own life would not improve matters."

She nodded. Remembered something. "I have to go," she said.

"How can I contact you?" I asked Vienna.

"You don't…"

"I can't just hang around the park," I protested.

"We know where you live."

"I'm sure you do…"

□ □ □

Winter was approaching fast. Blades of cold, carried by the wind, ran past my skin and chilled my bones. Soon, the avenues would be scoured by even harsher streams of freezing air as the island of Manhattan surrendered to another glacial season, and stood in all its decadent, spoiled and tarnished glory between rivers which had frozen for every single year in living memory, the cold would be marked by the appearance around Thanksgiving of the frost fair on the Hudson, not just a market through which you could skate but a place of assignations, illicit pleasures and laughter that reminded all of us survivors of better times.

It had been several weeks since I had first accepted the assignment from Alexandra and she had not been in contact with me since. Whether she was aware or not that her father, the Commander, was openly hostile to my endeavours on her behalf, I must confess I was annoyed by her absence, if only because of all the extra questions I now wanted to ask her, not least if she, or her missing sister, had ever known Giulia at some stage, and if so precisely when. The chronology of events bothered me greatly. It didn't make sense.

Had she lost interest?

Had she been the bait to get me involved in some greater game? Or had the Commander silenced her? I still recalled with a shudder the body of the photographer partly buried under the debris of his work, his throat still gushing blood, the rough edges of the cut, the metallic smell of his existence spreading like a red puddle around him.

I lived in a small room on the floor above my perfunctory office. Bed, cupboard, bedside table, a chest of drawers missing half of its handles, a breakfast counter, a fridge and a microwave oven. All the things that were my present life.

Why was I doing this job? To pay for the groceries, to afford the illusion that my life still had a purpose since Giulia had gone?

My dreams were crowded. Panicky. I woke up in sweat most nights. My moods shifted between blue and blue while the sky outside was gridlocked between grey and grey.

I evoked that ineffable colour of Giulia's nipples, which had me imagining in a thrice what the piercings in Cherise's would feel like under my exploring thumb, and my mind inevitably shifting, by association, to the texture of Alexandra's burn scars, and full circle to Giulia again and the geographical shape of her birthmark and then to the straw-coloured pale sun of Vienna's hair.

Visions of women assaulted me.

There was a knock at my door.

Where I lived, not the office below.

No one ever paid me a visit here. I stepped out of bed, wearing just an old T-shirt as I usually did to sleep. Vienna knew where I lived. Had she discovered something new?

Another knock. Peremptory.

"Yes… I'm coming. Hold on. Who is it?"

A woman's voice, calling my name.

"Let me slip something on," I protested.

"No need for that," she said. "Just come as you are." I could almost hear a mischievous smile curl around her lips.

4 – OUT FOR THE COUNT

My mind was still fogged by clouds of sleep and I couldn't think properly. I was foolish enough to open the door.

The woman who stood there with a broad grin on her face was unknown to me.

Tall, strong shouldered, dressed in a thin tunic of a dress, pale blue, that adhered to her body like a second skin and stopped just above the knees. Her legs went on forever all the way down to her flat, black ballet shoes. She certainly didn't need to wear heels to appear Amazonian in stature. Her ash blonde hair was held back, scrunched tight at the back so that her forehead was prominent above small, dark brown eyes, strongly delineated eyebrows of the same colour, cheekbones to kill and a square, almost masculine jaw. The sort of woman who one moment would look beautiful and captivating, and at others on the borderline of ugly, if not severe in a cruel sort of way.

She gave me a scornful look, taking in my unkempt appearance and gazing down with studied indifference at my limp and shrunken cock, barely dangling beneath the line of the crumpled grey T-shirt I had been sleeping in.

"Expecting someone?" she asked.

My instinct was to bring my hands down and cover my exposed genitalia, but then I reckoned it was way too late for that and decided to brazen things out for all the good that it would do me. She visibly wasn't impressed by the appearance, let alone the size of my penis.

"Who are you?"

"I'm April Lea," she said. She had a distinctive Canadian accent.

"What do you want?"

"The Commander sent me. You're proving too much of a nuisance and should be taught a lesson…according to him."

My heart dropped and if my cock could have shrunk even further, it would have done so.

I was at a massive disadvantage.

"And… according to you?" I managed to reply.

"Well, it all looks a bit too easy. You do seem a bit…vulnerable right now, don't you?" She slipped her foot between the door and the jamb, to prevent me closing it in her face. Which, stupidly enough, I hadn't even thought of doing yet.

"He sends a woman?"

She grinned.

"I have a certain set of skills," she said.

"And you intend to use them?"

"It's always advisable to follow the Commander's orders," she pointed out, stepping closer to me. I could smell the strong, musky perfume than ran across her skin, noticed a single strand of dark blonde hair loosened from her coiffure, for a brief moment my thoughts balancing delicately between primal, animal attraction to her and deep grown stomach rumbling fear.

The incongruous thought ran through my confused mind: should I fuck her, or should I let her kill me?

I was never allowed the chance to complete the illogical thought. Her hand clenched into a fist and, at the speed of light, rushed towards my midriff like a guided missile and caught me square in the kidneys.

The pain was abominable. I fell to my knees, clutching my stomach, bent in two, the impact radiating from the point of contact outwards through every nerve in my body. The strike had been surgical in its precision.

I would find out at a later stage that April Lea had enjoyed many semiprofessional fights as a mixed martial arts fighter, a craft that combined boxing, wrestling and whatever else was designed to inflict pain on suckers of my type, pummelling opponents both male and female in a cage in Toronto where she had acquired something of a fierce reputation. I would look her up later out of curiosity. She fought as Fille de Vega, whatever that meant. But then I hoped never to have to ask her.

Short of breath and silenced by her first punch, I stumbled on one knee, raised my hand for both balance and protection and gripped the outer edge of her skirt, just above the knee.

She brusquely pulled her leg away from my grasp, raised it high, her tight skirt hitching up and allowing me a blurred view of the darkness between her thighs. A view I had little time to enjoy or fix in my mind before the leg surged forward as if on a spring and made contact with my face. I tasted blood. My lips were cut, and my nose felt bruised if not broken.

I collapsed like a puppet sundered from its strings. Welcomed the wooden floor with a sense of relief in the knowledge that I couldn't fall any further, and its hard surface felt like a temporary safety net.

"Come on, you're making it too easy. Get up, man." April Lea said.

How could I refuse her? I tentatively pushed myself up, knees grazing the floor in a hopeless attempt to gain some sort of balance through the fuzzy equilibrium my whole body was navigating. The pain from the initial blow to my stomach had still left me breathless and I had to stop my painful rise.

April Lea provided unwanted assistance and took hold of my hair, bunching a handful into her grasp and forcibly pulled me up to my feet. I stood in front of her, legs spread-eagled to retain my balance as if I was on a ship fighting the choppy waves at sea.

She looked at me with pity, let go, took two steps back and before I could even blink her left leg rose high into the air and took murderous aim. It flew forward, catching me between the legs with the impact of a runaway train.

I shrieked out. Tears rushed to eyes. My lungs expelled a lifetime of breath. I fell to the ground, clutching my genitalia.

My whole crotch was first on fire, then roasting, then consumed by the flames of hell, moving between extremes of ice cold and supernatural heat, pulsing, fading into the distance in agony and then experiencing the ebb and flow of returning waves of excruciating pain, as if the blow from her hard ballet shoes clad foot was being repeated time and again. Surely, I would never function again, annihilated, emasculated that I was.

Then, to contradict me immediately, compound my humiliation, I felt my peeing, distantly, the warm liquid pearling across my thigh somehow not connected with the totally annihilated zone where my sex had been.

I tried to move my head sideways, peer up, anxious to see how April Lea was looking at me. Would she display an air of disgust, of triumph, of pleasure in her ability to erase me from sexual existence, or existence altogether? No. She appeared serene, clinical, like a doctor examining a patient. I thought that if she let her hair loose, it would reach down to well below her shoulders in a gorgeous shade of blonde and I would find her quite beautiful to behold.

Yet again, the uncontrollable thought—surely not a message from my probably ruined genitalia—never reached a conclusion as another blow came out of nowhere to the side of my face. Fist or foot, it was impossible to know.

I passed out.

□ □ □

Like a prehistoric beast slowly rising from the ocean's depth and, defying water and gravity, aiming for the distant white of the sun, floating up to the sea's surface, disembodied. Soon after becoming conscious, through a haze, memories of my body, echoes of the pain tapping a drumbeat against my temples and all over the surface of my skin.

I felt something damp brushing against my cheeks, my mouth, my nose, my face.

Half-opened my eyes.

Looking concerned, bent over me, was Vienna.

"You…?"

"I said I knew where you lived. I came around, found you like this on the floor," she explained. "How are you?"

I tried to mutter a few words, but my lips were dry and my throat drier. My lips also felt swollen and the size of sliced, ripe fruit.

She passed the wet handkerchief across my face again, reviving me with every soft stroke.

I twisted my head around in an attempt to see the rest of the small room, check if April Lea was still around. It was just me and her. Would have been crowded otherwise.

She sat back on her haunches, looking me over. I was still without pants, lying in a drying pool of my own urine. I couldn't smell anything, as if my nose was switched off somehow.

"Not good," I managed to say.

"I'm certain it's not my father or his crew," Vienna said. "I would have heard."

"I know." I nodded but every effort to move just my neck triggered pain in places I didn't even know I had.

Unavoidably, with just the hint of a grin, she looked down at my cock.

"I'd heard of blue balls," she said. "But it's the first time I've seen any..."

I peered down.

My ball sack was badly bruised. Black, purple, brown.

Anything but blue. Where April Lea had mercilessly struck me with the vicious force of a hurricane. If I could have blushed, I would have done so. She shouldn't have to see me like this, broken, battered, utterly shamed.

"I'll get you something to put on," Vienna said, indicating my nudity. She rose and picked up a pair of jeans that I'd left hanging on the room's only chair. "Here," she handed them over. "Oh," she remarked, "There's a note." A piece of paper had been stuck to the microwave window with chewing gum.

It was from April Lea. Signed with a heart traced around her name and a happy face. 'NEXT TIME I'LL HAVE TO USE MY OTHER SKILLS' it read.

Right then, I would have sold my soul never to discover what other mortal skills she possessed. My cock and balls would bear the marks of her assault for ages to come, I feared, and my bruised face, and the pit of my stomach. I couldn't think of anything worse she could inflict on me, bar killing me outright, which right now even sounded like a preferable alternative. Swift and probably painless.

Vienna helped me into the jeans. "I couldn't find underpants," she said. "You'll just have to go commando."

Actually, I often do.

"Liberating, isn't it?"

We both sat on the bed. She poured me a cup of water, then another. She drank with me.

"I've been asking around," she revealed. "Here's someone we could meet. He knows things about New Orleans."

I groaned as another stab to my stomach lining sharply raced across my midriff, an after tremor of April Lea's ministrations.

"Unless your little accident has put you off the case?"

It hadn't. I'm a contrary sort of bastard. Especially when it becomes personal. Which now it had certainly become.

I no doubt looked a total mess and left the apartment without taking a glance at myself in the mirror. I felt even worse, but there was no giving up.

Vienna had warily checked the rest of my body over and there didn't appear to be anything broken. A small mercy. On the way uptown, we stocked up on Advil and I swallowed a handful.

The further north we walked, the busier the cross streets and Avenues were with security and army personnel. Armed to the teeth. Green camouflage vans, with metal grills instead of windows, armoured SUVs, souped-up police cruisers crowding the intersections.

The tribes in Central Park were rebelling, they wanted to break out and reclaim the territory from the Plaza Hotel down to Times Square and 42nd Street. Another small war was brewing.

Whether it turned into a full-scale war or ended up as just another local skirmish was impossible to know. The old rules no longer existed. Logic was now illogical. I'd learned to accept our bright new world, I went with the flow. Did I, or anyone, have a choice?

The Dark had changed us.

Overnight it had taken so much from us. Goodbye data that had become a symbol of our lives, a crutch to make us feel alive.

Goodbye Facebook, Instagram, Flickr, chatrooms, websites, commerce made easy cyber-style, contactless, electronic life; farewell to everything we had delegated to that mythical cloud, wiped out without even ashes to mark its passing.

Some became angry. Angry at themselves for having allowed such a thing to pass, for having mortgaged all the things that made up their life, to be so obvious and vulnerable. Angry at others for the very same reasons, for having been part of some untold conspiracy or having caused it. Angry at religions. Angry at others. Angry at the whole world.

A minority welcomed the event, as it gave them another chance, the opportunity to be born again, without a past life, virgins again, no bank accounts, no criminal records or records altogether, their previous life erased with the swipe of an electromagnetic wave. But most were left bereft, desolate, orphans, vindictive and melancholy at the same time because the world they had once known, and trusted, was no more and would not be reconstructed.

Actually, nothing went dark: the sky at night retained its shade, the blind remained blind and the seeing didn't even need spectacles. I can't remember how the expression came to be attached to the aftermath of the event. Maybe someone had said or written that its momentous impact was a herald for a new dark age. But it became commonplace to use it. As I did: before the Dark, I loved Giulia; after the Dark, Giulia left me. It's all words, isn't it?

□ □ □

We reached the area of Grand Central. It had become a form of demarcation zone between the warring halves of Manhattan.

"It's Gabriel we're meeting," Vienna informed as we approached the block. "He used to lecture at Columbia but lost his job there when it all burned down. I was briefly a student of his."

"What did he teach?" I asked.

"History and Human Geography."

"That's what you studied?" She seemed too young to have attended university.

"No," Vienna replied. "I just sat at the back of the room for some of the courses and lectures. Things that interested me. He gave a lecture on Austria, so it caught my attention. Maybe the history of Vienna, the city, would provide me with clues to who my mother was."

Gabriel was waiting for us at the entrance to the Oyster Bar. It was still in operation, one of New York's grand traditions that had not been affected by the catastrophe, although not many could still afford to dine there and enjoy the succulent seafood or taste the expensive wine selection they were rumoured to stock. Few of the trains above still operated, just a handful to Connecticut or Philadelphia, with an unreliable timetable and often dodgy customers.

The Station was now under the control of the Emperor of Grand Central. That's what he called himself. It was said he had previously been a mere public office attorney down in Jamaica, Queens. The story of his rise was a maze of urban rumours, like so many Manhattan tales these days subject to a maximum level of disbelief. Why in days of desolation did all these maniacs want titles?

Gabriel greeted us by the bridge on the south side of the station and led us down the corridor. Everyone around seemed to know him well and didn't give us a second look. We followed him down a labyrinth of steps into the depths of the cavernous, partly abandoned building. Reached the shadowy bar area through a side entrance. All in silence, as if the place was a library and any conversation would see us banned for life. We sat down in an alcove. Shadows lurked in the corners, ignoring us.

He was tall and rangy, thin, straggling unwashed hair tied at the back into a ponytail, wore a moth-eaten heavy metal tee that had seen better days. His trainers had once been white. He looked nothing like a university lecturer.

"So, what do you do here?" I asked him, curious about his role at the Station. He didn't seem to fit in at all. All the others we'd seen in our underground journey here had been clean-cut, grey-suited and pulled from the same mould, uniformed executives at the bidding of the Emperor.

"I'm his memory," Gabriel said. "His living encyclopaedia. I have the knowledge stored away in here," He jabbed at his forehead. "These days information is the best currency."

"There are still books in the remaining libraries as well as the main one," I pointed out.

"True," he assented. "But you also have a need to interpret them."

Vienna protested. "Let's not argue, Gabriel. We need your help."

"Are you here on behalf of your Dad?"

"Not this time, and I'd rather he not find out. Call this a personal favour to me."

He brought a fingertip to the side of his nose and scratched it mechanically, his mind considering the request.

"Go ahead," Gabriel suggested.

I was uncertain of what to ask him first, unaware of what had previously transpired between Vienna and him that led to this encounter. Should I question him outright about Cherise and the photographs? But then how much did Vienna know about the nature of my case and what had she already told him?

"Someone we know appears to have taken refuge in New Orleans," I finally said. "We need to contact that person."

"Many people have flown to the Crescent City," Gabriel replied. "It's become a city of outlaws, each with his own laws and rules, a dangerous place from all I surmise."

"That's common knowledge," Vienna remarked.

"If they've journeyed there, I assume they don't wish to be found." He was prevaricating. I was growing impatient with him.

"Come on, Gabriel," Vienna interjected. "You owe me one. Badly."

I wondered what she had done for Gabriel in the past that had put him in her debt. Maybe I would rather not know.

"Spill," he finally said, with a heavy sigh.

Vienna nodded towards me.

"I'm seeking the daughter of Commander Helmsmark. I have reasons to believe she might be in New Orleans."

Vienna turned towards me, her eyes wide open, surprised, as if my question had come as a total shock.

"Oh dear, oh dear," Gabriel said. "You're not the only one. Word is out that the Commander has a contract out on her. Not just to find her, if you get my meaning."

"His own daughter?" Vienna exclaimed.

"There are rumours also that she might not be his daughter. But there is no proof." He turned towards me. "Why would the Commander employ you too?"

"He doesn't," I said.

Again, Vienna gave me a look of disbelief.

"Another party has contracted me," I pointed out, more to her than Gabriel.

"In which case you might have taken on more than you could handle," he said. "Murky waters indeed."

"Care to explain yourself?"

"There are alliances, plots, plans. They shift. Here one day, gone another. Friends now, enemies tomorrow. The Commander always appears to be at the centre of the spider's web, pulling the strings. A very dangerous man."

As if I didn't know this already to my peril. I could still feel the ebb and flow of irregular but powerful spasms of pain in my face and crotch.

"A most desired young lady, Tiffany Cherise," he continued, seeing me deep in thought.

"Is she the one who created waves with her porno pic?" Vienna asked.

"The one and only. Artistic nudes is the way I've heard them described," Gabriel pointed out.

"I don't suppose either of you has actually seen any of them?"

I asked.

The response was uniformly negative.

"Have you?" Gabriel enquired.

"Just one," I said.

"Before the Dark?"

"No."

"Interesting," Gabriel remarked. "Word on the streets is that the Commander was intent on getting them all destroyed. Eliminating the evidence, so to speak."

I didn't make any further comment but noted the sideways look that Vienna was giving me. Could she guess that the Polaroid was in my inside pocket, carefully wrapped inside a bunch of napkins?

I wanted to change the subject.

"So, how can one get to New Orleans?" I asked Gabriel.

According to him, it was not impossible, but I would need help. There were smuggling routes, a form of underground railway that people in the know and with the right combination of alliances and joint interests had been known to use. After all, Louisiana could not really survive on its own. Certain supplies, vital requirements had to be obtained from the outside, paid for in some form he was unable to determine. But it would be a slow journey. A dangerous one. By road, as planes no longer flew, or at any rate, commercial flight and privately-hired smaller craft were both few on the ground, and out of financial reach and carefully monitored by the warring authorities.

"And how do I make those necessary alliances?" I asked him.

"Well…" he hesitated, his glance moving between Vienna and me. "You might already have made one…" He smirked. Vienna shifted uncomfortably.

Once we had left him and reached the park and sat on a bench, the cold streams of winter circling us, she, hiding her straw-coloured hair under a knitted woollen beanie hat and me with my ears approaching freezing point, I questioned Vienna.

"Why did he hint that you could help me reach New Orleans?"

"My father's crew have arranged it previously, so I know part of the process. He's never told me exactly what, but he has had a close involvement with matters in New Orleans, dating back to well before the Dark. And if I read between the lines, some of it is even connected to the Commander. I suspect they were once in business together but might have come to a parting of the ways. What to avoid, some of the routes to Louisiana. But it was some time ago; the situation on the ground could have shifted."

"When?"

"A year ago. A woman was sent to the hotel by the Commander. My father agreed to smuggle her into Louisiana."

"Cherise?"

"No, she was dark-haired so couldn't have been her," Vienna indicated. Unless of course, she had dyed her hair for reasons of anonymity, I speculated.

Vienna shook her head. She told me that a girl knows those sort of things and would always spot a dye job from ten paces.

"You saw her?"

"Yes, I was loitering in the lobby. Had heard them discussing her earlier, so was curious to see what she looked like. Thick, curly hair. Italian."

My heart skipped a beat.

"How do you know that?"

"The others in the crew never referred to her by name. Just called her 'the Italian'."

I had to take my gloves off to unbutton my coat and pull out the bunch of napkins in which the photo was concealed.

I unveiled it slowly, fearful the daylight might accelerate its natural process of disappearance. I showed it to Vienna.

"Is this her?"

Her face was impassive as she examined the photograph.

"Well?"

"Yes," she pointed to Giulia. "That's the Italian woman. I don't know who the blonde is, I like her breasts though…"

"The blonde with the nice breasts is the Commander's daughter. The famous Cherise."

"Wow… And what's the Italian chick doing with her?"

"I'd pay a lot to have an answer to that question," I said.

She kept on gazing at the photo as if hypnotised by the nudity of the two models, the arc of their curves, the angle of their bodies against the background of Jackson Square, as fascinated as I was by what wasn't shown of their anatomies, of the story behind it.

"Who took the photograph?" she asked.

"Yet another question I don't have an answer to."

"So, I guess all the roads lead to New Orleans?"

They did.

I no longer had a choice in the matter.

We sat there in silence, the cold seeping into our veins, both lost in our own thoughts. Of others. Of another place all the way down south by the Gulf.

"Your mother?"

"Yes, what about her?" Vienna looked back at me, puzzled.

"Is she connected to all this?"

"I don't think so," Vienna said, a shadow falling over her pale features.

"Because there are a lot of coincidences at play here," I indicated.

"Not really. Actually, I was adopted. That's the only thing I know. Hence my curiosity about my origins. I'm not technically his daughter, but he's always treated me as if I were. He's an old softie, behind that rough exterior… He's never actually been married."

"I see."

"My birth mother must surely be dead, but it would be nice to find out who she was."

"Why so positive about that?"

"Because in my heart I know she is dead. But in my soul, I need some form of closure, to banish the ghost of her that always travels with me." Her sadness washed over her face.

"If you are convinced she is dead, why did you hint at paying in kind for my services when you first approached me, Vienna."

"Sometimes I like to pretend I'm a bad girl, you know… Mind you since I've seen you lying in a pool of your own pee and witnessed the sad, may I say inadequate, state of your cock and balls, I'm somewhat less attracted to the idea of sleeping with you now…" She grinned. A note of mischief illuminating her features.

"I'll heal… I think… I hope…"

"In which case you'll need a bodyguard to avoid a repetition or worse, having the whole package severed by the baddies," she stated. "Would be a waste."

"What do you mean?"

"I'll come with you to Louisiana. Help out."

"It might be dangerous."

"It WILL be dangerous," Vienna stated. "But I'm good with weapons," she pointed out.

"I don't doubt it."

□ □ □

We needed time. To plan. The route. The detours. The people who could help along the way and those to avoid. It would take a few weeks.

In the meantime, I knew I had to allow my body to heal, the marks to fade. They were already shifting from dark to yellow when I looked at myself in the full-length mirror of the office bathroom. I was still a shadow of my former self. Deep lines indented beneath my eyes, but more from lack of sleep and concern over the ramifications of the Cherise trail, crazy speculations that sometimes put me to shame, about who Giulia had been and what she had kept from me. This, allied with powerful fantasies of the photographs of Cherise and their pornographic nature together with Giulia's involvement in a whole set of images I could only dream of. If such images existed, I wanted to see them at least once before they were inevitably destroyed and all remaining traces of her betrayal erased.

Vienna had returned to the King of Washington Square's lair, in readiness for her own betrayal. We had agreed to not be seen together until the time came to hit the road.

I visited the 42nd Street Library again, delved into the archives and the microfiches, following cold trails and unfinished business. Found out quite at random about the ferocious April Lea, her talent as a mixed martial arts fighter and shuddered again at the memory of the beating she had given me. Christmas came and went, spent on my own in a diner by Gramercy. Then New Year's Eve when the rivers froze, and I slept through the night and woke up in a new decade, still the same man, not transformed overnight into a creature more handsome or at least brighter. Happier would have been too much of a bonus.

Time passed. I kept to myself.

I followed up existing data about the King and patching random pieces of information together, confirmed the fact about Vienna's adoption. It appeared that her mother had been an Austrian immigrant who had been taken under the King's wings after she had arrived penniless and pregnant from Vienna, she had died of natural causes, shortly after the child's birth. Reading between the lines, it sounded like a case of post-natal depression gone bad. I double-checked with the hospital information.

Maybe the King had tried to shield his adopted daughter from the facts to safeguard her from the ugly reality.

I then located her burial place to a cemetery in New Haven, Connecticut. I was uncertain how much of all this I should disclose to Vienna. If she reacted negatively to the news, she might pull out of the New Orleans expedition altogether and I was worried I might not even get near the Louisiana Republic without her assistance and contacts.

Decided I would play it by ear the next time I saw her. Maybe only parcel out the information as we approached the Republic's barricaded frontier.

I waited for her to make contact again.

All this time, I didn't hear from Alexandra and was absolutely determined I would not be approaching her with news of my relatively meagre progress with the case of her missing younger sister, let alone the fact that the enquiry had been subverted by my discovery of the photo of her and Giulia.

She was in no hurry for me to report back, it seemed, so there was no point informing her I was now no longer looking for one missing woman, but another one too, and that the latter took absolute priority in my mind. Maybe her father, the Commander, had nipped the whole affair in the bud anyway, and she was under strict orders not to see me again, or had been given the impression I had given up on the case.

The bruised Polaroid in my pocket was by now greasy with the lingering trails of my fingerprints as if by touching it again and again, padded my finger against the hollow of a neck, a calf, the sideways view of a breast might conjure her—and Cherise, of whom so much more skin could be seen—back into existence.

Had I perchance lost it, it would never leave the screen at the back of my mind, where it was now printed in indelible mental ink, the sort that never fades and even leaves a scar, like the sea marks the shore and anguish slashes the heart.

I slept the sleep of the guilty. Dreaming of immense seas with unthinkable depths. Of the way the sands of the Sahara seen from miles above in a plane when, pre-Dark, I had once travelled over them on my way to the Indian Ocean, danced in the air like living waves, a litany of movement hypnotic and with the power of a ritual unleashed that the human mind could barely fathom.

My dreams never made sense.

Do any dreams?

5 - FOG FATALE

I'm not a patient man.

Waiting for all the elements to click into place for the journey to Louisiana was hell on the nerves.

I was itching to get underway. Do something, While I was still stuck in Manhattan, what could be happening down in New Orleans to Giulia? To Cherise? Sometimes my twisted imagination could only conjure up the very worst-case scenarios and my stomach would twist into contorted shapes that only served to hurt me even more, the pain on overdrive, moving from the depths of my midriff to my feverish brain.

Painting images in my mind of the transformed Crescent City as a new incarnation of hell, with bleak and phantasmagorical landscapes and tortured victims inspired by both M.C. Escher and Hieronymus Bosch, a combination of dream art that made no sense at all and which any psychiatrist would consign me to the loony bin for even imagining.

I had faith that Vienna would deliver in the end but was curious how she was getting on with the preparations, frustrated by the fact I was unable to contact her first without endangering the project.

The frost melted on the Hudson. Then, the fog arrived.

The big fog.

Whether it was just the perennial scapegoat of global warming or another manifestation of what had provoked the Dark, it was unique and worrisome.

No one alive could remember Manhattan ever having been brought to a halt by the weather in such a drastic manner, a pea-souper of a shroud that, overnight, and coinciding with the arrival of spring surrounded the island, draping us all into a thick shroud of suffocating closeness, where you could barely extend your hand away from your face by an arm's length and still see it.

We'd fallen asleep to the familiar form of frozen darkness through which the sky carried veins of pink and woke up to a blurry morning of penumbra, a solid wall of grey in which every single breath made us feel like a swimmer struggling to reach the surface before his lungs would explode in protest at the thin nature of the air on offer. It was T.S. Eliot's "brown fog of a winter dawn" redux and everything ground to an immediate halt as we, remaining inhabitants of Manhattan, struggled to adapt to yet another set of catastrophic circumstances.

In a way it was fortunate that I was myself insulated from the outside world with my obsessive worry about Giulia and the head-scratching mysteries of the Cherise case that I filtered out this new endless night, wallowing as I did in my own misery.

Others were more vulnerable, and a shroud of depression wrapped itself around the island, when the black mist and murk had not lifted by Easter, there was an epidemic of suicides.

Would the fog achieve what the Dark hadn't totally succeeded in doing and wipe all hope from our lives?

Traffic had become impossible and food supplies problematic.

Fortunately, I could walk down to Chinatown, hands scraping against walls and doors every inch of the way, ever squinting and peering through the curtains of suspended particles that dotted the atmosphere for the recognisable sign of a familiar street corner or a malfunctioning traffic light. Here I could stock up on dry goods, all too often past by their sell-by date, which I could later rehydrate and consume. I wondered how others were surviving, how they were adapting to this new collective blindness where the impaired now held a distinct advantage over us able-bodied folk. This was certainly not the time to try and make my way back to Washington Square where the chances of being mugged by friends as well as foes was as likely as tripping over in the shadow of every tree.

From my distant memories of books read and vaguely digested, fog was supposed to smell of sulphur, but our New York fog was different, odourless but still noxious, life-draining in its nagging persistence.

Days spent indoors, on the sofa or just staying in bed, alone with my ghosts and anxieties. Sheets sticking to my naked body, pillow littered with strands of discarded hair, scalp sensitive, urging me to scratch away at its irritation. No knocks on the door, no one to see or reason to hit the misty streets, just the business of waiting.

I'm normally not a great conversationalist, more accustomed to short quips or dismissive remarks than the intricate flow of views exchanged and opinions weighed and deliberated, but the time quickly came that I got so stir crazy staying in my room or the office that I began to talk to myself. The way to madness. A word here, another there and then, to make matters worse, conversation between versions of me. The man who had convinced her to stay and took her to all the places we had once talked about: Barcelona, its beaches where you could go nude, the lakes north of Rome and the ruins of old cities, the walk in London between the South Bank complex and the Tate Modern, the sand of the Caribbean, the rain falling on the damp streets of Seattle and Vancouver... And then the man—the same one but for an accident of fate—who had lost her for reasons he still couldn't fathom and was now swimming through a living nightmare where fog, a semi-deserted Manhattan, pornographic images of women's bodies, and the spectre of distant New Orleans clouded his mind, orchestrating his despair. I was both those men, and neither of them was a sight to behold.

I had to get out.

I didn't make it past the front door. It was unlocked, so I pushed it open with my right foot, ready to face the cold, brown leather jacket zipped up, grey scarf wrapped around my neck, gloved hands deep in my pockets. I stepped forward and through the fog's haze saw a nearby silhouette in red emerging from the easel of the fog, at first diffuse, rounded along the edges then sharpening as it moved closer towards me. A person.

The scarlet red of a coat clouding its shape. I'd been planning to walk south, maybe make my way, inch by slow inch, to Battery Park, guiding myself from wall to wall using dimly flashing traffic lights as stepping stones, the sequence of which I had recently memorised, or hoped I had. But the red mass was moving towards me, in the door I was about to exit.

When it reached me, I could smell its breath hanging in the heavy air, fleetingly noted the matching scarlet of a woman's painted lips.

"You're on your way out?"

Her voice.

Alexandra Helmsmark.

My original client.

"That's what I was planning to do."

She was now so close to me we were almost touching, I could feel the heat radiating outwards from the tight bundle of her red coat, although I still couldn't see her eyes, half of her face obscured by a black scarf.

"I just caught you," she remarked.

"Indeed. It's been some time," I pointed out, peering through the fog in a forlorn attempt to catch the expression on her face.

"I thought you'd given up on me. Forgotten the case altogether."

"Have YOU given up on me?" she asked, sharply.

"Your father suggested I should. Rather forcefully..." I replied.

"And have you?"

"No."

"Good."

Despite the fact Alexandra was something of a moving blur just a few inches away from my eyes, her red coat phasing in and out of vision in the blink of an eyelid, I could feel a nervous hesitancy in her.

"I haven't much to report," I said. "It's proven trickier than I expected."

"I'm not surprised..."

Silence fell, cloaked in grey haze as we faced each other, as if both daring each other to say the next thing.

Alexandra stood there motionless.

I broke the spell first.

"Do you want to come inside and talk? At least we could see each other properly."

"No."

"So, what?"

"Maybe we could walk?"

"Walk? Through this? Where?"

In any direction, it would feel like stepping into a dark tunnel, only the sound of our voices and steps on the pavement forming a tenuous bridge between us, keeping us together.

"I don't know," she said.

"It's your call. You're the customer," I remarked.

Her hand took hold of mine. She wasn't wearing gloves. It was cold. She took a firm hold of me.

"Your hand is so warm," Alexandra said.

"All part of the service."

We walked for ten minutes in the general direction of the Bowery, in silence, hesitantly, grazing the walls, store windows and doors to guide our slow progress through the murk, like ships on a choppy sea, swaying to avoid unseen strangers and obstacles.

The warmth returned to her hand, draining the heat from mine, the remote beat of her heart coursing through her veins shooting echoes of her life-stream through our intertwined palms.

Inevitably, we reached an intersection that we hadn't foreseen and realised we were lost, stranded in the harbour of the fog, somewhere in the East Village, bearings confused, no doubt just a street or so away from familiar territory, but disoriented enough to feel shipwrecked.

Her hand still gripped mine, as if terrified by the prospect of me letting go and abandoning her to the desolation of the semi-empty streets.

We stopped.

"What is this all about?" I asked her. I pulled her back towards a boarded-up store's steel shutter as I heard an unseen car moving close by on the road, its engine rumbling in low gear, a danger to both itself and whichever bystanders were risking the outside in these conditions. Us. "You wanted me to find your sister and then you disappear out of sight for ages, as if the whole matter were unimportant..."

"Things happened."

"Your father?"

"Yes. Other things too..." she continued.

"I think he doesn't want her found. I discovered that to my personal detriment. He's rather adamant about it. Has persuasive methods."

"I heard."

"Anyway, I now have an idea of where she might be located. I was waiting to hear from you whether to pursue the matter," I lied.

"Really?"

"But everything is too murky for my liking," I said. "Your reasons, his reasons, it's as if the main story behind it all is being held back from me, for reasons I can't quite fathom. I can only work properly if I have all the information, the truth."

"I'm sorry," Alex said. Right then, I craved to see her eyes, because I knew they would finally tell me the true story, betray her. But the fog defeated me.

"So?"

□ □ □

It all came spilling out: a torrent of information, more random pieces of the jigsaw, some contradicting what I had been told originally, some new, some old. By the end, I didn't know what to think or believe any longer. We had by a stroke of luck and almost by accident found our way to an open 24-hours Korean grocery somewhere in Alphabet City and had taken refuge in one of its aisles. The will-o'-the-wisp scarlet of her lips a beacon in the outside obscurity, the hard grip of her fingers against mine a sign of her anxiety.

The strip lighting was on the blink and we parked ourselves between the hair products and the dental supplies. Alexandra pulled the scarf away from her face. Her eyes were metal grey.

Tiffany Cherise had always been the Commander's favourite child but had seldom done anything to justify this status, normally treating her father with disdain if not contempt, and an unhealthy rivalry had always existed between the two sisters as a result. There were dark hints, too, of something that might have happened between the younger child and the redoubtable Commander. Alexandra alluded to dark, unspeakable matters.

But, as if something was holding her back, her words were hesitant, unable to focus properly on the matter at hand. It all made no sense and there was no proof, but a terrible sense of wrongness hung in the air.

No, Cherise hadn't stolen anything from her, she confessed, it had just been a pretext to catch my attention, but she did have compromising information about their father's activities which he wanted suppressed. Alexandra had repeatedly heard them vigorously argue but couldn't pinpoint the principal reason for their antagonism in addition to

Tiffany's sexual existence as Cherise.

Yes, Cherise had slept with Alexandra's husband, had deliberately seduced him only to humiliate her, not that he had been by that stage a catch worth holding on to, a high school sweetheart who hadn't blossomed, as she had hoped for, into proper husband material.

When I queried her about the story of the car crash and the fire, she looked back at me blankly, neither confirming the tale or denying it, staring into the space behind me, the long line of shampoos, conditioners and lotions hardwiring the geometry of the shelf.

"So why do you want her back, why employ me to find her?" I asked.

"I don't know," Alex said. "Maybe I want her to say sorry to my face or feel it's my turn to apologize for the fact I didn't love her properly. Or this. Or that. Some form of closure. I'm just so confused."

A tear formed in the corner of her eye.

"It's so complicated," she said

She wiped the tear away with the back of her hand and gazed at me, as if she were asking for my forgiveness or, at any rate, some understanding. I was none the wiser now. She was visibly a mess, as was her relationship with her lost sister, her husband, indeed the whole world. And, resultingly, a dangerous client, harbouring secrets, unreliable. One I should have steered clear of. But there was that remote connection with Giulia. I couldn't let go. Not yet.

"You don't believe me," she remarked.

"Or trust you..."

The tear returned, welling up, about to spill down her pale cheeks. Her long hair was loose, ash blonde and uncombed, now freed from the sheath of the scarf, falling across her shoulders.

Under her red coat that she now undone, she wore a white silk shirt, buttoned tight around her neck, a grey cashmere cardigan and a loose black skirt that reached to just below her knees, nude-coloured stockings or tights and flat ballet shoes.

"You must find her," she continued, a note of pleading in her voice.

"Before he does?"

"Yes."

How could I refuse her? I've always been a sucker for women in distress. The way I was brought up, I reckon, or the fact I'm an unreconstructed romantic of the worst kind.

"I will." The words came out before I could think properly.

Whether I was responding to her pleading or was just convincing myself I was being professional and had to continue handling the case, I knew I was pulling the wool over my own eyes. I have a talent for self-delusion.

I could sense her relief.

"Come," she said.

She took hold of my hand, closed her red coat and pulled me gently down the aisle and towards the grocery's exit and we dived hand in hand into the fog. This time we didn't flounder much, her steps steady, her sense of direction as sharp as a GPS, as if our earlier floundering in the semi-darkness of the Manhattan day had just been a game. We walked in silence.

Half an hour later we arrived at the door of a medium-sized apartment block. It looked familiar the closer we approached.

Very familiar.

We climbed the steps.

I still had a key to that door. It was buried at the bottom of my pocket. I didn't have to use it. Alexandra had her own and unlocked the door to the building. It felt familiar although I hadn't felt as if we had actually travelled that far north.

"What is this place?" I asked her. I knew where we were, but I needed to hear her version.

"It's an apartment my family own. On the seventh floor. We can talk more, in total privacy."

Of course, it was on the seventh floor.

Where Giulia had once lived before moving into her university lodgings.

I had, needless to say, been a frequent visitor back then and returned several times after the Dark, following Giulia's disappearance. I had found nothing of course. Her clothes and belongings had long gone, together with any trace she had ever lived there. Just like in a bad mystery novel. All that was left and recognisable was the familiar furniture, the empty closet, the narrow kitchen and its bench, the flecked granite top on which we had often had our breakfast. I had once queried Giulia how she could afford such a pleasant apartment on her student funds, she had told me it belonged to the family of the friend she was sharing the premises with and was almost never present. The owners were living overseas for a lengthy period and the place was available to them rent-free.

The elevator wasn't working. Since the advent of the fog, power cuts were frequent.

We reached the right floor, both slightly out of breath.

Stepped down the short corridor. It was the first door on the left.

Alexandra had the key. The one I still retained was burning a hole in my pocket, rubbing against the key to the building on my key ring.

She opened. As always, the door offered minor resistance. It still hadn't been oiled.

For a brief moment, I half expected Giulia or even Cherise to greet us with a smile of surprise as we walked in, but the hallway was as empty as the last time I had come here on my own desperately searching for clues I might have missed on my earlier visits, but only the emptiness of the apartment faced us.

Alexandra shed her coat, letting it fall to the wooden floor, the red of its material spilling like a wet stain across the dark-brown varnished boards.

She turned to face me.

I couldn't read her face.

All that I knew is that she was beautiful, in a cruel but affecting way, both predator and prey, seductive and vulnerable.

"I'm so lonely," she said. Her lips moved closer to mine.

It felt as if I was seeing her for the first time, now that we were finally free of the fog, every angle of her face sharp and in focus, every shade of her skin a variation of white and pink and every degree in between.

Her eyes a metal grey landscape of grief, wet with emotion, inviting, tearful.

We kissed.

In the chiaroscuro of the apartment, the only light a dim haze of grey fog beyond the uncurtained window, caressed by shadows.

Alexandra's lips were like fire, unlike the now familiar coldness of her hands.

I couldn't resist and abandoned myself to the moment. Closed my eyes. Tasting her, the sickly-sweet flavour of her scarlet lipstick, a background of cherries behind the cushion of her moistness, the luscious ridges of her skin.

The kiss lingered, abolishing all notion of time. Both of us savouring the sudden intimacy.

I half-opened my eyes to find Alexandra peering straight into me, at such close range that the metal grey of her eyes felt like a searchlight drilling deep.

Our lips parted as she took a small step back.

"Indulge me," she asked.

I nodded, just a little bit puzzled.

She picked up the black scarf she had been wearing earlier outside from the floor where it had pooled beside the abandoned red coat. Straightened, brought it up to my face, and then tied it firmly around my head, blindfolding me. Its material was soft and woolly, impenetrable. I was in the fog again.

Blind.

"Love me," Alexandra asked.

Her hand reaching for my wrist, guiding me to the next room, to the bed I knew was there. A bed in which I had fucked Giulia more times than I could remember. By blinding me, Alexandra was forcing me to turn a new page. God only knew what my hypothetical psychiatrist would ever make of this, in terms of metaphors, symbolism and all that mixed-up jazz?

Her still cold hand brought mine to her face and I touched her, my eyes deliberately closed behind the blindfold, to experience this newly-acquired state of blindness at its most extreme.

Skin like silk, cheekbones rising like small hills beneath the epidermis, a new geography birthing beneath my fingers.

Grazing the curve of her cheek, the breeze from her breath gently flooding the back of my hand as it travelled across her features. She let go of my hand, allowing it to now roam freely, tracing the slope of her nose, moving to the softness and sponge-like nature of her earlobe, fingers dragging through the strands of hair, mentally comparing the thin threads of her blonde crown with the remembered thick dark curls of Giulia's hair and setting my mind wondering about all the other differences this exploration might lead me to.

I brought my other hand to Alexandra's face, washing over the hard, flat landscape of her forehead, lowering it against the geometrical close patterns of her eyebrows and encountering the delicate brush-like nature of her eyelashes. Her eyes were open, no doubt intent on recording every expression illuminating my face as I ventured by touch only across her features. Why did she want me to be blind?

One hand cupping her chin, another circling her neck, feeling the pulse of her heart as I roamed freely, I came upon the top button of her white shirt and loosened it. Her throat now naked, the flow of blood and air rushing through it, the tenseness in her whole body, begging me silently to move on to the next button, and the next and again. I pulled her shirt open, the back of my hand brushing against her freed breasts. I didn't linger there for now. I had all the time in the world. I resisted the strong temptation to touch her there and moved back up, my fingertips now drawn to the ravaged skin across her shoulder. She shivered when I touched it first. Took a deep breath. As did I.

Crossing the frontier between the hot smoothness of her skin and the cratered territory of her burn scars felt like moving into unknown land, I realised that ever since our first encounter I had been curious as to how it would feel touching her there, travelling across the no man's land of this other, dark side of her life. Maybe it was fetishistic, like the attraction of amputees or their stumps, but I couldn't help myself. I never said I was perfect, did I?

Finger-pads like lasers mapping every micro inch of her scars, experiencing each individual line, ridge, tear, crevice, like lingering across the landscape after the battle.

Alexandra kept on holding her breath, her whole body febrile, in a state of excitement and nervous expectancy.

"Do you mind if I touch you there?" I asked her.

"No," she sighed. "I've always wondered whether my errant husband would ever have wanted to do so, had he survived after the accident," she added. "It fascinates some men, attracts them in a morbid or sick way, while others draw back at the sight. Sometimes it gives me the measure of the man."

I couldn't pull my hand away, imprinting every detail of her map of destruction to my memory, embedding it within my own libido. Realised I was rock hard.

What sort of man did it make me?

Although she was frozen to the spot, Alexandra must have sensed this and lowered her arm, unzipped me and took me into her hand.

There we stood, she almost topless, holding my rigid cock, me entranced caressing the complex grid of her scars, remembering the full panorama I had once originally only glimpsed, of burnt skin, pink, rose, white and purple excrescences and destruction.

I imagined that the apartment's window on Broadway had been flung wide open and the fog was now invading the apartment and we were swimming against its currents, fish in a whirlpool, out of control and oblivious to the rest of the world.

I reluctantly pulled my hand away and took a step back.

"Fuck me," Alexandra asked.

Cloaked in the privacy of my own personal dark I finally reached out and undressed her. Taking my time. One item of clothing at a time, teasing, deliberate, exploring each revealed surface with sly touches and travels, shedding her layers of protection until she was fully nude and exposed to me, albeit still invisible, imagining each square inch of her body in its lush unbound perfection. I could feel her, smell her, bathed in the radiance of her naked heat.

Like an impaired sculptor I traced the hills of her breasts, the harder ridge of her nipples, the sculpted curve of her arse, the cup of her chin and the moist line dividing her back cheeks, one finger drawn to her increasing wetness.

She helped me out of my own clothing, momentarily letting go of my penis, pulling the sweatshirt above my head, pulling down my briefs and jeans, loosening the laces on my trainers and then slipping my socks off.

"The bed?"

She guided me towards it.

There was no linen on it. Just a quilt. In the heart of me I hoped it would not retain Giulia's scent. It didn't. Nothing lasts forever. For a brief moment I was relieved. This was no moment for guilt. She was the one who had left me. I didn't owe her anything, or did I?

We lay down.

She took me in her mouth, lullabied my lust with her lips and tongue. Made me gasp, time and again, in the acceptance of her hunger.

Later, I buried myself inside her. Deep. Hard and angry.

With every thrust I could feel her body tremble in my arms and beneath me her movements progressively in sync with mine.

Her nails digging hard in my shoulders, my breath racing against her scars, sweat rising from both our bodies and mingling in the usual ceremony of the flesh.

I could feel the wave rise inside me, the cruise to inevitable orgasm in full stride, seconds away from release. Still in full darkness.

"Please," I begged.

"What?"

"I want to see your face, your eyes. Now."

"No. You mustn't..."

I wanted that blindfold off. An uncontrollable urge to witness the veil that might fall across her metal grey eyes when I came, my way of communing with her.

"Please..."

"No."

So be it.

Was it her way of punishing me? Of imposing her will on me.

Telling me in the secret language of sex that she was the one taking her pleasure and I was just the instrument of her desire?

I came. With a terrible roar.

Had I ever been so loud with Giulia or others? Probably not, but then it had been months since I had last been with a woman, so what could I expect?

You know that feeling when you've come and you want the world to freeze, to remain embedded in her body forever in a parody of death, not wanting her to move either or rub against you further. That craving for absolute silence and motionless stasis.

Alexandra respected it. Made no move to disengage herself from the weight of my body. But neither did she say a word.

Both listening to the silence falling across the room and the messed-up bed where we lingered.

I finally slumped away from her. On my back. Prey to a thousand feelings and my mind too confused to analyse them.

I felt her move, a step on the floor, the bed emptying on my right side.

"Can I take the blindfold off, now?"

"No. Keep it on."

"Why?" I could hear her hastily dressing.

"I don't want you to see me."

"Regrets?"

"Not at all."

"So what?"

She didn't answer.

Lost in my fog, I pictured her slipping on her hold up stockings with all the grace of an ice queen, straightening the creases in her skirt and pulling on the red coat.

Her voice, finally, moving away towards the door, the acoustics of the apartment sadly familiar to me. Post-coital depression hitting me hard. Every move she was making, breaking me, wanting to ask her to stay with me. Lonely like seldom before.

"Just close the door when you leave. There's no rush. No need to lock it. There are realtors coming tomorrow. We're planning to put it on the market."

Did she know I owned a key?

I pulled the quilt up to cover my nakedness.

Heard the door slam shut.

Embraced sleep. For a while.

When I woke up, it was still dark, even when I pulled off the scarf that had kept me blind. It still smelled of her, a remote fragrance evoking green tropical flowers and citrus fruit. But it was a different type of darkness. I looked out of the window and the lights of Broadway were bright. The fog had gone, as mysteriously as it had first appeared.

I couldn't face the idea of taking a shower in this apartment again. Too many memories. I dressed briskly, the scent of cheap sex still rising from me and my parts. But there was no one around to sniff me or reproach my lack of cleanliness. Somehow, I knew that Philip Marlowe didn't indulge in frequent showers either!

The following morning there was a white envelope on the floor on my side of the office door.

It was a note from Alexandra Helmsmark formally advising me that she'd had second thoughts about the job, and no longer wished me to pursue the investigation into her sister's present location and thanking me for services already rendered. Along with it was a cheque to cover my fees and expenses already incurred. It was a most generous sum.

There was a PS: 'I changed my mind. Sorry.'

At first, I was angry. Felt used.

But then I also saw the funny side of things: I had inadvertently become a gigolo, a male escort, paid for my sexual services.

I could live with that. It certainly appeared to pay better than private investigations and carried less risk.

6 - I HEART NEW YORK

The arrival of spring in New York is normally a cause for celebration.

This was no longer the case.

The leaves growing on tree branches were stunted and dull, the budding flowers colourless and drained of life, and mounds of refuse sacks accumulated on alternate street corners for days, rotting, their obnoxious smell spreading ever further afield. It was as if the whole island was grinding to a halt under a shroud of hopelessness.

Vienna had still not been in touch and I was beginning to think she might not do so, for one reason or another. But I knew it would be best to steer clear of Washington Square for the time being. Chong, one of the identical twins who served at the counter of the Korean deli on the corner of Spring and Wooster, had informed me just the other day that the squirrels had vacated the park anyway.

"All the squirrels?"

"Yes. A few days after the fog lifted it seems they all disappeared overnight. God knows where they've gone to. But I suppose anywhere is better than New York right now, eh?"

I had no reason to disbelieve him. Animals know best to leave a sinking ship long before the sailors onboard realise their fate is sealed, I reckoned.

The rumour was circulating that some of the refugees from the camps in Central Park were escaping and now roaming the area between Columbus Circle and 44th Street, and that the army barricades around the Times Square area were being breached on a regular basis. Manhattan was descending into chaos. All the while, I knew that others were fleeing to upstate and the countryside. At this rate, the island would soon have a whole new population. Out with the old and in with new.

I was sitting in the Salt Well, a familiar bar on La Guardia Place, making a glass of rotgut last, while ruminating on my own fate.

I'd spent the whole day seeking out O'Carlson in his usual haunts, but no one had seen him now for a few weeks. It worried me, he was a creature of habits and always one of my best sources of information.

I was unfamiliar with the bartender. Myron, whom I was acquainted with and was also a repository of drunken wisdom and snippets of news was away in Florida, I was told, and wouldn't be back until after Easter. Thierry was French and had a nose ring and had seemingly never read the bartending manual where it stated that Greenwich Village baristas should be garrulous and not sullen and silent.

I sipped away in my corner, next to the old vintage jukebox which was all lit up with rainbow colours but was long past the stage where it could play music. I'd been visiting the Salt Well for years and it had never functioned properly throughout and the only form of entertainment had been the TV screens where baseball fixtures always seemed to be playing in a loop. The Dark had seen an end to that when all stations had gone off air never to return. I'd never properly understood the rules of baseball. I was more of a soccer man.

The thin stream of alcohol seeping down my throat was rough, probably illegally-distilled in some nearby bathtub, and gave me little pleasure. I could barely remember when the vodka or the gin flowed smoothly under the tongue and warmed my insides with a radiant glow. These days that sort of booze was out of my price range. But the tall glass was soon empty, and I called out for another.

I'll never be an alcoholic. Drink does little for me, and for some reason my metabolism processes the poison as if it was water. I've never been drunk or had a hangover. I suppose it makes me a dull person. I drink because I like bars. The fact that once you walk past the threshold, you become anonymous, one in a crowd, a member of an invisible and neglected community.

No one bothers you if you wish to remain on your own and just listen to and watch people speak too loud, stumble or make fools of themselves. It even beats television, even more so now that there were no stations on the air anywhere on the East Coast, although I'd heard there were a couple of pirate channels still in halting operation, respectively broadcasting old movies from the 1980s and non-stop pornography.

Giulia used to prefer spending time in coffee shops where she could linger for ages, her stickered laptop roaming the web, revising her Catalan literature essays and coursework, her headphones plugged in, listening to her favourite Pink Floyd, Clash and Talking Heads tracks, while I worked at the magazine, fact-checking and researching and constantly counting down to the end of the working day and the knowledge we would meet up in a coffee shop or at our apartment and be together again.

Telling each other stories, daydreaming, laughing, loving.

Unless, my mind now unhealthily perturbed by the new information, she had not actually been in the actual coffee shops but had run off the moment I looked away to a succession of seedy studios with Cherise or others, stripping or worse for photographers, living another life altogether, a parallel world of lies and secrets which I couldn't fathom, however hard I tried to understand it. Which still didn't explain the New Orleans photograph, or when it could have been taken.

She hadn't, it appeared, made a fool out of me; I was blind enough to have managed that all on my own.

I was deep in thought when someone slammed a glass down on my table and sat across from me.

I looked up.

It was 'Reservoir Dogs', the Commander's henchman. I struggled to recall whether I had ever been given his name.

He looked down at my own glass and its murky contents and sneered. His own drink was amber-coloured and anything but cloudy. The good stuff.

"That doesn't look very healthy," he said, pointing at my drink.

"It's all I can afford," I replied.

"Really? I thought Miss Alexandra had paid you off in full."

"I have expenses. Life these days is anything but cheap."

He chuckled.

"So, what brings you here?" I asked him.

"The Commander is feeling a bit guilty. Thought you might want to work for him."

"Who says I'm for hire?"

"Last I heard your client had terminated your assignment. I hope I haven't been misinformed. The Commander would be rather annoyed if that were the case. Surely someone like you doesn't work for free?"

From the smirk taking shape like a scar in the far corner of his lips, I could see the prospect of having to inform him I was still working the case would not amuse him and his employer in the least, and with it the myriad possibilities it opened for retribution. His knife? The redoubtable April Lea?

I remained silent.

"We can pay well."

"Tell me?"

"As a matter of fact, we wish you to work for us, be on retainer in some way, but to do nothing. Doesn't sound strenuous, does it? There will be no need for violence or anything unsavoury."

"Isn't the latter part of that your job? Or that mighty lady boxer you also have on your books?"

"The Commander says it's horses for courses. Some of us are more adept at certain jobs."

"I'm not sure sitting around doing nothing is quite up my alley," I said. "I find people, locate things. You might even say I'm a man of action."

"Surely, beggars can't be choosers?"

A sense of quiet menace oozed from him.

"Let me think about it," I said. "I know you know where to find me."

"Don't think too long."

I finished my drink and left the bar. I could feel his eyes following me all the way to the door.

□ □ □

We all have secrets.

You can spend ages with someone and never know them completely, skilfully kept unaware of the shadow zones they conceal from you. Was it my lack of curiosity?

I was a repeat offender.

Women would leave me, and in my forlorn loneliness my brain would turn and turn like a Ferris wheel, going nowhere and arriving back where the journey had begun, a loop that kept on repeating, before I truly could understand why, process the facts even when they were presented to me clear as daylight, come to my senses and identify my failures. But I seldom learned and would make the same mistakes again. Of loving too much, wanting too much, ignoring reality.

Before Giulia there was Kate. Before Kate, there had been Lisa, and then Lois, and others. I was maybe too much of a romantic, blinded each time by that mirage of emotions where lust and affection met.

I hadn't always been a fact checker and researcher.

Once—don't laugh—I had wanted to be a writer. It was a deep desire, something that consumed me for years. I even published a little: a few articles here, a couple of short stories there. But then I realised I had nothing to say. No message for the world, no insight into the ties that bound us or the state of society.

Some are content to just be storytellers, but then again, my tales, more or less, were always about the same subjects, the same emotions, the same losses and I concluded that the world at large had little interest in me and moved on. If I couldn't write, then I would live. And I tried. Sometimes it worked, for a few weeks, months or even longer, on other occasions I ended up with egg on my face. But I was persistent. Some would say living in a half-life, where memories and regrets reigned was not much of a life, but I would affirm that a half-life was better than no life at all.

There was always hope in tomorrow, even if after every bruising new relationship, that hope grew dimmer.

So, there you are, the digest version of the story of my life.

I told you I wasn't much of a storyteller.

□ □ □

I finally came across O'Carlson in a small trattoria on Thompson Street. He was sitting in a darkened corner booth, hunched over his table and a plate of spaghetti vongole in which the tomato sauce outnumbered the clams by a nautical mile. He'd lost weight, he looked ten years older than the last time I had seen him just some weeks ago and there was a splash of red on the tip of his nose. He was a messy eater at best.

"What's happened to you?" I asked him. "I've been looking everywhere. All your customary haunts. You've done something of a disappearing act."

He looked up at me, a worried look stretching across his gaunt features.

He wiped his lips clean with a paper napkin. I felt as if I should warn him of the sauce still staining the bulbous tip of his nose but decided against it. This was not a happy man.

"I've been looking after my health."

He avoided my gaze.

"Is it because of..."

He interrupted my question by putting his hand up and begging for my silence.

"Not here," he said.

We walked up to Broadway, O'Carlson nervous, regularly looking behind us as we made slow progress, checking if we were being observed or followed. I had suggested we speak at my office, but he had quickly turned down the suggestion.

Surely, I was not being bugged?

"You've been asking around too much. It's been noticed..."

"I know that," I remarked.

"And whoever is interested in those photographs also knows you often come to me for information."

"You've also been warned off?"

"I have. It wasn't pleasant. I just can't be seen with you any longer. I hope you understand."

I let him go on his way, now the shadow of himself, crossing Astor Place and stumbling towards St Mark's Place, where he had permanent lodgings in what used be a hotel at the intersection of the roads. As we parted, he'd told me he was planning to leave the city for a while. "A long while." He had a relative who lived outside New Haven, in Connecticut. I wished him well and apologised if I had been responsible for his new-found troubles. I knew I was. His shoulders were hunched, his step uncertain. I wasn't sorry, just angry at those responsible for his pain that they had acted in reaction to my enquiries and his easy availability. If only I knew why. It was more than just a set of compromising photographs, that now seemed evident. As if my investigation had just touched on the tip of the iceberg and there was a whole new dimension to the story that I was missing.

An overwhelming feeling washed over me, screaming out loud that everything around me turned to shit, a new magic power, a curse I had unwittingly acquired. Soon, I would be taking personal responsibility for the Dark itself at this rate.

I sighed.

I shrugged.

That night I had a dream. At least it wasn't a nightmare full of recurring loops and anxieties as was normally the case.

Ever since her disappearance, I had unconsciously never allowed Giulia to populate my sleepless nights, maybe in the knowledge it would just be too painful, but on this occasion, she made an appearance. A striking one.

We had once travelled to London where we had spent a handful of days in a house close to a park that belonged to an acquaintance, who was away at the time and offered his place for us to stay. There was a long corridor between the main bedroom and the toilet and bathroom, a pale wooden floor and white wood, with high bookshelves on both sides, full of books we couldn't even reach. We had both wakened at the same time with an urge to pee; I had, trying to control my bladder, let her rush to the toilet first and was waiting for her to emerge, standing in readiness at the top of the narrow corridor. She had pushed the door open and giggled seeing me there, legs crossed, naked as she was, and deliberately took her time to step in my direction and allow me passage. I playfully patted her warm rump as she slithered by so I could move forward. I relieved myself and left the small toilet space only to find Giulia standing at the opposite end, waiting for me, splendid and desirable, her nudity buried in shadows, the darker stain of her nipples and pubic hair like black stars in the pallor of her body. No doubt she saw the delight on my face and began to slowly dance for me, like a stripper, playful, gently provocative, out of reach, teasing, a parody of lust, innocence and obscenity that was so characteristic of her. It's an image I can never erase. A vision of her carved into my brain cells like an indelible photograph. Later she joked that I didn't even get hard at the sight of her exaggerated gyrations.

In the dream, she was dancing again, her movements now so much more suggestive, bordering on the pornographic, the curve of her silent lips—no one ever speaks in my dreams—like a Braille pattern of untold desire. The corridor was now illuminated in shades of red, like a stage in some seedy strip joint.

Her arms were similar in movement, deployed like wings, fingers undulating with the dance, dragging across her skin, grazing her breasts, her stomach, thighs, and then deliberately skimming through her pubes until I could clearly distinguish the slash of her sex, a darker red, a wound, seemingly wet under the pressure of her fingers parting it in offering. Then, in a flash she was no longer dancing alone, the even paler form of Cherise's body had joined her, and all of a sudden they were embedded into each other, dancing as one, skin against skin, sweat dripping from one onto the other, lips meeting in a kiss, eyes half closed in a pattern of mutual ecstasy. They were dancing, and then they were making love to each other, porcelain blonde against dusky brunette, and I was sitting in the audience like a voyeur, unable to move or speak, my mouth open, my words strangulated at birth, my heart beating wildly as if tied down.

The longer they danced, the more I found it difficult to breathe, my lungs weighted down, the air around me thick like treacle, my body immobilised.

On and on it went.

And, in the dream, this time my cock was hard, throbbing, threatening to explode. And no doubt between the sheets too as I shuffled and wriggled in my sleep. But release wouldn't come.

Part of me didn't want the dream to end, even if its oppression was making me breathless, while the other half of my brain just begged for it to end, afraid I would die of frustration, a helpless prisoner in the cage of my mind.

Somehow, I woke up.

Usually, the substance, the narrative of dreams and nightmares, fades quickly. This one wouldn't go away. For days it floated in my mind, striking, sexual beyond endurance, painful.

I realised there was an avenue of investigation I had not explored. Vienna had still not been in touch. I had all the time in the world.

□ □ □

It was the fourth strip club I'd visited in the past two days. A long time ago they had mostly been situated around the Times Square and 42nd Street area, but rents and gentrification had steadily contributed to their scattering all over Manhattan, as far down as Battery Park.

From the sparse number of spectators and drinkers in those I had passed through I couldn't see most surviving much longer.

They were depressing places with a strong scent of failure shrouding their interiors, badly-lit stages, faltering sound systems and the watered-down booze a pale approximation of the labels on the bottles it was poured from.

As for the dancers, they were a motley bunch. Once they had mostly been East European and reasonably attractive underneath the fortress of their make-up, with some ballet background lending a modicum of grace to their exertions, but all the Russian girls had, I was told, moved down to Florida where at least the weather was shiny and they could perfect their tans on the nearby beaches between the sets.

They now came in two distinct models: Latinas and Suicide Girls. Surprisingly, it was the latter category that I found more palatable, emo pixie girls with the saucer eyes of caffeinated students, pierced and tattooed, indifferent to the way they looked, going through the motions with a faraway look, mostly skinny, dark dyed hair shorn close to the scalp or worn short and geometrical, and with a better choice in music to dance to by far.

I was nursing a tall glass of soda which tasted of nothing, since the ice had melted and washed all the sweetness away, waiting for the next dancer to arrive. I'd seen her rush through the door, no doubt arriving from another club. Most of the dancers moved between clubs and I'd already recognised a couple I'd seen the day before on 6th and 19th. I was in no doubt that travel costs could, on bad days, cancel out their meagre tips.

The bartender looked so young I reckoned he needed I.D. to even enter the club, let alone serve drinks.

I'd shown him the battered Polaroid of Cherise and Giulia and asked if he recognised them or knew where I could find more featuring the same girls, or maybe even a movie. They hadn't looked familiar to him but he assured me that he had a contact who could supply movies of the sort I was seeking, and maybe he would recognise the models, as he euphemistically referred to them.

Still out of breath, the dancer I'd seen arriving ten minutes ago walked on to the stage, and the music in the tinny speakers on both sides of the stage began pouring out a Britney Spears song.

She had a cheerleader's outfit on. White shirt buttoned down to her midriff, finished off with a large bow, and a pleated skirt in Burberry patterns.

She had skinny legs, moved without grace fighting against the angle of her high heels and within a few beats had already loosened the shirt to reveal the sideways curves of her breasts.

She looked to me like a little girl with a bad complexion trying to act like a woman, a parody. I looked away and continued to sip my drink.

There was a pat on my shoulder.

"Hi..."

I turned around. Her voice was hoarse. It was the stripper who had been on stage earlier. She had cleaned most of her make-up off and now looked half attractive. Her CBGB T-shirt was holed in places, her skin beneath it a dull pink as if she had just vigorously scrubbed her skin clean under the shower with piping hot water. She hadn't been a bad dancer, gyrating with the right proportion of sensuality to Bowie's "Let's Dance", her loose limbs moving with the beat of Niles Rogers' bassline. Her jeans were tight and, close-up, she smelled of soap.

"Hello. What's your name?"

"It's Lily."

It might even have been her real name. At least she didn't try and call herself Sapphire, Lolita or by a ridiculous stage name, I wouldn't be able to take seriously.

"Keith said you were on the look-out for stuff..."

"Keith is right." I assumed Keith was the barman.

"Offer me a drink," she suggested. "A beer would do."

I ordered.

"I saw you yesterday," Lily said. "I was dancing at this other tittie bar in Midtown, I noticed you in the audience, thought you didn't look like the usual sort of punter."

"Why is that?" I asked.

"You're not the type we normally get. The way you look at the girls. Not that you didn't seem interested when we had our kit off, but it wasn't the same kind of hunger if you see what I mean. It was sort of detached but appreciative."

"Very observant. You're something of a philosopher..."

"Actually, no. I want to be a sociologist. That's what I'm studying. Post-graduate level. I do this for the rent money."

Her hair was dyed a shocking shade of orange, her eyes were dark green. I was beginning to like her.

"So... do you do other things when you're not dancing or studying?"

"What sort of things?"

"The sort I've been enquiring about: posing for photographs, private movies?"

"I don't, but I know gals who have done. I'm not that desperate; I still have my pride," Lily pointed out.

I took out the photo and showed it to her. "Do you know them?"

She pulled a pair of reading glasses from the voluminous side linen satchel in which she kept her performing clothes and make-up, squinted and examined the print. There was a hint of recognition. Time stretched as she deliberated.

"Yes or no?"

"I don't know her," she pointed to Giulia. I felt a pang of disappointment. "But the other woman is familiar."

"Is she?"

"Yes, but she's bad news."

"How come?"

"I've heard things. You know you're not the first guy to visit the clubs looking for her?"

"I reckon I'm not, but maybe my reasons for seeking her out are different. Is she, well... was she also a dancer?"

"No. We all know each other. She's never on the circuit, I'd know otherwise."

"What can you tell me about her?"

"Rich kid. In it for the kicks, not the cash, I heard some people say."

"Where did you come across her?"

"There was this guy. Also studied at Hunter College. Fine Arts. He was doing this photographic project for his thesis; a reportage about the Manhattan sex trade after the Dark. Thought he could offer a new approach to the Nan Goldin life on the wild side thing, you know. We had friends in common. He crossed her path. She posed for him. Then, within a few days, he was approached by some heavies and persuaded to sell them the negatives. Funny business."

"Any chance you could put me in contact with the guy?"

Maybe, I reasoned, he still had prints he had kept, or might have seen Giulia with Cherise, or had remained in touch with the Commander's daughter.

"It's not easy," Lily stated.

"Why?"

"Last I heard he was living in the park. Now working on a new project, documenting the tribes there."

Central Park was not the sort of place you just wandered into for a stroll these days.

"I really want to meet him," I told Lily. "Would you help me? It's important."

She agreed.

□ □ □

You had to negotiate past a series of barricades to reach the southern approaches to Central Park, but Lily knew most of the Home Security personnel on duty. They seemed more concerned about people leaving the area and leaking into Midtown or Lower Manhattan than bodies actually breaching their perimeter to enter the park. Once we had made our way past these official cordons, though, we had to face the obstacles put in place by the tribes occupying the park.

Lily went ahead. She suggested I wait for her in what had once been the luxurious lobby of the Plaza Hotel, which had now evolved into a thriving flea market of sorts where all kinds of legal and illegal foodstuffs, medicine, antiquated equipment and spare parts were being traded, services negotiated or in most instances bartered.

I watched her crossing the road, her baggy dark green camouflage cargo pants fluttering in the breeze sweeping down from the river which animated the sparse branches of the surviving trees on the park's periphery. She looked minuscule and I had difficulty recalling her naked body gyrating on one of the club stages. Her flaming hair was partly covered by an outsized baseball cap for a long defunct team. Off-duty she was another person altogether, more like the timid student she actually was when not working for rent money. Once on the park side, I saw her in discussion with a tall guy in military fatigues and a gun belt. They appeared to know each other. I wondered what park faction he belonged to, and if he would prove willing to allow us into the territory he was guarding. A large lorry passed between us, laden with construction material and by the time it had reached the corner, Lily and the man were no longer visible.

Aimlessly, I walked around the Plaza market, just on the off-chance someone there might be trading in photos or porn in any form. It was unlikely, but I had nothing else to do until I found out if I would be given a visa for the park, as if was a foreign country—which in a way it had become.

I was offered fake watches, exotic fruit well past its sell date, on the wrong side of rotting and even a gun, a Sig Sauer, a preppy-looking Frenchman with a Maurice Chevalier accent manifested from his side purse, under the impression I looked gullible enough to pay his exorbitant asking price. I was briefly tempted, although I had never used or owned a firearm before, I reckoned that the trek to Louisiana and what lay beyond its walls might require some form of insurance, but then I peered down at the weapon, taking a closer look and was quite unimpressed by its dull sheen, and I thought, traces of rust. I could just see it exploding in my face at the worst possible moment and declined the proposal. Did I look like the sort of guy who needed a gun?

Half an hour later, Lily hadn't returned, and I was beginning to regret having given her the photograph of Cherise and Giulia.

She had told me that she knew of a Canadian dealer who lived among the tribes who had connections with porn and had at one stage helped some of her dancing friends to arrange portfolios, whether legit or more explicit. He could prove a mine of information.

Dusk was falling, a grey sky spreading its heavy curtain over Manhattan, from where I stood on the pavement looking out at Central Park on the other side of the now empty road, the green inner expanses of the park were fading into the murky distance.

Personnel guarding the perimeter were changing watches.

Uniformed militiamen on one corner, Home Security armed to the teeth on the other, with night goggles covering half their face, Frankenstein-like monsters in the darkening gloom.

And still no sign of Lily.

Smoke was rising towards the centre of the park where I remembered the ponds, from campfires being lit by the various occupying tribes. I had a mental flash of the world I had lived in before the Dark, making me feel I was now living on another planet altogether.

I thought I recognised the tall man she had been speaking to earlier, walking amongst a group of khaki-clad guards and I crossed the road.

"Hey?"

"Do I know you?"

"Lily, the young girl you were speaking to earlier, with orange hair. Where is she?"

"You must be mistaken," he said, giving me a dirty look. "I wasn't here earlier. Anyway, gals are in short supply here," he smirked, "I'm sure I would have noticed one, especially with that sort of hair."

I knew he was lying. I was about to respond when I saw his companions approaching, as if ready to support him if I contradicted him. Each and every one was taller and bulkier than I was, so I prudently retreated.

I crossed the road back and stationed myself by the Plaza entrance, buttoned up my shirt and pulled up my collar against the cold. Trying to smuggle myself beyond the perimeter would be suicidal, even more so at night.

A few hours later, and night was already in its first quarter. Lily had not reappeared. I didn't know what to think. I was fearful for her and guilty at having despatched her into the park, conflicted at having handed her the bruised Polaroid which was my only link to the connection between Cherise and Giulia.

I made my way back home.

Hoping for some news. But then Lily had no clue where I lived and worked.

A couple of days later, I visited two of the clubs where I knew she danced. She hadn't come to work since the day I had seen her last. My heart sunk. The other dancers I warily approached had no clue where she lived. They also made it clear that I was distinctly unwelcome in their midst, what with all my questions.

It felt as if I was making my way blind through a cloud of treacle.

7 - HELPLESS IN COMBAT

For several days now, an atmosphere of febrile dread had taken hold of the island. Rumours were circulating that some of the tribes of Central Park were on the march and had broken through the cordons and descended south all the way down 5th to St Patrick's Cathedral level. According to hearsay, Home Security forces were in disarray and some of its elements had even joined up with the advancing tribes. Militia reinforcements were on their way from upstate, men with more experience in combat, ex-Feds with a reputation for brutality who shot first and asked questions later.

I had no wish to find out for myself the truth about the rumours. Even in normal circumstances, I seldom ventured further uptown than Times Square and even then, only when a job required me to do so. And, right now, I had no jobs. Work had dried up, as if news of my involuntary involvement with the Commander and his affairs, let alone with the Washington Square crew was now common knowledge and I had, as a result, become persona non grata, the sort of fool you steered clear of if you knew what was good for you.

Cash was tight but at least a few local Korean delis and rundown bars still supplied me with credit out of loyalty for favours past or ignorance.

People were leaving the city in droves, streets increasingly empty, commerces closed and shuttered. At this rate, it would soon be an island of ghosts, and guns. Some mornings I even wondered why I was still hanging around and why I hadn't yet gathered my stuff and hit the road to Louisiana to search for Giulia, and incidentally Tiffany Cherise Helmsmark as she was part of the puzzle. But I held faith in Vienna. I was hoping she would come good in the end and provide a way to travel there safely. I believed in her.

I had an itch to visit the park and her father's territory, enquire about her, but on every occasion reluctantly decided against it, not wishing to queer matters up, trying to rein in my impatience.

What was holding her up?

I wasn't that far away that day. Sitting in an isolated corner of one of the few remaining coffee bars on Houston, near the corner of Wooster, making a lukewarm lemonade last long enough so I could skim through the final chapters of the old paperback thriller I was reading to distract my mind from more important matters. It was, ironically, a private eye caper, albeit set in Los Angeles, and the protagonist who looked nothing like me, had a taste for chocolate and Cola without ice and always bedded the blonde, was about to uncover the web of conspiracy clouding his missing person's case. Through the corner of one eye, I noticed beyond the window onto Houston a dark limo pulling up to the kerb, its shadow casting a curtain across my yellowing page. I attached no importance to its arrival but soon after the coffee shop's door opened there was my old friend, Mr 'Reservoir Dogs' in his shabby black suit and fading white shirt and matching tie. The Commander's henchman.

"Shit!"

He walked up to my table. I looked up. There was no way to ignore him. I closed the paperback without even leaving a marker on my page, already knowing deep down inside I was never going to find out the ending.

"You've been asking questions again," he said. His voice was hoarse, his nose stuffed up from a cold or hay fever. Even gangsters are subject to the whims of nature and anatomy. I noticed a pale stain below the knot of his necktie.

"It's been a while," I answered. Which was true, ever since I had lost Lily to the park, I'd kept to myself.

"Makes no difference," he said. "Your orders were clear. You had to keep out of bloody sight. Retreat into your shell. What was there not to understand?"

I nodded. There was no point getting into an argument I was unlikely to win.

He gestured at me to get up and follow him out.

"Summoned by the Commander?" I ventured.

The suited henchman said nothing in response, just shrugged his shoulders.

"What if I refused to come with you?"

A cruel smile dawned across his thin lips, as if the idea of my resistance was an entertaining prospect and he was already relishing the idea of punishing me according to rules only he, and I assumed the Commander, followed.

"Your choice," he said. "There's pain and then there's more pain..." I knew which option he favoured, and briefly recalled the slumped body of the photographer, Hilton Willis, on the floor of his studio. I rose from my seat.

Stepping into the parked metal grey limo felt like entering a coffin. The air conditioning was turned up to the max and I had to turn my leather jacket collar up before I even sat down for fear of shivering. The windows were tinted, as was the panel that separated us from the unknown driver. The vehicle smoothly joined the sparse traffic, the rumour of the engine just a gentle, remote thud.

My unwelcome escort sat, immobile, alongside me on the back seat, silent, the faint scent of his cologne a hint of alcohol and flowers. I, on the other hand, squirmed, sweat drying under my armpits as the cool wave of the AC washed over me.

"It's freezing," I stated. "Mind if we open the window a little?"

"The condemned man's last wish?" he sniggered.

I struggled for a modicum of wit and failed. I just nodded. He hit a button on the control panel by his door and buzzed the window on my side down a few inches. We were gliding past Astor Place, heading north along a semi-deserted avenue. A faint drizzle peppered the air, the final breath of a fading winter.

We barely drove on for a further five minutes and the sleek limo turned right and eased into a side road leading on to 3rd Avenue, coming to a halt next to Webster Hall on East 11th Street.

I remembered seeing a whole load of groups there some years back before the city had turned to shit and joy had leaked away from music at an exponential rate. I didn't even know if the club was still functioning. At any rate, there were never any concerts here in the daytime, it being more of a night place.

"This is it," 'Reservoir Dogs' said. He gestured for me to open my door and exit the car.

The side pavement had debris piled high, uncollected refuse, bins full of bottles and discarded plants, even the desiccated remains of a Christmas tree. I stepped sideways to avoid the mess, noticing out of the corner of my eye the charred walls and ruins of the movie multiplex on the corner which had burned down the year before and left to stand and rot like a giant four-storeyed twisted metal sculpture, a legacy of the madness that had followed the Dark.

Webster Hall's main doors were barred, a heavy metal latticed grille nailed to the dark wooden frontispiece. I followed the Commander's henchman towards the steps where, to the left, a smaller entrance seemingly carved into the stone wall of the building, set back like an alcove, stood half open, a couple of guys in matching dark leather coats and jeans screening entrants.

They nodded in recognition to my unwelcome companion and allowed us inside.

The lobby was kept in part darkness and was mostly unchanged from my distant memories. Small groups of folks were congregating, soft whispers and furtive conversations blanketing, queuing on either side of a hastily hung set of purple velvet curtains leading to the auditorium. Men and women of all ages and appearances. A buzz of febrile expectation hung in the air. I slowed and Reservoir Dogs, noting my hesitation, grabbed hold of my sleeve and pulled me along.

Another door, marked 'Private—Staff Only' to the left of the curtain. He knocked three times, a pre-arranged signal. It opened. He indicated for me to walk ahead as we left the lobby and turned into a corridor which led to the side and backstage areas. Here, again, people stood in waiting on both sides of the narrow passage, eyeing us up as we passed along. I was perturbed by the way they gazed at us, as if they knew something I didn't, and should.

A large well-lit space, a dressing room now mostly stripped of furniture, just a few chairs, a tall mirror, a trestle table with a scattering of make-up paraphernalia, tubes, compact cases, bottles in all shapes, sizes and colours. An open, deep travelling trunk, with random items of clothing spilling from it. In the corner of the room, away from the light, another chair and someone sitting in it, watching us arrive, a thin smile scratched across his recognisable features. Commander Helmsmark. My heart jumped, even though I had sort of known this had always been who I was being led to. But why here? I could feel the presence of a handful of others in the room, but his presence obscured them by far, dominant, in charge.

"The man who just can't let go," he remarked. His features were impassive, as if neither amused nor annoyed at my attitude, just supremely indifferent.

For a brief moment, I thought of coming up with some excuses, pretending I had given up the case and was no longer seeking Cherise, but realised it was unwise. He knew exactly what I had been up to. It would have been pointless.

I kept my counsel. I could feel every eye in the room fixed on me. But the Commander's gaze was, I felt, the only one I had to worry about. For now.

"Haven't you been warned several times already?" he continued.

"There were loose ends," I argued, although I was unwilling to mention Giulia or that photograph.

Had he been a pantomime villain, he would have roared with laughter, but his features remained frozen in place, which made him even more menacing, as he processed the thin sliver of information.

"There are NO loose ends. End of story."

A sense of finality.

"You are becoming a terrible nuisance, Sir," the Commander stated. "Fast becoming a danger to yourself and to the other unfortunates you have been dragging into this sorry situation."

Lily?

"Do you know what's happened to her?"

"I guess you're referring to that young stripper you foolishly sent into the park on your behalf?"

My throat tightened.

I blinked. He took that as an answer.

"She's been taken care of," he said.

"What is that supposed to mean?"

"Do you really want to know? I have allies, you see. New York, Manhattan is, as you know, now under the control of a handful of groups. We have different aims, but we work together for the common good," he pointed out. "We communicate. Help each other out. And the only reason you are still alive is that one particular party has asked us to go easy on you, despite your failings, all your cumbersome questions. You're a lucky man."

I guessed he was referring to the Washington Square mob; maybe Vienna had the ears of her adoptive father and I had been under his or her protection. Until now.

"You haven't answered my question. Where's Lily?"

"Questions, questions. You'll never learn. So that's her name, then..."

"It is. She does have a name."

"I gather the park people have had their fun with her. I gather she's young, borderline attractive, I assume she's been sold off by now. I don't think she will be making a return to her old profession, or if so, it will be on an unpaid basis and merely as an appetizer for more serious sexual activities..."

Anger boiled up against me. It was well-known that some of the groups controlling the park were involved in slavery.

A hole in the pit of my stomach hollowed out as I stood there, making me sick to the core. I knew it was all my fault. I shouldn't have allowed

Lily to cross that road.

"Anyway, that's no longer your problem, is it?"

My throat was bone dry, words bitterly welling up against a dam of bile blocking access to my vocal chords.

"You're going to be taught a lesson. One that you will remember. And should you not, there won't be a next time, if you know what I mean. Protection or no protection."

I pictured the dead photographer.

There was movement behind me.

"I'm ready for the show," a husky woman's voice said. I detected a faint Canadian accent. She shuffled up against me, a brush of silk against my side. I turned my head.

It was April Lea.

Again, her hair was combed back into a tight, functional ponytail, her forehead free of lines, hair pulling the skin back, dark blonde, her make-up highlighting those killer cheekbones and the cruel, meaty mouth, that delicate balance between woman and androgyny that made her face so captivating. She was wearing a shiny silk dressing gown, like a boxer's. Which, I suppose, she was. In her way. One who obeyed no rules. What struck me at first was how broad her shoulders were, and the fact that she was a few inches taller than me and, as she approached nearer, the musky smell drifting from her body.

For a few seconds, I was puzzled by her appearance here. I was aware she worked for the Commander, but why was I brought here of all places? She could beat me up, and badly at that, pretty much anywhere, and I would be helpless to avoid it. Oh well, I reckoned, I've survived it once and I can do so again. It'll hurt.

Badly. Probably worse this time around. But bruises fade, bones heal. I'd grit my teeth, be a man and all that.

As if he had read my mind, the Commander remarked "Oh no, it won't be so pleasant this time. And it has to be public..."

He rose from his chair.

Walked past me, ignoring me altogether.

Reaching the door to the dressing room, "I'll be in the audience. Do put on a good show," he said. I wasn't sure which of us he was addressing, April Lea or me.

The others who had been lurking around the room followed him out and then only I, the Canadian mixed martial arts fighter and 'Reservoir Dogs' were left. I felt the temperature drop sharply.

His hands gripped my shoulder.

"So how do you want him?" he asked the ferocious young woman in her robe of blue silk.

She looked down at me.

"It's nothing personal," she said. "Just a job. Do understand that."

"We all have to make a living," I sighed, hoping it would not sound too ironic. Should I feel grateful for the fact that she was apologising in advance for hurting me badly?

The Commander's henchman let go of my shoulder, then turned towards April Lea. "Do you want him stripped?" he asked her.

What the fuck?

She considered. "Maybe not fully." A faint grin passed across her lips. "I've seen what he has to offer," she said. "First time we met..."

"So?"

"Leave him something. For his dignity, I suppose. It'll only be temporary, anyway."

All sorts of thoughts were jogging their way under my skull.

"I'm sure the Commander wants you two to put on a proper show," 'Reservoir Dogs' said. "There's an invited audience. They would enjoy a bit of drama."

April Lea sighed. "Oh well..." She moved to the trunk, bending over, dipping her hands into the confusions of clothes, her blue silk robe loosely held together by a belt in the same material and colour yawned open to reveal those long, sturdy legs I was finding difficult to forget, tanned, taut. She pulled some clothing, scarves, what looked like a dress and then small strands of material she dropped disinterestedly to the dressing room floor, dug deeper.

"Yes," she said, holding something minuscule, and crunched it in her hand. "This will do the trick." She waved it at the henchman and he chortled. "Perfect," he remarked, "unless he's wearing one already..." The sound of his amusement was deeply vulgar. I still couldn't see what they were referring to.

"I don't think he's that sort of guy," April Lea remarked.

April Lea turned on her heels, heading for the door, throwing her crunched up treasure find towards me. I surprise myself by catching it, as she makes her exit.

'Reservoir Dogs' sniggered, "Good catch, good reflexes."

"I reckon I'm going to need more than that," I remarked.

"You don't know how right you are," he said. "Now strip down and put it on."

I looked down at my open fist, uncrumpled the flimsy bit of material I'd been gifted with.

My eyes widened.

It was a jockstrap. I recognized it. Not something I'd ever wear.

Tiny, no more than a wide elasticated band and a thin strip of dirty turquoise corduroy. I'm average-sized but it didn't even look as if my balls, let alone my penis would fit into the abbreviated pouch it offered me.

"This is ridiculous," I exclaimed.

"Be that as it may," he said. "But those are the orders."

I was frozen to the spot. 'Reservoir' stared at me, malevolence rising behind the dark walls of his pupils.

"Hurry up. We haven't got all day. Your audience is waiting. Undress and slip that on. I promise I'll look away," he assured me mischievously.

Meekly, I followed my instructions. Unbuckled my belt, unbuttoned the jeans, pulled them down, lifted my sweatshirt above my head, stood a moment in nervous expectation. Kicked off my loafers.

I was down to my boxers. American Apparel. Grey survivors of a thousand wash cycles. And my socks. Black. Always black. I knew I looked patently absurd. Diminished. I'd often thought that naked men wearing just socks in movies, porn or whatever the circumstances, were a figure of ridicule. So, what was I now?

He lied. He hadn't looked away.

"The rest," he ordered.

The dressing room was not heated. My white skin was a panorama of goosebumps. My tufts of chest hair offered no protection from the cold.

First, I bent and pulled the cotton socks down, straightened out, now standing in my bare feet. Then, looking 'Reservoir Dogs' straight in the eyes in a gesture of unnecessary defiance, I dug my thumb into the waist of my boxer shorts, tugged them down and wriggled out of them.

The Commander's henchman held my stare, chortled gently as I cupped my hands in front of my crotch. He knew, and I knew that I was hopelessly limper than limp down there, no more imposing right then than a snail robbed of his shell. How could it be otherwise in these forced circumstances and the shrinking cold floating across the room?

"What are you waiting for?" he asked, hurrying me up.

I fully untangled the jockstrap, held it before me to puzzle out back from front.

"It'll fit perfectly…" he smirked.

Somehow, I managed to squeeze my meat into the tight pouch. I was terribly aware of the way the material cut into my crack and the fact that my arse-cheeks were fully exposed, just bisected by the minimalist strip of material.

"Good," he said. Had he uttered one more word, attempted a single joke about my appearance I would have ragefully leapt at him, no doubt attracting severe punishment. But I knew already I had to save all my energy, whatever reserves of hidden strength I could summon.

For April Lea.

□ □ □

I was led back to the auditorium through the maze of corridors, shivering, almost naked. Had he put a collar around my neck and led me by a leash, I couldn't have felt more vulnerable.

Webster Hall's geography had changed. The old stage had disappeared and in the very centre of the hall, a three feet or so high dais had been installed. Like a boxing ring set within a cage.

The ring stood brightly in a daze of spotlights, like a parade of suns shining on the battle to come. Two rows of seats circled the ring, partly illuminated by the main lighting. They were comfortable chairs, deeply upholstered, leather, the money seats.

As I was being led to the dais, I quickly recognised some of the folk sitting there, in place of honour. The Commander, of course, but also his eldest daughter, just a handful of seats away, her expression unreadable. Faces I didn't know, all with a touch of arrogance, the way they visibly dismissed me on sight, the way they sat or dressed, Manhattan's new aristocracy.

We approached. In another section of the small, selected audience, the King of Washington Square. And sitting by his side, Vienna.

My heart dropped.

'Reservoir Dog's' calloused hands slapped my rump.

"Up you get, now."

I climbed into the ring.

The fierce light focused on the ring now blinded me to anything beyond its perimeter. Once inside and bathed in its accusatory glow, I noted the presence of invisible spectators in the balcony by ear alone. The cheap seats. A rumble, a buzz, muted voices, conversations well beyond my understanding.

I stood there. Self-conscious in the extreme, like a gladiator who's been forcibly thrown into the arena

The jungle sounds rose.

April Lea was approaching the steps to the ring, still clad in her robe of blue silk. Like a champion entering her kingdom. She waved in response to the unseen crowds and the roar doubled in loudness. She appeared even taller now.

She was wearing red boxing gloves. I was bare-handed. For a brief moment, I wondered whether the punches would feel less painful this way.

Someone must have made a sign below. The crowd's rumour fell to a hush.

"Our first bout. A most delicious opener to today's entertainment. An amuse-bouche before the evening's usual cocktail of blood and mayhem and no mercy. The sumptuous April Lea, the exquisite Punisher, our mixed martial arts Canadian lass, with the killer legs and killer touches…" the stentorian voice paused. It didn't bother to introduce me. "Open rules, meaning there are no rules, all fight styles allowed. Loser pays in kind."

A mass of catcalls erupted.

I reckoned most were addressed at me.

I didn't have a good feeling about this.

I was still rooted to the spot. The ring's flooring under my bare feet felt unsteady, slippery, reminding me of the bouncy castles of my youth.

April Lea stood with her legs apart, like a leopard about to pounce. She pulled the belt from the robe and threw it off.

She was wearing black Lycra sports gear, a halter bra and figure-hugging high-waisted shorts. Her trainers were orange with blue laces, their soles adding a couple of inches to her height.

She winked at me.

Should I wait for her to come at me first, or should I please the audience and not play the sacrificial lamb, go down with at least a fight of some sorts? It wasn't as if I had too many options.

She began skipping from foot to foot, observing me, squinting.

I took a step forward.

Seeing me coming, she opened her guard, fluttered her gloved hands, inviting me to move closer.

I stopped in my tracks. Tried to blank out everything except for the female warrior now facing me. The Hall, the audience, Vienna looking on, the Commander, Alexandra, whoever else was in on the joke, the distant sounds, the jeers, the laughter.

Now she was just over an arm's length away, coiled, her breath just a rumour, clearly now waiting for me to take the first step.

I had never hit a woman in my life before.

Now it was the only thing I could do.

I tried to remember how boxers fought, the way they jabbed forward, swung their arms, attacked while all the time holding back to avert the counter-punch.

Our eyes met.

I was no longer scared. Whatever happened, happened.

I became indifferent to my fate.

Had I only known.

I threw a punch. Sideways in a forlorn attempt at disguising my intention and my target, her jaw.

She read me like a book, swung the top half of her body aside while not even moving her legs from their wide-opened stance and my fist just rushed through the air. I hadn't even pulled it back halfway to myself when I felt the thud of her glove in my side, taking me by surprise, the first wave of pain coming long after the shock of her counter-attack. I took a deep breath and rushed forward in the vain hope of overwhelming her, smothering her forward movements. Her arms opened, welcoming me, taking me against her in a parody of embrace, the searing heat from her body washing over mine like electricity unleashed from a Taser gun.

I tried to extricate my right arm from our involuntary entanglement, directing jabs at her stomach. I even managed to make contact, but her skin was like a washboard, hard, silken, a wall of flesh I was incapable of denting.

Finally, she pulled herself away and pushed me back. While I struggled for balance, she despatched a quick one-two of punches, right hand followed in a flash by her left hand. The first caught me on the shoulder, the other just above my navel in the fleshy area of my stomach. I was immediately breathless, struggling to breathe, my lungs flattened, emptied by the punches.

I had no time to consider my sorry situation after a single wave of April Lea's assault when her right leg surged towards mine, caught me at the ankle, bruising my bone what felt like permanently, I staggered to the floor, falling awkwardly on my side. Dust rose, my mouth wide open hungry for air and within seconds I was coughing on the spot like a medieval mendicant. I looked up and saw April Lea in all her magnificence, immense, sturdy legs, every curve in her body highlighted by the paper-thinness of the Lycra top and shorts, every line and topographical contour even, I couldn't help but notice the camel toe of her sex a deep indentation in the material.

I resigned myself then to another major kicking, and steeled myself, my whole body tightening in readiness for what was to be unleashed.

It never came.

This was a public fight; she had to give the crowd what they had come for and merely beating me to a pulp lacked originality.

And cruelty. After all, if what had been hinted at earlier by the master of ceremonies was correct, following my ineluctable pounding there were other bouts scheduled of a more murderous nature. I had come across rumours of gladiatorial jousts to the death; I just hadn't believed them.

Still straddling me, April Lea lowered herself down on me, jettisoned her boxing gloves, and with her hands around my neck positioned my head between her thighs in a choke hold.

Once again, the spectators on the balcony roared their approval.

She adjusted her position and with a few nudges pushed my legs out from under me, placing her weight against the crook of my bag, all the while keeping my head and neck firmly encircled between the throbbing muscles of her mighty thighs, my nose just inches away from her sex, a distinct scent of arousal reaching my nostrils. She paused for a moment. I tried to move, wriggle but I was fully immobilised.

Head pulled back, I saw her look up at the crowd of watchers upstairs as if beckoning their instructions, then towards the seated Commander. He gave her a sign.

She pushed harder against my back and, for a brief moment, I thought she was going to break me in half. Rather than fight the pressure, I attempted to lessen it by stretching myself out as best I could, thrusting my pelvis upwards, my resolutely shrunken genitalia pointing upwards to little avail.

This was what she had engineered.

Her hand moved to my jockstrap and, in one swift, hurried movement, tore it off, so that I was now totally naked in her clutches, exposed, exhibited almost.

My head was still held back so that I was incapable of seeing myself in such an obscene posture.

Without losing her grip on any part of my body, I felt her lips against my ear.

"Don't fight it," she said. "It'll be easier if you surrender, just give in."

I tried to relax, release the tension paralysing every one of my muscles.

She loosened her hold and I was able to breath more easily.

Not for very long.

Moving like lightning, she somehow grabbed one of my limbs before I could even realise what was happening, pulled, twisted, used her strength and, taking advantage of my own lack of balance and mental confusion, rearranged my position so I fell on all fours, still straddled by her imposing figure. I threw one of my arms about in search of support, but it just found air, my nails grazing against the slippery texture of her Lycra top, barely skimming against her hard nipple beneath it. It was as hard as diamond, as hard as the rest of her finely-tuned body.

A loud exhale rose from the crowd of spectators. Her right leg held me down, her foot pressing down against my most sensitive vertebrae.

I could feel the rest of her in slow motion above me.

I feebly attempted to raise my chin, my eyes fixing on the first rows of the audience, catching a faint glimpse of Alexandra who immediately looked away.

April Lea's foot ground into my spine.

She adjusted her stance. Stepped back, freeing me partly.

Walked around me. Faced me.

The buzz from the crowd was growing. Inescapable. Laughter and excitement blending in with obscene shout-outs. The spotlight was moving, focusing ever tighter on me, shining hot, drawing my anxious perspiration.

I reluctantly looked up, my gaze running up April Lea's legs all the way to her waist where she was now wearing a strap-on belt, dominated by an enormous dildo, black, organic-like, textured, deadly.

She moved closer to me until the sex toy jutted out from her and she offered it to my lips.

"Do I need to spell it out?" she said.

I opened my mouth.

It tasted like stone and rubber, smooth across my lips, gliding across my tongue but it was its sheer size that put the fear of death into me as I assiduously sucked on it, blanking out the sounds from the audience, appreciative and mocking in turn. I managed to control my gag reflex, only retching twice as the artificial cock hit against the back of my throat under the steady impetus of April Lea's thrusts.

It was humiliating, sure, but if my punishment stopped here, I reckoned I could live with it. But I doubted the ordeal would come to an end there.

I was right.

Five minutes later, once I had lubricated the toy enough for her ultimate purpose, the Canadian martial arts Amazon pulled it from my mouth, moved to my back, dragged me up on my knees a tad higher and, in one swift movement, dug her toy into my rectum.

I screamed.

Like a baby.

Feeling as if not only my anus was on fire but was also being torn from side to side, leaving bloody flaps of martyred flesh dangling on each side of the opening as the object was pressed deeper and deeper inside me.

I closed my eyes to stem the flow of tears.

I could swear it was growing larger inside me with every assault. Soon I would burst.

The crowd began to sing to the rhythm of the thrusts.

I never passed out totally, but my mind quickly switched off, my body now a sore puppet of flesh, my sides gripped by April Lea's hands to save me from collapsing to the ring's floor like a deflated cushion, as she fucked me relentlessly to the applause of the spectators.

Time moved on.

Slowly. Indifferent to my plight.

Under the pitiful gaze of women I knew: Alexandra, Vienna, others I couldn't see lost in the hubbub of balcony spectators.

Eyes that would never forget the spectacle of me on my knees being mounted from behind by a woman. All dignity and pride stripped forever. The acme of humiliation.

The Commander had chosen his punishment with exquisite cruelty. This was indeed a moment I would never forget.

Eyes closed shut. Mind disconnected from reality, I endured.

Until I could endure no longer. It was a new sort of pain, where pain no longer existed, it just was, it became me, its heart in my bruised rectum, marked, branded, eternally scarred.

Time freezes, but goes on forever.

8 – THE SACKING OF NEW YORK

I opened my eyes.

Felt dizzy.

Shapes floating in the ceiling, a Rorschach test in unsettling motion, maps of countries merging into each other, blurry faces with smiles turning into rictus echoing my pain.

Bile at the back of my throat.

Nausea. Mental and physical.

"Are you OK?"

A voice rising from the depths, out of focus, by my side.

I struggled to move my head to see my questioner. Every muscle in my body screaming bloody hell at the sheer effort, sinews in my neck resisting.

Words struggled, rising to the surface like wading through mud.

What came out of my mouth was more of an animal moan than a voice.

She placed the rim of a glass of water to my lips, and my tongue greedily darted towards it, then my lips understood what I was being offered, and I rose my head an inch to gain further access to the drink and began to sip the refreshing liquid as if there was no tomorrow. Clumsily, half of it pouring out across my chin and then the sheet under me on which I had been lying.

A stream of life gliding down my throat reaching parts of me I didn't know I had. The glass was now empty. Behind it, coming into focus, Vienna's face.

"Where … how?" I mumbled.

"You're safe," she stated. It didn't feel that way from the concern I read in her eyes. I knew I probably looked the same as I felt: gaunt, eyes sunken and rimmed with darkness, bone weary, shots of pain racing along my nerves.

With consciousness returning to my mind and body, so did reality. Through the layers of hurt came a desperately urgent need to urinate. I tried to sit up. Looked around. Just Vienna sitting on a chair by the side of the narrow bed in which I was tucked up, her features anxious and caring, wearing an old Ramones T-shirt.

"I need to pee… Badly…"

Her arm rose, indicating the door. "Over there," she indicated.

I struggled to push the bed covers back. Hesitated. I was fully naked. Just as I had been in the ring. Earlier today? Yesterday?

How had she got me here?

Noting my reluctance, Vienna half-smiled.

"Don't you think I've seen all of you before by now? I've probably had a better view of your cock from all angles than of any other man's…" Her smile broadened.

I gingerly set my feet down and tiptoed to the washroom.

□ □ □

"I couldn't do anything to stop it," Vienna explained. "I begged with my father to ensure you weren't killed, but that's as far as I could manage. He put you under his protection, but there were limits even he couldn't impose on the Commander. Look: it could have been worse, much worse. That Canadian chick is known to have broken the backs of several men already. She can be lethal. In exchange, we both had to agree to be present, watch the whole spectacle, endure your breaking."

"I suppose I should be thankful to you."

"Indeed. Neither of us stayed for the latter part of the show, but I know from reputation that the Webster Hall shows end up with many of the involuntary gladiators and cage fighters dead."

"Civilisation is breaking down," I remarked.

"If it's bare fists only, the loser once beaten to a pulp is usually disposed of. In some cases both the fighters are given blades, razors, knives. It's not pretty. I was also told that alongside you, as part of the arrangement to spare you, to compensate, he also punished his own daughter for recruiting you…"

"He didn't have her similarly exposed in the ring, did he?"

"No. But the agreement he'd reached with her was that she had to administer the coup de grace at the end of the next bout. Slit the loser's throat. Whether the victim was someone she knew, I don't know, but I would never put anything past the Commander. So, consider yourself lucky."

I was back in the bed, counting my bruises and cataloguing the areas that still hurt. My arse was still on fire and felt as if it was gaping open from the way that April Lea's monstrous toy had stretched it to its limits.

Vienna noticed my grimace.

"How does it feel?"

"I'm now truly sympathetic to others who've endured piles…"

"I have some medicine you might use." She handed me over a tube of cream. I glanced at its label. It was designed for babies' nappy rash. "It's all I could think of," Vienna apologised. I reckoned she'd never been anally forced. I was not about to smear it across my parts in her presence and compound my shame further.

"I'll use it later," I said.

A wave of despair washed over me as memories of Lily, as well as the way April Lea had turned me into a piece of meat for her fun and that of the Commander's audience, flowed through my mind. I just didn't want to picture what might have happened to her. Guilt assailed me.

Another random souvenir slammed against me like a wave and spread its poison further: how, when making love with Giulia, I often enjoyed the way she slipped a dainty finger into my rectum to stimulate me further. Damn. Not something I would ever want a woman to do to me again, even in lust.

I tried to snap out of the funk I was wallowing in. I asked Vienna what day it was. It was indeed the following day.

"We drove you here. It's a small hideaway we keep on Prince Street. Normally, I stay at the old hotel on the Washington Square; the first two floors are habitable, but it sometimes comes in useful to have somewhere discreet outside."

"Did you get my clothes?"

"No. They'd dragged you into the side stage area; you were semi-conscious. Abandoned you there to make space for the next bout. You were still naked. That horrible jockstrap you had to wear was thrown over you, but I'm sure you wouldn't have wanted us to bring it along."

"Jeez no. It made me feel more naked than actually being naked having to wear it."

"I'm sure that was the idea. It was too small for you. You kept on spilling out of it during the fight, long before the Canadian woman tore it off. We just found a blanket and draped it over you and helped you to the car."

"Thanks."

"Couldn't have you wandering the streets of Manhattan after dark. Even more so in the traumatised state you were in. It was one of those nights anyway. Blood in the air. As if the events in Webster Hall were inspiring bedlam just a dozen blocks or more further north. It seems the Central Park tribes have gone on the offensive and burst through the cordons and are heading south with a vengeance. Food is in short supply in their erstwhile territory, so hunger is driving them. There have been atrocities. I heard of bodies being strung up from posts close to Gramercy Park. Crucifixions…"

"Feels like the end of time…"

"Dangerous times, at any rate," Vienna agreed. "We have to get out of New York," she stated.

"Hadn't that always been our plan?"

"I know. But it took time to arrange. Things are mostly in place now."

"You mean it's going to happen?"

"If you still want it? Even outside of the city, the Commander wields influence. Has contacts, alliances, a whole network of informants and helpers. If he hears you're still on the trail of his daughter, he won't spare you next time. It'll be ugly."

"I know."

"Are you certain?"

"Absolutely. I realise the risk. But I can't give up now. They can only have me sodomised once, next time they'll have to kill me. I can live with that… Or die to be more precise."

"It's not just because of the daughter, is it?"

"No, there's someone else I must find in Louisiana."

"I hope she's worth it."

"She was. Whether she is now, is another matter. So, are you still willing to help me get there?"

"I don't think staying in New York is much of an alternative any longer. Even my father is thinking of giving up the park and moving his operations to the Florida Keys. He likes the heat…"

"Well, to begin, you'll have to find me some clothes."

Vienna smiled, and the gentle curl of her lips brought a touch of much-needed warmth into that small bedroom.

"I'll try and scoop something up," she said. "It's not as if I keep a whole garderobe on the premises. And, anyway, I don't think we wear quite the same sizes!"

"It's only six blocks or so to my place from here, I guess. I can bear the temporary ridicule, but I'd rather not have to walk another walk of shame in the altogether…"

She dug up a loose enough T-shirt, a pair of tight sandals and some wrap-around sarong that at least helped with my modesty.

None of the jeans she found fit.

We were walking down the stairs to Prince Street. The stairwell was a cauldron of cooking smells and badly lit, I had to keep the waist of the material wrapped around my midriff closed tight with my fingers or it would have slid off. I was not about to win a fashion contest.

It was mid-afternoon already and passers-by were scarce. We didn't come across anyone until we reached the Houston crossing. We separated there, me heading to my office and Vienna to the refuge of Washington Square Park. We had arranged to meet the following morning at 5 a.m. on the corner of Lafayette and Astor Place. Vienna would have transport and provisions.

After we parted, I gingerly made it to my apartment, attracting strange stares along the way. I expected witty and less jovial remarks, but I must have looked too much of a mess as well as a weirdo to invite verbal scorn. It was a relief, as I knew I would have had no sense of repartee in the current circumstances. My arse still hurt like hell.

□ □ □

The place was the usual mess. I half expected it to have been ransacked in my absence, but no one had bothered. The Commander's people knew they had the measure of me, and no doubt previous visits had not uncovered anything of interest, if only because, apart from the now lost print of Cherise and Giulia draped around each other in Jackson Square, New Orleans, I had found nothing of consequence and whatever useful information I harboured was all stored inside my head.

I wandered about in something of a daze, puzzling as to what I should be doing next: tidying up, selecting clothes for the journey to Louisiana, sleep, wallow in my despair…

But first I badly needed a shower. I was filthy, from head to toe, the soles of my feet literally black from all the barefoot walking, and falling, I had done since being stripped in the Webster Hall dressing room, a thin overall sheen of dried sweat curtained my whole body and my ravaged arse was probably a dubiously unsanitary sight to behold.

There was no hot water and I braved a cold shower, scrubbed, washed, wiped, scrubbed again, dried myself and then, sniffing under my armpits and my fingers, repeated the whole exercise all over again until I felt part way back to normal, if not totally presentable.

By then I felt hungry, but the prospect of real food, textures to chew on, swallow, actually taste and digest was not in the least appealing. The hollow in the pit of my gut screamed for something, sugar, some magic ingredient. A quick look at the inside of the fridge and a peep inside some of the drawers where I sometimes stored candy or chocolate bars revealed nothing. I rummaged in the washing basket and found a denim shirt which wasn't too dirty, and I buttoned it above my tee, slipped on a pair of old tasselled loafers and walked out of the apartment in search of a convenience store that might still be open. Down the corridor was the door to my office. There was a form slumped against it, sitting, head low, long blonde hair stuffed haphazardly into a Manhattan Kickers baseball cap. She was wrapped in a long black leather trench coat and wore fading Nike trainers.

"Who…?"

The woman looked up at me, her eyes deep wells of sorrow. It was Alexandra. A galaxy away and more from the paragon of fashion and poise she had always been in my presence. After the fall.

"What can I say?" a voice, plaintive, worn down by life.

For a moment, I felt bitter, mindful of the fact that everything that had happened to me, and others, had begun with her knocking on this very door, offering me the case. Was she now accepting the brunt of the responsibility?

"A fine mess you've caused, eh?"

"I know…"

"Have you come to say you're sorry? In which case it's way too late. Some things can't be undone you know, or parts of my anatomy restored to their primal virginity."

She remained silent.

She sat with her back to the door, her whole body folded on itself as if she was trying to make herself smaller, less of a target for my anger.

She took a deep breath. Gazed up at me, with just a touch of defiance.

"Help me up," she asked.

I extended my hand and, with my assistance, she rose from the floor. She had been crying, her eyes rimmed red and tired. I unlocked the office door and we stepped in. I sat behind the desk and Alexandra parked herself in the client chair. As if we were starting from scratch and she was about to make a proposal which would only end in tears, as we both well knew already.

"Don't tell me: you want me to find your sister…" I thought I was being facetious. From the glum look on her face, she didn't get the joke.

"Don't make fun of me," she said, a hint of her fire of old reappearing.

"So, have you come with some explanations this time around? I don't think I wish to be lied to again, Miss Helmsmark."

"I let you fuck me," Alexandra said.

"Was that planned or just an accident, an indulgence you thought you deserved because you'd paid for me? Get a detective to accept a case, and then throw him a few breadcrumbs on the side to motivate him further?"

"No," she replied. "It was good. A pleasant interlude. I was lonely. You were there, you were sympathetic, you were a man."

She appeared so detached now that it made me feel used as if anyone around at that moment would have done the trick and I just happened to be conveniently placed and owned the right plumbing.

"That doesn't make me feel any better," I remarked.

"You're free not to believe me. It no longer matters. I had to kill a man yesterday…"

"So I heard."

"The final bout of the evening, long after you'd been thrown out onto the streets, but alive. One of my father's associates who'd been tailing me. I'd somehow convinced him not to tell on me, the fact that I slept with you. The Commander found out. Ordered for him to be punished…"

"And he felt it wasn't enough for the poor guy to have his arsehole ripped open…"

"No. He had to be made an example of…"

I wondered how she'd describe what had happened to me.

"Was it April Lea he had to face?"

"No. She only does recreational stuff. It was a professional. He was butchered, literally. His blood was all over the floor of the ring, his face a mess, one eye left, the tendons on both his legs severed, he couldn't even crawl. I wanted to look away when my father said it was my turn to learn a lesson, handed me the knife and ordered me to finish him off. At first, I was struck dumb. Then I asked him: how? You just slit his throat, my father said. Pointing out the poor man was already partly unconscious and was unlikely to put up any resistance. Your baptism in blood, he pointed out."

"And you did it?"

"Did I have a choice? I thought it would be easier. I just couldn't look at him. My hand slipped. It felt as if it took ages. I almost vomited afterwards."

"Maybe. Had you refused what do you think your father would have then done? Had you punished too? Ceremonially stripped, fucked publicly, mutilated? Surely not?"

"You don't know what he's capable of," Alexandra argued.

"He's still your father."

"The Commander is a law unto himself," she said.

"So, tell me: why did you want me to locate Tiffany Cherise, what had she stolen, if that is what she actually did, or knew, and why was your father so against the idea?" I wanted to hold my knowledge of the Giulia connection back; ask her about that another time, once the main elements of the puzzle had properly been assembled.

She took a deep breath.

I held her gaze.

A flash of understanding running between us, the intuition that at last, I would be hearing the real story, the facts.

"She's not my sister."

The jigsaw immediately became clearer in my mind, the pieces reassembling themselves into a different configuration, albeit one that still didn't offer all the answers.

I made a quick mental calculation, estimating Alexandra's age in the mid to late thirties. It made sense, now.

"She's your daughter, isn't she?"

Alexandra nodded.

"I was fourteen."

"Did she know?"

"Not until very recently."

"And the father?" I knew the answer already.

Alexandra lowered her eyes.

"Him."

Silence fell like a ton of bricks, as if a balloon had been punctured and all the pestilential bad air within had been expelled, the boil lanced.

"So why did Tiffany Cherise leave?"

"I don't know… Somehow we were never very close. I found it difficult to bond with her when she was smaller. Maybe the fear lurking inside me that she would inevitably discover the truth one day. It held me back, muted my affection. And then as a teen, she seemed to take the wrong path. Rebellion, defiance… I was confused, didn't know what I should do or say. Felt so helpless. Became to feel responsible. So many words I should have said, and never did. Standing in the shadows observing her pain…"

"And the Commander?"

"What about him?"

"How did he react to Tiffany's wrong turn, the modelling and all the rest?"

"He was indifferent as if she was not his responsibility. He berated her, sure, but it felt as if he was just going through the motions."

"Do you think he also abused her?"

"I'm not sure. She wouldn't confide in me. Maybe…"

"A right proper mess," I ventured. "So why did you have to get me involved?"

"I felt as if I owed it to her. For the years of silence. I couldn't allow her to disappear from my life in that manner. When my father learned what

I had done, he was furious. For a moment I thought he would harm me, but he never did, not in that way. I thought that if you could locate her, maybe I could flee along with her, find a new life together, build something, erase all the mistakes."

The weight of guilt was like a ghostly shroud floating in the air above Alexandra's shoulders.

What did she expect me to do now, I wondered?

"I think I know where she is," I declared.

Her eyes looked up at me, saucers full of questions.

"Tell me," she said softly, her voice no more powerful than a spring breeze.

"In New Orleans," I said.

Alexandra went pale, gulped hard.

"In that case, she is lost forever," she said.

"Why?"

"Since the Louisiana Republic was established, it's become the most evil place in the country. I've heard a lot of things through listening in on my father's meetings and talking to his colleagues. He has, as you well know, a finger in many pies, but the one place he now ostensibly refuses to do business with is New Orleans. He was there once, and something went badly wrong. More or less at the time of the Dark..."

"So why would she move there?"

"Because it's the one place he would never set foot in."

I pondered.

"Did you know any of Tiffany's friends? Someone she might have escaped with?"

"Not really. She never did take me into her trust."

"A young Italian woman, a student here in Manhattan?"

"It doesn't sound like her sort of acquaintance. Her frequentations were more… down market, bohemian. Other models, photographers, artists on the lower rung of the ladder."

I guessed I wasn't going to get much more out of Alexandra and every minute I spent with her would attract further wrath from the Commander if he found out we were still communicating.

"I think you should go," I told her. I had no intention of telling her I was leaving for Louisiana the following morning. Or who with. It could cause problems I could do without.

She stood slowly.

"Walk with me a little," Alexandra asked. "I need company right now."

Dusk was falling on Manhattan. The sky was moving between blue and grey, and the sun was reluctantly setting behind the skyscrapers.

There was a sadness in the air.

"I will," I said. "But just a little. For old time's sake," I suggested. On one hand, I wanted to see the end of her, while on the other, I didn't want her to go. Call me sentimental.

□ □ □

I suggested we go west, towards the Piers, but Alexandra wanted to walk north.

"There's trouble up there," I said.

We went north.

As the early darkness fell and we crossed Union Square, we could hear rumours ahead. Crowds, movement, then in the air the acrid smell of smoke. Everyone else we passed was heading in a different direction and gave us strange looks as we persevered past them, albeit at a slow wandering pace. We didn't speak, but Alexandra was holding my hand, as if we were just tender lovers on a night out. Her grip was firm.

Home Security personnel retreating south, ammunition slung over their shoulders, heavy weaponry hanging on their sides, a feeling of panic controlling their movements.

"What is it?" I asked one of them as he rushed by. He couldn't be more than a teenager, spindly body occupying his fatigues, features still scarred with acne, young, scared.

"I wouldn't venture in that direction," he said. "The tribes are on the march. This is the big one…"

As he walked past, I suggested to Alexandra we turn back towards the Village, stay out of trouble.

She refused.

The Flatiron Building was in flames, and there wasn't a single fireman or truck in situ trying to control the blaze. Dark smoke flew from the lower story windows and onlookers gazed in awe at the destruction of the landmark building. We stood watching too, paralysed by the dreadful spectacle. Further up, all 5th Avenue was like a long line of insects, a sea of humanity in sickening motion, screams, shout-outs, desperate cries and war chants, and a thin line of militia and armed personnel standing behind an improvised barricade of turned over cars and whatever junk they could find to reinforce the barrier was all that separated us from the mob ahead.

Until recently the tribes had all operated individually, but now they appeared to have a single purpose, to conquer all of the island of Manhattan: the Arabs, the Jews, the Italians, the Greeks, The Irish, the out of work Wall Streeters, the unemployed, the Rainbow coalition and every minority group that had been resettled in Central Park over the past decade. All bent on revenge.

We moved across to Madison, and then 3rd Avenue in search of a passage north.

There were bodies on the ground, abandoned with no compassion. I didn't know how long they had been there, fresh or older victims of the troubles.

Further buildings had burned down, a mass of twisted metal and ebony black ruins. The other buildings were all shuttered, some with windows shuttered or protected by barbed wire. We only managed to move a further four blocks until we were stopped in our tracks by a terrible spectacle.

Bodies hanging from lamp posts or windows. Some still clothed, others in a state of disarray which was even more obscene, others stripped down to the flesh, skin still bloody, flayed, mutilated. Mostly men, and from what remained of their uniforms, military, but there was also the body of a young woman, her neck at an unnatural angle, rope strung under her chin, dangling like a puppet, her bottom half naked, a deep, gaping wound below her navel, where blood had now coagulated. It was unclear whether the cut had been inflicted before she had been strung up.

Alexandra stood, fascinated by the dreadful display of inhumanity.

"Don't," I begged her. "Just look away."

She let go of my hand, kept on gazing at the dead body obscenely displayed ahead of us. I wished I could do something, and maybe bring her down, cover her visibly ravaged intimacy, but there was no way I could reach that high.

"I wish it could be me," Alexandra whispered.

"No, you don't," I said.

"No more guilt, no more memories, no more waking in the middle of the night with a head full of sorrow and regret. She's been washed clean. She's at peace…"

"You're talking nonsense. Do you think that's what came to her mind in the last few moments of her life? Whoever she was, after she'd been raped by God knows how many, tortured and then unceremoniously pulled up by that noose and left to squirm while her consciousness was ebbing away, bereft of all dignity."

"Her problems are over," Alexandra said.

"We have to turn back," I insisted.

"No, I want to continue. Reach Central Park."

"You're crazy. That's where all the insurgencies are based. It would be suicidal. Can't you see?" I pointed to the bodies on the ground, strung up from the poles and dangling from the windows. "You'll end up dead.

Or worse. Being the Commander's daughter won't help any longer. Even his powers and influence have limits. This is the beginning of a new world. With new rules. Don't you realise that?"

"No one has to know I am the Commander's daughter," she said.

"Don't. Please."

There was the faint sound of a distant explosion to the west, then another. A child of no more than ten came running down the side street, with an open rucksack overflowing with booty, new trainers, sports gear, on his back. He rushed by us without even a glance.

Alexandra looked towards me and I knew she had made her mind up. I remembered that final glimpse of Lily disappearing across the road into the park. At least she'd been full of hope.

Alexandra had chosen to die. Her way of seeking penance, I suppose. What a fucking waste.

"I'm sorry I caused all the trouble," she said, blew me a kiss, and I saw tears in her eyes. Then, she turned and headed north.

I waited a few minutes. Thinking this could be an old-fashioned movie and maybe any second now, the strings on the soundtrack would surge in a rush of emotion and she would turn back, look at me, change her mind and come running in my direction as the music reached a crescendo and in slow motion take refuge in the harbour of my arms.

She didn't.

This was no movie.

I retraced my steps to Houston, carefully avoiding corners or streets where the mob were already on the rampage, trying to appear as innocuous as I could. The pain between my legs still hovered but tonight wasn't as sharp. Not that I would ever be able to erase the memory of what April Lea had done to me at the Commander's bidding.

I would never see or hear of Alexandra again, I knew. Or her actual fate.

That was the famous night Manhattan burned.

9 – FROM ROAD TO RIVER

The city in early morning smelled of death, a pungent, bitter fragrance that hung low from a crown of grey, smoke clouds.

When I reached the street it felt as if the metropolis was empty of life and all its inhabitants had fled from its wreath of ashes.

Or had died during the night while I survived a darkness littered with bad dreams and the faces of every single woman I had ever known. The silence was eerie and chilled me down to the bones.

I'd woken with a strong sense of disorientation emerging from the loop of nightmares, aware of the significance of today but somehow grasping at the reality. A quick shower and I gathered up an assortment of clothes, mostly shirts, tees and a change of underwear, I thought might prove appropriate for the long journey, stuffed it all into a rucksack I had lying around, stepped into a sturdy pair of boots which had seen me through past winters of blizzards and snowstorms. I put on a three quarters length brown leather jacket with a hood, and on impulse shoved all the candy bars, I had finally gotten hold of the previous evening after parting from Alexandra, deep into one of its pockets. I gave a final backwards glance at my apartment, felt a surge of adrenaline racing through my veins and knew there was no turning back.

Walking north towards Lafayette, I kept close to the buildings, trying to merge with the shadows, not wishing to be seen or bring attention to myself. The smell of ashes lingering in the air was pervasive and I regretted not having brought along some cloth to wrap around my face and protect my breathing, and then maybe a different pair of shoes as my feet were already sweating inside the heavy, laced-up boots and the thick woollen socks I normally wore with them.

Vienna was already waiting for me, parked on the corner of Astor Place. She was driving a grey SUV with Oregon plates, a squat vehicle with traces of wear, tear and rust scratched across its bodywork like badges of honour. She saw me approaching and waved me on. She drove, her hair tucked back into a ponytail, the visible part of her body still clad in her Ramones T-shirt.

"What's that you're wearing?" she said. "We're not going to the North Pole." She looked particularly amused when she looked down and saw my winter storm boots.

"I wasn't quite sure what to pack," I said. "Maybe I somehow expected a fair bit of walking…"

"All the way to New Orleans? You must be kidding. It's going to be tough, but not that tough!"

I must have looked embarrassed, feeling like something of a fool, as she burst out laughing. It was the best sound I'd heard in several days. "Jump on in."

I did, installing myself down next to her in the front seat.

"Snap," I said.

"What?"

I'd noticed a pile of candy bars alongside the dashboard and stuffed into the pocket, separating me from her seat.

"We had the same idea," I pointed out, pulling identical bars from my jacket pocket.

"Good, because I wasn't planning on sharing mine," Vienna said. She then continued "But I also have other provisions, a few guns, water and whatever I could think of. The only thing I'm concerned about is fuel. I have a few extra jerrycans in the back, but I'm uncertain whether they'll last all the way. This monster of a car could be a thirsty one."

"I'm sure we'll find a way…"

"By the way, do you drive?"

I looked at the gear stick. I'd only ever driven cars with auto transmission.

"I'll find a way."

"Good." She switched on the engine and the car rumbled and came to life. We pulled away from the kerb, angled into the road and within one block Vienna turned left, just a couple of streets before the Webster Hall street turn-off, to my great relief. There were no other cars on the road. We owned the city.

"So, what's our plan?" I asked her.

"First step is to get the fuck out of Manhattan. It's been a rough night, pure chaos. God knows what's going to happen next. All night, terrible reports were reaching us in Washington Square. Unbelievable stuff going on. Atrocities and all that. At one stage, even my father was thinking of upping sticks and abandoning his patch…"

She had to swerve without a word of warning, to avoid driving over a couple of bodies left lying in the middle of 3rd Avenue.

The SUV's tyres screamed, as she braked, a brief moment of panic.

"I witnessed some of it," I said. "Total desolation." I felt no need to tell her about Alexandra's visit and our parting.

Maybe another time.

"The Midtown Tunnel and most of the bridges further uptown are blocked or too dangerous to manoeuvre," Vienna pointed out. "I thought I'd try the Williamsburg Bridge."

We drove towards the Lower East Side. Cruising down the Bowery and turning on Houston, then making our way to Hester Street. Even this far south, small clouds of ash peppered the air, carried along by the breeze flying in from the nearby river. The road was severely potholed all the way to the bridge from years of urban neglect, the SUV's heavy-duty tyres and the car's suspension absorbed the impact, even though Vienna did her best to avoid the worst of them.

Three blocks from the bridge, we ran into a small, improvised barricade built out of two burned-out cars and piles of industrial junk. Two young men in identical mirrored sunglasses, khaki trousers, Doc Martens, Yankees baseball caps and wife-beater vests were guarding the obstacle.

"I think I know them," Vienna said. "Don't say a word."

She hit the brakes and the car slowed down. She lowered her window and greeted them.

"What's up?"

"No one leaves, no one comes in," the taller one said. He was no more than a teenager, his 'would-be' beard just the ghost of fuzz. They didn't appear to be armed.

"I'm not no one," Vienna said.

"Yes, we know you. You're with the Square crew…" the other said.

"I'm not with the Square. I'm THE Square. If you don't want trouble with us, just let me pass," Vienna suggested.

The two guards looked quizzically at each other. Evidently, they were part of another gang, but one with less power or influence than the Emperor of Washington Square's. They were whispering to each other, debating whether to accede to Vienna's orders or question them.

"Why are you leaving the city?" the shorter one asked.

"That's for me to know," Vienna replied.

He waved us along. Vienna had to drive onto the pavement to avoid the barricade before returning to the road a few metres beyond.

"That was easy," I remarked.

"It won't always be. They belong to a minor group, and their only function was to levy a tax on any supplies coming in. Outside New York, I'm not known, so we'll have to improvise if we meet similar obstacles."

"Aren't you afraid the news that you've left the island will filter back to your father?"

"He knows. Ain't happy about it, but he wouldn't stop me. Not in his nature. He has some old connections in New Orleans, so I have some messages to deliver. Multi-tasking!"

It had been ages since the bridge had been properly maintained and the drive across it was bumpy and slow as we watched the shores of Manhattan retreat behind us, as we rose first and then descended into the suburbs over the elevated section of the highway. There was a hollow feeling about the landscape, grey, abandoned, like a demarcation zone between an old way of life and an uncertain new one.

"So, we'll be heading south? You've settled on a route?" I asked Vienna.

"Actually, no. Just an hour's drive at most, I expect, if there are no surprises in wait and then we'll be making a detour. The major roads should be avoided, so we'll be taking the scenic route. Slower but safer."

The highway out of Manhattan was like a nest of interlaced snakes, an intricate network of curves and levels, but we stuck to our three-lane blacktop and haltingly made it to Queens, as if we were heading for Long Island. There were wrecks along the road, so progress was slow, but the only cars we passed were on the other side, heading for the city. I remembered briefly how busy these roads had once been, from pre-Dark airport runs when the traffic ground to a screeching halt every few miles for no apparent reason before rushing into life again.

The night was falling away and a clear light emerging in contrast to the ash grey skies of Manhattan, the sort of light we hadn't witnessed for years, crystalline, clear, virgin-like in its sense of peace.

We were almost at JFK level, roads increasingly pitted and access to the airport now blocked, when Vienna pointed to the glove compartment and asked me to pull out a sheaf of maps.

"You have to navigate from now on," she said.

"Sure. I'm happy to take over the driving when you feel tired."

"You'll be able to manage the stick gear?"

"I'm confident I'll manage."

"We have to reach the Chicago area," she revealed. "Keeping off the main highways and the Interstates." I pictured the Eastern seaboard in my mind.

"That's a hell of a detour," I pointed out.

"Baltimore and D.C. are off the menu," Vienna said.

"Cesspits. Totally out of control. Don't want to be anywhere close to them, their outliers reach far and wide, I was told."

"So what's in Chicago?" I asked.

"Nothing. But the river is close."

"The river?"

"Da mighty Mississippi, man…"

I had unfolded one of the maps and quickly understood what she intended.

"We'll catch a boat?"

"Exactly. I've made loose arrangements. If we can get the timing right, there is a transport in three days by East Dubuque. It will take us down all the way to Louisiana. We'll have to disembark at some stage, before we hit the walls, which is when it will get dicey. Until then, we should be OK."

It was a plan.

I wondered whether she had come up with it all on her own, or whether she was playing a game, had different interests at heart.

But I had no better plan.

□ □ □

The country roads flew by as we distanced ourselves from the city, the day a haze of silence and greenery, bucolic woods and bushes, an orange sun that exploded into streaks when pierced by a passing cloud, every variety of tree I was unable to find a name for, cumulus formations drifting aimlessly, the horizon a straight line where sky and land merged in a fog of unknowingness.

I'd taken a short turn at the wheel while Vienna snacked on potato chips, an energy bar, sipped avidly from a bottle of soda water and rested briefly, holding out the map on her lap and checking on it at regular intervals, ticking off signs for obscure villages we passed or saw in the distance against the itinerary we had agreed on. There wasn't much to it, once I forced the stick into the right gear and just cruised along for a couple of hours.

By then Vienna was a bit antsy and decided to drive again. It was late afternoon and I had no clue where we were, just on a quiet country road between nowhere and nowhere mark two, the quiet rumble of the SUV's engine purring along like a precision piece of machinery, our only entertainment being the occasional insect splattering itself against our windshield in kamikaze fashion.

I was shaken from my torpor by Vienna's voice.

"The fuel gauge shows we're down to just a third of the tank," she remarked. "I'd rather keep the jerrycans untouched until we near Illinois. Keep an eye out for any form of fuel stop."

I took a cloth, wetted it and ran it across my face to energise myself. Outside, the quality of the light was changing, the sun in its final quarter in the sky above before it would set and the road would darken. The problem with local roads would be a lack of light, but then the interstates were now similarly without electricity.

"Plans for overnight?" I asked Vienna.

"We'll sleep in the car," she said. "Maybe take it in turns for safety's sake, one of us looking out. I don't know how safe these hillbilly regions are." We were only just under a day's drive from New York, but I took her point. The borders of civilisation as we once knew it were now blurred, and the barely inhabited country plains we were navigating through might prove as dangerous as the Ozarks or further perilous territories afield.

Things had changed, for the worse.

A road sign for a nearby town. Just three miles away. Streaks of pink painting the sky.

"Might we find fuel?" I asked Vienna. She pondered. Looked at the gauge again. Weighed the delay the detour would cause against our likely needs.

"Let's do it."

She braked. Took the left turn. A small country road alternately bordered with low hedges and cornfields in studied disarray, a palette of uninterrupted variations of yellow and brown.

The road narrowed, our all-terrain SUV riding the bumps and potholes, swinging from side to side. All the time it was growing darker, as if countryside time ran ahead of big city time. I glanced at my watch. It was only 5 p.m.

Close ahead a cluster of lights flickering like far away stars. It seemed too isolated a place to have a fuel station, I was beginning to believe, I was not looking forward to the journey back in complete darkness.

Vienna slowed down.

"What do you think?"

"Haven't a clue."

It didn't deserve to be called a village, just barely a hamlet. A ghost of a place, a dozen fragile edifices strung along the main street, half unlit, the others with pink and yellow windows, curtains pulled, secrets and people hidden from sight. The lights we had observed from afar now muted, and scarce. Just a couple of buildings with windows reflecting the pale glare of weak electric bulbs in some of the curtained rooms. A few cars were parked. A Buick, an Audi, something that looked more like a tractor from the Middle Ages, a Cadillac with fins, like a vintage car out of *American Graffiti*. That sort of town. But cars meant fuel. We cruised down the main drag in low gear, our engine barely on the wrong end of silent, discreet, tentative. We quickly reached the other end of the main drag and there it was. A small one pump fuel station, an empty forecourt with a corrugated shack by its side, once a convenience store according to the signage. It was empty. Shelves void, spinners stuck in place.

Vienna slid the car into position by the pump. Switched the engine off.

"It might be dry," she said, as the hint of a smile was breaking across my lips. "Reason there's no one here, manning things."

"I'll check."

I opened the door and climbed down. Walked around our vehicle to the pump and the long rubber hose and nozzle hanging by it. Vienna sat in the driver's seat, alert, ready for trouble.

The heat and smell of the engine, which had been running non-stop all day, assaulted me, chemical, heavy, acrid.

I unhooked the rubber hose. It wasn't locked in place. An indistinct buzz rose from the clockwork dial on the face of the pump's main body. There was no indication whether it was normal fuel or diesel. I could only hope for the best that I wouldn't fuck up our engine by drowning it in the wrong kind of liquid ammunition.

"It's working," I shouted out to Vienna, and loosened our hubcap and planted the hose's nozzle down our intake hole.

The fuel gurgled through the rubber hose into our tank. I heaved a sigh of relief. Not hearing back from Vienna, I turned my head back towards her while holding on firmly to the plastic tube through which the fuel streamed.

There was a reason she'd remained silent: there was a shotgun pointed at her face. A small, red-haired and freckle-faced kid, of about ten, was holding it, firmly, his aim steady.

As I noticed him, I heard footsteps creeping up behind me and I was also being threatened, a small girl this time, dressed in a floral smock and opening hours knee-high boots of faded leather, also holding a weapon, a .22 revolver, small in size but at this range powerful enough to make a sizeable hole in me.

"Trying to sneak up and steal our fuel, fucker?" she said. Her voice was squeaky but firm in its menace and intent.

Vienna was ordered to climb out of her seat and manoeuvred herself down to the ground, the shotgun following her movements every inch of the way. The girl waved her weapon at me.

"If I let go of the hose, the fuel will spill everywhere," I pointed out to the diminutive girl. She allowed me to pull it out of the tank slowly and hook it in its place of rest.

"So, what do you have to say for yourselves?" the boy said.

His denim shirt was a constellation of stains and much too long for him, reaching down to almost his knees.

"We were going to pay," Vienna said. "We're honest people, look at us. Not scavengers. Just needed to refuel, that's all."

"Pay with what?" the young girl asked.

"We have cash," I said.

"Money's no use any longer," the boy replied. "It doesn't mean a thing."

Vienna intervened. "Where are your parents? Let us talk to them. Take us."

"There ain't any adults in this here town. Just us kids…"

"Since when?"

"Weeks."

They had been abandoned there, in charge of nowhere. The fact that the station still had fuel was incidental since none of them was in a position to drive the vehicles we'd seen parked or stranded here. Their feet wouldn't reach the pedals. Unless there were older kids around.

We were led to a nearby building, its front doors wide open and directed to a large room on the ground floor, in which four other kids of similar age were sitting in a circle, haggard and hollow-eyed.

Every set of eyes in the room were fixed on us and there was an uncomfortable lull. As if they now didn't know what to do with us. Or to us.

I noticed the guns had been lowered. The young ones stared at us.

Vienna whispered softly in my ears. "They're hungry, that's what it is."

I tried to picture the scenario: adults without food supplies leaving the village and the children behind as too much of a burden and the kids abandoned without quite understanding why, having maybe been asked to guard the buildings or whatever precious was left there.

"We have some food," I said.

They all looked at me, as if disbelieving.

"And candy. Quite a lot of candy." added Vienna. "We can swap for the fuel we need."

The younger ones stirred. They conferred. Soon, we had a deal.

Vienna had mostly packed cans: stewed meat, beans, corned beef, and powdered soup sachets. We all ate together and agreed to leave our surplus with them. Hopefully, we'd be reaching Chicago within a day or two, and we'd be able to replenish our supplies here, if only thanks to Vienna's contacts.

We slept all huddled together for warmth in the large room. I tried to talk to some of the kids, learn more about their past, the circumstances that had led them here, but they were not eager to converse, sad-eyed and seemingly resigned to their fate. All I found out was that the weapons we had been threatened with were worthless as they had no bullets or ammunition. They'd just put up a front.

In the morning, we departed early at the first crack of dawn, voluntarily dumping our combined stock of candy bars with the children. I knew the provisions we'd jettisoned wouldn't last long and was concerned that the next supply of food they might come across was problematic. I tried not to think of the children's fate, but it brought a knot to my throat. I also realised we'd never asked any of them for their actual names.

We'd left the SUV by the fuel station and completed filling the tank. On the counter, the cogs turned and turned, indicating the amount we would normally have to pay, a bill we would leave unpaid, a memory of when fuel was cheap and flowed freely. Just to be on the safe side, we found a few extra cans at the back of the station and filled them too. The pump hiccupped and ran dry just as I was filling the final metal can. I reckoned we now had enough fuel for the rest of the journey unless anything unforeseen occurred.

We backtracked through the bumpy, narrow road bordered with cornfields and hedges, soon finding ourselves back on the main country road. It always feels shorter on the return journey, I noted.

Vienna was silent, and I was likewise in no mood for conversation.

□ □ □

The road unfurling under our wheels. The horizon stretching into the distance, never getting nearer, an unattainable target, ever on the retreat, as much as we moved forward.

The patterned sound of the wheels over concrete and gravel, the swish of the wind when we lowered the windows to air out the car and expel the cool, recycled curtain of the AC. Glancing at my watch at regular intervals and feeling as if time had ground to a halt, progress slow, halting, agonising. A sense of being at a standstill even though the dashboard bore witness to the fact we were moving at a regular 50 mph.

Fields, rusting agricultural equipment here and there on the side of the road, wild, unkempt greenery going to seed, the monotonous rattle of the journey kept on repeating itself, leaving me to my thoughts as the rhythms of silence took their toll.

Passing through this landscape gave me the feeling nothing had changed in the world and that we could possibly still be in the 1930s or so, the Great Depression years, before we'd become slaves to technology. A world untainted.

I tried to voluntarily banish all images and feelings about Giulia and my life of the past few years until the Dark had ripped our lives apart in a single moment. I regressed, mulled over the further past.

I had foolishly always thought of my life as a movie, or at a stretch a book. With a story, a beginning, eventually an end.

Ordered, tidy, on an onward trajectory and I was, by default, the main character. No, I didn't hear the swell of violins or a symphonic orchestra in the background at moments of importance, but I could imagine what it would all look like in the eyes of a spectator: undramatic but nonetheless fascinating.

But my life, maybe unlike the life of others, was not a plot, or divided into acts, it was more like a series of unremarkable episodes, the importance of which was never clear at the time.

Fragments that could be seen as part of an unremarkable whole, only in retrospect.

Maybe it was that lost romance that had led me after everything changed, to become a private investigator, to become the hero of my own days and nights again, as well as a natural use of my resources, skills and knowledge.

There was nothing remarkable about me. Had never been.

Apart from the propensity to get hurt by the world of women.

Bruises that became internal scars long after any hypothetical physical evidence had been erased by the passage of time.

Each woman a chapter.

Each one a bittersweet regret, for what had not happened or, if it perchance had, for losing her, having not allowed myself to be fully open to her affection or confusing lust with love, leaving only memories that became deeply imprinted in my psyche.

"You're very quiet," Vienna said from behind the wheel. "Are you okay?"

"Just tired."

"Is that all?"

We'd just passed the halfway mark on the map in our journey to the river, the road widening, a trace of dark grey over the horizon crisscrossing the low clouds, as if something was on fire in the distance.

"I'm uncertain about Chicago," she said. "Whether to make a significant detour to avoid it, or just drive straight through. There was sparse information about the situation there."

"Your call."

"Do you remember how many cans we have in the back?"

"Six or seven, what with those we filled up at the kid's village."

"You're not still thinking about New York?" she asked. I assumed she meant what had happened at Webster Hall.

"No."

I was thinking about my mother and how I had never visited her grave, how the vegetation surrounding it must be running wild from neglect, headstone smothered in moss, weeds on the rampage, inscription fading with every passing day. A hollow feeling in my stomach. Wandering in a daze, never knowing where she was or who I was, manic at times, placid at others, travelling deeper and deeper into her own private world, a country we had no access to, like a traveller through the circles of hell. How she had almost turned into a skeleton during her final days, gaunt, emaciated, eyes wide, cheeks sunken, her dark gypsy hair laced with streaks of white, the pain eating her from inside, drying her lips, begging for who knows what, words forming and un-forming at the back of her throat. I was still only a child, dimly unaware of how bad things were and still daydreaming of a day when she might return home and life could resume in all its normality. Which it never did.

Of course.

Becoming familiar with a grief that was not physical pain.

A girl I once worshipped from afar openly admitting she had slept with another. Another whom I fell madly in love with moving on after just a few weeks together, no doubt defeated by my own immaturity. The married woman who when given a choice returned to her husband, did so.

Each set of dreamy eyes, each perfect body fading into the limbo of recollection.

Moving to New York, the writing, the fact-checking, peace at last.

Giulia, with the Sicily-shaped stain on the back of her calf.

Nights of joy, drowning in her eyes, learning the shape of her body, the taste of her sighs, the scent of her sex, still not without guilt because of the age difference but living in hope. Again, thinking this was a movie, a novel and there could be a happy ending despite the rumblings of the cello on the soundtrack with all its omens of danger, echoes of stalker movies, ah the smoothness of her arse, the medusa jungle of her curly hair, the way she moaned when I entered her, the questions, the dialogue, the wonderful curiosity, the crazy, idealistic dreams she narrated when she was stoned.

Even the way she looked, from a certain angle, like photographs of my mother…

“Snap out of it,” Vienna shouted. Her voice reached me from a distant land.

“I don’t even know what day it is or what time of year,” I blurted out, without thinking.

In the dawn hush, the towers of Chicago could already be seen above the line of the lake.

Vienna stopped the car, opened the glove compartment and passed me one of the guns she kept there.

“It’s unknown territory,” she said. “Just in case.”

She dropped the other on to her lap.

Cold metal. The first a small calibre Sig Sauer, the other a larger weapon I couldn’t recognise by make. Looked lethal, though.

As we entered an industrial area full of crumbling run-down buildings and warehouses, Vienna slowed our speed down to a crawl, as we both looked out for clues, trying to recognise possible dangers lurking around us as we neared the metropolis of the Windy City.

We were driving in parallel to the lake, a few early morning joggers pounding the pavement as we neared South Michigan.

“Looks almost normal,” I remarked.

And the city was. We found a discreet, isolated parking spot close to Grant Park, and ventured into the centre, to find life as we had once known it: commuters ambling along in suits and otherwise, food stands open, most stores also functioning, just the occasional boarded-up establishment and a general sense of doom hanging in the air. What did Chicago know that New York didn’t? Just another indication that all the rumours swirling around weren’t always accurate.

We stocked up with food supplies, even some extra clothing from a Goodwill that was doing roaring business in used goods and shared a room with two beds at the nearest Best Western, which only took cash, but then Vienna had tons of it, bounty from her Manhattan scavenging days where the greenback had mostly fallen out of use and barter was more the order of the day. We took our bottles of soda, cheeses, sausages and fruit to the room and ate with an appetite I had forgotten I was capable of.

It was good to sleep in a bed again, lullabied by the soft purr of Vienna's breath in the other bed. In the morning, she declared that I snored and if there was to be a next time, that we would have to do something about it, or find me a separate room. I somehow doubted hotels would be plentiful during the rest of our journey. I even fell asleep fully dressed while waiting for Vienna to have her shower. She nudged me awake and insisted I follow her example, intimating that after several days on the road my odour was not as pleasant as it should have been. By the time I got back to the bedroom, she was already fast asleep. I quickly followed in her footsteps. It was a night without dreams. Or nightmares.

Early in the morning, we took the road again, left the city behind and sped down the first interstate in our journey. The world felt curiously normal. By afternoon, we had reached East Dubuque and, around the bend of the road, arrived at the banks of the Mississippi.

10 – WE ARE SAILING, WE ARE SAILING

We had to wait two days by the bank for the boat to arrive. The message when we reached East Dubuque was that it had veered off course the previous week to take on supplies and would now pick us up near Davenport, in Iowa. Vienna explained to me that there were often problems at the dams sited above Minneapolis and the Twin Cities, and our crew might have had to make detours through some of the tributaries of the river. Control of the locks regulating the river flow was changing from day to day in some areas.

The weather had turned cold and the stock of blankets we had picked up in Chicago was put to good use, as we spent the extra days hunched up inside the SUV's cabin, the heating switched off to save our fuel which was getting perilously low. Once the ship was here, we would have no further roads to travel, but Vienna had a contingency plan should our planned transport not be on schedule, which would entail moving on to Cedar Rapids and catching a series of trains. In which case, what was left in the fuel tank would just about get us to that destination.

We were just two miles out of town, parked on a promontory overlooking a bend in the river. The sound of cicadas interrupted the silence, an overwhelming, squeaky concerto of metronomic monotony interrupted by the rare sound of a bird in flight and song as it dive-bombed across the waters in the direction of the setting cold sun.

Vienna was huddled against me, just the tip of her nose peering out of the anorak hood, a thick woollen scarf draped around her neck and chin. She looked a bit like an elf, her eyes wide open.

For the past few days our conversations had been at best utilitarian, but we had settled into a fluid form of companionship, and even though there was a core of steel at the heart of her, I couldn't help liking her like a sister. On occasions, I would catch a strange expression in her eyes as she looked at me, but then she would quickly look away and nothing more was said. We both knew all too well that this was not the time for lengthy discussions about why we were now stuck together, with different motives and aims. The priority was reaching New Orleans.

"I think that's it," she said.

A pale light on the river inching closer from the north, moving between white and red and reflected in the churning waters as the embarkation dragged itself nearer with every passing minute, at first a speck of darkness and, quickly, an indistinct form topped by the navigation light, emerging from the dusk.

"How do you know it's the right boat?"

"Right time, right place," she remarked, so full of confidence in her plans slotting into place. She moved her head from my shoulder and unlocked the car door.

Ten minutes later, the boat had slowed to a halt in the middle of the river and a small tender was lowered from its side and began its journey to the bank where we were now standing and where Vienna was pointing a torchlight to indicate our presence.

"Let's get our stuff together," she said, heading to the boot and pulling out rucksacks, more blankets and other items she had been storing there.

I followed her out of the SUV and began gathering our paraphernalia.

The tender reached the sandy bank on our side of the shore.

There was a single occupant, clad all in black.

Vienna waved at him.

"You from the Washington Square crew?" he asked, in a gruff, weather-beaten voice.

"Yes, that's us."

"Hop aboard, then."

The small embarkation was barely large enough for the three of us and the bags we had brought along. There was a small engine attached to the wooden flank of the tender, but the guy navigated us back to the main boat with oars, as if the sound of an engine would betray our presence on this narrow stretch of the river.

We hauled ourselves aboard.

Two other men, similarly dressed in the dark colours of night, awaited us. A trio of undertakers on a river cruise. Not quite three men on a boat.

One of them came forward. In the penumbra, I could barely make out his face but could see it was lined and tanned under his beany cap.

"I'm Ripley," he introduced himself. "This is my boat."

"It's a good-looking boat," I said, trying to ingratiate myself. "Feels sturdy." The deck under my feet felt firm and reliable.

"It's not an 'it', it's a 'she'," Ripley replied, with an air of total disdain.

"Sorry."

"And has she got a name?" Vienna butted in, trying to divert any tension away from my ill-advised intervention.

"*Pride of Malabar*."

The boat was 25 feet across and I reckoned 100 feet in length.

Well-maintained, deep holds, just a navigation cabin at its centre, and a well-scrubbed deck with heavy, padlocked trunks scattered across its surface. Looked overall like a shipping vessel but without the smell, the filth or the equipment, pulleys, nets and all that one would associate with that kind of boat.

Ripley pointed us to a corner of the deck that had been cleared of cargo. "You can sleep there," he stated, indicating the aft area.

I'd been hoping we could a find a place to settle in the hold, maybe, but realised quickly this was not a situation where we were in a position to negotiate. Later, Vienna explained.

"Just steer clear of the hold," she told me. "That's where they keep their main cargo. Don't ask any of them about it. We just keep to ourselves, OK? They might be touchy. Best ignore them and enjoy the journey, without trying to make friends or whatever; understand?"

"What's so precious down there then?"

"Guns, ammunition."

"Oh…"

They were gunrunners, carrying a load of illegal arms obtained in the demarcation zone between the Great Lakes and the Canadian border, bound for the factions in Louisiana. I didn't even want to think of what cargo they would be taking on board for the return journey. Both New Orleans and the demarcation zone were no-go areas everyone steered clear of these days, and the stories coming out of those lands made what was happening in Manhattan child's play.

The three smugglers slept in the navigation cabin, and we had the deck. Settled. No argument. Now I knew why Vienna had stocked up on blankets and that I'd no doubt be in dire need of a shower when we reached our eventual destination.

Meals were taken together, stews, dry biscuits, all of us taciturn around the square, rickety table in the cabin cleared of navigation maps and papers.

First night aboard. The sky full of stars.

"So far, so good, no?" Vienna said, a faint smile written across her full lips.

"That's a matter of opinion. If you include me being beaten up, raped, held up at gunpoint by kids half our size, two women probably dead or worse..."

"Who?"

I hadn't told her about Lily or Alexandra. That was a cross for me to bear alone, I'd decided.

"You don't know them... Collateral damage, as they say." It felt odious to say.

"Anyway, we're OK. That's all that matters."

"I suppose so."

"Do you think we'd make a good team?"

"A team? Like Batman and Robin?"

"Why not? After all this is over, maybe I can be your assistant, receptionist, sidekick, whatever. You can't have a private eye without his trusted assistant, can you? I was thinking more of Mike Hammer and Velda, no?"

"You're not blonde or fatale. Yet..."

Vienna laughed aloud.

"There's always peroxide. And I'm armed to the teeth. Give me a chance."

"There's always something. Let's try and get some sleep."

□ □ □

We sailed past St. Louis, Missouri, dawn peering timidly through a mass of clouds, the full moon retreating step by step into the disappearing night. The boat gliding down the waters, the tall buildings looming around us like giants, the eerie silence a heavy reproach. It felt as if both sides of the city, particularly the East shore, were totally empty, ghost cities emerging from a thousand-year sleep like urban stone and steel incarnations of Snow White. We didn't stop and talk, the three sailors glanced nervously at the shores throughout, as if expecting trouble and only displayed a sense of relief when we left St. Louis well behind us. Ever since we had boarded the *Pride of Malabar*, we had been navigating our way through a wide channel formed by a series of man-made lakes. We were now approaching the free-flowing Middle Mississippi.

To say that the three stooges in black who controlled the boat resented us wasn't quite accurate: they downright ignored us, just a grunt here and there or a withering look across the table when we all ate together. I was initially worried that the presence of a woman on board might prove a bone of contention or a disturbing factor, but aside from a few sideways, questioning glances at Vienna from the self-appointed captain whenever she moved nearby or bent over and exposed a line of white skin between her sweatshirt and her jeans, they kept their thoughts and emotions under control. I assumed they were being paid well for transporting us and that money, or whatever was changing hands in kind, talked. It still didn't make me feel comfortable in their presence or having them around, knowing we could always come across a party who could offer more and we'd land in deep shit.

On the third day of our journey south, a handful of miles past the confluence with the Ohio River, ambling down the wide waterway, with dredgers and barges our only infrequent company, Vex, who was on look-out, cried out.

The others rushed to the front of the boat and Vienna and I who'd been playing cards to pass the time on the back deck followed, albeit in less of a rush.

"What is it?"

"Activity ahead," he said.

"Suspicious?" the skipper asked.

"Not normal…"

He despatched the other sailor to the cabin. The man promptly returned, holding a number of rifles and other assorted weapons, and a box of ammunition.

They walked to the front of the boat, all crouched down and held their guns in readiness.

As an afterthought, the captain called back to Vienna and me.

"Know how to handle a gun, do you?"

We both nodded in affirmation. As far as I was concerned, I knew how to hold one but had never fired one in anger.

Somehow, I guessed Vienna had more experience.

We were handed two of the remaining rifles, and given positions on either side of the deck, as a second row of fire behind two of the smugglers, while one of them climbed into the cabin and took the wheel. Ahead I could see nothing abnormal but deferred gladly to their certainty.

Moments later, I heard the boat's engines rumble, cough and sputter into a higher gear and within seconds the boat was now coursing down the river at much-increased speed. We kept our eyes peeled on the expanse ahead, through which we were heading now.

There was some smoke rising from the right shore ahead, but no sign of other human activity.

Right then, as I swept my eyes away from the upward rivulets of dense smoke, I saw them.

Pulling away from both shores to catch us in a pincer movement, two small motor crafts racing towards us, three in each, camouflaged in improvised khaki and camouflage-coloured uniforms of sorts. They were heavily armed.

Vex cried out to us. "You two, to the back, pronto."

Vienna and I turned around and noticed a third sleek motor craft racing towards our vessel. This one only had two attackers on board.

Three sets of attackers. Surrounding us.

The menace barely registered when the gunfire began. It was our captain aiming at both the embarkations now partly blocking our progress, taking the initiative while he still could.

Vienna took this as a signal and began firing in the direction of the small boat coming towards us from the back. Within seconds, we were enveloped in a cloud of thundering gunfire.

An attacker in the following craft fell overboard. Vienna was definitely a better shot than me, as I'd been aiming at his companion, who was still firing away wildly in our direction.

As the *Pride of Malabar* surged forward, creating a trail of foamy waves in its wake, Vienna managed another bulls-eye and must have hit the pursuing boat's fuel tank, and a jet of flames came spurting out of the white craft and its progress ground to a halt, its remaining occupant still firing at us as we outpaced him until we were out of his firing range.

At the front of the boat, the gunfire battle was still going on.

Our smugglers were taking potshots at the attackers from the safety of the deck, carefully keeping out of sight below the wood and metal sections extending upwards from the hull.

Having disposed of the menace behind us, Vienna and I crawled back forward to assist the two smugglers. The third was still barely visible in the cabin above of us, just his hands visible on the wheel while he crouched down and navigated the boat almost blind.

Each of the two remaining enemy craft was down to two men, the body of one of the attackers in the motor craft that had launched from the left bank lying slumped across the embarkation, his arm still tangled in the strap of his semi-automatic.

The captain hauled himself up and threw something at the nearest opposing craft, then quickly squatted back down, out of reach of the attacker's storm of bullets. Seconds later, the enemy boat exploded with a mad roar of thunder, and fire, the grenade having reached its target. The smell of cordite and burned flesh spread through the warm air.

The remaining enemy craft slowed down, admitting defeat and within half a minute we had raced past it into free waters and we were heading towards Cairo. We didn't slow down for some time, though, until Vex and the others were confident they had beaten off the attacks and there was no immediate further danger ahead.

"Fucking river pirates…" the Captain swore loudly. "They must have known what our cargo was. A leak somewhere in the system. Damn and damn again. The return journey is going to be a fucking big problem."

Maybe, I thought, that having unloaded his cargo of weapons and ammunition at his destination in Louisiana, the prospect of an empty hold would be of less interest to mercenaries. I mentioned this to Vienna that night as we lay huddled on the deck, under a speckled moon.

"I suspect not," she said. "They're not transporting arms for the sake of it. They're going to be paid. And not in cash. I suspect it'll be a hold full of drugs. They come in from South America through the cities on the Gulf of Mexico. It makes sense. Arms go south and drugs go north. The perfect swap."

How did she know all this?

"Things should be quiet until we go past Memphis," she said.

"Then we're in unknown territory."

It was common knowledge that Memphis had been burned to the ground eighteen months earlier.

Following the incident and our unavoidable involvement, our relationship with the smugglers eased somewhat, our having earned a degree of respect by virtue of not having panicked and, even more so, Vienna's straight aim during the river battle.

"That was a great shot," I complimented her. "Where did you learn to shoot?" I asked Vienna.

"In Washington Square, of course. We trained shooting squirrels."

"You're kidding me..." Her crinkly smile was unrestrained as she saw my eyes widen.

"Of course."

She passed a Hershey Bar over, offering to share it with me. I gladly obliged. The chocolate was a bit soft but what the hell, chocolate is chocolate and I'm sure I wasn't the first private eye who had vices other than booze and broads.

□ □ □

The *Pride of Malabar's* progress down the wide river came to a halt a couple of days later. We anchored just fifty yards away from a beach head, while one of the smugglers waded ashore to go searching for fuel. When we enquired how long this would take we were informed we would remain stationary overnight, as the depot was a fair few miles inland.

Both Vienna and I had been growing tired of being on board and welcomed the possibility of spending a few hours on dry land, although the captain was reluctant to see us go ashore.

Arguing it was no more dangerous for us to be on land than his colleague, and that anyway we would be armed, he agreed to our demand and so, we made our way through the shallow, muddy waters and walked to the shore, holding our arms, sleeping bags and some provisions.

The cove where we stepped onto the shore was just a tongue of land creeping free from a tangle of dense vegetation, a seemingly impenetrable wall of trees, through which narrow passages led to the heart of the forest and beyond, awkward trails of sand and rock and dead leaves, one of which the departed smuggler had used and which must lead to open spaces beyond with the prospect of fuel and provision supplies. We had no intention of venturing into the greenery, just intent on lying down on the beach, cleaning up, relaxing away from the constant sway of the boat and the metronomic rumblings of its engine, a deep bass sound which I couldn't imagine hearing on any other river than the Mississippi.

The tiny beach angled away from the river and, sitting on its left to keep away from the fierce dying rays of the day's sun, we couldn't see the boat anchored further out in the middle of the mighty stream or be seen by it. Vienna suggested we take a swim.

I was hesitant, not wishing to have to spend the night in wet clothes, and not having brought a change from the boat when we had disembarked.

"Come on," she chuckled. "We can skinny dip!"

Noting the mild grimace on my face, she burst out in laughter.

"I've seen all of you and more already," she reminded me. "Another peek won't pervert me..." And eagerly pulled her sweatshirt above her head and unzipped her trousers, then kicked away her knickers. I couldn't help but gaze lingeringly at her. She was minuscule, a doll of a body, fragile but sturdy, all in straight lines, coiled like a spring, her calves thin like matchsticks, but matchsticks made of steel. Her small breasts, small hillocks, heavy-nippled, pale like milk and her delta a sprawling ebony triangle of thick curls. The shapeless clothes I had always seen her wear had been a perfect disguise, concealing the delicate treasure of her body.

"What are you waiting for?"

My feet digging into the rough sand, my eyes fixed on her, awed and admiring.

Slowly, I undressed and finally stood there naked, facing her and the water where she was wading knee high with gentle laughter peeling from her lips. The first time I had been nude in public since that unfortunate last time. Still, I couldn't move towards her, as if tendrils of earth were holding me in place.

"Don't you dare go hard on me," she shouted out.

It was as if she could read my mind. I broke into a run and splashed heavily into the river, joining her, confident the cold water would dampen my ardour. Her laugh was crystalline, racing across the waters like a bird in flight, swooping, soaring, joyous and so full of innocence for someone whom I knew was anything but innocent. The daughter of the King of Washington Square was born a warrior, armoured against danger and naivety from the cot onwards. That I knew.

Later, we dined on dry beef jerky sticks, succulent green apples we'd picked up from a basket of fruit in the navigation cabin none of the others even seemed to explore, and the last of the chocolate bars both of us had been carrying in our rucksacks since Manhattan.

We moved our sleeping bags to the edge of the shore where we could see the boat and, faintly lullabied by a cloud of southern birds skipping across the canopy of the nearby forest, shuffled inside them, and promptly fell asleep.

Normally I'm a heavy sleeper, the veil of nightmares finding me an easy and welcoming target, but ever since that day when Alexandra Helmsmark had walked into my office and my life, I'd been finding the relief of sleep difficult, halting, assaulted by a barrage of images from the world of women: my mother, Giulia, others whose faces had long erased their names in the halls of my memory, Cherise, Lily, and now

Vienna, faces and bodies glaring at me with intimations of reproach, features and limbs merging like prehistoric monsters on an uncontrolled rampage, the cesspool of my past guilt stirring like an unholy witch's cauldron.

Reaching me through a veil of white noise, new sounds superimposed over the distant cries of the river birds, whispers, steps partly silenced by the softness of the sand. I opened my eyes and felt a heavy object hit the back of my skull. First an explosion of light inside my head, then cresting along the next wave of sensations the shock of the pain, moving from point of impact down every vein my body, irradiating my flesh with hurt.

I cried out feebly, then allowed my face to collapse down into the humid sand.

"That's him taken care of," I heard a voice say. I couldn't place its accent and somehow even half-conscious that innate streak of curiosity to place the voice alongside a precise geographical location must have saved me from passing out completely. I hovered briefly between the temptation to abandon myself to the blinding pain and faint and the will to remain conscious.

Through the fog still clutching my grey cells, the sound of a struggle somewhere to my right; unable to recognise how far away, my mind still a jumble. Then, Vienna's voice. Crying out

"No, no…" A slap, hard hand against skin. Silence again, then a series of vibrations in my ear, feet treading into the sand, trampling down, disturbing its harmony, the echo of a fight running across the sand like a silent wave.

It then dawned on me: the struggle was taking place where I had remembered Vienna's sleeping bag being.

I tried to open my eyes.

Everything was blurred, the river on one side and the busy, tangled forest on the other, one big cloud of dark shapes, indistinguishable from each other.

I blinked.

Realised my eyes were wet. My cheeks too.

Raised one hand. Felt every muscle in my body shriek out in pain.

Wiped my face.

Blood.

Fuck!

Wiped again until the veil in front of my eyes lifted.

Turned my head slowly in the direction of the scuffle.

Worried I could no longer hear Vienna's voice, just muffled sounds.

Every glance in her direction was streaked with pain, echoing back from the base of my skull where I had been hit.

Summoning all the willpower I could dredge up from the depths of my distress.

There: moving forms in the darkness, just a couple of arms' lengths from me.

Forcing my eyes to stay open and acclimatise to the night's dark.

Vienna. On the ground. Torn from her sleeping bag. Some dirty red rag forced into her mouth, blocking out every sound she no doubt was trying to broadcast, her frantic protests. Two men towering above her. One behind her pulling her two arms towards him above her head, stretching her, the other, bearded and gaunt as a skeleton, standing between her legs, half kneeling attempting to force her to part her limbs wide, with one free hand already busily unzipping his trousers.

I managed to raise my head an inch or two. Her jeans had been forcibly rolled down to her ankles, bunched up like an accordion, her knickers torn off, in shreds on the ground by her side, one trainer jettisoned a yard away, her brown socks the only last item of clothing protecting her lower body.

The guy immobilising her hands extended one of his in an attempt to pull up her shirt, but Vienna was writhing like a worm and he gave up on unveiling her breasts lest she partly free herself in the process.

I didn't need subtitles. The strangers who had attacked her were planning to rape her.

In the periphery of my vision, I caught a glimpse of my rucksack and silently began to crawl towards it as best I could. The men were too busy to notice my fumbling movements. I reached it with my extended right arm, and my fingers went searching blindly for the Browning the captain had loaned us during the attack. It felt like an eternity flowing by until I reached it, the cold metal under the pad of my fingers infusing me with energy, electricity. With my eyes still fixed on what was happening to Vienna, I slowly extricated the automatic from the bag.

Now, the man straddling her had lowered his trousers to his knees and was getting down on all fours, roughly kicking Vienna's legs apart, positioning himself to violate her. She was still struggling like the devil, slowing him down, but the acolyte holding her hands behind her shoulders now had a firm grip on her. For a second or so, I feared he was going to strike her with his booted foot to calm her down and defeat the final throws of her resistance.

I leaned forward. Finger on the Browning's trigger. Who should I shoot first?

The rapist lowered himself closer, about to reach the point of no return, the white flabby skin of his hairy arse catching the light of the moon as he positioned himself above Vienna in readiness to thrust.

It was an easy choice.

I aimed.

I fired.

The noise was deafening, the recoil more powerful than I was expecting or was ready for in my own reduced circumstance.

The back of his head exploded, fire-working pieces of skin, hair and brain matter like a halo around his collapsing skull. He fell down across Vienna, still shaken by tremors, then inert.

Surprised by the powerful recoil caused by the shot, I had been forced to let go of the Browning, which had fallen to the ground.

The other stranger quickly let go of Vienna and turned towards me, his hands moving to his back where a shotgun had been strapped which I hadn't seen earlier, and I realised with shock that I should have shot him first and kept the actual rapist second in line.

I scrambled in the dirt ground for the automatic but already the other man was raising the shotgun horizontally and pointing it at me, with a look of disgust on his face.

I could see the look of horror on Vienna's face, her huge eyes wide with dread, but there was nothing she could do, pinned as she was under the heavy body of the dead man, and still unable to shift him off to run for her own bag and weapon.

I was dead meat.

And, with a sinking feeling, I realised she was too, next in line.

Time ground to a standstill, my eyes fixed on the stranger's trigger finger and the helpless look of despair colouring Vienna's face.

The man with the shotgun smiled. His mouth opened. He was missing a front tooth.

Just as his finger began its downwards arc to meet the trigger, there was another loud sound, like thunder, echoing between river and forest and, with a look of surprise on his ugly face, the man with the shotgun looked down at his chest, where a red flower of blood was spreading quickly.

He gasped. Let go of his weapon and crumbled to the ground.

Both Vienna and I looked to where the shot had originated.

Moving out of the cover of the trees was the sailor who had gone looking for fuel. He was accompanied by a black guy, pulling a cart heavy with fuel cans. He lowered the semi-automatic he had just fired.

Vienna finally managed to shove the body of her attacker aside, rose to her feet, hastily pulling her trousers back on, and then vengefully gave a kick in the face to the dead body.

"Thank you," she said, looking first at me and then to our opportune rescuers.

I was frozen to the spot, still on the ground, a terrible headache launching its stealth rockets under my skull, as the adrenaline rush settled and began to ebb.

I had just killed a man for the first time.

They say you always remember the first one.

I felt no guilt. I'd had no choice in the matter. But the realisation stunned me. How many more would I have to kill until I found Giulia? Or Tiffany Cherise?

I reasoned that the first one is always the most difficult. The one you remember.

We made our way back to our boat in mutual silence, now painfully aware we were no Huck Finn or Tom Sawyer cruising the mighty Mississippi in all innocence. From now onwards, we agreed we would remain on board and steer clear of terra firma.

Until we reached Louisiana.

11 - MOONSHINE MILES

I'd lost count of the number of bridges we'd sailed under, irregular punctuation stops in our journey along the river breaking up the monotony of muddy banks, pontoons and industrial buildings abandoned to the rules of nature. The calm waters went on forever, widening at times as if we were approaching the sea and readying to become part of it, even though we were still, I reckoned, days away. But then I'd lost count of the days we'd been travelling.

The sounds of the birds had changed, as had the humidity in the air, and the colours of the land dotting both shores.

Since the incident on shore, Vienna had been surly and uncommunicative, lost in thoughts as she sat in a corner of the bridge at the back of the boat, no doubt mulling about what had brought her here and questioning her decision to escort me on this journey, realising it was no longer a game.

All my attempts to engage with her, distract her from her torpor, had been in vain as she turned her face away from me and kept on staring at the waters we were gliding down.

It was early morning, mist rising from the river, when the Captain tapped me on the shoulder, snapping me out of my daydream.

"We're getting close," he warned me. "Best wake your lady."

I squinted, looking ahead at the shapes of morning emerging through the thin curtain of cloud. The tallest of bridges began to take form in the distance.

"Which one is it?" I asked.

"The Natchez-Vidalia."

We were now actually drifting between the states of Mississippi and Louisiana, close to Highway 61 which led south to Baton Rouge.

The bridge rose in the dawning light to its full extent, massive, dwarfing us, wide eleven foot-lanes with both inside and outside shoulders bulking its mass.

Vienna tiptoed towards us, wearing thick woollen socks, holding her desert boots in her left hand.

"It gets tricky from now on," the sailor informed us.

The mist was lifting and I could see men in dark outfits standing on the bridge, armed, perusing the river and then, hanging down from the bridge, a series of long nets that reached down to the water, in which any embarkation would get tangled if they tried to breach the navigation lane.

"Get down in the hold, and make yourself scarce," he ordered Vienna. "Best if they don't see you. It will save on explanations."

She hastily retreated and climbed down, finding a space between some of the boxes of ammunition and pulling a blanket above her.

The captain called out and the sailor navigating the boat in the cabin above slowed us down and we reached the nets.

Within seconds, a group of rough-looking men had grappled their way down from the bridge and stepped onto the boat. They all wore the same sort of improvised militia uniform, sported beards and looked mean as hell. They were also heavily armed, ammunition belts threaded around their waists or hanging from their shoulders, shotguns and samurai-like swords on display.

Their leader faced up to the captain and greeted him. They visibly knew each other.

I tried to make myself invisible, remaining dead silent a few steps back, hoping not to draw attention to myself. I knew I didn't fit.

The two men walked away from me, walking up the gangway to the navigation cabin together, while the other militiamen stayed behind, eyeing me up, their gaze impassive but menacing.

When the leader and our captain walked back down a few minutes later, a deal of some sorts appeared to have been reached and there was just a cursory glance from the visitors down at the hold where our precious cargo was stored. It was clear they knew what we were carrying and approved. They made their way in silence to the nets and climbed up to the bridge, the middle net was lifted from above, allowing us clear passage through the bridge.

We were now in the Louisiana Republic.

Ahead of us, the river widened until it looked like a plain.

"We'll be docking in Baton Rouge," the Captain said. "It would be best if you left us before. I don't want you to be seen getting off the boat."

Vienna was now back on deck with us. She thanked him.

"And if anyone should ask how you arrived down here, you keep your pretty mouth shut," he said to her. "You have no knowledge of my boat."

"We understand," she said.

"It's another few hours to Baton Rouge," he said. "There's a place where you can go ashore. Halfway there. It's a bit muddy but discreet."

We nodded.

We painstakingly assembled our belongings. There wasn't much left in the way of food supplies any longer, just the clothes we had brought along, in various states of cleanliness. We'd have to somehow stock up on the essentials once on land again, a task I was apprehensive about. The boat drifted ponderously along the heavy currents and veered to the left bank of the river. We waited until we reached shallow depths from where we could wade ashore on bare feet holding our bags and boots above our head. It was difficult not to stumble as the underfoot suction of the mud gripped our ankles with frightening strength.

Finally, we set foot on the bank and watched as the boat returned to the central navigation canal and began to move away into the distance while we sat and dried ourselves as best we could.

"We're on our own, now," Vienna said.

I knew we had to avoid passing through Baton Rouge. It was the newly created Louisiana Republic's self-appointed capital, a place where visitors would stand out awkwardly and not prove welcome, lest we were taken for spies, or worse.

"Do you still have some of the maps," I asked her. "To find a way to reach New Orleans?"

"I do," she said. "But getting into the city will be the problem. Once inside, I have some people we can contact who could help, but until then we have to make the best of it." She looked down, as if the spirit had been punched clean out of her, all her verve wiped away, vulnerable, showing her age for the first time. I wanted to hug her but knew she would take exception if I attempted to do so. She mustn't know I was feeling almost as bereft and hopeless right now.

□ □ □

They call them dust roads and now I knew why. My throat was parched, aching for water, my forehead drenched with sweat, my hair sticking disagreeably to my scalp, and thin as my clothing was, it felt like a heavy curtain and I would have willingly stripped right there and then were it not for the fact that once naked I'd just roast in the fierce sun and appear totally ridiculous if not obscene.

The sun, the dry fields surrounding us, a rare bird cry and, most of all, the silence. Trudging along. The walls of New Orleans still a distant thought.

I'd asked Vienna if our dollars would still be accepted down here in Louisiana, now that the state had seceded from the rest of the country. I was worried that when we reached the next village we would be unable to purchase any water or obtain much-needed provisions. She was uncertain. Ever since the country had fractured after the Dark, reliable information about the way others lived was piecemeal and not always accurate.

There was a major question mark looming in my mind. How could we have been so unprepared?

A faint noise in the distance, at first indistinct but then becoming clearer, interrupting the muted tread of our footsteps. A purr, a gentle rumble, the sound of an engine revving quietly. A car emerging from the heat haze. We stopped. Turned. Looked at each other. A thin smile ran across Vienna's lips. I could see her deliberating with herself, weighing the risks against the odds of assistance.

She extended her arm. Put her thumb up.

It wasn't actually a car, but a pickup truck. A squat mass of grey metal and oversized tyres, with a partly-shredded Confederate flag flapping around its radio aerial.

Noticing us ahead, the driver slowed down, turned the vehicle right in our direction, tyres crunching the gravel, and came to a stop just a few meters ahead of us.

We looked ahead expectantly.

"You folks sure look as if you need a lift; this ain't walking country."

His voice sounded southern, but that was as far as I could situate it. I've never been good on accents. The sun's reflection on the windscreen
I've never been good on accents. The sun's reflection on the windscreen
prevented us from seeing his face. In the periphery of my vision, I noted that Vienna's right hand was inside her side bag, probably gripping her gun, and realised I should be doing the same, but it would be too obvious if I moved to do so now.

I tried to say something, but my throat was just too dry and the words faded away long before they reached my mouth.

"Car problem," I heard Vienna say.

"I didn't see no abandoned car down the road," the man queried.

"The breakdown happened on another road, way off from here," Vienna pointed out. "We thought this one would bring us nearer to civilisation or some form of help."

"Ah..."

He stayed put inside the truck's cabin, his features still a shadow.

"Not many strangers around these parts in this day and age," he remarked. "So, what brings you two down here. I wonder?"

"We have business here," I managed to say.

"And how did you drive past our border controls?" he said.

"They're not known for allowing out of state visitors in without a good reason."

"We sort of missed them," Vienna said.

"Sneaky..."

I heard his door open, and a long pair of jean-clad legs stepped out of the truck's cabin. He wore tall orange-brown cowboy boots with heels that extended his height by a few inches, an unbuttoned checked shirt baring his tanned chest and a red-striped bandana across his head. His face was equally suntanned and lined, thin-lipped and deep blue-eyed.

He wore his handsomeness like a tight-fitting uniform, a smile that dripped irony topped by a thin, trimmed dark blonde moustache, and the pale white slash of an old scar across his right cheek.

"I'm Luke," he said.

He appeared to have stepped straight out of a Hollywood movie with a technicolour carefully accessorized garderobe to match.

We both mumbled our names in response.

"Welcome to the Republic of Louisiana," Luke said. "So what can I do for you guys?"

"We wouldn't mind some water, actually," I said. "We weren't expecting this sort of heat. We're pretty thirsty."

"If water is truly all you want, can do..." He waved us over to the truck and stepped back and pulled up the tarpaulin concealing his cargo. There were crates of bottles piled up high.

He ignored them, dug into a corner and pulled out a large plastic container half full of water and handed it over to Vienna first.

"No refrigeration, so it'll be a bit tepid, I fear, but beggars can't be choosers, can they?" His blue eyes were twinkling with malice.

Vienna hastily unscrewed the top of the 20-litre jerry-can and brought it up to her lips.

I glanced at the rest of his cargo.

"Is it what I think it is?" I asked Luke.

"The elixir of life," he replied. "Locally brewed and potent stuff. Always in demand when times are rough. Want to try some?"

"I think I'll stick to water for now. I feel hot enough as it is."

Vienna handed over the jerrycan and it was my turn to refresh my dry throat. Even tepid, the water felt like liquid gold.

"Have as much as you want," Luke remarked. "I have more."

Vienna asked for the jerrycan and drank again.

"So where are you from?"

Between hasty sips, she said "New York."

"Wowzers, that's sure a way from here. Did you drive all the way?"

She exchanged glances with me, inviting discretion.

"Part of the way," she revealed.

"And how's the situation up there?" Luke asked. "News doesn't filter down this way with much accuracy or timeliness."

"Weird. Dangerous. Not the best place to be right now..." I ventured.

"So you came to Louisiana instead? That sounds even weirder. You know strangers are not particularly welcome down these parts, don't you? Sounds to me like you're deliberately moving from the frying pan into the fire, or whatever the saying is..."

"We know. But we have our reasons."

"Have you indeed. And what might they be?"

"We're searching for someone. She might be in New Orleans."

"Damn it," Luke roared. "Even I wouldn't voluntarily set foot in New Orleans, and I'm from these parts. You must be crazy."

"Aren't you taking your booze there?" Vienna asked, indicating his cargo.

"No way. The nearest I'd go is Metairie or, at worst, Algiers. That city is totally out of control. I'd turn back now if I were you. I really would."

I exchanged glances with Vienna.

"I can't," I said. "It's personal."

Vienna had handed the jerrycan of water back to him. It was now only a quarter full. He threw it into the back of the truck where it bounced around briefly between the tightly arranged crates of moonshine liquor and finally settled in place.

"What about you? Is it personal too?"

"No. I'm just along for the ride."

Luke burst out laughing.

"That's just too much. So, what are you two? Father and daughter? Something else?"

It was Vienna's time to laugh.

"He ain't that old, you know..."

I was squirming, crazy and shameful thoughts running through my mind.

"And I ain't that young either," she continued.

"Really?"

"Just friends."

"Friends?"

"Not what you might be thinking," I indicated. "A business partnership of sorts."

Luke gave us a quizzical look, as if disbelieving the nature of our relationship, his lips locked into a permanent grin, assessing the situation.

"Mighty interesting," he said. "So, you're not..."

"No, we're not," Vienna confirmed.

"OK. I'll believe you for now."

"Can you give us a ride?" I asked.

"To where?"

"As close to New Orleans as you are going? You mentioned Metairie or Algiers. Either would do." The names of the places were familiar to me from maps I'd glanced at, but I had no idea where exactly they were situated in relation to the French Quarter which was our intended destination.

"You're both downright crazy," he said.

"Crazy we might be but we're heading that way whether you help or not."

"How are you going to manage once I drop you off?" he asked. "I presume you have greenbacks?"

"We do."

"They're not worth anything down here any longer. The Republic has its own currency. They call them exchange credits. And there's no fancy bureau de change to convert your worthless dollars. It's a new barter economy they've set up."

"We'll find a way."

We would have to but, right now, I had no idea how. I'd improvise and keep my fingers or other parts of my anatomy, crossed and hope for the best.

Already New York felt like a century away.

"Hop in. You'll fit in if you squeeze together."

We joined Luke in the pickup truck's cab. It smelt of tobacco.

A hand-sized plastic skeleton with painted lips hung above the dashboard and began dancing a jitterbug as soon as we began rolling across the pitted road ahead.

□ □ □

It took us the best part of the day to reach the New Orleans area. We would stop at regular intervals along the way to drop off the liquor at isolated country mansions, hidden away down the end of long corridors of overgrown greenery or standing untouched by centuries of eternity alongside muddy bayous. We stopped twice for fuel at isolated pumps, Luke wordlessly exchanging one type of liquid for another, always greeted by the expectant locals with a smile and a quizzical look at us strangers journeying with him, but no one aggressively questioned our presence, as if he was in the habit of transporting lame ducks along his usual route. The sun shone down throughout with utter ferocity, its heat percolating ruthlessly through the truck's metal roof and our clothes were permanently drenched with sweat and adhering to our bodies as we sat there like tender meat in a pan.

There was, of course, no AC in the truck.

We conversed cautiously, unwilling to reveal too much about ourselves and our presence here, but nonetheless eager for information about the area and what might be lying in wait for us ahead in the Crescent City.

Luke was local, his family having settled by the Mississippi border generations ago, they had always been involved in some form or another, in the bootleg liquor manufacturing and smuggling trade, and his activities had barely been affected by the Dark.

I could see Vienna warming to him as our journey neared its destination, engaging with more warmth and curiosity unlike her initial cold reticence when we had come across Luke on the road.

Once, while he was unloading a couple of crates of rattling bottles in a farmyard under the watchful eyes of a trio of small kids circling the truck like dervishes, she even remarked to me that she felt he looked like a pirate or a cowboy and reminded her of Johnny Depp in those movies.

"I bet you he's bald under that bandana. That's why he never takes it off," I remarked.

Vienna giggled. "You're just jealous."

I was.

And I was wrong anyway. We were invited into the house by the farmers to refresh ourselves and have some mint tea and when Luke returned from the bathroom, he had indeed gotten rid of the dusty bandana and sported a whole head of hair, straw-blonde, suspiciously straight out of a bottle as far as I was concerned. Looked quite unreal, setting off his lined tan with scientific-like precision.

Late afternoon and the sun was losing some of its fury as we slowed down and negotiated a warren of roads, the pickup truck's stocks of illicit alcohol now almost fully depleted, barbed-wire fences standing high, isolating us from fenced-off industrial areas and the concrete plains biting into the landscape.

"This is the old airport," Luke revealed, juggling the many potholes with nervous braking and sudden turns of the steering wheel. "The walls to the city are just a few miles further ahead. We're entering no man's land. As far as I'm willing to go," he pointed out.

"You're dropping us off here?" I asked him.

"Your decision," he said. "Maybe you should wait for morning. At night they're always on the look-out for intruders and stay on their guard. Powerful flashlights, more guards."

"You don't sound as if you're giving us much of a choice,"

Vienna pointed out.

"There are only two ways in," Luke said. "Either you have to find a direct way through here and somehow get past the fortifications... or..."

"Or what?"

"There's always the river."

The truck took a sudden turn and we entered a narrow, sheltered alley leading to a massive, shuttered warehouse building, all red brick and corrugated steel roof and sidings.

The truck crunched to a halt on the gravel. Luke hopped out, dialled a number on the padlock immobilising the sliding door and when the cogs all fell into place, pulled it aside.

"We can stay here overnight. It's safe," he announced. "I keep some food here in reserve. My base. The nearest I'll ever go to the city. And tomorrow, I'm hitting the road back and you're on your own again."

He drove the truck into the dark jaw of the warehouse, parked it against one of the far walls and we all disembarked.

"Bring those maps of yours along. I'll show you how to get to the river from here," Luke suggested. "Make it a bit easier, at least. Give you a better chance."

He moved the padlock to our sheltered side of the sliding door, pulled it shut and locked us in. We were briefly plunged into darkness, but he lit a couple of gas lamps which had been left by the sliding doors and the cavernous space glimmered into a semblance of life.

We ate straight from an assortment of cans Luke had stored here on past journeys: some stew, rice pudding, corned beef and munched on dried fruit. It wasn't quite the cuisine Louisiana was reputedly famous for, but right now it felt like culinary heaven, all washed down with lukewarm soda water. We declined Luke's moonshine liquor though.

I felt tired and apprehensive as the next day loomed. The journey from New York had been unreal, like an unsettling step out of time before I reached a point of no return.

Being so close to Vienna all along was disturbing, an awkward situation reminding me in a weird fashion of that old Italian black and white movie about a couple searching on a Sicilian island or somewhere close for the man's lover who had disappeared and becoming closer and closer in the process, one form of affection (or could it be a malicious form of lust?) superseding another, testing the limits of what they knew as love.

Similarly, I was now floundering like a puppet with no strings in the world of women, Giulia's face and body supernaturally merging into those of Cherise's and then Vienna's voice and smile superimposing themselves across the eerie composite, vying for my feelings in a morass of confusion.

Vienna and Luke were in deep conversation, pouring over an unfolded map they had laid out on the warehouse's concrete floor, their voices barely a rumour as fatigue began to overcome me, and the adrenaline that had been sustaining me for longer than I would have admitted to melted away inside my veins like water in the sun.

"I think I need to sleep," I said.

They barely gave me a second look and continued with their examination of the routes into New Orleans.

There was a bunch of old blankets bunched up in a corner and I pulled one out of the pile and spread it across the floor and lay down on it, ignoring the musty smell rising from its folds. My increasing tiredness and the general veil of darkness dominating the cavernous warehouse soon delivered me to sleep.

If I had dreams, let alone nightmares, I remembered nothing by the time I was awakened by Vienna's voice and her hands digging into my shoulders, shaking me out of my torpor.

"Get up, get up," she begged me.

Willing the cobwebs away and rubbing my eyes, I rose from the hard floor, feeling as if my body was bruised from head to feet.

"What is it?"

"We have to go. NOW."

The warehouse was still plunged deep in darkness and all I could see was a pinpoint of light in Vienna's eyes as my own vision slowly returned and adapted to the penumbra surrounding us.

She was wearing Luke's red bandana tied across her throat. It was unmistakable.

"Why are you in such a hurry?" I stretched my limbs and straightened out.

"Stop bloody asking questions and hurry along," Vienna insisted, helping me get to my feet. She was nervy, as if riding a high.

Our rucksacks were by the sliding doors, awaiting us. I did not recall us leaving them there the evening before.

Against the corrugated steel back wall of the warehouse I noticed Luke's shape, spread out across the floor. Still sleeping.

"Shouldn't we at least say goodbye? Thank him?"

"No need," Vienna whispered. "I've done that already."

We were just a few steps from the doors.

"When?"

"No matter. I'll tell you later."

We reached the door. A sliver of light battled its way through like a beacon from the nearby boarded-up windows. I noticed the padlock was unlocked and just hanging from the metal bar.

Vienna pulled the doors open and the day rushed in, light and a humid form of heat jousting for the attention of our senses.

We stepped briskly towards Luke's truck, parked on the heavy gravel of the path. Vienna pulled a pair of keys from her pocket.

"What are you doing?" I asked her.

"We need transport," she said.

"What about Luke?"

"He won't mind."

"How come? Surely he hasn't loaned you the truck?"

We climbed into the cabin, throwing our rucksacks into the back, which was now empty of crates and bottles.

"He won't mind..."

The engine roared to life. Surely that would wake Luke from his slumber, I reckoned.

"What is that supposed to mean?"

We drove off, away from the airport hangar.

"I suppose you could call it a business transaction..."

We reached a fork in the narrow road, and Vienna braked, hesitating.

"I remember we came that way," I indicated the road to our left.

"I know," she said. "But that direction will inevitably lead to the fortification walls." She turned right, and we crossed over a tall bridge that overlooked a spaghetti-like intersection of highways. We headed towards the river.

"So, what's the deal?" I asked her, as the distance between us and Luke's hangar grew.

"I fucked him," she said.

"No..."

"Yes. I thought you would have heard us," she pointed out. "I'm the silent type, but he was a bit of a grunter. You must be a heavy sleeper."

"You didn't?"

"I liked him, so why not? It was good." I kept on staring at her as if trying to read her features and get a line on the joke she was playing on me, but she was deadly serious.

"Look," Vienna said. "You're not my keeper. I'm free to act as I wish, no?"

I must have looked sheepish, words caught in my throat.

"Anyway," she continued. "I managed to combine pleasure with business."

Part of me was aching to hear all the sordid details, even if I knew that every single word would prove painful and leave a lasting scar on my mind, while the other wished to be shielded from this new reality. I managed to turn around in my seat and glance at her. She was grinning.

"I'm not sure I know what you're talking about."

"I slipped him a post-coital couple of sleeping pills. Put him out for the count..."

"Is that how you got hold of the keys to the truck?"

"Indeed, And not just that..."

"What else?"

"His cash. The money he picked up along the way for the cargo of booze."

"Really?"

"Yes, it's in my rucksack, every note and credit."

"He's going to be furious when he wakes up."

"I suppose he will. But he's not likely to follow us into the city, is he? He'll come to the conclusion I was just an expensive piece of ass, I guess, and put it all down to experience" she chortled.

"You have no shame," I said.

"We Washington Square kids learn how to survive from an early age."

"Surely you could have put him out of action some other way, stolen the keys to the truck and his local cash? I could have helped, had you asked."

"Maybe. Anyway, it's happened so just live with it, OK? Once we break into the city, how were you expecting to pay for things? Work? Had you ever thought that far ahead?"

I bowed my head, knowing she was right.

We were leaving the industrial area that surrounded the old airport behind us and making our way through a new geography, a low plain where the land merged with the sky in the heat haze, isolated one-storeyed buildings shimmering in the distance.

The truck's cab windows were rolled down and the smells of the delta came wafting towards us, a distinct scent of rotten flowers, sea air and industrial effluent, tickling our throats, washing invisible across our faces.

"I have a few possible contacts, but they are inside the city and first we have to get into it," she reminded me. "It was a means to an end. Money talks, even Louisiana Napoleons. Apparently, that's what they call these exchange credits, I found out. Looks like Monopoly money to me, but what the damn!"

She had to brake suddenly, I was carried forward and almost hit the windscreen, having forgotten in the earlier confusion of our conversation to strap myself in. The truck's tyres protested loudly but dug deep into the dirt.

"Whoa..."

The small road we had been following had come to an abrupt halt. Wild vegetation surrounded us and the cry of birds above.

We had been following a narrow track and it had dwindled into nothing with no notice or road sign to warn us.

"As far as we can go," I pointed out.

"How insightful of you," Vienna said. She jumped out of the cabin and retrieved her rucksack. Pulled out one of the maps and sat down in the grass, unfolded it and examined its details. I followed her out.

"It said nothing about the road running out," she said. "But according to this, we're barely a mile from the actual river bank. There used to be a ferry. It could lead us to Algiers."

"Sounds good," I said. "Let's walk then."

I tightened my boot laces and we began our trek.

My heart felt bruised and my soul sad, betrayed by Vienna's practical fancy.

What had I been expecting, a fairy tale and a happy ever after in which sex played no part? This was after the Dark, the rules had changed.

I sighed and walked on, now leading, Vienna's short, regular breaths like an echo behind me as we staggered along, dodging weeds and clumps of thick grass down the overgrown path that led to the Mississippi's bank.

12 - FRENCH QUARTER CONFIDENTIAL

We had spent most of the day and following night crouched behind an elevated sandbank just a stone's throw away from the river, observing the landscape and trying to figure the best way of reaching the city on the other side. Vienna reckoned we were south of Algiers and we had a clear view of the vast bridge connecting our side of the shore with New Orleans proper, spanning the waters in oval grandeur. There was no way we could use it to cross over. A tall barricade of abandoned cars and debris had been erected to block its access to any form of motorised vehicles, and further along, stood groups of armed men guarding its passage along the walkways.

We had ventured earlier further upstream only to cautiously take note of the fortifications, the jagged wall of metal and barbed wire still partly under construction, that would eventually spread to where we were sat now and make the city impregnable all the way from Lake Pontchartrain further north down to the Delta.

We watched from a safe distance, Vienna having found a pair of binoculars inside the stolen truck's glove compartment, alongside a couple of convenient weapons Luke had left there, a Bowie knife and a switchblade, which I hoped we would not have to use. They now sat in our rucksacks, alongside the guns we had journeyed from New York with. An army of two.

"Any ideas?" I asked Vienna.

"Not yet. I need time to think."

The only movement on the bridge consisted of patrols relaying each other at irregular intervals, but at no time was the surveillance fully lifted that could have allowed us to rush across in between shifts.

We were fast running out of water and food and had no wish to backtrack. We had got so close and it felt maddening to fail at this final hurdle.

"There is no fixed pattern," I observed. "The men come and go totally at random; no way we could slip through between shifts and, anyway, the bridge is too long and we haven't a clear enough view of the other side or what might be waiting for us there."

Vienna sighed in agreement.

I began weighing the alternatives and realised there was only one available to us.

"It just leaves the river. Remaining around here would just be a dead end."

"Crossing it?"

"What else?"

"Where? How?"

"Maybe if we made our way further downstream, we could find some boat. Cross over at night, under cover of darkness?"

"Easier said than done."

"Can you think of anything better?"

She didn't.

We gathered our belongings and retreated into the shadows. For a couple of hours, we hopscotched south, zigzagging like drunken hitchhikers to stay under some sort of cover while not losing sight of the river, feet deep in sludge or treading dirt.

A skein of birds seemed to be following us, high above, darting across the open sky, either guiding or misleading us, their distant cries a fleeting lullaby, like us heading towards the sea, heeding its ever-closer call. On occasion, we'd spy people ambling by the river bank, or groups busy in the distance at some unknown task, and held ourselves back, in silence, to avoid being spotted. It was a stop and go walking through irregular terrain and my boots were already leaking, an uncomfortable feeling, my feet squishing between the leather of the sole and the dampening cotton of my socks, a most disagreeable sensation.

The river appeared to be widening with every passing step.

Had we already reached the alluvial plain where it joined the Gulf of Mexico? Gone too far?

We almost missed it: a shack, almost falling apart, roof partly holed, timbers hanging in disarray around a door held together by rope.

"What is it?"

It was fifty yards inland from the embankment by which we were ambling. Just some abandoned building that appeared to have been untouched by human hands for years. We could easily have missed it.

"I think it might be an old boathouse..."

"Surely, it's empty?"

We halted our progress, climbed the bank to the ruin of a building that stood there. Upfront it was even more of a wreck, vegetation growing freely along its perimeter, planks broken and covered by mould. There was a window on its left side, the glass shattered and thick with dirt. I peered inside and was met with partial darkness.

It looked empty at first. But then my eyes focused. Spotted odd objects, jettisoned pieces of machinery piled up against the back wall, indistinct shapes littering the floor.

"We have to get inside."

It was easy work opening the door, cutting through the damp knots of the fraying rope holding the door in place.

Pushing it open, it creaked, disturbing the embankment's overall silence.

A strong smell of decay wafted past our noses as we stepped inside, light pouring in through the opening we'd created.

My heart froze.

Sheltered in the far left-hand corner of the decaying shack, a recognisable shape. It was small, upside down but recognisably a small craft. A canoe, a kayak, whatever the hell it technically was.

"Is it?" Vienna enquired.

"I think so."

Dropping our rucksacks to the ground, we both rushed forward, taking a grip on the craft and gently turning it over. It was surprisingly lightweight, wooden, although it felt fragile, the planks holding its hull together still damp, even though it had visibly not been used for ages. There was nothing sophisticated about it, it was just about functional. The question was whether it would sink instantly or last long enough to carry us across successfully to the other shore.

A sense of excitement was building inside my head.

"Let's drag this wreck outside. Get a closer look at it."

"Hopefully, it might be river-worthy..."

"We can but hope..."

By dusk we had thoroughly examined the canoe, patched up its frailties as best we could with some old repairs material left lying around the shack and, tested it briefly on the edge of the water to assess how much water it might take in if launched carrying the two of us on the river. It was far from reassuring. We'd get our feet, or considerably more, wet, but how quickly we couldn't determine. We pulled the small craft back to the shore and agreed that we would attempt to cross the river after dark.

We sat in a patch of grass away from the embankment's mud waiting for the opportune moment, my eyes fixed on the curtain of microscopic lights shimmering in the distance which I reckoned was the outline of New Orleans.

Where I would find Giulia at last.

□ □ □

We made the crossing around midnight. A three-quarters moon illuminated our watery path, tiptoeing along us in the current, making us feel as if we were captured in the beam of a burning spotlight, but by chance no observer on either bank caught a sight of us as we manoeuvred in silence, using our hands as paddles to guide the fragile craft in the general direction of the opposite shore. We were drenched by the time we reached our approximate destination, having drifted even further south in the clumsy process, allowing water to fill the leaking hull to a dangerous level, up to our knees. Had it taken us another ten minutes or so to span the width of the river, we would have had to jettison our flimsy embarkation and swim the final leg to the shore. As it was, we looked and felt like survivors of a powerful storm by the time we set foot on the muddy bank we had been aiming for, drained of energy, filthy and cold.

We pushed the canoe back into the stream and watched it float away towards the sea. I doubted it would stay afloat long enough and reckoned it would sink within minutes, erasing any evidence of our illegal journey.

There was nowhere to shelter and both Vienna and I were now shivering as a faint breeze cruised in from the Gulf and washed over our wet clothing. The rucksacks were equally sodden and there was nothing dry we could change into. We were in no fit state to move on and aim for the city. Hopefully, the night would not get any colder.

We retreated towards the wasteland that bordered the river where we had landed and soon found ourselves wandering onto a long grassy knoll. Not having to trudge through mud any longer brought a sense of relief. We soon came to a fence separating the wild grass from a somewhat better cared for lawn which led up to a white colonial mansion sitting at the top of a moderate incline.

There were no lights on in the building, although it was, of course, the dead of night so there was no guarantee of it being empty.

"Should we?" I asked Vienna.

"We're armed," she pointed out. "We're going to freeze to death or catch pneumonia if we stay like this all night. It's a calculated risk."

We hopped over the low fence and furtively made our way to the building.

It was less than imposing up front, in bad need of maintenance and a fresh coat of paint, the white facade veering to dirty grey in the shadow of the leering moonlight.

We made a tour of the perimeter. There were no cars at the front or any signs of occupancy.

We broke in through a bathroom window at the back of the property where the latch had loosened. A quick exploration of the house confirmed there was no one in, dust sheets pulled over the furniture, electricity switched off, no food in the kitchen but, to our relief, the water was running, albeit cold.

We came across a towering pile of clean towels stored in an airing cupboard and quickly stripped down to our underwear and, with our backs to each other out of undue discretion, began to vigorously dry ourselves and banish the creeping cold from our bones.

Because of the lack of heating, we pulled some of the throws off the furniture and wrapped ourselves in as many sheets as we could. Hopefully, our clothes would be a little drier by morning.

Vienna collapsed onto one the beds in the principal bedroom upstairs while I remained on the ground floor, to doze fitfully in a semi-foetal position on one of the sprawling leather sofas.

Both of us were so physically tired and emotionally drained that neither of us saw morning come and go, and by the time we were fully awake, our watches indicated it was nearer to noon.

We explored the abandoned house more thoroughly now that daylight was rushing bright through the curtained windows. We found no food in the kitchen area and its cabinets, nor spare clothes in the bedroom closets. Fortunately, our own clothing had dried almost fully, although it still retained the muddy tang of the river, a scent of dirt and crushed flowers that bordered on the unpleasant.

Our maps of the area also had to be dried out before we could consult them again.

For the rest of the day and another full night under the same roof, we survived on water from the tap. It was painful but we both knew that even though we had somehow come so far, we weren't yet ready to find our way to New Orleans and face the likely obstacles and problems that would arise after our arrival.

On the second morning, we both were up before dawn, nervous, hunger digging into the pit of our stomachs, and readily agreed to finally leave our temporary shelter. We'd prepared our itinerary with care. We estimated we had crossed the river by Westwego so our route to the French Quarter would have to take us through the Garden District and possibly the old Arts District. But they were pretty ancient maps and we assumed the reality on the ground would be different, if we believed all the rumours about the chaos that had taken hold in New Orleans since the Dark. We'd cleaned up. I'd even managed to shave for the first time in a week and felt like a new man. The main thing was not to draw undue attention to ourselves.

We ventured forth.

Wide empty spaces, empty roads, at first it was eerie, like a ghost town, but then we remembered that of course it was still barely past dawn, not a time for folk to be walking around or going about their lives. At times, it felt like a city deserted post-apocalypse movie-style and, with just a smidgeon of fantasy, we could have imagined, or feared, vampires or zombies lurking behind a door or a window, ready to pounce.

And then our first encounter with a human being. An old, white-haired lady in a paisley dressing gown, with a small black dog on a leash walking in our direction, a voluminous shopping bag slung over her shoulders, wearing indoor slippers.

She nodded at us as we passed her, continuing in the direction she was coming from. It seemed we passed for normal. A moment later, the sound of canned music reached our ears as we arrived at an intersection with a wider avenue bordered with lush trees in bloom, and we noticed, carved into the road, the steel treads of a streetcar track. The music came from a corner store, outside of which a group of four men were standing around, shooting the breeze and smoking. Vienna and I conferred briefly, debating whether we might find food in the store. The increasingly hollow feeling in our guts didn't allow us to be cautious any longer and we made our way towards the corner store. The music grew louder as we neared the store's entrance, a 3/4-time waltz, a zydeco accordion and a brass section. None of the men even looked up at us as we passed them and entered. I could barely understand what they were idly chattering about, their local accents being so pronounced.

A wall of cans, a counter with fresh produce, apples, tomatoes, heavenly green varieties of salad. My mouth was watering already.

A rotund black woman wearing a purple turban, from which strands of dreadlocks peered out, greeted us effusively.

"Hello, my darlings. So, what's your pleasure?"

"We need some water," Vienna rasped out, while I made a beeline for the fruit and grabbed a couple of green apples.

"I also have all sorts of soda," the woman said, pointing at the wall to her left where the shelves were bursting with bottles and cans, most with labels I had never come across before.

"Just water will be fine," Vienna said.

The woman smiled at us. Her teeth were shining brilliant white as if she'd just walked from an orthodontist's chair that very moment.

"Where are you visiting from?" she asked me, as Vienna busied herself along the shelves, visibly dazzled by the choice of food and supplies on display.

"Just another parish," I improvised. "Near Metairie."

"Oh," the storekeeper said. I wasn't sure whether she believed me or not. "Passing through then? On your way to the Walls? I hear they're always short of labour. But not sure if you should be taking your girlfriend along..."

The fragrant scent of weed was carried by a morning breeze, tickling my nostrils, as the group of locals outside the door smoked away to their heart's content.

We piled up our purchases on the glass counter behind which she officiated. The woman counted things up and quoted a figure that meant nothing to either of us. Vienna dug into her jeans pocket and pulled out a wad of notes, some of the money she had stolen from Luke, his proceeds from the liquor-running.

Time held still while we waited to see if the storekeeper would accept it.

"That's much too much," she remarked, only taking a couple of the banknotes.

One thing less to worry about.

□ □ □

We crossed Canal in mid-afternoon.

Stepping into the French Quarter was like venturing into the past. No more tall buildings or skyscrapers, just a heavy sky floating like a shroud over a village dropped like a splash of paint in the heart of a metropolis, an oasis of penumbra, of furtive crowds minding their own business, the smell of beer and rotting magnolias, the wrought iron balconies, the shuttered bars and eateries, and the presence of centuries of memories hanging above you like a welcoming embrace.

It hadn't changed since I'd been here last.

The same architecture, a studied blend of Spanish colonial and country French, the atmosphere verging on the agreeable side of seedy, the ornate rectangular tiled street signs in both languages.

The only thing missing now were the throngs of tourists in shoddy clothes and clumpy trainers juggling plastic glasses of beer or colourful cocktails or, when inebriated more often than not, throwing beads from the hotel balconies to crowds of similar common descent in the hope the women might jovially bare their breasts, expose rolls of flesh that were best kept private in matrons of their age. There was still music pounding inside the few remaining bars that bothered to open in the afternoon now that the visitors to the city were no longer welcome, the resonant twang of steel guitars and the metronomic beat of drums and bass that reached all the way down to the pit of your stomach and begged for your limbs to twitch and shake and dance to the relentless rhythm.

"Where are you meeting your contact?" I asked Vienna.

"A place called the Napoleon House," she replied.

"I know where it is," I informed her.

I led her down Decatur and took a turn until we reached the crossing for Magazine and we headed towards Jackson Square.

"It's one of the oldest bars in the city," I said to Vienna.

"Sounds right," she said. "The sort of place people who have dealings with my father would hang around in. When were you here last?"

"Years ago. Long before the Dark. It's not so crowded now," I pointed out.

The brickwork on the wall outside was fraying at the corners and the small windows to the bar were grimy with soot. The door was locked.

"Maybe it opens only in the evenings, these days," I suggested.

Vienna ignored me. Banged against the door. Once. No response. A second time, louder. Waited. We heard steps inside, someone shambling towards the door, dragging their heels.

"Moment, moment..." the voice protested, irritated by the intrusion.

The lock creaked, it badly needed oil. The door opened halfway. The man inside pushed his face through the opening.

He was the palest guy I had ever come across, as if he had assiduously avoided contact with the sun or even the wilderness of the outside of the bar for decades on end. An unhealthy pallor conjugating every shade of off-white and grey, including his bushy eyebrows and matching sideburns. He was wearing a Panama hat so there was no clue if he was similarly coiffed or totally bald. He wore an ill-fitting khaki-coloured dressing gown and was barefoot. His toenails were seriously overgrown, I noticed. Which drew my attention to his hands which, surprisingly, were impeccably manicured.

"What the fuck," he groaned, looking dismissively at us. "We're not opening today. What do you want?"

Vienna introduced herself.

"I was told to come here. I need to talk to Sebastian Wallace. We've come a long way."

The old guy's eyes focused on us, his annoyance now fading, no longer dismissive of our presence.

The door yawned fully open and he ushered us in. A few candles were lit above the bar, the smell of strong incense, maybe patchouli, heavy in the air mingling with the manifold ghosts of liquor past and present. He locked the front door behind us and, dragging his feet along, guided us towards the restaurant area on the left-hand side of the bar, through a small arch.

He sat himself down and we followed suit.

"Wallace isn't here. I'm not sure when he will be in next," he said. "He's not a regular hours sort of guy, you know."

"We need somewhere to stay," Vienna said.

He offered us drinks, which we turned down. He helped himself to a tall glass of absinthe and avidly gulped it down, no doubt shortening his lifespan by another hour in the process as the rotgut cascaded down his throat and his whole body shook in response before he took a deep breath and returned wide-eyed to the land of the living.

"Needed that," he remarked. "Badly." He glanced at his watch. "This is an absolutely indecent hour to be up and about." Then as an afterthought, "There's a room going spare next door. I have the key. There's only one bed, though. Oh, and by the way, my name is Shearwater."

"That'll be fine, Mr Shearwater," Vienna said.

"Just Shearwater," he replied. "Absolutely no need for the Mr. Do I look like a Mr?"

He didn't, but I kept my lips closed.

"How long do you think it will take for Wallace to make an appearance?"

"Haven't a clue."

□ □ □

And so we waited. Again.

Almost made me feel as if I was a character in a play by Samuel Beckett on loan from a Raymond Chandler yarn.

The room was all light when the curtains were drawn in the morning. The furnishings chintzy and Belle Époque. I had suggested to Vienna I could sleep on the floor, but she insisted we share the bed, pointing out its size.

"I know I can trust you," she pointed out.

I was less certain about that, her constant presence in various states of casual undress a distracting factor, just about tempered by the memory of her tryst with Luke which, to my surprise, evoked much jealousy and envy in my heart and loins.

Shearwater brought us up to scratch on the state of things in New Orleans, or to be more precise the Vieux Carré. Where the self-proclaimed Republic practiced a policy of laissez-faire and did not interfere in the running of the territory. The area was controlled by a coalition of local gangs I had difficulty making sense of: The Voodoo Runners, The Bourbon Revival Team, The Preservation Hall Singers, The Oyster Cannibals, The Pontalba Chiefs and other minor groups including the La Stanza Justice League and the Pontchartrain Rollers. We were advised to stay well clear of the latter two, who were reportedly crazies in his opinion, wildly out of control and right now persona non grata anywhere between Canal and Ramparts according to him.

But, he explained, the shifts in power were subtle and frequent, and we had to tread carefully, even with our useful New York connections.

There was a hint that the King of Washington Square, and by inference Vienna, held favour with the Oyster mob.

"What about this Sebastian Wallace guy?" I queried Shearwater on an occasion when Vienna was downstairs, devouring a po' boy no doubt stuffed to the gills with deep-fried crawfish, mayonnaise and coleslaw, a local delicacy she had fallen head over heels for after the thin fare we'd been painfully restricted to on our journey here. Not that the improvement in our diet had any visible influence on her weight or appearance as she remained steadfastly thin as a rake. I, on the other hand, already felt bloated after just a few days here.

"He works for the Republic. A fixer. Keeps the peace, so to speak."

Until Wallace made an appearance, Shearwater had suggested we didn't stray too far from the Napoleon House, call undue attention to ourselves, so we never roamed much further than Jackson Square and the Café du Monde, not even venturing beyond the deserted railway tracks to the river. Anyway, we attracted strange, curious looks when we did go out, as if the local folk knew by instinct that we didn't fit in and I found the general atmosphere disturbing, like gliding across the surface of a quiet pond, under the surface of which all sorts of evil and conspiracies were brewing away, out of reach, and knowing that a single wrong word or gesture would set loose some cataclysm we would never survive.

Or maybe it was just that I wasn't very good at waiting, feeling helpless and anxious.

I asked Shearwater about Cherise and Giulia, but he had no clue. He had never heard of them, nor seen them or come across anyone, within his circle of acquaintances frequenting the Napoleon House, who had. The bar opened around dusk every day, a squad of taciturn bar staff trooping in, serving the stray evening customers with sullen indifference. The joint stayed open until 2 or 3 in the morning, and no longer served food as in days of old. Just another bar, and with no music, poor competition for all the continued animation a few blocks away on Bourbon Street. Most of the customers were regulars who equally sought silence and didn't wish to be bothered with conversation, seeking peace in the bottom of their glasses. Most stuck to hard liquor, with just the occasional beer chaser. Not a cheerful crowd. Shearwater didn't introduce us to the staff and they ignored us.

In the dark of the night, the sounds of the French Quarter a faint murmur at the back of my consciousness, the room's window wide open and the air heavy with heat, not a breeze within miles to disturb the heavy pressure bearing down on us.

Vienna, wearing just thin cotton panties, on the other side of the bed, almost hanging over the edge, sheets pulled aside to keep her lithe body uncovered and cool, her gossamer breath a whisper, my T-shirt damp around my neck, wiping my forehead clean as I twisted and turned in discomfort, unable to keep my eyes away from the delicate shape of her body, to halt her when still in her sleep, she rolled over and spooned against me, the silkiness of her skin like a salve, a nectar, a liberation.

All my being screamed to move my hand away from the pillar under which I'd buried it and touch her, run my fingers across her spine, linger around the hollow of her neck, wash my palm across the length of her thigh, hunt for the delirious heat radiating from between her legs. I bit my lip. Sighed. Struggled.

With thoughts, words unsaid, feelings, terrible lust.

I came here for Giulia.

Vienna was just a distraction, I reminded myself. I was just acting, thinking like a fool. Allowing my cock to take control, my lust, not that it translated into any form of erection: it was just too hot, or I had erectile dysfunction, or alternatively the last shred of decency in my head was reminding me she was half my age. But, then, hadn't Giulia also been?

She rubbed against me, unaware of her actions. I almost burst out in tears. Clenched my jaw. My throat was dry, my body revolting, numb, hungry.

I moved away to the edge of the bed on my own side, fleeing her.

She did not react. I wondered what she was dreaming of.

In the morning we were both woken by a sharp knock at our bedroom door. It was Shearwater.

"I've had news," he said. "Wallace will be here in an hour."

We wiped the drowsiness from our eyes. Vienna stepped out of the bed, the spectacle of her body yet another challenge to my sanity as I followed her movements while she tiptoed daintily across to the bathroom, shedding her panties on the way, an incandescent flash of the white cushions of her arse and an infinitesimal glimpse of the dark hairs of her outgrown delta before she closed the door behind her. I heard the shower in full flow and could only imagine her soaping herself, stretching, a standing siren out of reach but so close, impossible.

I was the king of longing.

Sebastian Wallace was initially a bit of a disappointment, a dapper little man in his fifties, his hair thinning on top, and wearing a tired light beige linen suit, creased white shirt, colourful tie and brown loafers, dark-rimmed glasses and with the demeanour of an accountant or a tax official.

"I was expecting you ages ago," he mentioned. "Didn't think you'd make it."

"Well, here we are," I said.

"Have you had breakfast?" Wallace asked us. "Best not talk on an empty stomach." He suggested we go around the corner of Jackson Square to the Café du Monde for beignets and coffee.

I had earlier dressed all in black, hardly an ideal outfit for the Café du Monde as the caster sugar on the beignets inevitably ended up powdered all over customer's clothing. But it was close and convenient.

"You've grown up," Wallace remarked, as we bit into the warm beignets, looking across to Vienna.

"You two have met already?" I queried.

"A long time ago, in New York," he said. "I think Vienna had just celebrated her 10th birthday," he added. He smiled. "I had business dealings with her father." He hand-rolled a cigarette and began smoking. I wiped some of the sugar from my sleeve.

The Asian waitress cleared our table, cleaning the debris away with a wet cloth. I quickly gulped down the dregs of my orange juice before she could steal the glass away. The place was only half-full. Once there were tourists queuing, jazz musicians busking outside and clowns juggling with balloons. Now, post-Dark, the Café had lost much of its buzz.

"He needs your assistance," Vienna said, glancing back at me for Wallace's benefit. "I'm calling in a favour."

"And you?" Sebastian Wallace asked Vienna. "What's in it for you? He your boyfriend?" The look he gave me was somewhat dismissive.

"No. Just a friend I've agreed to help out," she stated.

Wallace's features were a mask of doubt.

He turned towards me, loosened his paisley-patterned tie.

"Tell me then..."

There was no point in revealing the whole story behind my presence here. I described Tiffany Cherise, and provided a redacted version of the story behind her flight from New York, her modelling and the type of photos she had been involved in and described the Polaroid print in which she had been portrayed, with another dark-haired girl I did not identify on purpose—I hadn't told Vienna that it was someone I had known and still badly hankered for—and how I had recognized the location, off Jackson Square, facing one of the Pontalba buildings. I also confirmed I no longer had a copy of the snapshot.

"The Pontalba Chiefs must have known the photograph was being taken," he said, as if talking to himself. "Hmmm..." he pondered.

"You know them?" I asked.

"I know everyone, but they're not a group to treat lightly," he said. "Such a pity you no longer have the photo. I could have asked around if anyone around town had caught recent sight of Cherise..."

"Or the other young woman?" I added.

"Indeed."

Vienna had kept silent.

"And what happens when you find her? If you find her."

"I'll speak to her. Assess the situation. Then we'll see..."

"Maybe she won't want to return to New York? The news from there is pretty rough, I hear."

"I just want to talk to her. Or the other girl."

Vienna gave me a strange look.

"I'll ask around," Sebastian Wallace announced. "In the meantime, keep away from the Pontalba area. And what about you, young lady, do you have any plans?"

"I'll stick around. For now," Vienna said.

"You do that," Wallace remarked and bid us goodbye.

Later that morning, as we walked along Magazine Street, Vienna asked me what was so special about the other girl in the photograph and why I hadn't mentioned her before.

I lied.

And from the look in her eyes, I knew she knew I had.

The sky that night was streaked with shades of pink.

13 - DOCTOR, DOCTOR...

I had heard Shearwater refer to Wallace as a magician and queried him about this.

"Why a magician? Was he... is he still some sort of performer?"

"Not traditional sort of magic," Shearwater had revealed. "His is all too real. He has the power to make people disappear. Even the Voodoo crowd are wary of him."

I found this hard to believe. Nothing about Sebastian Wallace appeared in the least remarkable, even less menacing. And as far as disappearances were concerned, I was more interested in seeing whether he could succeed in making certain parties reappear.

"The folk who look normal are often those carrying the deepest secrets," Vienna remarked and gave me an oblique look, as if I fell into that category. We had been waiting for a couple of days for Wallace to get in touch again, and throughout Vienna had become more distant, the closeness we had enjoyed throughout our journey here fading rapidly, to be replaced by some sense of resentment as she had become aware of the facts I had been holding back about my true motivation in pursuing Cherise.

We had fallen into a routine, sleeping in late, circling Jackson Square, breakfasting at the Café du Monde, idle window shopping on Magazine and then returning to the Napoleon House to nurse a few drinks until nightfall, when Shearwater opened the bar and we could people watch from our darkened alcove at the back while we sat in silence, never finding the right words to say, just like a married couple who had run out of conversation subjects. The bar attracted folk from all the diverse factions that had carved the French Quarter, and the city at large, into separate enclaves, common ground where they could parley, argue, negotiate truces and disputes.

Most punters took little notice of us in our corner, although there was no doubt our presence had been noted, or at any rate, Vienna's, who attracted both lingering glances and a wary attention, her New York connection, heralded by Shearwater, no doubt preceding her and keeping us safe from questions or undue suspicion.

When I was finally summoned to a further audience with Wallace, Vienna declined to accompany me, pretexting a headache. Eager to see the fixer again, I had no wish to argue with her and left her alone in the apartment we'd been sharing.

Shortly after we had installed ourselves there, she had found a pile of old pulp paperbacks packed away in a large travel trunk and was reading her way through them. Most of them went back more than half a century and Vienna had this theory that the city, and even more so the Vieux Carré, must be a treasure trove of old books that had been left in hotel rooms from the days when there still had been tourists. The covers were garish and colourful, but for me they were just a reminder of how different my own version of sleuthing had become, in no way as romantic and straightforward as between the pages.

"This one's rather intriguing," Vienna said, brandishing the paperback. "I've only a few chapters left and want to find out how it's all going to pan out. Although I reckon that yet again things won't be truly explained by the author. Anyway, you just go ahead and see Wallace. You'll tell me all about it."

Wallace had an office just a few blocks away, it turned out, in a spacious back room of an art gallery on Magazine Street which opened only by appointment and appeared to trade in pre-Dark paraphernalia: vinyl records, movie and rock concert posters, signed photographs of mostly forgotten celebrities from the worlds of sports and theatre.

Waiting outside for him to open the door, I tried to identify the faces of some of the folk in the signed photos in the gallery window and barely recognised a handful.

It wasn't Wallace who opened the door for me, but a female assistant.

"He's expecting you," the older woman said, ushering me in.

She was in her mid to late 30s, tall, the tattoo of a black teardrop etched into the skin below her left eye, dressed in a simple combination of holed jeans, David Bowie-Ziggy Stardust era T-shirt and red braces holding up the baggy jeans. She was also shaven-headed.

"What's your name?" I asked her as she locked the gallery doors behind us.

"I don't need one," she answered, showing me the way between the piles of objects littered across the gallery's floor.

"I'm just the magician's assistant." Her voice was a deep baritone, almost man-like, every word accompanied by an ironic turn of her lips, an enigmatic smile.

I followed her.

Her square shoulders, height and narrow waistline reminded me of April Lea. I looked down and noticed she wasn't wearing any shoes. Had she been, she would have towered above me.

"There you are," Wallace greeted me. He was in his eyrie of an office, walls carpeted with book-laden shelves, sitting behind a desk, his glasses lowered, balanced on the bridge of his nose, still wearing the same drab linen suit and crumpled shirt from our first encounter. "Thank you, dear," he dismissed the older woman. He invited me to sit and I had to clear the only other chair in the room of its accumulation of folders and cushions before I could settle in it.

"There's only one person who could have taken the Polaroid photograph you described to me the other day," Wallace stated.

"His name is Jeff Fishburne. He normally works under the protection of the Pontalba people. He has a studio in the Business District. Isn't known for outdoor shoots, though, so I can't be certain."

"Normally?"

"No one has seen or heard from him for several weeks."

"What about the models?"

"I've also been asking around, but without an actual photo it's not easy. I think I might have a possible line on the blonde; if it's who I think, she has something of a reputation, but the brunette is impossible to identify."

"How would I go about locating the blonde?"

"You don't. Anything you do that alerts or disturbs the Pontalba faction could easily see you ending up floating head down in the river one of these sunny mornings. You're a stranger, an unknown quantity.

You stay put. I'll put the word out and maybe she'll come to you."

It was progress of sorts, but I was frustrated I couldn't do anything myself and had to rely on the kindness, or any rate the assistance of strangers.

I rose from my chair. Wallace looked down and went back to perusing the folders he had been examining earlier. A moth darted from table lamp to ceiling and he waved it away with an air of irritation.

His shaven-headed Amazonian assistant was waiting on the other side of the office door, as if she had been listening all along to the conversation. She looked at me with concern.

"You're entering muddy waters," she said to me.

"Do you know something I don't?" I asked her.

"I think that goes without saying," she answered.

"And what would it take for you to be more forthcoming?"

Still guiding me across the gallery floor towards the door that led back to Magazine Street, she considered my question. A faint whiff of her perfume reached my nostrils. It smelled familiar, a fragrance I had come across before but which, right then, I couldn't place.

I stepped out of the gallery and could feel the heat of the day bearing down on me. The magician's assistant still held the door open behind me, standing there with an air of hesitancy.

"I know the girl," she said.

"Which one?"

"The blonde."

I was both pleased and disappointed by her revelation. Trust a magician's assistant to come up with some sleight of hand.

□ □ □

Doctor Gustawsson was a collector.

Long before the catastrophe had shattered the world as we once knew it, New Orleans had been a hotbed of vice and excess, and you didn't have to be a genius to realise this was even more the case now.

But this was of no consequence to the Doctor.

He was a man of more refined taste and had no wish to partake in the varied menu on offer on the streets and behind closed doors.

He collected photographs.

Some could be considered pornographic while others could be described as fine art nudes, but the important thing was that each item in his collection was unique and no one else owned any of the prints. Unlike other collectors, the Doctor didn't trade but instead commissioned his photographs so that they became exclusive to him.

The magician's assistant had been spotted one evening by the Doctor at the House of Blues on Decatur and he had made her an offer she couldn't refuse to pose for his collection. Knowing only his eyes would ever witness the outcome, she had accepted and had participated in a handful of photo sessions, with local photographers the Doctor had recruited, mostly Fishburne. Most of the work had featured her solo, but on a few rare occasions, the Doctor—who never attended the shoots—had requested she pose with other models, twice in succession with young women he had carefully selected to complement her looks, and once with a man. The assistant had refused to participate in the latter and had not been offered further work since.

Tiffany Cherise had been one of the young women she had agreed to pose with. There was no mistaking her description. She had called herself Cherise, so there was no doubt about her identity, in addition to the fact she had revealed in passing during the course of the shoot that she had recently arrived from New York. Both of their sessions together had taken place at Fishburne's studio in the Garden District. I quickly queried the magician's assistant about the other models she had come across, but none resembled Giulia.

"Why are you looking for her?" she asked.

"Her family are concerned," I explained. There was no need to go into unnecessary details.

"She was nice. Although she never said much."

"Why is he called the Doctor?" I thought to ask.

"He is one. The word on the street is he might actually once have been a plastic surgeon. Now he's the first port of call for the various gangs. Private practice. Illegal stuff, you know. Patching people up who'd rather not be seen in a hospital. Knife and gun wounds. Rumour has it even disposing of the bodies, if they can't be salvaged. Otherwise, he's harmless, just enjoys his pictures. Pays well, though."

I had a lot more questions for her, but it quickly became clear she had told me all she was willing to.

There was a shout from the back of the store, the magician calling out for her.

"What sort of magic do the two of you get involved with?"

She was about to close the door on me. "That's our secret. Of course, he cuts me in half, and also in fours, amongst other tricks" she said, with a bright smile. "But don't trust him," she said. "He serves many masters, and not all of them are likely to be your friends."

When I arrived back at our room, I found Vienna in a state of total despondency. Her face was as pale as a sheet and there were tremors agitating her hands as she sobbed quietly and refused to look me in the eyes.

"What is it?"

"We're in deep shit," she said.

"Somehow, that's not news to me, Vienna."

"No, really."

"Has something happened? Shearwater said something? News from New York?"

Ever since we'd been here, she'd eyed with much amused curiosity a little cubbyhole of a store two blocks away on Royal.

One of the many so-called Voodoo museums in the Quarter.

Bored, after my departure for the gallery this morning, she'd decided it would be fun to visit and agreed to have her palms read.

The palm reader, whom she naturally expected to predict the future appearance in her life of a handsome man around the corner and love and fertility ever after, had instead proven a prophet of absolute gloom. According to her and witnessing the look of terror in the pseudo-gipsy's eyes, Vienna had had to forcibly drag the information out of her.

She had seen death.

Stating the fact that Vienna would not be alive beyond the coming Mardi-Gras festivities.

"Come on, it's a con of some sorts," I reacted. "Did she then try and sell you some amulets or talismans to keep the danger away?"

"She didn't. She was utterly convinced, said it was the strongest of visions, like a cloud surrounding me."

"Surely you don't believe her?"

"I don't know what to believe any longer."

Vienna was visibly terrified.

"What else did she say?"

"What do you mean?"

"How? Where? When?"

"It doesn't work that way."

"Exactly. It's all smokes and mirrors. So, you want to come back, get a second opinion or something. Pay all over again. A scam."

"I'm not sure. She knew other things..."

"What sort of things?"

"About New York, my father, you..."

"Look, we aren't invisible. Maybe we stand out down here. The word has spread. People see us. We're newcomers, questions being asked and all that."

I had to do something. I had never seen Vienna in such a state of despondency.

"Listen. Come with me. We're going back there and I'm going to sort this out. OK?"

I held out my hand to her, pulled her up from the bed where she had been sitting balanced on the edge. She was reluctant to follow me, but I gave her no choice.

We hit the street.

"So where is the damn place?"

Vienna remembered it being situated on Royal Street, just a few blocks away. We set off towards it at a brusque pace dictated by my anger. The growing crowds easily parted to make way for us. With the approach of Mardi-Gras, there were more people about, but it was as if they were insubstantial, transparent, shimmering in the midday heat like a hazy curtain of beads animated by the breeze, superimposed onto the landscape of the Vieux Carré streets. The whole city appeared to be descending into another realm, an insubstantial cloak of enchantment that came in changed colours and even made the surrounding air taste different as we travelled through it.

Vienna's agitation had increased as she looked around, a growing air of uncertainty spreading across her frowning features. She looked at me questioningly.

"What is it, Vienna?"

"I can't find it... The palm reader's cubbyhole..."

"But you were there just a moment ago..."

"I know. I'm all unsure now."

"Are you sure it was actually on Royal?" We had ground to a halt, stationary, and now the passers-by circled us, flowing around us as if we were a stray obstacle on a beach over which the tide was spreading.

"Definitely. It was between an antique dealer—I remember because there was an amber brooch on display I took a strong liking to, before I walked in to have my reading—and a clothes store selling used clothes, mostly linen jackets and scarves in the window."

I glanced around us.

On the opposite side of the street were the two other stores she had mentioned.

I took her hand and we crossed over, examined the windows and their displays. "There," Vienna said. "The brooch. That's the one..." She looked puzzled, every cog in her brain running on overdrive as she attempted to process what was happening.

But there was no palm reading or voodoo store between the two stores. No alley, no missing space, just the wall they shared.

"I swear it was here. I do," she was almost on the verge of tears again.

I believed her.

I had seen the palm reading cubbyhole some days before and although

I couldn't be totally certain it had precisely been situated between the antique dealer and the used clothes store, a vague memory placed it around here.

The antique dealer was closed, but the clothing store wasn't.

"Wait for me," I told Vienna, and pushed past its door. A teenager was sitting behind the cash register, smoking something herbal, the smell floating in the air, heavy, slightly intoxicating.

"I'm looking for a voodoo store, where they do palm and tarot readings and such, that sells paraphernalia," I stated. "I was under the impression it was very close to here. Maybe even next door?"

"You must be mistaken," the young girl said. She wore a nose ring. "I think there's one three blocks away on Chartres. That's definitely the nearest. I get my incense sticks there."

When I queried her further, she confirmed that her store and the antique dealer had both been next to each other ever since she remembered. She looked at me as if I was downright stupid in my insistence in placing the palm reading joint in between them. "You're wrong," she said. "Just wrong." I walked out.

Vienna stood, rooted to the spot, still in a state of deep perplexity.

"I didn't imagine it," she insisted. I tried to console her, but the right words failed me.

We returned to our room. Vienna walked in a daze, her steps mechanical as if she was heading, Alice-like, for a descent into a rabbit hole.

I felt the same. But for different reasons. Ever since we had been in New Orleans, I'd had this unsettling feeling of being disconnected, of having entered a new world through the servant's entrance, a place where new rules, I couldn't quite understand, operated.

"How do you explain it?" Vienna asked me, as I warmed up the coffee.

"I don't. This has always been a strange place..."

"You can say that again... I feel emotionally drained," she said.

I wouldn't have felt any differently if someone had told me to my face I'd likely be dead within days. I wanted to comfort her but felt so helpless.

Vienna took a sip from the cup of coffee I handed her and grimaced. "This is foul," she said. I brought my own cup to my lips, tasted and agreed. It had been sitting untouched on the stove for several days and heating it up had done nothing to improve it. Neither of us were coffee drinkers of any substance.

I would have to brew some more. She walked over to the sink and filled a glass with tap water and washed her mouth out.

"I need to think," she said. "I think I'll just go to bed, sleep on it. Was there anything you had planned to do?"

I was about to tell her I had to see a doctor, but I thought better of it.

□ □ □

"You don't appear surprised to see me."

Gustawsson's office was all white and black and elegant IKEA straight lines and made you feel you were maybe in Scandinavia rather than New Orleans in its uncluttered functionality.

"Wallace warned me you'd be coming," he said.

"I thought his assistant might have done so, rather."

"Does it matter who warned me? She's his creature; they're inseparable."

"She modelled for you," I stated.

"Many women have."

"This is not about her. A blonde, Cherise, participated in one of the same sessions you commissioned. She's the one I'm seeking."

"I'm aware of that."

"Where can I find her?"

"Aren't you curious?"

"What about?"

"The photos from the session? Or Cherise's other shoots?"

I was. I couldn't conceal the fact. An unhealthy curiosity.

He was wearing a white coat, a white shirt with a black tie, pinstriped trousers and shoes polished to within inches of shiny perfection. He was clean-shaven, his thin hair cut short and he wore rimless glasses. He looked just like a doctor. Someone I could have passed in the street a dozen times and never recognised again.

He rose from his chair and stepped across to the wall and the row of stainless steel cabinets.

There was an electronic lock and, with his back to me, obscuring the numbers pad, he tapped in the combination and I heard a click. He pulled the middle drawer out. A valley of orderly yellow folders with variously coloured tags filled the space. I briefly wondered about the significance of the colours he used. Did each individual colour represent a specific model, or a given perversion, a sex act, or a progression in the levels of pornography each folder harboured?

He pulled a thin folder out. It was tagged purple.

He returned to his impeccably tidy desk and laid out the folder in front of him, then sat down, facing me, with an enigmatic smile shaping his thin lips.

"It's a hobby," he declared.

"You wouldn't be the only one," I said, hoping he would understand I was anything but critical of his tastes.

"I love the bodies of women."

Make that two of us, I thought, the bittersweet yearning that underpinned my soul vibrating in sympathy.

"Nothing wrong about that."

"But that's as far as it goes," Doctor Gustawsson continued. "It's all in the mind, the body can't follow. And no amount of blue pills of any shape or strength can help. I can look and sigh and that's all I can do."

I tried to appear sympathetic, remembering how, after I'd been beaten up by April Lea, I had also been unable to function for days on end. Let alone capable of having any thoughts of sexual congress after our second encounter, the memory of which still made me nervously clench my buttocks whenever I thought of it, or my sphincter choke whenever I had to go to the toilet.

Taking my silence for approval, Gustawsson continued. "I so much prefer photography to film, don't you?" I nodded. "It's the stillness, you see, the way bodies and skin shine, the angle that light falls on flesh and brings it to life, the God-like geometry of curves and hollows, highlighting a blemish, a dimple, a shadow, the thousand mute words contained in a woman's eye. It moves me, like no animated hydraulics ever could in the sheer vulgarity of their inevitable and clichéd movements. Once there was a wealth of images all readily available, at the drop of a keyboard, of course, dragged down from the clouds of the web, but now, since the Dark, it's become so much more unattainable. So, I have the money and nothing much to spend it on, and I commission my own. There's no one to share it with, of course, but that doesn't matter. I look, I worship. No need to touch, no necessity to invite disappointment and hear the actual sound of their voices, approach the broken nature of their lives. It becomes a private ceremony. Me and the image of women, the heart of beauty."

In a strange way, I could understand him. This was a man whose intimate knowledge of flesh was probably like a scar on the soul, from all the cutting, the stitching, the blood, bones and guts he had delved in, butchered, patched up in his lifetime of practice. He had retreated into a passive form of worship, at the altar of women's immaculate bodies. Why did I feel so much empathy for him?

He pushed the folder over. I picked it up. Opened it. There were just a dozen prints inside it. All in black and white. I slowly leafed through them, one at a time. Absorbing every image with all the reverence they deserved.

Fishburne had a good eye for composition and light, capturing moments like a butterfly in a net, or maybe Gustawsson had selected just the right micro-second from the contact sheets, ignoring every stolen image that preceded or followed it, homing with surgical precision on the photo that stood head and shoulders above the others because of its uniqueness and splendour.

A shot of Cherise's back, bending over to slip out of her panties, her arse square and regal, right at the centre of the image, the faint shadow of her spine like a ridge in her skin, a symphony of whiteness.

On all fours, presenting herself to the lens. Looking up towards the camera, her eyes like a supplicant, her mouth half open, an arc of liquid—urine, I wondered?—cascading towards her face but still inches away, about to splash against her.

Another image taken from the rear, still on all fours, the thick line of her sex lips, the dark pucker of her anus, the pale crown of her arse cheeks like a target, an offering.

A close-up of her breasts. Small, delicately pierced, like a Saharan landscape seen from the air, all gentle dunes and shadows and the memory of movement.

Another, this time with the magician's assistant. Her shining, shaven scalp, buried in Cherise's crotch, her invisible mouth, tongue and lips pleasuring her no doubt, but with the feeling of an abstract nature of death. A Mondrian-like symphony of shapes, where curves have overcome the straight lines and repopulated the canvas.

Cherise and the assistant, both facing the camera, as if caught in the glare of a powerful spotlight, the contrast between the shades of white of their skin, the dead pool of their eyes, like trophies against a bare wall, the only elements of darkness the focused stain of their nipples, the 3-D indent of their navels and the abbreviated ley lines of their sex lips.

"They're genuinely beautiful," I confessed.

Gustawsson's smile spread to his eyes.

"Both the pictures and the women," I emphasised.

"Aren't they just?"

I gathered up the prints and slotted them back inside the folder and pushed it across the desk back towards him.

"I have others. Of Cherise," he said.

I remembered how some of the photos she'd featured in had been meticulously described to me by O'Carlson back in Manhattan. If they were even a patch on those I had just seen, I wouldn't be able to move for hours because of a raging erection forever spoiling the line of my slacks. It wasn't that Tiffany Helmsmark was voluptuous; she was actually rather skinny, and her arse was just that one small degree too large and out of proportion with the rest of her slender body. Her breasts were on the small side, although for men like me and sundry others that was actually a desirable plus. Her face was a naked canvas which could, in turn, look pretty, at others angular and sharp, while her expression moved between a studied pout and a come-hither form of provocation and would never equate with outright cheesecake sexiness or innocence.

"She's modelled a lot for you?"

"Yes, she needed the money. Arrived here with nothing but the clothes on her back."

"I see they soon came off." Not my best repartee.

"She has 'something'. Some women do, others just don't, even if they have the right face and body. It's ineffable, something few can capture. How they react to the lens pointed at them, move, espouse its gaze. There are others. Or were. Before it all fell down," Gustawsson continued. "But I don't have access to them: Nettie, June Ann, Cam Damage, Kathlyn, Trish Noir... Our modern-day sirens..."

"I need to see her. Is she still in New Orleans?"

"She is."

"Good."

"You mustn't harm her," the Doctor said.

"I wouldn't."

"She dances at the Locked Room Club."

□ □ □

I was rushing back to Vienna following my encounter with Doctor Gustawsson. Jackson Square was cordoned off because of the Mardi-Gras preparations, floats parked in front of the museum under dirty tarpaulins, tents and canopies being erected inside the Square in a flurry of activity. The security was being enforced by the Pontalba people, recognisable by the distinctive square badges with the image of a snake they sported on their lapels. I had to find a long way around.

I detoured through Dauphine Street and tried to make my way back through Pirate's Alley. There was a crowd gathering outside the Faulkner House, mostly bikers, in heavy riding gear and ritual chains, tattooed to the max, bearded and menacing. They were a long way from their normal patch, I knew. Maybe alliances were shifting, or a truce had been established in view of the coming celebrations? I studiously avoided them but still attracted some curious looks.

I emerged on Royal, just a handful of blocks from the location where Vienna and I had been puzzled by the seemingly disappearing fortune-telling store. I couldn't avoid glancing across the street. Damn!

The store was there. Just as she had described it, nuzzled between the antique dealer and the used clothes emporium, its narrow door painted dark red, a 'closed' sign hanging askew behind the glass. How could it just appear and disappear? Surely no proper way to do business.

I looked up. Long cursive letters dotted across the storefront.

'The Future', and in a smaller size along the bottom of the narrow window 'Voodoo, Magic and the art of the Impossible'.

I ran past, I had to get to Vienna, bring her back and show her it had not been an illusion, an affront to her sanity. Somehow, we just hadn't seen it, for some ineffable reason. And then, if we could, find whoever was running the scam and get her to take back the awful verdict she had delivered, which had shaken Vienna so much.

The crowds were gathering, trooping down the streets with a sense of expectation, ambling with quiet purpose down the Vieux Carré streets.

I caught sight of the Napoleon House as I passed the nearby corner. Unusually, it was open. Long before evening. Which didn't surprise me with the amount of folk already around. Even in our new reality, Carnival retained its attraction.

Which is when I saw him, walking briskly out of the bar.

The same dark suit with narrow lapels, the white shirt and skinny black tie, the sharp crease of his trousers, the brisk step and his cadaverous face concealed behind the dark glasses.

Recalled I had never actually seen his eyes. Assumed they were as hard as steel in their coldness.

'Reservoir Dogs'.

The Commander's lethal henchman.

What the fuck was he doing here?

A cold sweat broke out along the edges of my soul and I rushed towards the Napoleon House. He was facing the other direction and moving away from me.

I reached the side door. It wasn't locked. I quickly tried to recall whether I had left it that way, pushed it open and ran up the stairs.

Vienna was not in the room.

Right then I was unsure whether I was relieved or whether I should be worrying.

14 - ALL SHADES OF SHADY

Shearwater was in the bar's back office and knew nothing of either 'Reservoir Dogs's visit or Vienna's whereabouts.

I had no initial idea of where to begin searching for Vienna.

Her few belongings had been left untouched in the room, bundled under the bed where she normally kept them, including the roll of local currency she had stolen from Luke. I knew she had not departed with 'Reservoir Dogs', so maybe his appearance and her absence were merely coincidental? Part of me argued this was too good to be true and there must be some connection.

Maybe she'd felt the need for some fresh air and had just gone out for a wander to clear her head?

I hoped this was the case.

In the meantime, I had to find the club where Cherise supposedly danced. It was barely midday and the sun floated in oppressive splendour above the Mississippi, the heat shimmering across the waters and radiating in all directions. It was going to be a hot, sticky afternoon where the minutes ticked away so slowly you'd feel like you'd been walking through treacle, glancing at your watch at regular intervals in the vain hope a whole hour had passed instead of the mere handful of minutes you'd just survived, shirt sticking to your skin, collar wet and lethargy insidiously attacking all your senses.

Gustawsson had provided me with the Locked Room Club's location and a modicum of information.

It wasn't open to the public and didn't advertise its existence.

But he had suggested I use his name as an introduction. I'd also slipped much of our cash into my pocket, should further inducements be needed. It felt like I was stealing from Vienna, but she wasn't around to argue with. I hoped she would understand when she reappeared. If I found Cherise, we could soon leave the Louisiana Republic and the money might not be required any longer, although the thought of the journey back was another nightmare I wasn't ready to face yet.

Bourbon Street was one of the few places in New Orleans, and in all likelihood the whole country, that had barely been affected by the Dark. Most of the bars remained open, the scores of eateries offering gumbo, jambalaya, seafood, oysters and calorie-heavy po' boys in competition with each other, as did the seedy strip joints and redundant souvenir stores and stalls, even though tourists were now few and far between. It was just that the inebriated crowds were different these days. No longer in the majority consisting of tourists in inappropriate clothing and footwear, stumbling, plastic glasses in hand from one joint to the other to the sound of duelling bands in the bars facing each other on both sides of the street, all the way from Canal Street for almost two-dozen blocks.

Instead Bourbon was crowded by an assortment of gang members patrolling up and down, wary of each other, displaying their colours, uniforms, badges, scars, tattoos with evident pride, with an air of surprise that none were being challenged, the imminent Mardi-Gras celebrations the occasion of a rare truce when the city was open to all and the territories of New Orleans no longer had any enforced borders.

I was still on Pontalba patch, the area immediately surrounding Jackson Square, circumscribed by the banks of the river just a stone's throw from Jackson Square all the way back to North Rampart, and ranging across from Conti to Ursulines Avenue.

The reigning gang's headquarters were located on the top floor of one of the Pontalba buildings, and each member wore a badge with the figure of a snake. Once I had even come across two women stepping across Chartres both wearing, or at any rate sharing, an actual live snake, green and viscous. One end of the snake circling the neck of the gang moll and its endless tail wrapped around the waist of the other, making them into some form of conjoined twins. Their teetering steps restricted by the reptile's embrace, their eyes dead to the world, parading like chattel. They had looked alike, possibly a mother and daughter, both worn and broken, their gang owners walking a few yards behind them, clad in tight back T-shirts and heavy boots.

A loud and energetic blues band was playing in the bar on the right-hand corner of Bourbon and Toulouse. The resonant echo of the bass rhythm reverberating across its low ceiling being spat out into the street, followed like a shadow a second later by the accompanying beats of the snare drum and the hi-hat, as the gravel-voiced singer on the raised dais sang about faraway crossroads and melancholy women who'd left his heart shattered in a million pieces.

One block later and the blues had faded, to be replaced by the sound of a soul band in full flight gliding across the fabled midnight hour. The singer a shimmying black mama in a voluminous kaftan performing to a totally empty bar, where even the barman appeared to have deserted his quarters.

As I made progress down Bourbon, the bars, eateries and stores thinned down, until I was walking past normal Vieux Carré buildings. Shuttered, wrought-iron balconies with dead flowers hanging forlornly down their sides and the noise behind me thinned.

I passed Ursulines Avenue and was now out of Pontalba territory. I wasn't quite certain which realm I was now entering. I had never listened too carefully to Shearwater's explanations as to who controlled which areas. Compared to ten minutes ago, it was dead quiet, surprisingly so, a few blocks ahead the demarcation line of Ramparts and beyond the faded splendour of Esplanade Avenue.

I knew I must be nearing the club. It was one of the few blocks of Bourbon which lived in darkness, even right now with the sun at its apogee, shadows running into shadows, silence wrapping itself like a curtain around the old buildings.

There was nothing to indicate the club's existence. Just a steel door, with no sign or lettering, rusting in the corners, worn, anonymous. Not a place that advertised itself.

A door in the middle of nowhere, away from hustle and bustle of the French Quarter, even though it was still technically within its perimeter.

I knew there was no point in knocking. It wasn't the sort of place that would be open until well after dark.

I considered a brief while whether I should stick around, hide in the shade somewhere close and observe, wait for people to arrive, the staff, the dancers, even Cherise, but I knew I would, however discreet, be too obvious. I would return in the evening.

In the meantime, I wanted to find Vienna.

□ □ □

She hadn't returned to the room we had been sharing and there was no indication either that she had come and gone. Everything was in exactly the same place I had left things before my trip down Bourbon Street in search of the club.

I went downstairs to see Shearwater and ask for his advice.

"Ah," he said, as I walked in to his badly-lit den, "There was someone looking for you earlier..."

"The man in the black suit?" I said. "I caught a sight of him on the street. I don't think I care to speak to him," I continued.

He looked up at me, puzzled.

"Not a man. It was a woman. A rather striking one, if you ask me..."

"What did she look like?"

He described her, in loving detail.

It was April Lea. There could be no doubt about it. The only thing that hadn't somehow caught his inquisitive attention was the minuscule scar bisecting the corner of her right highbrow. A minute imperfection I had noticed as her blows had rained down on me on the occasion of our first, unfortunate, encounter.

"Was she just asking after me, or did she also enquire about Vienna?" I asked Shearwater.

"Just you," he confirmed.

"You didn't tell her about Vienna, did you?"

"My lips were sealed. And neither did I inform her you were enjoying the fruits of my hospitality. But I know she didn't believe me; why would she have come through my door in search of you had she not information already about your whereabouts."

He had a point.

"Did she say if she was coming back? Later?"

"She didn't. But she had a smile on her lips as she walked out. As if the whole affair was funny."

I could just picture that ironic smile on those full lips. My heart skipped a beat.

I should have gathered my stuff, and Vienna's, that very moment. But I had nowhere else to go.

Shearwater looked at me, quizzically.

"So, who's the man in the suit?" he asked.

"No one you'd want to know. He works for Commander Helmsmark."

"Oh," Shearwater remarked, "Not a very nice man, then."

I nodded.

I walked back upstairs and found one of our guns, which we'd concealed in the bread cupboard. I had a feeling it was advisable to be armed from now on. Quickly cleaned it. Checked it was loaded and, after engaging the safety, dropped it into my jacket pocket.

□ □ □

The lights went out.

The sound system roared to life. I recognised the song: Bowie's "Let's Dance". Uplifting, joyous.

A thin spotlight illuminated the raised stage at the back of the room. The club had only opened an hour ago around midnight and there wasn't much of a crowd yet. It was the sort of confidential place that probably didn't get into its proper stride until the twilight hours of the night when the rest of the city was sleeping tight.

The interior of the club was as sparse as its outside walls and a front door that first led to a shaded courtyard at the end of which was a separate building, which now functioned as the locale for festivities. It was deliberately stripped of character, markedly anonymous, in a possible attempt to deter the curious or the uninitiated. It sat three blocks beyond the animation and bright lights of Bourbon Street's main drag, and just yards away from the once residential side of Rampart, where now most houses were boarded up and abandoned. Just illegal shelter for clandestine lovers, drug-runners and all shades of shady and dangerous.

It had taken some persuasion to get in, as well as a handful of notes from the stash. But the drinks were free until midnight and I'd never been much of a drinker anyway. I nursed my glass as the place slowly began to fill up. The private areas beyond the main room were still roped off. I had expected the usual lingering smell of stale beer tempered by the invasive ghost of tobacco generations, but the Locked Room Club had a unique feel to it. As if by walking in you were entering into a different world, where sweat had been banished to the outer circles and just a touch of green fragrance floated freely, with a sweet but powerful back-note that reminded me of very dark chocolate. It was surprisingly soothing, putting the visitor at ease in an instant.

The staff were equally unpredictable, drawn from the various New Orleans gangs that controlled the city, but here appearing harmless and even welcoming. The guys at the door and those roaming around acting as security were clearly from the Mud Bug Team, which controlled most of the Garden District and were headquartered in the Audubon Zoo, while the bar staff and waitresses were part of the Tujague Crew, recognisable by their single pendant earring in the shape of a skull.

The previous dancer had been a petite young woman with a fierce buzz cut that undermined her femininity. She had stripped, professionally enough, down from her fringed pirate outfit to her G-string to the sound of some hearty zydeco music. I couldn't help notice that on her left arse cheek she had been branded, a deep indentation cutting into her skin in the shape of an infinity sign. There was also a small barcode tattooed across the narrow valley separating her breasts.

It had been all of five minutes since she had left the stage and I was wondering whether my visit here was going to be a total waste of time, when the Bowie song sprang to life, its hiccupy bassline vibrating along the club's ceiling, spreading the rhythm through the room.

My eyes followed the spotlight. A long, tall body, white as milk against the dark background, straw-coloured hair halfway down to her shoulders, that distinctive aquiline nose. Tiffany Cherise Helmsmark. Finally. In the flesh. She was already nude. At first glance, she was damn perfect, not a blemish in sight, just the discreet studs on each side of her nipples, held in place I assumed by a small metal bar. Had I not known of them previously in the description of some of the Hilton Willis photographs, I might not even have noticed them considering how tiny they were.

She didn't actually dance, but undulated, feet planted firmly on the ground. Medium-sized heels, a wedge, a buckle holding them in place below sculpted ankles.

My eyes were attracted to her bush, a dark, warm shade of light brown, growing wild and free, just a hint when the spotlight moved and focused on her genitalia of the thin, distantly pink-red, line of her gash.

She was elegance and class, sexual but in a reserved sort of way, allowing one's imagination full-range even though she was quite naked to conjure further hints of lustful perversions and speculative delights.

Another punter brushed against my shoulder. Turned to me to apologize silently. I nodded. His eyes were fixed on Tiffany, as were mine.

"Damn it, she's beautiful," he whispered, as if speaking any louder would interrupt the magic or derail the Bowie song as it unfolded, its divine guitar riff now in full flow.

"Absolutely," I said in reply.

"A great pity she only sticks to dancing," he remarked. "I'd love to see her involved in the other sports," he grinned.

All too soon, the song came to an end, the spotlight faded into darkness and, in the shadows, Tiffany left the stage as I squinted, following her fluid movements.

I asked the guy who had spoken to me if he wanted to join me at the bar for another drink. He was happy to do so. I quizzed him at length, more about the club and its activities than Tiffany, not wishing to draw undue attention to my presence there tonight. I noticed the Pontalba badge on the lapel of his jacket.

At any rate, he didn't appear to know who I was.

He confirmed that the club's main activities didn't get into full flow until later, when the actual shows began. He breezily mentioned the cage fights, the dark rooms at the back which would be opening, sometimes auctions, even the dogs. I didn't wish to appear too curious, even though some of the things he was referring to sounded quite out of the ordinary and, feeling somewhat proprietary even though I still hadn't actually met Tiffany, I thanked the unseen gods she only danced.

Soon, various acquaintances of his filtered in and he moved away from me to meet them, with a nod I should join him and his friends which I politely declined, just in time to avoid the inevitable questions it would have been awkward to answer. I found an alcove and sat myself down and observed the growing crowd. Soon, the stage was lit again and the petite stripper from earlier returned. On this occasion, the heat rising in the room, she disposed of her G-string at the end of her set to reveal smooth pudenda and was soon followed by a tall guy festooned from tattoos from neck to feet, already stripped to his socks and Doc Martens and sporting a fierce erection. He dragged along behind him a couple of chairs and the pair soon began to embrace in a simulacrum of theatrical desire and ten minutes later were artlessly making love on the stage to the total indifference of the sparse spectators. Maybe the dog shows later would attract more interest, I reckoned, feeling ill at ease with myself at the thought, both repulsed and also curious.

From where I sat, I had a good view of the entrance and clocked all the new arrivals, as well as the rare departures, in the hope Cherise might be amongst them. Would she be performing again? Doing what this time? Or was there an exit I was unaware of, and could miss her altogether?

I was thinking of posting myself outside the main building, lurking in the courtyard just in case so as not to miss her should she leave before dawn, when an announcement over the sound system informed us that tonight's auction would soon be beginning, and we should take our seats and consult the menu.

The Tujague Crew of bar staff and waitresses were circulating between the tables, dropping a single foolscap sheet of paper on each. "Good luck," my waitress murmured as she shuffled by and let the page float down across my table. I picked it up. Just five photos. Four women, one man. Black and white, faces caught like deer in a spotlight, images with all the artistry of a passport photo booth machine on the blink. Two of them I recognised, the petite stripper and her recent fuck partner. Equal opportunities, then. I was relieved to see that Tiffany was not part of the programme, or should it have been described as merchandise. I was surprised to see that one of the women was actually the waitress who had dropped off the leaflet.

It felt as if I was inhabiting a strange, twilight world where the rules were different, and the decorum of civilisation as I knew it was fading in incremental units as the night progressed. As if New Orleans now only half-belonged to the real world, and part of it was submerged in a form of insidious darkness.

The events of the past week were swirling around my head, unsettling, bizarre, illogical, making me doubt my sanity, like quicksand sucking away at me.

I was about to rise from my table and move towards the door when, out of the corner of my eye I noticed a slight, pale form at the back of the room, hunched, head down, shuffling its way in that same direction and recognised Cherise.

I quickly followed her out. Caught up with her in the courtyard.

"Hey?"

She turned around to face me, her features set in a rictus of anguish. "Who are you?" Pulling out a switchblade from somewhere on her person. She wore a white T-shirt and skinny jeans. She was shorter than I had expected in the flesh, wearing only ballet pumps. "Keep away from me..."

"You're Tiffany," I stated.

"It's Cherise, actually" she protested, but I could see her heart was not in it, and a look of surprise was spreading across her face, alarmed as she was that I was aware of her true identity.

"Once known as Princess Sensuality..." I continued. She was still holding the blade dangerously close to my stomach. The courtyard was so deep in silence after the hubbub of the club's interior you could clearly hear the sound of every leaf fluttering in the breeze that flew in from the nearby river.

"Who the fuck are you?" she asked. She raised the blade towards me. "And don't come any nearer, or I might perform an open throat tonsillectomy on you."

"I'm just the poor guy who agreed to come down here and find you, and most days I feel I should have known better..."

"You work for my father?"

"No. It was your sister who got in touch with me."

She fell momentarily silent.

"Can we talk?" I asked her. "I mean you no harm."

"I'm not going back to New York," Cherise said. "Willingly."

"That's not my intention," I said.

She scrutinised me as best she could in the shadows of the courtyard. I hoped I didn't look too sinister. I hadn't shaved for several days and feared I was not at my best reassuring.

She finally came to a decision and lowered her switchblade.

"OK," she said.

"Anywhere we can talk?" I suggested. "Have a drink and a chat?"

"This is the French Quarter, the place that never sleeps. Where do you want to go?"

"Maybe somewhere without music, might make the conversation easier."

We exited the courtyard into the silence of Bourbon Street and walked towards the bright lights in uncomfortable silence.

"How is my sister?"

"I can't be certain, but I suspect not in a good way. The last time I saw her, she was heading towards Central Park where all the troubles were. I begged her not to; it was suicidal..."

"She always had a flair for the dramatic," Cherise said with little warmth in her voice.

We found a deserted bar, well away from what was left of the nocturnal crowds, close to the Cabildo. Ordered a tall mug of iced tea and sat facing each other across the marble-topped table as the solitary night barman followed a football game on the overhead TV screen with the sound off. Cherise had been hungry, and he'd served us a plate of wilting day-old pastries which I didn't touch but which she gulped down.

"So, what did she tell you?" Cherise asked.

"She just wanted me to find you. She was worried."

"How kind-hearted of her."

"Why New Orleans?" I asked Cherise. "How did you make the journey?"

"I could well ask you the same question."

"I suppose we both found ways..."

"The Commander was once heavily involved with some of the factions down here, so I took advantage of that, pretended I had his approval and used his contacts," Cherise said. I found it interesting that she referred to her father by his rank rather than something more personal or affectionate, but didn't raise a flag, considering what I'd learned about their relationship.

"You and your father do not get on, I hear."

"You could say that. I know I'm self-destructive, but who wouldn't be if you'd grown up the way I did. He disapproved of my modelling. Said it shamed him."

"I've heard about that."

"The body is beautiful, and I felt no shame allowing photographers to use me. It was always art. Despite what he thought, I never slept with any of them... Well, there was this one guy in Baltimore, but it had nothing to do with his photography..."

"He's had most of the prints destroyed, you know. And Hilton Willis is now dead."

"The Commander's revenge... "

"I heard the Willis photos were rather explicit..."

"So what?"

"Listen, I felt I had an obligation to find you and now I have. My job is done. You're alive and safe..." I hesitated.

"There is one more thing, though..."

"All you have to do is ask."

"I briefly came across a photo of you and another young woman, a relatively chaste one, in fact, taken on a bench facing one of the Pontalba apartment buildings, off Jackson Square. What can you tell me about her?"

"I remember that session. It was Fishburne who organised it..."

"No one I've contacted knows where he might be...."

"She was Italian. Very pretty. Didn't say much. All he wanted was for us to hold each other, embrace. She had a lovely smell, her skin was warm even though we shot at dawn and it was rather cold. She only agreed to take her top off and pull her skirt up, so she could cradle her thighs in my lap; it was a specific image Jeff was hoping to recreate which he'd seen in some book, a painting of sorts, I think."

"Do you know where she is staying in the city? If she is still here?"

"I haven't a clue. He paid us cash and we parted. I think I remember him saying he'd come across her late at night sitting in the Café du Monde, as if she had nowhere to stay."

"Her name is Giulia."

"I wasn't even aware of that. We barely spoke, just posed, followed the photographer's instructions."

I felt deflated. I'd come this far, experienced so many emotions and pain, and now had seemingly nowhere further to go.

"He was involved, you know..."

"Who?"

"My father, the Commander..."

"With Giulia? How is that possible?"

"No, not her. The Dark. The night the Internet was wiped out. It was all part of a plan, but it went badly wrong."

She held my full attention.

"There was someone here who offered my father and those who followed him access to some incredible source of power. They referred to him as the magician..."

The cogs were beginning to fall into place, as I listened to Cherise.

"What sort of power?"

"I never knew, but he'd always mentioned New Orleans as a place where magic worked, you know. Maybe because of the old Voodoo traditions and all that. I'd never believed in it of course. But I was aware it had always been a city on the edge, where things functioned differently. The Commander was here on the night of the Dark. When everything collapsed. After he returned, and the whole world was becoming illogical, he made everyone swear to never reveal the fact. Didn't wish to attract attention to himself, to a possible connection between the catastrophe and him. But he'd become haunted, possessed in some way, and life around him became unbearable. As it is, he'd always treated me so ambiguously while I was growing up with so little affection, wariness even, his disapproval of me never far from the surface. He did mention he could never set foot here again, so when I decided to flee I thought it was the best place to come to."

Did Cherise know who was her real mother? I had no wish to inform her and worsen her distress. Even more so now that Alexandra was in all likelihood dead.

"Is that why you ran away and came down here?"

"No. I just had to get out of New York. He was becoming increasingly irrational. I couldn't think of anywhere better to come."

Fire and frying pan came to mind.

I kept on querying Cherise about the supposed connection between the Commander and the fateful events of the Dark, but she could provide no added proof or details; it was all vague, suspicions, words overheard passing between him and acolytes before and after the night when it all collapsed, hints of things impossible, supernatural.

"I will never return to New York," she stated.

"That's fine with me," I said. "It was never my intention to drag you back. How will you manage here?"

"I've managed so far. I'll continue. I've tired of modelling and, anyway, the Commander has put the word out and most of the remaining practising photographers around are nervous using me again, and so few of them are active anyway. An art form that went down the pan after the events. As so many others did. I've a series of gigs, at the Locked Room Club, although the owners are keen for me to do more than dance, and I don't know how long I can resist their pressure. But I've a few waitressing slots I do whenever there is a chance and someone drops out at short notice because of illness or some problem. You can live for very little in New Orleans these days."

I almost offered her some money, but remembered I had limited funds already and half belonged to Vienna, wherever she might be, and if I were to return to New York or get out of New Orleans some cash would definitely be required for bribes, transport or food.

I just paid the cheque and we tramped into the night. I checked my watch: it was four in the morning already. There was a quiet in the air that was soothing. The streets we walked through were deserted.

Cherise lived in the Business District beyond Canal in an office building top floor squat with three other women she'd met while waitressing. I offered to walk her there. Neither of us was in much of a hurry and we took the long way around, by the river, past the moorings for the large riverboats which no longer served tourists these troubled days but had, respectively, been turned into a notorious floating brothel and a refuge for the homeless.

We passed the Cajun Queen, bobbing against the shoreline.

"I lived there," Cherise remarked, "during my first two weeks here. There was nowhere else to stay. I had no clue where to go. But it was OK. Men and women were segregated at least. It's run by the church. A paddle boat functioning as a charity hostel."

We had reached the Holocaust Memorial and were approaching the now derelict Aquarium. Beyond it and the Algiers ferry stood the old Riverwalk Mall, which I knew had become the Audubon Bikers' headquarters and not a place to approach lightly. We would be turning back onto Canal well before we reached it. Lines of early light were cutting into the sky, the moon a thin crescent high above. The peace was overwhelming. Out of the blue, Cherise put her hand in mine. In silence. As if the gesture sufficed, needed no words to pass our lips. An expression of trust.

It felt as if we were orphans in the storm.

An instant later, I felt a terrible blow to the back of my legs and, felled, I collapsed to the ground, letting go of Cherise's hand, her fingers slipping through mine as the intense pain ran like lightning through every nerve in my body and I felt like screaming.

Before I could react, and the very moment my face made contact with the cold concrete of the walk, another blow struck my shoulder, a black shoe unleashed in full swing, its crunching momentum racing through my bruised flesh like butter and making my bones shriek in agony. I curled up like a foetus, a seductive feeling of lightness in my head, an invitation to fainting right there and then.

I heard the shuffle of feet around me.

Cherise's voice.

Plaintive.

"No, no. Not that."

15 - COME TO THE CARNIVAL

I tried desperately to keep my eyes open. I knew that if I allowed the pain to overtake me completely, I'd pass out. Maybe never to wake again.

Every bone inside me felt as if it had been hit by a hammer, the pain dancing along my limbs and stabbing away with wild abandon at every sinew of skin, nerve and muscle and places I didn't even know I had.

My head was facing the river. I dragged my chin across the concrete, slowly twisted my neck and tried to lift my jaw and turn my face round full circle.

The silhouette was unmistakable: my old friend, 'Reservoir Dogs'. Who else could it have been? And was the similarly ubiquitous April Lea not far behind?

She didn't appear to be on the scene. Only the black-clad, cadaverous-looking 'Reservoir Dogs'—he must have a name, but I was in no hurry to find out—stood, with his back to me, looming menacingly over Cherise's cringing, retreating form.

I squinted, focused on his silhouette.

Saw he held a blade of some sort in his left hand, its serrated edge catching a fleeting reflection of the dying moon overlooking us.

Banishing the pain still animating every part of my body, I dug into my jacket pocket and retrieved the gun.

Everything seemed to be moving in slow motion.

My hand.

Steadying the weight of the weapon.

Releasing the safety catch.

Aiming.

'Reservoir' moved forward, approaching the frightened young woman I had been escorting home, not so much out of gallantry but in the hope that I might glean some further information about Giulia and her whereabouts. I shouldn't have been here.

He raised his arm.

She drew her hands up to protect her face.

I adjusted my aim.

The knife, held high, now his arm fully extended, the coming arc of descent of the blade drawn like an invisible line in the air.

My finger pressed the trigger.

The shot was loud, my ears ringing, its echo settling inside my skull.

He heard it, tried to brusquely turn his head back towards me but the bullet hit him before he could finalise even a fraction of the movement.

He dropped the knife, rushing his hands to his own neck, where a rapidly expanding small red crater had appeared. He stumbled. Next to him, Cherise was staring at me and the gun I was holding, her eyes wide open in fear and amazement.

'Reservoir' stumbled, first to his knees, then his hands now deserting his neck and the wound in a vain attempt to avoid the fall and his head hitting the ground. He rolled over. Lay there motionless. The sound of my shot reverberating across the still river bank.

Both Cherise and I were motionless. She, standing on the small ridge she had run towards, me still sprawled across the promenade.

Our assailant was now similarly immobile.

Cherise snapped out of her stupor and, gingerly, took a couple of steps towards the man's prone body, got down on her knees and took a closer look at him. She rose. Stared at me.

"You've killed him," she said.

My throat tightened. I'd managed almost four decades without killing anyone and now I had a second notch on my belt within the space of a few weeks. I was just a fact checker, not a killer.

This really was becoming a crazy world.

"I didn't have a choice," I managed to say, struggling for an explanation. "I thought it was either him or you. He was about to knife you."

"Mr Black. He works for the Commander... worked..." Cherise said. "I knew him in New York. I never thought he would follow me here. Or that my father would sanction him killing me."

"I came across him back there too," I said. "It wasn't pleasant." What I didn't mention was my theory that I was the one who had been followed here. That I had merely been allowed to escape Manhattan in the hope I would lead the Commander's thugs to Cherise. As to why he wanted her dead, was it because she was an incestuous embarrassment or maybe she knew too much about his involvement with the Dark? I doubted I'd ever find out the true reasons.

I painfully rose to my feet, the pain ebbing with the realisation I had, against all odds, survived the attack. Looked around to check the sound of the gunshot had not attracted anyone. The promenade was still deserted, and no lights had come on the nearby riverboat.

"We have to go," Cherise said, a look of panic on her face. She was paler than white right now, like a ghost about to be devoured by what was left of the night.

"We can't leave him here."

"What do you suggest, then?"

"We could roll the body into the water," I suggested. "It might delay its discovery. I'm not sure if there are any currents, tides that might move him away from here, but I think it would be advisable. Don't you?"

Cherise agreed.

It was a gruesome task and the splash 'Reservoir's body made as it hit the river created barely a ripple on the water's surface. We watched him sink quickly into its muddy depths. It occurred to me I should have taken his wallet, stolen whatever money he had, both for personal profit (which I could have shared with Cherise) and to muddy the scene, make it appear as if he had been mugged and robbed, but the thought came too late.

I saw Cherise to her building.

The sun was now rising.

"What are you going to do now?" I asked her.

"I don't think I should tell you, actually. I feel it's better if we don't see each other again," she said. "Stay apart."

I agreed.

□ □ □

I moved in a daze back towards the heart of the Vieux Carré, still clumsily processing the events of the night in my mind, half expecting April Lea to be lurking around, spying on me around each successive street corner, bent on revenge and mayhem which I would not survive.

I came across the first Carnival procession as I crossed Decatur, its musicians all similarly uninformed as if they were circus attendants with bright-coloured red tunics and white bell-bottomed trousers with a dashing red stripe along the side.

Preceded by a young girl of no more than fifteen in a football cheerleader's outfit twirling a beribboned baton, came the brass sections, tubas, trombones, trumpets, a quartet of flutes, a handful of clarinets, followed as they moved along like soldiers by rows of resonant percussion, drums in every size and shape.

Making up the tail of the procession was a couple of chained prisoners, a man and a woman, whose heads were covered by hoods, their civilian clothes torn and in disarray. He was barefoot and sleeveless and she with her blouse torn open and hanging in threads, heavy, pendulous breasts hanging and visibly scarred from recent cuts or burns. Both the captives ceremonially festooned with chains of beads like a Xmas tree.

Prisoners. Crowds were aggregating on the sidewalk. I heard a whisper run through from mouth to mouth, ear to ear. This was the Pontchartrain Crew, and the two chained individuals were trespassers from another faction, who had strayed into their territory by the Lake. They would later at the end of Mardi-Gras festivities either be exchanged for similar hostages the other gangs might hold or, failing that, found unwanted, be sacrificed in an appropriate manner to the gang's chosen gods or deities.

Walking at a funeral pace behind the musicians and the prisoners were the gang members themselves. Armed to the teeth, all dressed in ceremonial white from head to toe, even their moccasin shoes, heads held high, all painted in war stripes, heads shaven clean, exuding menace from all their pores in this open demonstration of power.

I had a ton of questions I was begging to ask, but reasoned it was best not to interrogate any of the other onlookers standing around me for fear of advertising the fact I was a stranger in these parts, having no desire to end up in chains and paraded around the city myself in such a humiliating manner.

I was unable to cross the street while the Pontchartrain crew moved along and the gap between them and the next crew was insufficient, so I had to stay rooted in place while the next gang followed. From my scant knowledge of local folklore, I was unable to identify them, but they looked absolutely fearsome.

Their band, who outshone the preceding Pontchartrain gang in loudness and clarity, well-drilled, slick and strident even though they were half the number, were playing something I recognised by Arcade Fire. They were all dressed in jet black, like undertakers, their faces artfully made up to make them appear like skeletons or ghosts, eyes ringed with dark paint, lips almost blue and clown-like, hair wet and slicked back. The gang members in the following section of the parade were made up in a similar manner, all topless, even the women, their skin caked in dry mud, nipples pierced and ringed both men and women, thick gun belts cinching their waists and skin-tight jeans like a common uniform. Behind them, a large float which inched along the street, again under a cascade of beads hanging from the lorry's front cabin, fluttering around with every forward motion of the vehicle, and in the truck's bed four improvised wooden crucifixes had been raised and were held in place with steel pulleys, from each of which hung four pitiful forms, alternately clothed in rags or stark naked, more dead than alive, emaciated and similarly caked in dry mud which made identifying who was male and who was female difficult from my distance, although I was sure one was a woman from the length of her hanging hair.

In their position and condition, I thought it was unlikely they would even survive the next few hours of the parade if the sun came out in full force. The image of the crucified soul I had witnessed that terrible night in New York appeared in my mind and I shivered.

I felt a knot in my throat at the thought that I could end up like this. And, worse, the image of Vienna's face flashed in front of my eyes and the terrible possibility she might be the next sacrificial body in the next float in the parade. And that I might be helpless to do anything about it. And what about Giulia? All these dreadful thoughts boiled away inside my head, feeding my growing anxiety. It was all like a bad dream come to life.

There was a significant gap behind the float carrying the crucified prisoners and the next crew along the parade whose music was still an approaching echo, and I was able to rush across the narrow street and quickly forced my way through the crowds converging on the Mardi-Gras route, and reached Chartres.

I felt frantic, a wave of premonitions drowning any rational thoughts I might be able to conjure up, let alone express.

Even though it was early morning, the Napoleon House's doors were open and there were already small groups of customers drinking at tables or standing at the bar counter. Nothing closes for Mardi-Gras, I guessed. I didn't recognise the barman, a barrel-chested black guy I hadn't seen working here before. He ignored me as I rushed through the kitchen door and made for the back office. The door was locked. I knocked a few times, each time harder and louder than before, but to no effect.

Shearwater was not in. Maybe he was with the crowds somewhere watching the ongoing parade. I retraced my steps to the bar and asked the barman.

"Who is Shearwater?" he said. He had a lisp and it came out mangled.

"The owner, the guy who runs the place... He's always in the office at the back." I described him.

"No such person works here," he protested. "What sort of name is Shearwater, anyway? We haven't even got an office."

I felt that drowning feeling again.

I was also angry. I tried to control my temper and convinced him to leave his station for a minute and took him through the kitchen to the office door and showed him there was actually an office situated there. Maybe he only worked here on occasional shifts and wasn't aware of the place's layout. He looked at me as if I was crazy, not for the first time and pulled out a set of keys from his waistcoat pocket, scrutinised them and inserted the one he had selected into the door's Yale lock and opened. There was no office behind the door. Just some storage space for cleaning materials.

My throat was running dry.

I had been inside the damn office, spent hours there actually.

With Shearwater, with Vienna. I could describe every item of furniture in the room, the colour of the walls, the Rorschach-patterned stains in the ceiling. This was just crazy, defied the senses. Was I going mad?

I thanked the black barman and ran out of the Napoleon House, making a beeline to the side of the building where the stairs to the room we had been staying in were situated.

They were no longer there.

The wall was an undisturbed line of tightly-packed sienna-coloured bricks, with surviving shards of broken cladding hanging on in its far corners. There was no opening in sight.

Could never have been. Following all the other discoveries I had been making or the things I was encountering at almost every turn, this almost made sense. As if the joke being played on me was directed by some irrefutable logic of its own well beyond my comprehension.

I wandered for the rest of the day, unable to cope with the situation, steering as clear as I could from the Mardi-Gras parades weaving their way through the city in an unpredictable serpentine circuit. On every corner, the geography of the French Quarter seemed to be shifting, buildings, places I knew now moved or totally absent, the streets a quicksand of unreliable memories embedded through a problematic present.

Smoke rose in the distance, thin columns of smoke drifting upwards over the low rooftops like uncertain vertical clouds reaching for the vast sky. In my troubled circumstances, all I could think of were funeral pyres. Somehow, I had no wish to have that hypothesis confirmed or go anywhere close.

I found refuge on the other side of Canal, close to the old Casino now isolated behind high barbwire fences, in a small oyster bar where the coffee tasted artificial and acrid, or maybe it was the particles of smoke floating across the streets forcing their way down my throat. Finally, dusk came. I left the bar. The streets here were deserted, not a soul in sight, sounds of revelry echoing over from the other side of the Vieux Carré, music, the dull murmur of crowds and savage celebrations rising and falling.

I felt bone tired. But had nowhere to stay. I began walking north, always keeping the width of Canal Street between me and the Quarter until I reached the intersection with Ramparts and remembered the park. The weather was mild; maybe I could spend the night there? Would it be safe enough? In the morning I might be able to collect my thoughts and decide on some form of action, whatever the alternatives had become for the stranger in a strange land I had unwittingly become.

□ □ □

I woke in Louis Armstrong Park with renewed energy, wiped away the dirt from my clothes. I had slept sitting against the wall of the bandstand but must at some stage have slid down to the ground, and my slacks were damp around the ankles. I reckoned it could have been worse and I could well have been assaulted or robbed.

I retraced my steps to yesterday's oyster bar and, a sucker for punishment, had another coffee. It hadn't improved overnight. I also gulped down a couple of doughnuts to pacify my empty stomach and proceeded at a brisk pace towards the magician's gallery.

Somehow, I knew his lair would still be where it had previously been and not vanished into thin air, even if he was a master in the art of disappearing.

It was. And was also closed. I rapped repeatedly on the glass door but there was no response. Neither he or his curious assistant appeared to be present.

I crouched down and decided to wait. I had no other alternative. I had to learn to be patient.

Time flew by. The French Quarter was slowly coming back to life after the excesses of the previous day and night, passers-by strolling past me with no interest in my presence, like daytime ghosts with an unknown agenda.

I'm unsure how long I dozed off for, but I was shaken out of a low-level daydream,—in which I was still a child and pestering my aunt for a peanut butter sandwich on the day of my mother's funeral and being chided for my lack of sensitivity,—by the gentle nudge of a foot against my side. I brushed the sleep away from my eyes and looked up. It was the magician. He looked down at me with amusement but no hint of surprise in his eyes.

"An early visitor, I see," Wallace remarked.

I pulled myself up.

"We need to talk."

He nodded as I moved away from the door to allow him to unlock it.

"That's not a problem," he said, pushing the door open and dropping the long, golden key he had used into his waistcoat pocket. It was only then that I became conscious of the way he was dressed today. He wore a dapper Panama hat and an immaculately white linen suit with golden coin-like buttons, his waistcoat was a rainbow of colours, an orchestra of shimmering sequins in perpetual movement, a skinny turquoise green tie hung from his neck against the equally detergent white of his frilly shirt, and his tall boots were polished to within an inch of a diamond-like shine and reached all the way up to his knees.

"Your professional attire?" I said.

"Mardi-Gras is always a busy time for me," the magician said.

We stepped into the art gallery that served as his headquarters.

"Aren't you locking up behind us?" I queried.

"There is nothing to steal," Wallace said. I looked around at the piles of prints and frames piled around the floor and hanging on the walls, and the glass cabinets with all sorts of shiny paraphernalia and must have looked dubious. "Anyway, no one would dare," he added.

We moved into his small office.

"No assistant today?"

"She comes and she goes," the magician said. "She was a bit of a naughty girl, the other day, passing you information I hadn't yet decided you were ready for..." he smiled.

I thought it wise not to respond.

"So?" he looked up at me.

"I want to know what the fuck is happening."

"Is that all?"

"It would be a beginning."

"You do have a point, I suppose. Although I'm unsure what help the information would be to you," the magician said.

"Try me."

He sat there thinking. Took his hat off and set it down on the otherwise empty desk.

"So how is the lovely Tiffany?" he asked.

"I think she now prefers to be known as Cherise."

"Of course," he said. "But for me, she will always be Tiffany. I just adore her photos. Did you know I probably own the last remaining complete set? The Commander would be annoyed if he only knew. You must never tell him, of course. I particularly love the images that came out of the sessions she did for the late, much-unlamented Hilton Willis. The girl pees in public with such wonderful abandon, makes her look almost innocent. Ah, that spine stretched under the skin, the pallor, the exquisite curves of her arse. So delightful. And those with the hand-marks still adorning her butt cheeks, that almost perfect equilibrium between the red indentations and the white of her skin. Hmmm... I've always wondered what goes through the minds of women when they are being spanked. Never done it myself. Such a pity she came here to turn a new leaf. Oh well..."

"She told me you knew the Commander. The connection with the Dark?"

"Oh, that..."

He looked me straight in the eyes.

"I thought it was the other girl who was your main concern," he said. "Not Tiffany. Or the problems caused by the Commander's stupid interference and ambitions."

"Giulia."

"That is indeed the name she adopted when I sent her to New York. Normally, my assistants don't actually require a name. Makes no sense. They're just pretty creatures I summon from the Crossroads."

"You sent her?"

"She was my previous assistant, you know. I needed someone in Manhattan to keep an eye on Commander Helmsmark. To ensure he kept his mouth shut about the events that led to the Dark."

I interrupted him. "What do you mean, you summon your assistants? From where?"

"From the other side," he said.

A pit opened under me.

"You don't believe in magic, do you?" he continued.

"It's all sleight of hand and smokes and mirrors, I believe, with all due respect to your profession..."

"What about the supernatural?"

I had felt this question coming. Had you asked me the same one a few weeks earlier, I would have been adamant in my rejection. Now I was troubled. So many things that made absolutely no sense had occurred, that I was wavering on the edge of what I had once considered fundamental reality.

My life had once been normal and then, overnight, had turned into a pulp novel. Was I ready to accept I had now turned a further page and become a helpless protagonist in a ghost tale?

That I was drifting on the waves of popular fiction, tossed around by the whims of the impossible.

"I see the seeds of doubt have been sown," the magician said, noting my evident disarray.

For the next half-an-hour, I was like a studious schoolboy sitting at attention on his wooden bench listening to the teacher explain matters new, finding it difficult to process news that made him examine his own life and the whole world he lived in, in a new way.

The magician's family had emigrated all the way from Quebec down to Louisiana a couple of centuries ago. They were authentic Acadians, who in the fullness of time became the Cajuns who thrived in this new environment, as much as the mudbugs, the crawfish that had allegedly also made the long journey down the Mississippi River to the Gulf of Mexico.

Their new land was already steeped in legends and superstition from successive waves of arrivals and interlopers, the native folk whose memories were immemorial and were at one with the nearby swamps and Badlands of Florida, the Spanish, the French, the whole spirit of the warm Caribbean seas nearby, bloods mixing, beliefs entwining with each other's in a climate that bred madness, Catholicism facing up to Voodoo traditions, irrationality leaking into the fabric of everyday life.

It was a place where anything could happen and often did.

Legends abounded.

Of old Gods, of new Gods, of the way the dead were still mysteriously a part of the living, an invisible foundation stone of the land, through which they travelled, unseen by most but casting a net of wonder over others, communicating, interfering, secretly running affairs even.

It had all become part and parcel of the way the city and the region had acquired its alluring image beyond its physical frontiers: gaudy, dangerous, a set of attractors dutifully enhanced by the delights of his music, its food and the inviting atmosphere it conjured, a tourist attraction with the right balance of risk and delight.

And so it had been for generations. But, for some, the old truths had never disappeared or become a glittering mirage behind the commercial facade on view to the outside world.

They believed in the old Gods, or the Devil, or whatever held the balance of power. The magician's folk were amongst them.

The true believers.

They knew there was something intangible beneath the voodoo shop, juju talismans, magic powders, feathers and beads of folklore.

They became the conduit between the forgotten world and ours, protectors of both realms. Monitoring the peace between magic and reality.

Obtained powers which they concealed from others in order to freeze the status quo, using it in moderation and with discretion to maintain that exquisite balance that kept the world on an even keel.

Magic was one manifestation. The ability to communicate with the dead another. But they knew it was best to live in the shadows and not advertise these minor powers or, worse, acquire greater ones which they knew most would be unable to control.

But no secrets eternally remain so.

Words slip out. Drink, envy, the fear of physical death, vanity are all powerful instruments of revelation.

On most occasions, it all turns out to be quite harmless and the revelations are not taken seriously or just considered to be a bunch of lies, tall stories to keep the children entertained, campfire tales, speculation, obfuscation. There is no evidence.

But people have ears, and too many coincidences over the decades soon alert the uninvited.

Commander Helmsmark was one. A man of towering ambition. Imbued with the conviction that he was born to rule, but unconcerned with the normal trappings of power: politics, mere money, the Presidency. A man who burned with an inner fire, an obsession to control.

Rumours had reached him.

He had come to New Orleans.

Met the magician and some of his colleagues in the vast conspiracy of silence. Engineered his way into their trust, then forced them to reveal where the physical portal was which connected our world with the next, the Crossroads, a tenuous Rubicon they had protected for centuries. In the hope it would become a new source of power and control.

It had gone horribly wrong. As if nature, or the powers below had recognized the falseness, the selfishness of his intentions and violently rejected him.

As if something or someone on the other side had surmised his intentions or the blackness of his heart and unleashed a terrible punishment on his world for daring to even try and manipulate them.

"The Dark?"

"Yes."

It made sense. In a twisted way. Few people had ever believed the authorities' explanations, the sunspots, the surge of electromagnetism that had knocked things out, it was all too pat.

"So, he was partly responsible?"

He bowed his head with an air of sadness.

"Is that also why Cherise ended up down here?"

"Maybe. She is his blood; it runs deep the attraction."

I wanted to unbelieve. Return to the comforts of reality.

"So, what now?" I asked the magician.

"It's a stand-off. He has retreated. Maybe he is still plotting but in the meantime it's been a terrible warning for us not to interfere with the balance of things…and so it should be."

"He's an angry man, a dangerous man," I said.

"We're sadly aware of the fact. We should never have welcomed him or led him to the point of passage..."

"The point of passage?"

"There is a place where a bridge stands that separates our two worlds, the real and the unreal one. In legend, it's the gate to hell, but that's just being melodramatic. It's fluid. Neither an actual bridge nor a gate or a door. Just a form of portal. Some can move between the planes of existence at their will; others with more difficulty, while some will never be able to do so. We've never understood the rules, if rules they are."

Something was bothering me. Which he had said earlier.

"Your assistants?"

"Exactly."

"That doesn't answer my question."

"You'd... hinted they came from the... other side... I just don't understand that."

"It's complicated... "

"And Giulia was one?"

"Yes."

"But neither she, nor your present assistant who saw me in on my first visit here, were, how should I put it, insubstantial. They were women, flesh and blood, not spirits or ghosts."

"Indeed. They can be what they wish to be. After the Dark, they all returned back to where they had come from. It's only recently, now that matters have settled down, that some are returning. But, still, they come and go for no apparent reason. They walk among us, you could say, but they never say why. Look just like us. Normal. I said I summoned them and that's not quite right. The thought occurs to me that I am in need of an assistant when I am asked to work my sleight of hand, and sometimes one appears and stays for a few weeks, and at other times doesn't, as if my need is being responded to, judged valid or not. She was called Eurydice, or at any rate, it was the name she wanted to be known as..."

"And the one I came to know, did she also call herself Giulia, when she worked for you?"

"She had many names," the magician said.

"I loved her, you know."

"I'm not surprised. She was delightfully charming. But all of them are just women, visitors, tourists from the Crossroads.

They have no magic powers, as if once they cross into our world they become human, flesh and blood, emotions, they assimilate."

"I have to see her again. Hear her part of the story. Why, after working with you, she came to New York. And why, of all people, she met up with me..." I wanted to also say that she had stayed a little while and had changed my reasons for living, but I was sure the magician also knew that. He knew a lot of things, I realised, in his quiet, unassuming manner.

"I think it would be better if you just accepted the state of things," he said.

"I'm unwilling to do that," I answered with determination, almost surprising myself. "Where can I find this point of passage?"

"It will find you," the magician said.

16 - THE PRICE TO PAY

The trail was growing cold.

It had been several weeks since I had consulted the magician. I had found a place to stay at night on Conti, a large top floor room which a passing acquaintance in a Bourbon Street bar had made me aware of. The door didn't have a key, but then I had no belongings to speak of. The French Quarter was full of abandoned locales and, in the absence of outside visitors, squatting was neither frowned upon let alone generally noticed.

I had come here with Vienna to seek out two other women.

Vienna had gone, one of the women no longer wanted to have anything to do with me, and the third one, the most important one, was just the rumour of a rumour.

Spring was getting closer and the heavy curtain of humidity was rising.

Drunks ambled up and down the narrow pavements of Iberville Street clutching cans of beer or empty bottles of cheap whatever. Piles of refuse mounted on the sidewalks, overflowing with oyster shells from the nearby Acme Bar, one of the Vieux Carré's institutions which had seemingly not been affected by the catastrophe or the secession of the state from the rest of the United States.

I crossed an empty Royal and made my way towards Decatur.

For some time, I had been spending a few hours on most days, unless my morale had hit a cyclical low and my heart just wasn't in it, consulting dusty old tomes about the city, its past and traditions in the vast cavern of Beckham's Bookstore, a used book emporium which had survived to this day even though it was seldom full of customers or the curious. The young guy at the desk with the Voodoo Gang earring tolerating my presence as he listened to music on his earphones. He never told me his name but when he heard that I was investigating New Orleans lore, he proved most helpful, allowing me to peruse even dustier tomes kept in the glass display cabinet or behind lock and key, and when my research more often than not hit a brick wall, gave me directions to the Historical Museum beyond the French Market where rarer volumes might be found which could provide me with answers.

Doctor Gustawsson was standing on the corner, sheltering from the rising heat of the day under an awning. As if he had been waiting for me for ages.

Slung over his shoulder was a cavernous Strand Bookshop tote bag. I somehow guessed there were no books in it. Call it gut instinct. Under his black leather ankle-length coat, he was similarly dressed in black slacks and a black cashmere long-armed sweater.

"Our young investigator," he remarked, looking in my direction. "A man who asks a lot of questions."

I nodded to him, acknowledging his presence and, without a further word, we walked on to the nearest bar on the corner of Bienville and Decatur.

He ordered. We drank. He paid.

Within minutes I knew the trail I had been following for some days had grown cold as ice. The Italian girl who'd been glimpsed a month or so before by a contact of his—a student hard up on her luck who was stripping in the top rooms of local disreputable clubs to make ends meet, and was on the slippery, druggy slide to oblivion—was not the one I sought. She was blonde and called Grazia, or at any rate that's the name he had been given, but more importantly, she was blonde. An easy case of mistaken identity what with the nationality and closeness of the name to Giulia's.

"Maybe she's dyed her hair?" I suggested to him, "and is using another name?" I was clutching at straws.

Gustawsson roared with laughter, and thin pearls of beer spluttered in a falling arc from his open mouth all the way across to the shoulder of my jacket. He was a fair few inches taller than me.

"The lass was stripping, young man. I'm a doctor, I can assure you she was a natural blonde," he winked at me, mischief illuminating his now ruddy face, as the alcohol infiltrated his bloodstream. "This Italian dancer stood out, you know. As a lover of beauty, I remain observant. Most working girls like to shave down there, you see. She didn't. She was different..."

I was about to interject, but he silenced me.

"Nah, I can tell when a woman colours her pubes, young man. Looks damn unnatural, if you see what I mean," he gulped down another sip of beer. "And I had a front seat view. Real blonde. You could tell. No doubt about it. Absolutely."

He put his glass down on the bar counter and smiled. No doubt recalling the proximity of Grazia's pudenda. Waxing rhapsodic as he attempted to explain his certainty. "The colour of the skin around, the inner folds of the cunt a touch darker, the curls, the hair, it all sort of conjugates, you just sort of know when part of it is artificial..."

A thin veil of hopelessness began rippling in my mind. I was getting nowhere fast. Again.

"Hmmm," I muttered under my breath. My glass of orange juice was empty.

Gustawsson jettisoned his obscene memories and gave me a sharp look.

"I'm sorry, young man."

All of a sudden it felt to me that a terrible weight had fallen across my shoulders, that I had finally reached the last dead end.

Had I not been in a public place, I would have allowed the tears welling up inside my eyes to flow.

"Just forget her, young man," Gustawsson said. "There are other women. The world is full of them."

"But some are special..." I interjected.

"You can say that again," he remarked, with a deep sigh. "I gather you've been consorting with our friend the magician?"

"Yes."

"So, you know the story of his assistants?"

"Not that I believe it completely," I pointed out. "It's too extraordinary. Neither does it make sense. These women who come from another realm and, in their exile, become all too human..."

"Exactly..."

"According to him, Giulia was one of them. I just find it so difficult to believe. I knew her well and there was just no hint of anything of that nature. She was warm, loving, young... Real."

"Hmmm..." Dr Gustawsson muttered, as if approving of my words. "But isn't the concept just fascinating: another species of woman. What I would give to see inside one, examine her, analyse her, dissect her, peer into her eyes, establish how she might be different..."

"That sounds ghoulish," I said to him.

"Maybe..."

He looked at me briefly as if he wanted to ask me a host of questions about Giulia, but then a shadow passed across his eyes and he drew back.

"Let me get you another drink before we both go our own ways," he suggested.

I was tired. "Why not?"

I took a long sip of the glass he had brought me, while he downed his cognac, and I knew straight away there was something wrong with it. The taste had a bitter streak. He'd drugged me.

A whirlpool of questions raced through my mind as I lost rapid control of my body and my consciousness receded.

□ □ □

I knew I was dreaming but it also felt all too real. Shards of truth merged with fantasies until everything blurred.

It would be midnight in an hour or so, and the streets were still fat with crowds, milling shiftlessly, ambling, parading up and down with drinks in tow as the night deepened. It was getting colder and I turned my coat's collar up. I quickly left the bright lights of Bourbon behind me and reached the darkened block where the club was situated.

The doorway beckoned.

I was recognised from my previous visit and allowed into the courtyard. I approached the main building and entered. Things were still quiet.

It was like a mirror image of my first time here, the same stripper indolently shaking her bones on stage, a gaggle of bored punters struggling to keep their eyes open. A moment in time fixed in amber. I sat myself down in the same alcove and waited for the next stage turn, in the vain hope it might prove to be Cherise. But she didn't make an appearance. Instead, a squat, thunder-thighed teenager whose body was a canvas of unnatural piercings and tattoos lumbered into the spotlight and began going through the motions of lust according to her own diminished standards.

I somehow intuited that Eurydice must be upstairs, or at least that's where her office might be. Having studied the ground floor's geography, there could be no other alternative.

I waited until none of the staff were looking and slipped through the side door marked 'Private', which I knew was on the way to the washrooms. Sighed in relief: it wasn't locked.

Peering through semidarkness I noted a flight of wooden stairs. I walked up its steps. On the first floor to the right, what sounded like a private drinking room. Quiet noises of glasses clinking on counters and serious drinkers mumbling against a background of muffled traditional music. A welcoming night shrouded the deep room. And the prevalent smell of stale beer. Not my favourite fragrance.

Beyond the landing, the stairs continued. Which didn't make any sense, as from the courtyard the building housing the club had no further storeys. But by now, nothing surprised me in the French Quarter any longer.

Further upwards, a gallery on each side of the stairs of yellowing posters advertising long forgotten House of Blues gigs featuring prestigious artists from the past and Blues idols in black and white. Finally, I reached the top.

A sliver of light beneath a closed door. I moved towards it.

Listened. Utter silence on the other side of the door. I knocked.

There was no response. Standing there, I felt a deep chill in the air. Knocked again.

This time there was a rustle of fabric beyond the closed door, then steps. The door opened.

"Yes?"

It was a woman's voice, not that I could see a damn thing in the heavy penumbra spreading beyond the threshold. There was a soft country accent to her voice. Not local to Louisiana.

"I'm seeking Eurydice," I said.

At first, she didn't react to my question.

I waited. There was no point repeating myself.

The darkness lifted in part. I began to see her eyes. Green. Catlike. Piercing.

"Which one?" she finally answered.

"Just Eurydice," I said.

"There are many of us," she answered, as if surprised I was not aware of the fact.

"I don't know," I indicated. "I was sent here. I was only provided with her name. As someone who could assist me. I have some questions I need answered."

"Ah..." she paused. "In that case, it's one of my other sisters you need."

Her eyes backed off towards the furthest end of the dark room.

And another set of eyes neared. As green and piercing. It might as well have been the same woman, since all I could distinguish in the surrounding darkness were her eyes. The shadow approached me. Loomed. There was something familiar about her.

"And what is it you wanted to know?" Her voice was sharper, sustained by quiet anger.

By now I was becoming used to the darkness inside the dank room. I had begun to distinguish her shape. Tall, wild-haired, a velvet robe of indeterminate colour ending at her feet.

"There's a young girl. Italian. She's been seen around here. I seek her."

The woman sighed.

And it came to me: this was April Lea... Although her eyes had not been such a distinctive green on our previous encounters.

Definitely not. It was her and then it wasn't her. Go figure.

"Then it's another of our sisters you require," she said.

How many of them were there, I wondered, the whole sister charade beginning to get on my nerves. But she did not retreat, standing her ground. I waited for her to say more. But she failed to do so. Just quizzically peering at me through the silence, as if this was the first time we had come face to face.

"And is your third sister here?" I asked.

"We are not three. We are many," she replied.

"Should I wait for her?" I enquired.

"That's entirely up to you," the initial sister said, her green eyes now shining at me, beside her sister, like parallel sets of beacons on a highway night. Now that I was becoming increasingly familiar with the darkness, I was beginning to see both of them better. Had it not been for the remarkable eyes, one was the mirror image of April Lea, in her stance, body movements and lingering sense of menace. Contact lenses, maybe? The other was slight in build, but similar, with a petulant turn of the lips that reminded me a little of Vienna.

"In that case, I shall wait," I said to the two of them.

A pale light came on as she flipped a switch on the wall to our left. A meagre 30-watt bulb illuminated the room. It was larger than I imagined.

As the meagre light revealed the room in which we all stood, there was a sudden movement in the corner of my eye. I just caught the swift movement of a small black bird racing across the room just below the ceiling. A crow. But when I looked for it again, it was nowhere to be seen. Maybe a trick of the pale light.

The two sisters were clothed in identical garb. Heavy, green cloaks almost like monks' cloaks. Tall, slender but what stood out most was the burning fire of the first woman's hair. Myriads of untamed curls clustered together as well as exploding like a galaxy of circular stars in every possible direction, as if her head had never felt the caress or the pull of a comb or a hairbrush.

For a brief moment, I thought of Medusa and the representations of the twisted divinity I had come across in books and paintings. And indeed, standing there in sepulchral silence, gazing at me, they were truly in the image of goddesses.

Imperious. Returned to Earth. Or was it the other way around and she had risen to the surface from the depths of hell, or wherever this mythical other side she was a product of lay.

April Lea was as blonde as ever, but in similar exploded-like disarray. Her gaze was unstinting. Full of anger. Like a goddess of war.

And then there was the new arrival. Slight. Short-haired but carried along by the same halo of fierceness. My breath stopped.

It was Vienna. But from the way she looked at me, intent, on her guard, it was evident she did not recognize me.

One of them spoke.

"There will be a price to pay," she said. I no longer knew which of the three women had uttered the words, my mind in complete meltdown as all the terrible contradictions of the moment overwhelmed me.

There was a strange coldness, almost indifference in her tone of voice.

"I know," I replied. "If it means I can see Giulia again, any price will be worth paying."

Vienna smiled. My glance ran across her two companions.

They were smiling too. Wise, enigmatic, ironic.

The suddenly amplified sounds of bacchanalian oceans of drunkards parading further down Bourbon Street outside began to fade in the distance, as if banished in time, the whole world rearranging itself into a new configuration.

"So be it," the three sisters whispered in unison.

They moved towards me. Steps in unison. Three silhouettes merging into a single cloud, fragrant, hypnotic.

A different sort of music appeared to replace the confused, faraway sounds of blues, rock and zydeco in the distance or filtering upwards from the club's dance floor. Like an ancient, alien melody rising from the depths of time.

They were now so close to me that I could smell their breath.

Eurydice. April Lea. Vienna. Or versions of them.

Sweet, strong, intoxicating.

In one rapid movement, they both shed their cloaks and stood naked, facing me.

I drank in the regal pallor of their skin, the jutting angles of their breasts, the way their lower deltas shared the same shade of fire that adorned their heads.

It was beauty untamed. Consuming. Dangerous.

"Pay the price," one of them said.

I undressed.

They converged toward me in a single coordinated movement and smothered me in their embrace.

□ □ □

When I awoke in the bleak cold morning, the memories of the past night made me retch, as if the abominable obscenities of what we had all done had literally sucked my soul out and spat it back into my body forever deformed, tainted.

In no way did it feel as if it had been a dream.

As we had fiercely fucked, as they shared me among themselves, they had feasted on my flesh, my secretions, my emotions and left me empty, an abandoned shell of a man.

I knew they were creatures from another world, that the feminine beauty of their appearance was just a cloak of deceit, that the forms they had taken had, all along, been designed to deceived and baffle me. But also enchant me. No matter.

Goosebumps spread across my naked flesh. My penis looked even more shrivelled than ever, the surface of my skin a terrible shade of grey. I looked around for the clothes I had shed and dressed quickly, as if ashamed of my pitiful nudity, as if I had been used.

I remembered little of our lovemaking, save the tangle of limbs, the gaping of openings, the hunger of their kisses, but what I did clearly recall were the strange dreams I had travelled through shortly after between the repeated fucks, images of bloody battlefields, of despair and pestilence, war and pain. And surveying our intimate pornography in motion was the bird, the crow, flying high above the battleground as if giving us his blessing, his damnation, his approval.

I shook the torpor out of my limbs as I tied my shoelaces and straightened my crumpled trousers.

Checked my pockets. The gun was still there, as were the Louisiana credits I still owned; nothing had been taken from me.

So why did I feel I was now less of a man?

And I remembered about Giulia.

The reason for my quest.

Paused for a moment's thought.

Looked around the now empty bar room I had woken in as a thin sliver of daytime peered hesitantly through the crack of a shuttered window in the far corner. There was a sheet of paper lying on the dirty wooden floor. The same filthy floor I had spent hours writhing on, rolling around, thrusting, being spread and flayed by the women's sexual greed.

I walked over.

It was just a crumpled sheet with rough drawings of an eel, a wolf and a cow. A curious trinity of animals. A child's bestiary? I peered at the page again. Turned it round.

On the back of the sketch was a map of the nearby bayous.

With a pencilled cross seemingly designating the intersection of two roads.

An address?

Their parting gift. I knew I would never see them again. They had returned to the other side. For good, I knew; don't ask me why.

I made my way to the door and the stairs and holding unsteadily on to the rail stepped hesitantly down the stairs. The ground floor area of the club was empty, but the front door unlocked and I stepped out into the courtyard. The magnolia leaves were unfolding to greet the morning.

Outside, on Bourbon two hundred yards further down the road, the smell of booze still lingered in the air. Here and there, men with bloodshot eyes stumbled along the road, sometimes accompanied by hiccupping young women with short skirts hiked even higher, vulgar, hungover. This was the landscape after the bacchanalia. But did I look any better, I wondered?

I stole a bike which had not been chained to a railing. I had no other options as the location I had was clearly out of town.

It took me the best of two hours to get there. A crossroads in the middle of nowhere. Wasn't this where the legend told us that Robert Johnson met the devil himself? I was in a sweat and every muscle in my body screaming for relief.

The actual farmhouse was a stone's throw from the roads and the only building standing as far as the eye could see and I made my way towards it. Stepping through the dry mud led me to an outer building, a sort of barn.

The man was still sleeping. Snoring loudly, empty bottles were strewn across the ground, his attire in disarray. In one corner, a naked woman, hands cuffed to a low beam, hung like a puppet.

As if crucified.

I stopped breathing.

I tiptoed silently towards her.

Dark blood still dripped down to the straw-covered floor of the barn from between her legs.

I pushed her chin up gently so that I could see her face.

Her eyes were open.

It was Giulia.

She was dead.

Her dyed-blonde hair hung limply, the ebony roots clearly showing through her centre parting, curls like funeral wreaths.

It was the Italian girl Gustawsson had described. But he had lied to me. About the true colour of her hair.

I had no need to check her genitalia to confirm Gustawsson's lies. I would have recognised Giulia anywhere, regardless of her hair colour. I knew every contour of her body, every mole and blemish, every square inch of silken skin and more. Not that I could actually see much due to the horrendous mutilations she had suffered there.

I felt sick to the core.

I closed her eyes as delicately as I could. There were dried tears on her cheeks, like tiny diamonds now shining in the emerging light of the day through the open door of the barn.

I turned towards the sleeping man.

It was, of course, Gustawsson.

How could I have not guessed?

I took my gun, my blood at boiling point but steadied my aim and depressed the trigger.

Nothing.

It was out of bullets.

I'd never even bothered to check.

I kept my calm. No way was I going to abandon my resolve.

I picked up a pitchfork and with no hesitation dug it deep into his gut. He woke up, a look of pain and despair spreading across his distorted features. I pulled the pitchfork out in one rapid movement and then plunged it straight into his face. The noise it made as it embedded itself in his flesh was one I would never forget. Strange how killing was becoming second nature to me.

He never had the chance to utter a single word.

Not that I required any explanation.

I searched for the key to the handcuffs still holding Giulia's dead body up but couldn't find it in the dead man's pockets.

I just couldn't allow her to be found this way, strung up, defiled. There was a can of petrol in the nearby garage. The whole place would be consumed before anyone in the area even spotted the fire. Better that way.

The blaze was beautiful, flames rising high towards the sun as the barn shattered and crumpled, a funeral pyre worthy of an Egyptian God.

I sat watching the conflagration, dusk came and ashes hung in the air until the winds from the bayou rose and carried them towards the river and then the sea and it was time for me to go.

I walked back to New Orleans with bile burning sharp in my throat. My thoughts frozen in place, balancing between despair and abominable sadness.

Yes, Eurydice and her sisters had been right. There had been a price to pay.

□ □ □

When I went to visit the magician, the following day, he didn't appear surprised. He already seemed to be aware of most of the recent developments.

"You came across three of my former assistants in one night? You certainly have been a busy man," he remarked, as I sat myself down in the pokey office at the back of the art gallery.

Today he was wearing a pin-striped suit, a scarlet bow tie, and a pair of horn-rimmed spectacles were perched high on his forehead, holding his hair back.

I nodded, feeling too exhausted to even respond.

"I'm sorry," he said.

Whether he was saying that because of Giulia or just seeing me in such a state of dejection, I wasn't sure.

"It's over," I finally said. "There's nothing left for me down here. But I haven't a clue as to how to get back to New York," I added.

"Maybe there is no longer a New York to return to," the magician said.

"Who cares?"

"So, what do you plan to do now? Although I must declare I have no pressing need for male assistants," he added, a faint smile racing across his lips.

He looked at me with genuine concern.

Pondered at length.

"You could start anew, you know..."

"Sorry?"

"New Orleans can be a beautiful place, if you ignore some of its obvious drawbacks and the silliness of all these gang wars; I expect they will soon come to an end anyway, when they all come to their senses. Balance has a way of re-establishing itself of its own accord, I find. Or maybe with a suitable nudge here and there..."

"I should stick around?" I asked him.

"Why not?"

He stood up, brought out a bottle of amber liquid and two glasses from out of nowhere. Poured us a drink each. Whatever it was it would taste better than a rabbit, I supposed.

The bourbon was strong but warmed my body. I'd needed it.

"Too many memories," I said. "Things I've seen, experienced. I'd be reminded daily, on every street corner, little things here and there. It's inescapable," I pointed out.

"Even if it was possible to escape back to New York, wouldn't the situation there present you with the same problems?" he said.

I reflected.

"You're right."

"There is a solution," the magician said. "It's not foolproof, but you might be interested."

"Tell me."

"The oldest form of magic. I could make those bad memories go away... It doesn't always work and pieces of them stick around like bad pennies, but they would feel no more than dreams."

"More sleight of hand?"

"You could say that."

I thought long and hard. Was it the only way out of the nightmare? Would I wake the same man or a different one? At any rate, I wasn't that fond of the man I had become or even had initially been...

"Do it," I said to the magician.

If he'd smiled in reaction to my demand, ironically or not, I would have punched him in the face. As it is, he didn't. He just looked sad as he raised his hands towards me and opened his mouth...

17 - NEW ORLEANS WHEN IT RAINS

Some cities smell of diesel fumes, others of cats, and then there is the smell of the sea, or mown grass, or the sharp odour of curry cooking endlessly in basement flats, or again the acrid combination of industrial waste and low-hanging fog.

New Orleans smells of spices, the humid twang of nearby Mississippi bayous and swamps and, in early morning, the unpleasant waft of stale beer on the Bourbon Street sidewalk following yet another night of drunkenness and minor league wildness before the high-speed hoses complete their work and sweep away the detritus of the previous evening's boisterous excesses. Mardi-Gras adds yet another dimension of smells and spills and noise, or the Jazz Festival or New Year's Eve when it can take almost a quarter of an hour to walk through the massed crowds from Jackson Square to the corner of Toulouse and Bourbon. A cocktail like no other.

Even the music rising from bar to bar on each side of the street, battling for your attention, blues against jazz, show-tunes fighting hard rock, Broadway schmaltz wrestling with tentative folk melodies, it all seems to hold yet more fragrant promise of sensuality unbound.

There is no place like New Orleans.

It was a city that talked to me, whispered to me from far away, its seductive voice reaching the melancholy shores of my soul.

Some cities are male. Others are distinctly feminine. New Orleans was assuredly the latter.

The way it tempted you, licked you, kissed your emotions, sultrily caressed your soul, fed you with sumptuous plates of jambalaya, warmed your stomach with okra—sticky but succulent bowls of gumbo and its raw oysters, once chucked open, made you think of a woman's cunt as you sucked on them with undisguised greed and swallowed their juice and spongey flesh in one swift and easy movement.

It was a city I had brought women to.

Often.

In a spacious 12th floor room at the Monteleone, I had undressed a preacher's wife from the Baton Rouge suburbs I had met on the Internet. Which only goes to show how far back in time this was. She had driven down in her SUV to join me and timidly tapped on my shoulder while I examined the shelves at Beckham's on Decatur, where you could once often find some interesting first editions amongst the morass of worthless book club editions. That was where we had arranged to meet. I turned around.

"It's you?" Comparing what she saw with an old snap I had sent her, early in our dialogue.

"Hi..."

She was voluptuous, a lovely face, somewhat bigger than I had expected from the photos she had sent me, but I knew those curves and the demure clothes she was wearing concealed terribly guilty urges and a determination to be bad.

Once in the hotel bedroom I stripped her and buried my face between her high but generous breasts, licked and bit her nipples to gauge her reaction while I cupped her cunt with my hands.

She was terribly wet. Her kisses tasted of cotton candy.

When I undressed, she looked down at my half tumescent cock and exclaimed that it was so big. Which warmed my heart of course, although I knew it wasn't particularly so, just that her husband's (she had known no other man, she had once confessed) happened to be smaller.

I drowned in the folds of her flesh, my thrusts inside the cauldron of her innards setting off concentric waves of shimmering movement across the surface of her skin.

We fucked ceaselessly, between walks through the Vieux Carré in search of beignets and praline-led sustenance. She only had two free days before family duties required her to be home.

"Where have you told him you are?" My finger inserting itself into her anus, feeling her squirm with added pleasure.

"It's not important. I don't want to talk about him." Her regal thighs clinching me in a mighty vice, her hand roaming hungrily across my balls, nail extensions dangerously grazing me.

Even though she lived barely a couple of hours away, it was only her third time ever in New Orleans. A city of sin that represented everything that was evil in the eyes of her social set.

Which made her brief affair with me even more of a thing of the night, and a temptation her frustrations had been unable to resist. Meeting a strange man with a quaint accent for purposes of the flesh in such a den of iniquity somehow felt right. We would never meet again after those frantic two days but before we lost contact I heard that she had left her husband and shacked up with a pharmaceutical salesman who was happy to fuck her once a day at least unlike the monthly diet her religious fanatic of a man had restricted himself to, and always in the dark at that. I had, inadvertently lit the fire and set her on the right (or wrong) path.

Then there was Natalia, a Lithuanian waif and single parent who had moved from Delft in Holland to Manhattan in search of a better life, who became a regular fuck buddy. My evocative tales of New Orleans and its sweet craziness had convinced her to accompany me south. She made it a regular habit to meet men she came across in chat rooms and I knew all too well I was not her only sexual companion. (I was aware of the Korean business student she had been giving Russian lessons to; the English engineering export rep; the married car dealer who wanted to leave his wife and live with her; and the many others she had no doubt omitted to inform me about).

She also fell in love with New Orleans. The hotel I had booked us into upgraded us to a suite and she wandered naked and free across the lush carpet, the angle below her pert white buttocks always just that touch apart, a sheer invitation to grab her and do my worst. She was playful, capricious, deliciously wanton. No post-coital sadness for Natalia: the moment I'd withdraw from her following each frantic fuck, she was up and about, eager to go out and sample more French Quarter atmosphere, tip-toeing away from the bed towards the open window and looking out from the balcony in the buff, attracting whistles and cries from the street beneath on most occasions, and then rushing back with a cheeky smile on her face at having exposed herself and straddling me, or standing above my still exhausted form on the bed, her legs obscenely spread, affording me a voyeuristic close-up of her still wet cunt and her luxuriant and curly dark pubic thatch.

One morning, she had arranged for a local pen pal to pick her up from the hotel in his car. We shook hands, both introduced to each other as just friends. He was supposed to take her for a drive along the nearby bayous, but I suspect they spent most of that morning in his bed. No matter, it gave me a handful of hours to rest.

In my memory, Natalia and New Orleans went hand in hand in perfect harmony. The fragrance of Southern flowers, magnolias et al., and the intoxicating smell of her body. The delicate curlicues of wrought steel of the Crescent City balconies and architecture and the cheerful curve of her snubbed nose and the gap between her front teeth. The Queen of the blow jobs who always insisted on going pantie-less when we went out for walks or to eat. I stayed in touch with her for a long time, until she returned to Europe shortly before the Dark. Good timing.

She finally gave in to his advances and actually married the car dealer and had a son with him, although I later learned it hadn't worked out and they were now separated.

Another bittersweet New Orleans memory is the Finnish interpreter from Seattle. High cheekbones, square jaw and a monstrous tease, it took me ages to finally get her into bed proper (days of foreplay and petting until she finally agreed that having spent an eternity in bed naked together, we should finally fuck...).

She knew of my attraction to New Orleans and suggested I join her there; she was in town for a conference and had a large room in one of the massive impersonal hotels on Canal Street, with a view of the Mississippi from her window.

By then, she was beginning to lose her looks and I was no longer as much attracted to her, I must shamefully confess, but the lure of New Orleans was too much to turn the opportunity down. I entered her from behind, her pale body squashed against the bay window, suspended above the void, like in a bad erotic movie (which is probably why I enjoyed fucking her thus...). Her plaintive voice endlessly calling out my name, invoking it in fear, in lust, as I dug roughly into her, slapping myself into her, against her. She liked it rough, made you know wordlessly that she wished to be manhandled, to end up with bruises across her arms, on her rump after the deed was done, although in private conversation before or after, during meals, or normal social interaction, she would always refrain quite religiously from raising any matters sexual. For ages she kept on sending me birthday and Xmas wishes.

And then there was Pamela, who was married to a famous experimental jazz trumpet player. We'd met on the Upper East Side at a party. She was a friend of a friend who worked for a publishing house I was doing some research for. We would get together on a regular basis when her husband was out of town gigging in an apartment she shared with a girlfriend near the Columbia campus. Her husband was often away on tour. God, Pamela, so many years ago now! Dark, lustrous, long hair, sublime arse, heavy breasts, how we fitted together so well! She joined me for a Bourbon Street Mardi-Gras folly, walking up and down the alcohol-soaked road at a snail's pace, screams from the balconies for women to lift their tops and display their breasts and be rewarded with cheap, colourful beads. Which she did, roaring with laughter, on a couple of occasions. Her breasts so shapely. Dead drunk, we finished up in someone else's hotel room with a group of local acquaintances of hers, which ended in a fumbled orgy in which all present ended up in bed together; I even think her husband might have been there too and watched us fuck before dutifully taking his turn with her, while I was being indifferently blown by his blonde companion, my cock likely still coated with Pamela's sweet juices. New Orleans madness!

All this to explain the guilty attraction for New Orleans that simmers uncontrollably beneath my skin.

The spicy food, the oysters and crawfish diet I could live on, the voodoo fumes, the rumbling and heavy flow of the river, the fireworks off Jackson Square on New Year's Eve as all the riverboats on the Mississippi toot their horns on the stroke of midnight as the traditional Glitterball concludes its descent on the sidewall of the old Jackson Brewery. The drunks and druggies in Louis Armstrong Park, the endless causeway across Pontchartrain Lake, the antique shop windows on Royal Street, the antebellum mansions of the Garden District, the halting tramways, the diners dotted across Magazine, the sounds of every conceivable sort of music filtering like smoke from the bars and clubs, the noise, the warmth, the humidity, these have all become the foundation stones of who I have become and entrenched New Orleans in my blood.

The only memories from before the magician allowed me to keep.

□ □ □

When it rains in New Orleans, it pours. The skies open wide. It's the climate, you see, a sheer avalanche of water. Within a minute or so, the streets are like rivers. It never lasts very long, and in late spring or summer, within minutes, it has all evaporated as if by a miracle of science.

But if you happen to get caught, you're drenched from head to toe in the blink of an eye. Best take shelter fast.

I was wandering aimlessly through the French Quarter, smelling the smells, drinking the sights, my mind both at rest and empty, although my soul, as ever, yearned for things unsaid. I'd already strayed beyond the main Vieux Carré area which is always so full of bars and stuff, walking by mostly boarded-up buildings and all-night groceries. I recalled that there was a small park a few blocks further to the north. Maybe I'd sit for a while, collect my thoughts, read a bit from the old pulp paperback I'd picked up earlier at the Rue Dauphine Librairie Bookshop.

My short-sleeve shirt stuck to my skin and sweat painted a sheen on my bare skin. I took a sip of water from the Coke bottle I carried along in my tote bag and looked up at the sky. A mass of dark clouds was passing across the sun, and there was a touch of electricity in the air. A big storm was nearing. I knew from experience how quickly it could break and looked around for possible shelter. The park I remembered was too far, even if my memory of its location was correct.

A drop of water cascaded over the tip of my nose. None of the buildings nearby had extended canopies across the pavement, unlike in other areas of the French Quarter. I darted down a side street, hoping for a bar or a store where I could take refuge. The sky darkened.

There.

A small neon light advertising something just fifty yards away on the other side of the street. I hastened my pace. Reached the door of the joint just as the heavens opened, water splashing against my loafers.

Inside, the smell of stale beer and centuries of cigarettes impregnating wood and bodies.

I'd thought it was just a bar but noticed the small badly-lit stage at the back of the room. A titty bar! A strip joint away from the normal beat. The sort of place I'd never really cared for much, whether in New Orleans or elsewhere. Muted sounds of a Rolling Stones' song shuffling in the background. "Sympathy for the Devil", I recognized. My eyes were becoming accustomed to the ambient darkness.

Men along the bar, or at small tables, nursing drinks, hushed conversations. I found a gap at the bar. Ordered a Coke and was told they only had Pepsi. Fine with me. "No ice, please."

As the barman, a swarthy red-haired bull of a man, delivered my glass, the lights illuminating the stage area at the back were switched on proper. The music on the jukebox fell to an abrupt halt and with an asthmatic click, the club's sound system came to life. Conversations ceased, punters shifted in their seats, glasses clinked.

Just as the new music took flight, I briefly heard the monotonous sounds of the rain outside beating against the pavement and the club's unsheltered windows. It was a major storm.

As the sound of the echoing rain quickly faded into the distance, I realized that the music now spreading like a wave through the room was not the sleazy sort I'd somehow expected.

No sweaty rock 'n' roll, or brassy big band tune or jazzy effluvia.

It was actually classical. I closed my eyes for an instant in an attempt to dredge some form of recognition from my memory.

Lazy strings, shimmering beaches of melody lapping against each other, Ravel or maybe Debussy.

A spotlight appeared out of nowhere.

Highlighting a dancer who had also materialized from the undefinable contours of the surrounding darkness.

Again, she was not some identikit stripper, all crude make-up, vulgar attitudes and gaudy minimalistic apparel.

She was clothed in billowing white gossamer material, a flowing dress or sheet suspended in an imaginary breeze.

Reminded me of Isadora Duncan in photos I'd seen in books or magazines, or maybe in a movie. Her face was even paler than her thin dress. Just a savage slash of red lipstick, like a still bleeding wound, highlighting a set of perfect features.

Cheekbones to kill for. Eyes deep with ebony darkness. A luxuriant jungle of dark curls like a royal crown, falling all the way down to her shoulders, framing her face in total harmony.

She was almost motionless at first.

I looked up.

Met her eyes.

An endless well of sadness.

Her face expressionless.

The billowing white dress concealed any hint of the shape of her body, just thin legs and delicately-shaped ankles and below her bare feet.

Again, skin of abominable pallor.

One shoulder moved imperceptibly to the rising beat of the strings carrying the melody.

I held my breath.

Hypnotized.

The next five minutes saw me transported to another time and place altogether as I watched the young woman's set. Similarly, every other spectator in the room had fallen silent as we all watched transfixed by the spectacle of her dance and gradual disrobing, as her movements invisibly accelerated and she began to dance, sashay, sway, shiver, perform, display herself, lullaby of desire, conjugating the geometry of her sexuality to a factor of infinity, stripping, moving, flying even, suspended in the winds of desire, spreading herself with both grace and total obscenity and making the whole spectacle a thing of both innocence and unashamed pornography.

Her slender neck.

Firm small breasts. Nipples adorned with the same fierce shade of lipstick. Fiery. Hard.

Her washboard stomach. The miniature crevice of her navel where the steep descent towards her delta began.

Her shaven mons.

The highlighted straight vertical scar of her cunt opening, again defined by the scarlet hue of lipstick. The coral depths peering with every other movement inside her as she floated between the billowing flow of the thin white material of the dress, she had now shed, and swum through a word emptiness and gauzy material to the quiet, peaceful beat of the music.

Darker, brown inner labia, teasing our eyes.

An imperceptible tattoo just an inch or so along to the left of the opening of her cunt. Looked like a gun, or maybe more traditionally a flower.

The harmony of her thighs. The golden down in the small of her back caught by the spotlight. The symmetrical orbs of her arse. The darker pucker of her anal opening as she bent forward and spread herself wide for our edification.

It could have been offensive, vulgar, dirty but it was anything but.

She was confident with her body. Knew how beautiful she was. Remained in control of every square inch of her immaculately white skin and she was gifting us with its vision.

At no moment did she stray more than a few metres from the fixed spotlight. No need for wasteful moments or poles for acrobatics or seeking tips from the audience. Not that there was anywhere they could be tucked as she had been quite naked underneath the white Grecian-like dress. No exotic lingerie or suspenders or garter belts. No superfluous items of clothing.

Once she was naked, it was something so natural, the way a woman should always be.

And her face, ever expressionless. Distant. At peace.

The melody began to fade, the strings shimmering as the journey ended. I felt as if my heart had stopped.

The young dark-haired and pale-skinned woman's motion slowed.

Her legs open at a revealing angle.

Her arms spread wide in both directions.

Christ-like. Crucified.

I held my breath. As if a distant memory was burrowing its way from deep inside me towards the surface of my consciousness. A forbidden memory. Something terrible buried within.

The spotlight sharply disappeared and the darkness that took over the room was blacker than ever.

By the time our eyes adjusted, the dancer was no longer there, and the small stage was empty.

Every spectator present was silent.

I finished my drink and walked outside.

The storm had passed, and the street was almost dry already, thin clouds of steam rising from the gutters as the rain evaporated in overdrive.

It was late afternoon.

In the distance, the calliope of a steamboat on the Mississippi chimed.

Damn, who was she?

I walked all the way back to Toulouse and then, impulsively, backtracked to the small strip club. The stage was occupied by a black girl with silicone tits and an over-prominent Jennifer Lopez or Beyoncé throne of a backside and the customers were now few, as if all the previous punters knew no one could properly follow the preceding beauty and there was no point lingering.

The barman glanced at me. His eyes twinkled with malice.

"She only performs once a day," he said, anticipating my question.

"Oh..."

"She's dressing right now. Should be coming out any moment," he added.

"I'll wait, then."

Away from the stage, she appeared taller, straight-backed, imperious if fragile, now that she had wiped the savage lipstick away, her whole face a symphony of whiteness. I was unable to recognize the fragrance she wore.

She seemed to be still wearing the white gauzy dress she had begun her dance in, under a floor-length transparent plastic mac.

And she was still barefoot. A large canvas bag hung from her shoulders. It appeared to be full of books and silk scarves in every colour of the rainbow.

"Loved your set. Can I offer you a drink?"

"I just had a sip of water in the dressing room," she said. "No thanks." Looked at me blankly. There was the trace of an accent.

Spanish? Italian?

"Returning home?"

"Maybe..."

"Are you hungry?"

"A bit. Dancing does eat up all your energy," she said.

"My treat. Anywhere in particular you might want to go."

She agreed to share an oyster po' boy at the Napoleon House.

Even now, I remember very little of our conversation although we must have spent more than an hour together eating and conversing. She never would tell me what her name was or anything about her life. I recall discussing books, she loved F. Scott Fitzgerald and let slip she had once lived in Manhattan as a student. Every attempt on my part to find out how come she was a now a stripper failed. She wasn't rude or offended by my questions, just indifferent. The time passed quickly, and I assumed that yet again, I must have done too much of the talking, and bored her stiff with my usual stories and feeble anecdotes and jokes.

We walked from the Napoleon House to the small Faulkner House bookstore in the alley by Jackson Square where I failed to find a copy of a book I had been singing the praises of and had hoped to buy for her.

"Sorry."

"It's fine," she said, with a faint smile. "So?"

"So?"

"Do you wish to come back to mine?"

My heart skipped a beat.

"That would be lovely," I replied.

It was a walk-up in a decaying building that might once have been a mansion's slave quarters just off Dumaine.

She closed the door and took my hand in hers.

"Kiss me," she asked.

How could I say no?

It wasn't fucking. It was making love in the most absolute sense of the term. It could only have happened in New Orleans.

Her bed became our battlefield.

I knew how pale her skin was but never guessed how soft and pliant her body would prove, a feathered cushion firm and languorous, a perfect treasure offered up for plunder and worse.

Oh, the satin of her skin, the marrow-like texture of her lips, the way her fingers caressed my cock with shameless impunity and coaxed it to full length and thickness before she took me into the oven of her mouth, nibbling, teasing, biting with kindness, her tongue delving into my pee-hole with exquisite, measured probing, riding my lust, controlling it.

Her sex, a map of untold treasure. Yes, it was a tattoo of a gun there, no larger than a nail, a Chinese miniature in the heavenly pornographic landscape of her intimacy, inner and outer folds delineated with mathematical precision, a medical sketch where every feature was drawn with close attention to detail and colour.

Beckoning me. Opening for me like a flower of the tropics, swallowing me whole, feeding on me, feeding me.

New Orleans night.

The sound of her moans, the tightness in our throats as we pushed boundaries and held each other in the darkness like orphans in a storm. Every single woman I had touched, loved, brought to New Orleans led to this moment, this epiphany.

Fuck! Why wasn't it always like this?

Morning. Lazing spread-eagled in a crazy geography amongst the tangled sheets of the bed. Our smells mingling, our sweat a potent cocktail of spent lust.

"Hello. Shouldn't I at least know your name?" I asked, a fingertip lingering indecently across the ridge of her nether lips.

"Good morning, lover."

She rose from the bed, brushing away my greedy hands. Regal.

Pale. Naked. My cock hardened again in an instant, despite its rawness.

She smiled and tut-tutted.

"Later," she said. "Offer me breakfast."

We dressed and walked out into the hesitant early morning sun to Jackson Square for traditional beignets and coffee at the Café du Monde.

She still wore the white, billowing dress, a slight, pale ivory figure making her way across Decatur.

Wiping away the powdered sugar that had spilt across my dark shirt, I looked up to see the sun fading.

She followed my eyes.

"Seems like another storm is on the way," I said.

She nodded.

We began to make our way back to her apartment, hastening our pace as the dark clouds gathered menacingly above.

We only made it halfway there before the heavens opened.

I laughed as the first drops fell on my tousled hair, turned towards her expecting a similar smile. But the look on her face was one of sheer terror.

"It's only rain, just water," I said.

And, one final time, I witnessed the despair that lingered deep down in the dark pit of her eyes.

The rain fell, implacable, surrounding us, submerging us.

Quickly soaking the thin material of her dress, instantly revealing the sweet contours of her body, the now transparent gauze sticking to her skin, betraying the dark hardness of her nipples and when she attempted to move, the unmistakable cleft of her cunt. At any other time, I would have found this highly erotic and arousing. But not right now.

As soon as her total nudity beneath the dress was betrayed, she began to fade.

It only took a few seconds.

Fading.

Like melting in the rain.

Her contours losing their firmness, their definition. Her pale skin disappearing with every successive drop of rain.

I stood there with my mouth agape.

Her lips parted as if she wanted to tell me something but not a sound emerged and then she was gone.

The rain beat against the pavement with monotonous regularity, cutting through the air where once she had stood. And soon, as ever, the storm passed, and the water just evaporated and disappeared in little swishes of thin steam. Just like she had. And I was left alone, on the corner of Conti and Royal, standing like a fool in front of the Federal Building.

I didn't know what to think at first.

Was this a joke? Was this illusion, sorcery of some sort?

My mind in a tizzy, I ran back towards her apartment but was unable to find it again. But then, in New Orleans, so many houses looked alike and my mind had been on other things when we had first made our way there.

I tried to compose myself.

Went to my own place to change clothes. Take a shower, reluctantly washing away her scent from my body, from my cock.

Then rushed out to look for the strip joint where I had first stumbled across her. Half believing it also would have disappeared from the map. Vague premonitions of a New Orleans where things, places, people came and went with no sense of logic.

But it was there. In the same place as the previous day.

Closed. Of course, it was still only mid-morning.

I found a second-hand copy of *The Beautiful and the Damned* at the bookshop on Dauphine. Hadn't read it in decades. It helped me pass the time until the bar opened.

Standing on the opposite pavement, late afternoon, I saw the blinds rising and the click, click of the door's lock.

A short, greying man was wiping the tables clean with a wet cloth, and no sign of the customary barman.

My questions hit a blank wall.

No, it had been ages since they'd featured dancers.

No, they no longer even had a license.

Elderly regulars slowly streamed in.

None of them had any memory of when, if ever, the place had been a strip joint. Just knew it as a good place for a quiet drink these days.

Somehow, it was what I expected.

Made a strange sort of sense.

I finally sat at the bar and asked the middle-aged woman now serving for a drink.

As she bent down to get the bottle from the lowest shelf of her glass-fronted fridge, I caught sight of a fading framed photograph crookedly stuck to the large mirror which formed the back wall of the bar.

Squinted.

Recognized the pale features of my heavenly dark-haired stranger behind the patina of the sepia tones.

"Who is that?"

"Oh, that... Just an old photo taken some sixty years ago when the bar was a thriving private club for respectable gentlemen," I was told. "Must have been one of the dancers."

I gulped down my drink and walked out.

I wandered in a daze.

Much later I found myself in Jackson Square, disoriented, forlorn, my thoughts going around in a circle, like a bad dream, shards of memory clashing against others, my heart ravaged.

The fortune-tellers were out in force, sitting at their tables facing the Pontalba buildings, idling the time of day away until tourists returned.

There was one with a top hat and a multi-coloured waistcoat.

Our eyes met.

"Do we know each other?" I asked him, as I approached his table. "You're looking at me as if you did."

"Probably not," he said, but there was an unmistakable twinkle in his eye, a sense of mischief, as if any moment now he was going to bring a wand out of his bag and accomplish magic.

I was in no mood for magic.

□ □ □

Tomorrow, I will slowly walk away from the Mississippi, stroll down Royal Street and head towards Canal, leaving the mighty flow of the river behind me, and I will wait for the rain to come and maybe I will melt away and meet her again on the other side of the humid New Orleans curtain of rain.

For sure…

Acknowledgments for the Stark House edition

Books don't come out of nowhere, fashioned for better or worse by a writer's imagination and will power.

They are made possible by the encouragement and support of those close to you.

So this is where I get the opportunity to thank people without whom this novel might not have existed in its present form:

The real Giulia, who broke my heart and never went to New Orleans.

My wife Dolores who will always be by my side even when she is no longer able to be so due to the horrors of fate, my agent Sarah Such who goes to battle on my behalf, my friend and erstwhile collaborator Ngaire Mason-Wenn Wallace and the whole crime and thriller community of which I am proud to be a part of, including my colleagues on the Crime Writers' Association board.

And even though some of them don't normally read my books or won't for a number of years. I owe an invaluable debt to Natasha, Adam, Silas, Taylor, Lark, Evie and Millie. They know who they are.

And last, but not least, a nod of thanks to Darren Laws who published the first edition and to Greg Shepard of Stark House for rescuing this novel that falls between so many stalls, but was one I had to write and still hold close to my heart.

Made in the USA
Columbia, SC
13 March 2022